BEYOND TRIVAR

Book One
of The Third Daughter Prophecy Trilogy

By L. M. Christenson

Acknowledgments

Thank you to Robert Brown, who has always been there for me and has provided valuable counsel and endless hours of support. I really couldn't have done this without you.

Thank you to Josh Allen at BYU-Idaho and his junior-level technical writing class, who took my manuscript in its infancy for an entire semester project. I learned so much from you.

Thank you to Karey Shane, my Twinkling friend, who has been there, done that, and selflessly paid it forward.

Thank you to Roxane Colburn and my Mothers Who Know home school moms and children, who have taught me how to slow down and just be.

Thank you to Grandpa and Judy, who have loved me and believed in me.

Thank you to Connie McKinley, whose mother's heart helped early on to make my dreams a possibility.

Thank you to Woody Woodward and Davy Rigby, who helped pick me up, dust me off, and remind me how to live with all my soul again.

Thank you to Sherlyn Howlett, who has been by my side through everything, read my manuscript multiple times, and believed in my book and in me.

Thank you to my mother and father, who always believed in me, who have read and re-read my manuscript, and who have always been my friends.

Thank you to my beautiful children, who have read my manuscript, prayed for me, cheered me on, and supported my seemingly endless work to complete this book.

Thank you to Erin Martineau, a kindred spirit, who saw the vision of what I was trying to create early on and helped me refine it. You are a wonderful editor, counselor, and friend.

Thank you to all my dear family and friends who have been so excited for me to complete this book. Your love and support has lifted me.

I also want to thank my grandmothers. It may seem strange, but writing this book has brought me closer to them as I have realized how much they are a part of me. I am blessed with amazing examples of faithful, determined, talented, beautiful, strong, and tender women in my life who have nurtured me, my parents, and grandparents, and have left an imprint on my heart.

And finally, I would be remiss if I did not thank my Heavenly Father for His love and guiding hand in my life. Without Him I truly am nothing.

- L. M. Christenson

Hiraeth

No tears shed I for feet trod raw,
No grief for the coat that I lack.
I cinch my belt, condemn the gnaw,
Square the burden upon my back.

No regret when lantern oil failed,
No remorse for the compass lost.
How the body's misery pales
When poor heart and soul pay the cost.

Why did I covet lands afar?
Could they match for safety and peace?
Lead me, lead me, oh guiding star,
Or hiraeth's haunting will ne'er cease!

I long for home's rugged landscape
Of vibrant green under wild sky,
The rock-hewn shores and rough seascape,
Where cliffs rise treacherously high.

I miss her untamed wilderness,
Calderon forest near the vale
Of wildflowers that gaily rest
Near steep slopes of Glen Alladale.

And, yet, she will never leave me –
Hiraeth is the bond in my heart –
That makes me regret I left thee.
But I'll return, no more to part.

She, Nature, reigns in the Highlands.
She will welcome me to her shore.
At long last bound for my homeland,
Hiraeth, longing, shall be no more.

By Erin M. Martineau
© 2013 Erin Martineau. All rights reserved.

Prologue

A Beloved Child

"It's the only way," he whispered in the dark.

"But she's not even seen her first fortnight," she pleaded.

"You know it is the only way to protect her," he said more urgently.

"It is so far away…" A sob caught in her throat.

Another man opened the bedchamber door and whispered desperately, "Now! You must leave now…shadows on the horizon! We'll hold them off as long as we can, but you must go."

He shut the door quickly. Heavy boots sounded through the halls and out of the house. Anxious neighing and hoof beats faded into the quiet morning. The first man exhaled slowly as he knelt down next to the bed.

"Don't say anymore. You will be well soon, as though nothing ever happened. We will return her to you when the danger has passed. I promise to keep her safe. If I don't leave now, I will miss the boat's departure."

The man reached for the baby.

"Wait…"

The mother gazed painfully, longingly at her little red-headed daughter. A few tears escaped. "Remember your mother loves you," she whispered.

Placing a gentle kiss on her child's soft cheek, she lingered. Finally, she looked up at the man and relinquished. Now tears streamed freely down her cheeks as he tenderly took the child. He stole one last glance at the woman. She buried her face in her pillows as he disappeared out the bedchamber door.

Utilizing the baby's blanket, he tucked the infant securely in a sling-wrap that held her snug against his chest. Covering the wrap and baby under his cloak, he rushed down the stairs and ran out into the cold autumn morning. Quickly, but carefully, he mounted his horse.

Riding north, he refused to look back, despite the distant yells of men and creatures and the echoes of crashing steel. Urging his horse faster, he held his precious charge tightly, aware that all of Trivar depended on him.

After two hours, the baby began to fuss. He rode on, hoping that she would settle down. But after a short time he slowed his horse. For the first time, he turned his gaze southward. The wind blowing across the moor tossed his silver hair and blew it in the direction of large plumes of black smoke that poured into the light grey sky.

He looked at the child sadly before dismounting. He hoped that some of her kinsman had escaped. At least this precious girl is safe, he thought. His mind wandered to another young girl, and he hoped his brother was doing well and that the plan would be successful.

He opened his saddlebag and felt around. His battle-worn hands found a leather water pouch with a cheesecloth nipple. He looked toward the sky before finding a smooth, dry place to sit. He smiled at the irony of feeding this beautiful Trivarian child. But his thoughts were cut short as the baby realized that food was near and began to cry intensely.

Carefully, as if afraid he might accidentally break her, he aimed the nipple toward the wide, upset mouth and awkwardly pulled her close to his chest. As the cheesecloth nipple reached her lips, she began sucking frantically. He relaxed as her body curled into his. She drank happily.

As he had been instructed, he pulled her away from the nipple every few minutes and put her tiny body over his shoulder to gently but firmly pat her back. Each time he returned her to his cradling arms the process became easier and more natural to him.

He fed her peacefully for a time until she began to fuss again. He remembered the rest of his instructions and wrinkled his nose. He checked the baby's pants, wondering how anyone could get used to this part. After cleaning her off, he wrapped her tiny body and carefully closed the pins to her pants.

He pulled her clothes over her bare legs and swaddled the blankets securely around her. He fed her for another minute. Sure enough, she fell into a peaceful sleep. Watching her dear, rosy face as she slept changed something in his ancient heart. He no longer felt that this was just a mission for Trivar.

He carefully returned the leather and cheesecloth baby bottle to the saddle bag and mounted his horse with the little one once again tucked securely in her blanket, snug against his strong chest. All day he traveled over green hills, brown moors, and swampy valleys in an intermittent drizzle. Every few hours he fed and changed the child. He felt grateful that she was so young and slept most of the time. His thoughts wandered again to his brother.

By evening, a slice of the setting sun escaped through clouds at the horizon to illuminate the rider as he entered a forest. Riding between branches of evergreens, he breathed deeply and looked back at the open land behind him. Allowing relief to wash over him and smooth the anxious lines on his forehead, he turned forward again and let the horse walk slowly.

"We're nearly there," he said as he heard the distant roaring surf and smelled the fresh salty air from the North Sea. Snuggling the baby close, they made their way through the moss-covered trees.

As darkness gradually wrapped its tendrils around them, a strange but not unfamiliar sound flooded the air, like a rainstorm on a wooden shelter as it grew into a downpour. However, the rumbling came from the earth below him. He recognized the sound as thickly padded, quick-moving feet – hundreds of them.

Without hesitation, he kicked his heels into his steed's sides and leaned over the baby. In and out through the trees they galloped without looking back or slowing. Branches whipped his face and grasped at his white hair, but he urged the horse on.

Shortly, the woods began thinning. Brambles covered the ground. His faithful horse found an el-kirin trail and followed it swiftly. The old warrior could see ahead where dirt mixed with sand, and tall grasses replaced brambles and trees. As his path became sandier, his horse's footing was no longer sure.

Out of necessity, he slowed and checked behind him. Shadows moved at the far edges of the forest. His brow furrowed. He looked down at his charge and back at the shadows. In one smooth motion, he shot a bright white light from his hand in the direction of the shadows.

The thin arrow of light spread into a wide shield and flashed in an explosion of blinding light, forcing the shadows to scurry back into the darkness of the woods for safety. He could hear their screeching as the explosion forced their small beady pupils to open painfully. The light hit some of them, killing them instantly. He smiled, but his head and shoulders sagged.

In front of him lay a row of small but daunting sand dunes covered with grass. A flock of seagulls squawked mockingly overhead. He slowly breathed in the fresh sea air in an attempt to regain some strength as his horse climbed the nearest sand dune. Arriving at the top, at last he saw the North Sea.

It was growing dark, but the waters seemed lit by an internal flame. Each crashing wave erupted into big white plumes. The sky above had cleared to reveal early stars. Aurora Borealis shimmered in the sky behind a ship resting at anchor in the bay. But there were no boats on-shore. His countenance fell.

He rode his horse down the dune through soft sand, then onto the wet compact sand, all the way to the edge of the sea. Stopping short of the frothy waters, he yelled toward the boat, but the turbulent sea engulfed his cry. Again he tried, but his voice trailed off.

Looking at his charge and then at the shifting colors in the sky, he whispered a quick prayer before raising his hand and shooting out three lights, simple arrows of light with no explosion, over the ship's bow. His head drooped over the baby, and he looked lovingly at her.

With his last bit of strength, he dismounted, clutching the child, and dropped to his knees. As carefully as he could, he fell onto his back in the wet sand and untied the blanket, leaving the baby asleep on his chest. He watched the ship. It was dark. No one stirred.

"Gillantri, no!" he whispered to the surf. "I can't do anymore. Please protect this child. Please make up for my weakness. Let them come and get her."

A light appeared on the upper deck. Men with lanterns ran to a small rowboat that they lowered to the sea and rowed to shore. The rider had no strength to do anything but watch the boat and hope they would beat the shadows to him. The sound of the ground storm had returned and rumbled with a vengeance behind him. The baby woke and began to cry.

"Please be still, little one. It is going to be all right. Gillantri is watching over you. It is going to be all right." He tried to reach for her bottle in the saddlebag but could barely lift his arms from her fragile body.

Men from the rowboat ran up the beach with lanterns in their hands. As the men with the lanterns arrived, the now thundering sound from behind reached its climax. Short, thick, hideous looking creatures like black shadows appeared on the crest of the dune but hesitated. The elf knew their features well: their large noses, beady eyes, fat feet, and muscular bodies. Their stench.

The child cried louder. Trying to send one more explosion of light at the shadows, he moved his fingers...but nothing happened. His eyes widened as rough-looking strangers from the ship approached. Once they were standing around him, he confronted them with his little remaining strength.

"You aren't whom I expected."

"Well, I can't say that a Silver Elf with a baby is what I expected either," the man from the ship said. "And strangely it appears that we now have another Highland baby to sell. Thank you!"

"Another baby?" Images of his brother flashed through his mind.

"It happens to be our business to trade worthless Trivarians for things of greater value."

All the men laughed.

"You can't have her. I was expecting someone else." The elf's voice was faint and frustrated.

"But you have no power to stop us. Besides, your bulbane friends won't be kinder to her than we will be."

"My bulbane friends won't be kind to you either."

"From the looks of things, our light will keep them in check until we are safely on our way. My guess is that you might be the one in the most danger from them."

"Don't take her," the elf pleaded helplessly.

"And leave her to the bulbanes? What kind of a pirate do you think I am?"

The pirate picked up the child, startling her and causing her to cry again. With the sobbing infant in tow, the pirate and his men ran spryly to the rowboat, the ancient dance of the Auroras lighting their escape. The elf watched sadly, unable to do more for the child.

Something intuitively drew his attention back toward the shadows. At the top of the hill, a dark, ghastly figure of a man emerged, the dark figure he feared more than any other. Daman, he whispered. The elf closed his eyes and prayed.

1

To Xannellion

Jaden sat up sharply. Her green eyes wet with tears, she struggled to reclaim her bearings. A single torch on the tent post near her bed illuminated her surroundings. Silks blowing in the cool night breeze and the simple travel tapestries on her tent wall reminded her that she was finally on her way to Xannellion. She sighed heavily. She listened momentarily to the never-ending chorus of trilling frogs and the occasional shrill cry of a wild animal. The jungle never slept.

Jaden brushed the tears from her face and tossed her thick auburn curls. Feeling melancholy, she reluctantly pushed the covers away from her and put her feet over the edge of the bed. She picked up her silk night shoes and shook them out before placing them on her feet.

Jaden took the torch, opened her tent door, and passed into the darkness. She ignored the insects that blindly flew into her. At least these northern jungles were tamer. The insects were smaller and it rained less than in Yamis.

At the edge of the light, a shadow moved slowly. Jaden froze. Breathing deliberately, she said to herself, "Jaguars cannot get to the inner circle of camp."

"Mother, it's me, Zachariah."

Jaden took a quick breath. "What are you doing up?"

Zachariah came into the light. He was handsome with blond wavy hair, a strong physique like his father's, and green eyes like his mother's. His eyes narrowed good-naturedly.

"I couldn't sleep. Too many chariots racing through my head."

Jaden heard the concern in her son's voice. "I wondered. You have a big day today."

"Well, I'd hate to disappoint Xzavier."

"Your father."

"Of course. My beloved father."

"I wonder if Cannote has a navy," Jaden mused, trying to change the subject.

"If he is anything like his son, he will have a ban on ships and anyone who appreciates them," Zachariah scoffed.

"Your father insists that his father is nothing like him, so maybe there is hope."

Jaden fixed her gaze upon Zachariah. "You will meet Cannote this afternoon at the race. Please treat your grandfather and your father with respect. We need to make a good impression."

"I will behave. I haven't argued with father since we left Yamis, and if Cannote is so very different than Xzavier, we might get along handsomely."

"You have done well. Thank you," Jaden said wearily. She fell silent.

"Why are you up anyway?"

Jaden smiled sadly. "I needed some fresh air. I had more dreams."

"The same dreams again? About your parents?"

"Yes. But this time there was much more." Jaden paused as her dream began replaying in her mind. "I stood aboard the most exquisite ship. I wish you could have seen it. You wouldn't believe how masterfully it was built, right down to the lilies carved into the railings. Only people who love their work could have created such a fine ship. She cut so smoothly through the waters of the sea.

"They were out in the open sea, and at night, luminous bows of light moved across the sky. It sometimes looked like an iridescent curtain and at other times like radiant arcs of colored light. It was breathtaking.

"The men on board were strong, stronger than any army I have seen. But they were also quiet, nervous, and traveling fast, as if they were fleeing from something. I looked around for an enemy pursuing them, but all I saw was their enormous fleet of magnificent vessels," she paused, breathless. "You will sail the seas someday."

"My fleet will be the greatest."

Jaden nodded sadly. "They arrived at an inlet that appeared to be deep enough for their ships, but the inlet was terribly narrow. I thought the captain was crazy, but he led his ships one by one without any trouble through the channel, past mist-shrouded hills of the brightest green foliage. The ships made their way to a very large inland lake surrounded with evergreen trees and grassy fields. The brilliant green reminded me of Yamis, but I sensed a lonely barrenness, a forsakenness that filled me with sadness. And yet, I felt inescapably drawn to this place. It called to me.

"Next I was caught away to a galley ship somewhere in the middle of the fleet where two women stood at the railing staring far away. A drizzly rain fell, but they seemed to disregard it. The older of the two may have been in her late thirties, like me. The younger woman held a baby. You can imagine my surprise and curiosity at the sight of gentlewomen aboard a war ship and with a fleet so large and grand.

"They wore thick, heavy earth-toned clothing of simple but high-quality tailoring. Their beautiful pink faces gazed into the wind. Everything began to grow blurry except for the woman that held the baby, who seemed to glow. I looked into her crystal blue eyes and felt a familiar sadness overtake me, when I was suddenly swept away to a far different place.

"I stood surrounded by an army in a burned out wasteland that spread out all around us. The edges of the enormous valley revealed patches of glorious, lush flora far superior to even Yamis. But someone or something had destroyed most of it.

"Directly in front of me stood a beautiful woman with curly blond hair blowing in the wind. She had those same striking blue eyes as the woman holding the baby whom I saw on the ship. The woman wore armor. It may sound funny, but I think she resembled me, and I felt love for her like I would for a sister, if I had a real sister. But her every feature, from her glaring eyes to her lowered head and clenched fists, told me that she hated me.

"I reached out to her, but she lunged at me. At that same moment, someone from my army restrained her from behind. She struggled but couldn't free herself. My heart ached. We were not on the same side. I couldn't do anything as they tied her up and began to kick her with their heavy boots... Betrayal and sadness poured out from her soul and condemned mine."

She winced. Jaden's chest rose and fell.

"Is there more?"

Jaden brushed away an escaping tear. "Yes. I watched them beat her until I begged to be freed from the dream. At that moment something changed. The place changed, the feeling changed, and I have no idea where I went in this final part of the dream.

"Both the man and the woman appeared, as well as the blue-eyed man, the same who always appear in my other dreams. They wore beautiful, flowing garments, pale-colored, rather than bright, like in Yamis, and so fine as to be almost transparent. The man with the auburn hair and green eyes held hands with the woman, whom I presume to be his wife.

"The woman had black hair and green eyes. They were both filled with and radiated light, although their faces were sad. I could not understand their language, yet they spoke to me as if they were trying to tell me something important. The blue-eyed man emanated profound calmness and peace. He reached out to me, but I pulled back, and they disappeared. That's all. I woke up crying."

"I hope you can find your parents when we arrive in Xannellion."

"I have dreamed about this day for years now. They have to be there." Jaden's eyes narrowed. "I have one more thing I need to tell you. Xzavier requested that you and I ride together tomorrow. He doesn't want to seem 'encumbered' by us... You understand, right?"

Zachariah turned to face his mother squarely, his green eyes burning in the torch light. "I suppose Arabetta and Luana will not encumber him?"

Jaden lowered her voice. "All of this is for you. My greatest hope is that you will become king. You have to overlook your father's passions. You have to mind yourself...no matter what."

"No matter what?" Zachariah looked incredulously at his mother. "You have suffered too much. The women, the lies, the killing."

"Son, I can handle it. I always have."

Zachariah stared sadly at his mother. "I wish he didn't hurt you. If I were king, you'd never cry again." He clenched his jaw.

Jaden reached out and brushed her hand over the side of his strong face. "You will be king. You will be. Please watch yourself tomorrow at the races."

As he turned to leave, Zachariah teased over his shoulder, "Don't I always?" Exhausted with emotion, Jaden returned to her tent and got back into bed. Lying back on her silk pillows, her heart beat in her throat. She tried to close her eyes, but sleep wouldn't come. The chattering of the monkeys and repeating bird whistles crescendoed as the light began slowly filtering through the canopy above her tent.

Later that morning, the company broke camp and traveled for some time. Jaden and Zachariah rode in comfortable lounges, called litters, carried by large Yamis warriors. They followed far behind Xzavier in the long train of travelers.

"So are those skirts comfortable?" Jaden said.

"I like Xannellion fashion," he answered. "This tunic is pleated handsomely. How do you like your new wraps?"

"Actually, they are very comfortable. Much finer material than anything in Yamis. I wonder why Cannote sent us these gifts. It is suspicious."

"I agree." Zachariah pointed ahead of them toward a massive archway with the word Xannellion in large letters engraved on it.

"Xannellion," he said. "I am grateful to my father for one thing."

"What is that?"

"That I learned to speak his language. It might come in handy here."

As they approached, Jaden watched the walls of Xannellion grow until they towered over her as tall as the emergent trees that broke through the canopy of her jungle home. The city walls were made of grey stones that were cut large and rectangular. Admiring the archway, she wondered aloud, "How did they build that?"

"A lot of slave labor, I am sure."

Looking ahead, Jaden caught a glimmer of Xzavier's purple and gold robe that caught the sunlight through the mist of water evaporating off the pathway.

"We'll definitely make a scene."

"Indeed. Xzavier surely carried every last statue out of Yamis and many species of plants," Zachariah noted with disgust.

"Even some potted trees."

"Yes, who would have thought? He also brought as many animals as he could capture."

"Hunter though he may be, he restrained himself and brought them alive," Jaden added triumphantly.

"Only because you insisted, and you still paid a price for that," Zachariah added.

Jaden softly touched her right eyebrow.

"Not to mention," Zachariah continued, "the endless rows of remarkable Yamis male and female warriors and more slaves than I can count, and casks upon casks of precious metals and gems from our kingdom to flaunt when he makes his grand entrance. He didn't even leave the gold on Teeku's grave," Zachariah spat out sourly.

"Justine and her counterparts alone will make for quite a show here. However, I do hope that Cannote will be impressed."

Jaden lifted her chin and smoothed her sheer red dress accented in gold, thinking how well it offset her auburn hair, which was carefully twisted around her head and inlaid with delicate, vibrant orchids from Yamis.

As they passed under the giant arch that was guarded by soldiers, Jaden pointed out to Zachariah several creatures atop the city walls that stared down upon the newcomers. Zachariah's wide eyes told her he had already noticed them. They had the bodies of black jaguars, the heads of ravens, and eagle talons.

"Those must be the black gryphons that Xzavier talked about."

"Yes. They are fiercely beautiful."

Absorbed by their dark beauty, Jaden watched them until they faded into the distance behind her. Inside the city walls, the terrain transformed into jungle swampland from horizon to horizon. Mossy treetops, plants growing out of the trees, and flora fortunate enough to get sunlight on the jungle floor were all filled with spring blooms. Green light pervaded. Simple bridges or raised earth led the caravan over bodies of water filled with alligators and crocodiles.

Near midday they emerged from the swamps. Cottages with grass roofs appeared a few at a time until they filled every empty space. Curious people in rough togas tied at the waist with simple leather straps lined the roadway or stood staring from their doors or from their labors. A man pounding out metal on an anvil and glistening with sweat in front of a hot fire stopped and stared with suspicious eyes at Xzavier's entourage.

Men pulling handcrafted, two-wheeled carts stacked with hay, produce, or cages of doves or bats moved aside to yield to the parade from Yamis. Children in rags ran along the dirt streets with no indication that their parents were anywhere nearby. Rough men darkened from hard labor and hard lives stared lustfully at Jaden.

Masculine-looking women with their skin darkened by sun, unkempt hair, and shapeless apparel spat at her as she passed. Perched in her litter carried by servants and draped in soft, colorful linens that accentuated her shape, Jaden could feel their contempt. She turned from the crowds to find Justine.

Justine walked slowly behind them, large and midnight purple with yellow horns. Even for one of Teeku's dragons, Justine was massive. Jaden was grateful that the other dragons were taken into Xanellion by a secret route in order to avoid overwhelming and terrifying the people. The additional thirteen dragons and their offspring would likely have caused mass hysteria. That was one thing Xzavier did right.

The pressing crowd yielded plenty of room for Justine to traverse through their city. When the Xannellion citizens saw Justine, they gasped in amazement, and some withdrew into the crowd. Women covered their eyes, and men stood in front of their women and children as if they could protect them. Only a few of the bravest and most foolish dared move in for a closer look.

Jaden smiled as Justine caught sight of her, stood to her full height, and let out a fierce and intense bird-like call. The crowd jumped in one body and moved farther away from her. Jaden gave Justine a stern stare, causing Justine to slump back down and plod along faithfully.

Zachariah chuckled. "This just might be Xannellion's first encounter with the great dragons of Yamis."

"She is impressive, isn't she?"

As they moved through Xannellion, the muted thudding of the servants' sandals on the dirt road changed to the slap of leather on stone. Stone buildings replaced grass and bamboo huts. Occasionally, statues of Cannote, some as tall as many of the buildings, loomed over the streets.

The roads grew wide enough for three groups like theirs to pass through side by side, if not for the throngs of people filling all the extra space. Some of their togas had the edges dyed with bright designs. Many wore beautifully crafted leather sandals and belts. Mothers stood by their children, and fathers were often near, as well. Jaden observed an occasional smile and felt glad to be farther from the suffering masses.

"Mother, can you believe the size of Xannellion? The entrance gate and walls were enormous, but everything grows bigger as we travel..." Zachariah halted mid-sentence. Both Jaden and Zachariah forgot the crowds and stared ahead to the right of their litter.

"It has to be the Xannellion Stadium Xzavier talked about," Zachariah said. They both breathed in awe as they rounded a corner and the colossal stadium came into full view.

"Stop calling him Xzavier. He is your father," Jaden responded, suddenly very weary.

Zachariah turned to his mother. "I am going to be all right, mother, I promise. I don't care how oversized this place is. I am the best."

"I know you are. I just want you to be the best alive."

Zachariah changed the subject. "Did you ever get back to sleep this morning?"

Jaden returned to studying the buildings. "Did you?"

He lightly scoffed and stared at the stadium. Jaden felt the heat rising from the stone road beneath them, while the moist, hot air pressed in around them.

2

"Where We Always Wanted to Be"

They passed into the stadium's shadow, and Jaden's good feelings faded. The shade cooled them but gave Jaden no comfort. The exterior walls boasted exquisitely carved reliefs of Cannote's conquest of Xannellion, as well as bigger-than-life representations of his many battles and acquisitions of other cities.

Two enormous gold-plated statues proudly bearing Cannote's name flanked the stadium entrance. Banners and smaller festive flags adorned the passageway. Masterfully detailed designs decorated the ceiling under the arches. As they entered the arena, Jaden took in a quick breath at her first sight of the tens of thousands of spectators.

"Oh, Zachariah…"

He tried to sound casual. "Mother, I have been racing chariots since I could walk. I have never lost. I'll make a good impression, don't worry."

"That isn't what concerns me, and you know it."

Zachariah winked at his mother.

Jaden studied the scene in horrified wonder. They followed Xzavier's litter in a circle around the stadium's inner track. All of Xzavier's spoils from Yamis fit inside the massive arena and looked like children's toys compared to the oversized stone walls full of cheering legions that surrounded them. The people from Yamis left their circle and settled into free-standing bleachers in the middle arena to watch the race at ground level.

Zachariah helped his mother out of the litter before jogging toward the chariots. As an afterthought, he called back to her, "I'll wave to you around the last lap."

Thirty-five young men from Yamis stood in their chariots waiting for Zachariah. Jaden watched as he found his place among the charioteers from their jungle home. After he situated himself in his chariot, they raced toward the starting line where fifty of Cannote's best charioteers readied themselves.

Jaden spotted Cannote in the middle of the stands in his comfortable box half-way up the north side of the stadium. From a distance she couldn't be sure, but Cannote appeared older than his statues portrayed him. Colorful fabrics were draped everywhere inside the box. Beautiful women surrounded him, a few soldiers congregated around the edges, and two male advisors stood next to him.

She scanned the crowds as she walked toward Xzavier. The faces of the onlookers reminded her of berries on a colossal bush waving in the wind. As she and her attendants neared the designated sitting area for their sizeable court, she focused on Xzavier. He was handsome with sandy brown hair and brown eyes. He lounged, casually laughing, flanked by two women.

Flashbacks of Luana and Arabetta as children made Jaden's blood rise in her cheeks. How mercilessly they teased her for having fair skin and red hair! Why had she let them make her feel so inferior? Why had Xzavier chosen them, of all the women in her father's court, for concubines? Jaden hated them and hated him, but she reminded herself that if she were patient, someday she would be free, truly free.

"Good afternoon, Xzavier," Jaden said civilly as she took her seat.

"Everything is going as I planned. Now if our son can just do as he is told..." From his other side Arabetta whispered something to Xzavier and laughed.

He replied to Arabetta, "I expect it to go better than that."

Jaden held her tongue as Cannote raised his hands to the crowd. "Welcome, Xannellion's people!"

The crowd cheered loudly. Cannote, with his hands still raised, announced, "Fifteen laps of the best entertainment in Trivar!"

The crowd erupted into chanting, "Best in Trivar! Best in Trivar! Best in Trivar!"

Jaden rolled her eyes. She searched for Zachariah and found him below, his golden hair shining in the Xannellion sun.

Cannote held up his hand to begin the race, teasing the crowd who kept up the chant, "Best in Trivar! Best in Trivar!" In a decrescendo, they softened, quieter and quieter until they barely whispered it, waiting for Cannote to start the race. Everyone was leaning toward him in great anticipation, when his hand finally fell.

The horses lurched, their hooves digging into the gravel, and the chariots pulled free from their stationary positions. With so many chariots, it took a few minutes for everyone to get going, but the speed steadily increased until the dust, horses, and men were swirling around the track.

The pounding of horses' hooves reverberated through the stadium and through Jaden's body as she rose to watch. She turned to follow Zachariah on the track behind her as he pushed past one charioteer after another. From the corner of her right eye, she saw a charioteer in the back of the pack lose control.

She turned to see him fly from his chariot and get trampled by the last ten riders. Two others fell because of the wreckage. The three lifeless drivers and most of the wreckage were quickly removed by the attendant servants before the leaders of the race circled around again.

As Jaden whipped her head from the wreck back to Zachariah on the opposite side of the track, her eyes passed over Xzavier, who was still seated and receiving a foot massage from Luana. He whispered something to his top advisor, the Scorpion, who had been known in his earlier days as Phillip.

Jaden searched again for her son. When she found him, he was three-quarters of the way to the front of the pack. The first quarter, about twenty chariots, ran more tightly together. Zachariah skillfully maneuvered around one of them, causing Jaden to hold her breath. He continued passing one or two each lap until halfway into the tenth lap, finally jockeying for the lead.

Between lap eleven and twelve, he seemed stuck behind the leader, a large, suntanned Xannellion man who kept looking back with a shocked expression at Zachariah, as if no one had ever before challenged him so. By the beginning of the thirteenth lap, the man whipped his horse desperately with a heartless scowl on his face.

"Zachariah looks frustrated," Jaden commented.

"Well, he should be. He's about to lose this race and ruin everything!" Xzavier glanced up at the track.

"Does it always have to be about you?" Jaden couldn't hold her tongue any longer. "You know that when Zachariah gets frustrated he takes crazy risks. Would you at least act like you care?"

"Oh, you underestimate how much I really do care, dear Jaden," he said. "I care more than you know."

Jaden faced him. His cold stare told her that she was close to pushing him too far, but he suddenly turned his attention to the race, as they both realized Zachariah was heading into his last lap. Anger simmering, Jaden watched as Zachariah still trailed the leader on the outside by just the length of his horse.

"Ride hard, son, ride hard," Jaden whispered. He didn't seem to be riding full-bore as he headed into the last corner around the east side of the stadium. It was there that he unexpectedly accelerated to get around the leader.

"No, Zachariah!" Jaden gasped.

The centrifugal force and the acceleration rocked Zachariah's chariot dangerously. Jaden took in a sharp breath and held it, snatching her scarf from around her shoulders and putting it to her mouth.

In seconds he was out in front and on the northern straightaway, barely in the lead. Jaden realized she wasn't breathing and forced herself to exhale, refusing to observe how Xzavier was handling his son's near-death experience. Zachariah waved to her as he crossed the finish-line decidedly in the lead.

She sat down exhausted as everyone else jumped to their feet and cheered. Zachariah took a victory lap, and the noise was deafening. Cannote stood as Zachariah approached the place just below Cannote's box. Cannote lifted his hands to still the crowd. Once they quieted, he began, "Welcome young man from the south, winner of the largest chariot race in all of Trivar!"

The crowd roared. Cannote raised his hands to silence them, but this time they delayed their obedience. When they finally quieted again, Cannote inquired, "What is your name, young man?"

"I am Zachariah. Your grandson."

Silence stilled the crowd for a moment, and Cannote seemed genuinely moved. "Well, you are a champion. Welcome to Xannellion!"

The crowd exploded with obvious pride, sending another burst of deafening noise throughout the stadium. Relieved that the race had finished with Zachariah unharmed, Jaden looked aside to check on Justine and realized the dragon was noticeably jumpy.

But when Justine connected with Jaden's gaze, Justine relaxed and bowed her long, purple, serpentine head, making her bright yellow horns stand out against the backdrop of her midnight purple body.

Jaden mouthed, "You are a good dragon."

She turned back to the throngs of cheering Xannellions. Surrounded by tens of thousands of people with fair skin like her own, Jaden thought longingly, "I wonder if my family is really from this place?"

Jaden returned to the present as Cannote invited "...my long lost son, Xzavier, my champion grandson, and the mother of my grandson, and all Xzavier's company to a feast, the likes of which they have never seen!"

The crowd erupted again. Jaden put her hands over her ears to block some of the noise. Thoughts of the blue-eyed man and the couple in her dream crossed her mind as she scanned the crowds.

A short time later, Zachariah returned, glistening all over and radiant. He teased her, "You really do thrive on this kind of stuff don't you?"

"You did well, son."

"Thanks, but you know I'd rather be on the sea. This is just a hobby," he joked with an arrogant shrug.

Xzavier heard Zachariah and responded, "A sea-going man is a fool-hardy man. Besides, you need more practice on land. You almost lost that race." Without saying more, he left and got in his litter.

Jaden gently put her hand on Zachariah's hand, which was touching the hilt of his sword. "Son, you made a good impression. Let's go."

Resentful of his father, Zachariah walked beside her. He helped his mother into their litter. He walked over to his side, ascended it, and leaned over to give Jaden a hug. She dodged the sweaty young man and gave him a warning look. He chuckled as the litter was raised and Xzavier's treasures began moving again.

They followed Xzavier's litter, a trail of warriors, exotic animals, breathtaking plants, and pots of treasures from the stadium, through the wide streets, and to the gates of Cannote's palace. The palace was a cave-like structure with tall stone archways and high walls that receded into the hillside behind. Jaden counted ten rows of archways. Cannote, who had gone ahead of them, stood on a balcony welcoming the guests invited to his feast.

As they approached the palace, Zachariah's eyes widened. "Have you ever seen anything so immense?"

"Only our mountain back home. Do you see your grandfather waiting on the balcony?"

"Yes. Doesn't he look old? My father made him sound immortal," Zachariah mocked with a tip of his head, adding emphasis to my father for Jaden's sake. Her eye's twinkled sadly.

Jaden and Zachariah were brought forward near Xzavier's litter, though he had already departed from it and was walking toward the palace arm-in-arm with the ladies, followed by Phillip, the Scorpion. A servant brought a step stool to Jaden's side of the litter as Zachariah jumped out and walked quickly around to his mother's side, offering his mother his hand. Jaden stepped down onto Xannellion stone and into the intense Xannellion sunlight, her delicate, vibrant red silks blowing in the hot breeze.

Jaden put her shoulders back and raised her head. Zachariah walked just behind his mother and observed the scenery. When they reached the door of the palace, one of Xzavier's servants obediently showed them in. They followed the servant up a large winding staircase into an extravagant, exorbitantly wide hallway through which Zachariah's chariot could have easily maneuvered.

At the end of the large hallway, double doors opened to reveal a stunning, lavish dining hall with ceilings at least forty feet high. Ten long, bold chandeliers of wrought iron holding clear candles spanned the length of the room. The chandeliers hung by hefty thirty-foot chains and filled the space with light. Spacious, bulky rectangular tables anchored the room. Five fireplaces filled the wall on the left side of the hall, but no fires burned, as it was a hot spring day. The right wall displayed several tapestries of tremendous size and color variance.

Jaden leaned over to Zachariah. "Nothing is small in Xanellion, is it?"

Zachariah gave no response as he scanned the room. Jaden poked him with her elbow. Without looking at her, Zachariah quietly announced, "Mother, something is wrong. Stay close to me." He reached for his sword as Xzavier approached them.

"Come meet my father," Xzavier said. He leaned in close to Zachariah. "You can relax, son. The premise is secure."

Zachariah looked at Xzavier questioningly. Jaden glanced at Cannote who was noticeably curious about the exchange. Breaking away from Xzavier and Zachariah in an attempt to distract Cannote, she reached her hands out to him. He ignored her hands and took her shoulders, pulling her in close.

"My, my, Xzavier, you have your father's taste for exotic females, but this one doesn't look like the other Yamis beauties. Where did you find her?"

"She was brought to Yamis as an infant, but we don't know from where," Xzavier answered, feigning interest.

"Well, I would say that you are from north of Alexandria, if my travels serve me at all. Yes, the Great Northlands. I can see the spirited look in your eyes, and no one has hair of this shade and sheen except those from the north."

Jaden drank in this new piece of information.

"You are a spectacular prize," Cannote said. He touched her hair and made her skin crawl. "I look forward to having you – as a guest – in my palace, Jaden," he said her name slowly and sent shivers down her spine. He kissed her on both cheeks, as was Xannellion custom.

"Please sit beside me, over here." Cannote motioned for Jaden to sit on his left. Relieved to be free of his grasp, she moved quickly to her chair.

"And you, grandson, who embarrassed my best charioteers, sit next to your mother. Finally, my son, can we let the past stay in the past? Let's start new – today. When you sent word that you were still alive, I sent my fastest runners to invite you home. Please, sit on my right side and be my son as it always should have been."

He motioned for Xzavier to sit down next to him on his right side and took his place at the head of the enormous table. Jaden caught a surreptitious look that passed between Xzavier and the Scorpion and quickly turned away. She had seen those looks before.

Cannote's highest nobles sat along the table nearest to him. Farther down the row of tables sat all of Cannote's remaining nobles, intermingled with Xzavier's nobles and servants, at least all who were not "securing the premise." Jaden observed Zachariah, who shifted uneasily in his seat.

Servants began pouring drinks before bringing in the food.

Xzavier stood. "I would like to offer gifts to my father, Cannote, and to the nobles of this great land of Xannellion. I have waited many years for this opportunity. I am most rewarded by the reception we have received and anticipate a great future in our new home."

Here, Xzavier tipped his head toward the Scorpion, who waited for permission to rise. When Cannote acknowledged their request, Phillip, the Scorpion, walked to the door of the grand room, opened it, and whispered to a guard outside.

After nodding to Jaden, Xzavier resumed, "My beautiful companion came from a most lush and vibrant land named Yamis, which is in the southern jungles. Her father, bless his memory, loved a creature that can only be described as king of all beasts, for there is none that compares to it. This creature came to the land of Yamis each spring to mate and produce two precious eggs. The mated pair would keep and nurture the larger of the two eggs, always letting the weaker fall prey to the elements. The one surviving offspring would grow quickly, and before the end of summer, all three would fly south to their feeding grounds."

As Xzavier spoke, the great doors to the room opened and one hundred of Xzavier's servants entered, each carrying a sizeable lidded platter made of delicate, thin ceramic inlaid with precious metals, stones, and gems. The largest platter was placed before Cannote, while the others were set before each of his nobles and servants.

"Father, I have wanted to share my feelings with you for these twenty years, and now I am able to do so in a way I once only dreamed possible."

A concerned expression crossed Cannote's face. Before he could say anything, Xzavier shouted with a flourish, "Open your gifts, Xannellion's finest!"

Cannote and his nobles lifted their lids. Jeweled colors shone from the iridescent, scaly bodies of irresistibly dazzling and mesmerizing creatures. Every noble exclaimed at the beauty before them, but Jaden gasped.

Yellow eyes peered intently at the person in front of them, and before Zachariah could unsheathe his sword, the baby dragons lunged at the necks of each noble, including Cannote, who looked at Xzavier with wild eyes as he tried to disengage the vicious creature. Xzavier sat back in his seat smugly. He winked at Jaden who gaped helplessly. Cannote struggled for a short time and died without another word.

Once the struggle ended, Xzavier stood and gently, almost reverently, handled Cannote's crown.

"I would like to present myself as King of Xannellion," he said flatly, mockingly understating the pride he clearly felt in the success of his coup d'état.

Everyone cheered, except for Jaden and Zachariah, as Xzavier placed the crown on his own head. Xzavier's nobles and servants bowed as he declared with relish, "Never look a dragon in the eye."

His loyalists laughed and he continued, "Perfectly executed. We will tell the people of Xannellion later. But right now it is time to eat!"

They cheered again.

"Well, you know what to do."

Xzavier's servants detached the dragons from their prey and placed the deadly creatures under the lids of their platters. Xzavier's earlier command now haunted Jaden. "Make a good impression on Cannote," he had said.

With death all around her, Jaden felt faint. Zachariah put his hand on hers and firmly squeezed. Because the noise around them covered his voice, he leaned close to Jaden and spoke clearly, confident that only she would hear. "I think Cannote was up to something, as well. Xzavier just got to him first."

The dead Xannellion nobles were hauled to the back of the room and loaded into wheelbarrows.

"Place them in the dungeon. The dragons have earned their dinner," Xzavier ordered, and his servants carted them away. Some of his other servants draped tarps over the bloodstained tables and resumed meal preparations. Xzavier sat at the head of the tables, and his nobles moved closer to him. After drinks were poured and sumptuous entrees were placed before them, Xzavier rose once more, this time as king.

"All food was tested on Cannote's servants, and we can eat what hasn't killed them. Let's feast."

Xzavier's men and women roared. Xzavier sat down and madly tore off a bite of juicy, rare meat with his teeth. He chewed for a moment and then spoke to Jaden.

"Finally, we are here, where we always wanted to be."

3

Caged

"I hate this dress. This one won't do either...pink looks awful with red hair. Zoie, these dresses are horrible! I cannot wear any of them. Tell Xzavier I need something fresher and more modern if I am to look like the Queen of Xannellion and not just another courtier. And I am not just another courtier!" Jaden flung her last dress at the door as her attendant, Zoie, quickly scuffled away.

Jaden stormed to her balcony and thrust opened the gold shutters, taking in the fresh air that blew in from over the jungle. Her eyes scanned the sky, and she wished that she could take Justine for a flight. "But no! I must play the good queen today," she said to herself aloud.

She retreated into her room. Unimpressed with the lavishly ornate gold filigree that Xzavier's craftsmen had recently installed, she fingered the delicate, fanciful woodwork gilded in gold leaf that was laced around her entire room. The designs on the high arches of her ceiling interplayed with each other so intricately that it made her dizzy to follow their patterns.

Jaden paced the room waiting for Zoie to return. Although the room was actually quite spacious, Jaden felt cramped, most likely because she spent much of her time in her room. She certainly never felt at home anywhere else in Xzavier's stolen castle. The only other place Jaden preferred was with Justine, whether attending to her in the dungeon or flying upon her back over the surrounding jungle.

The feeling of suffocation was what motivated Jaden to install more mirrors in her room. The mirrors made the room feel bigger, and Jaden bought into that illusion with relief. She stopped in front of one of her oversized mirrors made of many sections that craftsmen had fitted with precision to the curved shape of the wall from floor to ceiling.

You're bored, Jaden. You need to find a better distraction than picking on poor Zoie, she thought. Jaden laughed and then looked at herself in the mirror. "Not bad for an old queen," she said aloud, turning to the side and examining her thin midsection and curves.

Zoie knocked and entered carrying a flowing gold gown and a birdcage-like structure.

"My lady, here is the dress that Xzavier commands you to wear. I...well, I told him you needed something new."

"How did he get it so quickly? Never mind. I don't want to know that this is another of Luana's castoffs. I actually like it. But what is that thing?"

"It goes around your waist and flairs the skirt out at the bottom. It is the latest fashion. Xzavier said he wants his women to be the first to wear them."

"Who would wear that awful cage?"

"If you don't mind, I can help you," Zoie tentatively offered.

After a long struggle, Jaden emerged from her room with the cage under the gold dress and her hair done up high atop her head.

"I can barely breathe, Zoie. How am I supposed to walk?"

"Carefully, my lady," Zoie urged.

Jaden turned too quickly to give her a harsh look, but instead compulsively cried out, "Owww! It pinches!"

Zoie stifled a giggle and headed down to the maid's quarters. Jaden slowly made her way in the other direction to the ballroom. She passed hall after hall adorned with Xzavier's eccentric artwork, vases, and exorbitantly carved marble statues without noticing any of it.

At a window, Jaden paused and looked out, taking a moment to catch her breath. She took in the view of the huge city of Xannellion with all of its stone and dust. She scanned the horizon longingly. Her gaze turned to the front of the castle. "That hideous statue! Xzavier is crazy!"

Xzavier loved wrought iron and gathered the best smiths in the south of Trivar to work this iron until it looked like delicate lace. Wrought iron framed windows and pictures, was made into banisters for circular staircases, and formed tables, chairs, and chandeliers. It was everywhere. Worst of all was the black wrought iron statue of Xzavier at the front of his castle.

"He has no taste. That's for certain," Jaden said, shaking her head disapprovingly.

The sun rested heavily in the western sky, and she knew that if she did not keep moving she would be late and Xzavier would be angry. "Not that he pays any attention to me once I am present," she mused to herself. With one last gaze at the sunset, Jaden took a shallow breath and marched on.

"Mother, you do look spectacular."

Jaden fortunately remembered to turn around slowly to avoid getting pinched.

"A little stiff?" Zachariah asked. He was accompanied by two young ladies, one on each arm who wore the same style of dress as Jaden.

"This new fashion is an insult to women! Don't tease me. I am in no mood. You poor girls!"

Zachariah passed by his mother with his companions. "I am not that bad!" Zachariah smirked.

"No, you aren't. But these dresses are."

The girls smiled curtly.

"Mother, content yourself. Tonight is going to be full of glorious food, elegant company, and entertainment that promises to amuse even you. Maybe there are benefits to Xzavier's arrogant flaunting of our wealth and his paranoid obsession with declaring his status to the world!"

"It is probably a good thing that there are still a few rich but weak kingdoms for Xzavier to rape, pillage, and plunder. Otherwise, he might become as bored as me, and then what worse diabolical plans might he pursue?" Jaden said.

Zachariah leaned in close to Jaden, "If you have to be here, you may as well enjoy it. Try." He kissed her cheek and waltzed off with the girls.

Approaching the dance floor, Jaden thought the music sounded less like music and more like dying swans or angry elephants. The musicians came from a village south of Yamis, Xzavier's latest conquest. Reed instruments blown loudly were underscored with primitive drums and large rattles. Although two or three different flutes whistled an almost-pleasant melody, the combination of sounds still reminded Jaden of raucous animals.

She walked over to Xzavier and sat in her ornate seat of satin, less able to breathe while sitting.

"You call this fashion? I call it torture!"

"Maybe it will keep you quiet tonight, my pleasant Jaden."

Jaden ignored him and watched the young couples dancing around the band. The combination of harsh music and intoxicating drinks turned the party into a wild display of inhuman behavior. Two women began cat-fighting in front of the royal couple. Xzavier allowed it to go on, seeming to enjoy their bodies becoming more and more exposed, until Jaden realized he was going to do nothing and called for the guards to break it up.

"Remove them from the castle immediately," she ordered.

Xzavier glared at her but said nothing. As the night progressed, more and more disorderly behavior erupted like fire that refused to be put out. Before long, Jaden felt exhausted by it all. The gaudy gold, the overused wrought iron, the obnoxious music, the drunken women and men who acted like untamed beasts. She sat by Xzavier long enough to satisfy him and then stood to go.

"Leaving so soon? We have some jugglers coming to entertain us. You don't want to miss the jugglers, do you?"

"Of course not, but I am concerned that the circulation in my legs may never return if I don't get out of this awful dress. Goodnight, Xzavier."

Xzavier laughed, waved Jaden away, and kissed a young lady whom Jaden had never before seen at the palace or elsewhere.

Jaden fought her way through the drunken crowds and was about to make her final escape when someone grabbed her shoulders from behind.

Jaden turned carefully to see Zachariah, rosy cheeked and smiling, "Where are you going?"

"Away from this insanity."

"But it is fun."

"No, Zachariah, this is not fun. It is insufferably unfulfilling. But if you are enjoying it, I am glad for you."

Zachariah's countenance fell. "I'll walk with you."

"You don't have to. You might miss the jugglers," she scoffed.

"I like jugglers." Zachariah glanced back toward the chaos and then turned to his mother, "You don't like jugglers?"

"I don't like any of this. I just want to find out where I'm from."

"Well, you don't have to get angry about it."

"Go enjoy your jugglers!" Jaden whisked the other way too suddenly, and the metal cage dug into her midsection. She gasped and slowed down, refusing to look back. She hated arguing with her son. He was the one bright spot in her life, next to Justine.

She walked as quickly as she could back to her room and changed into a comfortable gown. Out of spite, she threw the cage off her balcony and laughed. She turned back toward her confines with its golden perimeter and stopped.

She buried her face in her hands. Without thinking more, she ran out her chamber door. She hurried through the back hallways toward the dungeon, talking aloud to herself en route.

"I have to find my real home. The dreams I have...the blue-eyed man...I know I belong somewhere. There must be people out there, family who will care for me. I hoped I would learn more in Xannellion, but there is nothing! And now I am trapped here, surrounded by stone and filth with no hope for freedom! Xzavier will never leave Xannellion, and he'll never allow me to find my home.

"So many years I lived in the splendid, lush Yamis jungle and yet longed to be free of it. They called me a princess. But it was a lie! I was a servant! I washed and cleaned and lived with the slaves! Now look at me. I am Queen of Xannellion, and I'm still not free!"

Jaden arrived at the heavy dungeon door and tried to open it but was too upset to muster the strength necessary. Suddenly, a hand from behind opened it.

"Who..."

"Mother, it is me."

Jaden fell silent, momentarily lost for words.

"I was debating," Zachariah explained, "whether or not to knock on your chamber door when you flew out. I was worried and followed. I heard everything."

Jaden grabbed handfuls of her hair and screamed a muted scream. "You aren't supposed to see me like this. Leave me alone!"

She hoped to get to the dungeon alone, but Zachariah followed. A few steps down, she turned around and said, "Aren't there some jugglers to entertain you back there?"

Zachariah halted on the top step, brooding like a puppy that had been kicked by its master. Deflated, he obediently pivoted to leave.

Jaden crumbled to the stairs. "Don't go. I am not angry at you. I am just angry. I feel trapped, and I can't take much more."

Zachariah hung his head and shifted his footing. "Can I ask you a question? Why did you say you were a slave in Yamis?"

Jaden forced herself to stand. "Come with me," she said, holding her hand out to her son.

Jaden and Zachariah descended into the dungeon. In the semi-darkness, they heard a man's voice and froze. They inched forward slowly and silently, but the voice faded into the dark.

"Did you hear that?" Jaden whispered.

"Yes." Zachariah called out, "Is someone there?"

"It is just me, Phillip. I am feeding the dragons."

Zachariah looked questioningly at Jaden, who shrugged. A soft golden-orange glow appeared in the darkness and moved toward them. As Phillip approached them, the semidarkness revealed the Scorpion wearing an amber bracelet. Jaden stared at the bracelet, and he immediately put both hands behind his back.

Phillip came out of the darkness looking sickly. "What are you two doing?"

"We needed a reprieve from the party. I wanted to look after Justine. The jugglers are performing. You shouldn't miss them."

Phillip looked suspiciously at them but seemed equally pleased with an escape. "Yes, the jugglers."

When the dungeon door closed behind the Scorpion, Jaden sat down on a step. Zachariah sat beside her.

Jaden said, "Why did you leave the party to come find me?"

"I wanted to see the jugglers. But when Xzavier tried to join them, I couldn't watch. He was wearing one of those new dress cages over his clothes while trying to juggle. He is embarrassing us. He is embarrassing the whole kingdom. It makes me so angry. But there will be more jugglers, more wine, more lavish parties, and more embarrassment for our kingdom, I am sure. You know, I really can't think about it more, or I might escape on his dragon and leave forever!"

"Please don't do that. I can't bear this by myself."

"Then come with me," he said. "We really should, you know. Let's go somewhere pleasant and wait out Xzavier's life. We don't have to be hurt and embarrassed by him ever again."

"We'd have to stage another coup when we returned to claim the throne. I'd rather not have to fight and kill in order to rule here. No, we need to stay. We have to stay. You will be king, and then we can do things right."

Silence passed between them.

"Mother, why did say you were a servant or slave when you were a child?"

"I hated my childhood."

"What? How could you hate growing up in Yamis?"

"You were a prince and had everything you wanted. You wouldn't understand."

"But you were a princess and had everything you wanted – didn't you?"

"As a child I felt so alone, so uncared for, so different. My skin was pale and ugly compared to everyone else's copper skin, and my red curly hair never laid flat like Talla's black hair did. Yes, I was a princess, but in name only. After Tallu was born, I slept in the maidservant quarters, where I felt neither comfortable nor safe."

"You are lying. Talla would never make you sleep with the servants."

"Talla loved you, but she never loved me."

A gloomy heaviness entered Jaden's voice. "My earliest childhood memories are living on a pirate ship."

Zachariah sat speechless, causing Jaden to chuckle quietly. "Xzavier forbade me to tell you that part of my story, but it is time you knew."

She let her comments settle in and started again. "I remember when I was very young walking behind the pirate captain into Teeku's large open-air hut. The pirate captain was the first guardian I recall. Teeku and Talla were being fanned with palm branches. They seemed so old to me, and I remember how dark their skin looked but how beautiful they were. Once the captain was allowed to speak, he said, 'This one is my special one. Look at her jade eyes. Have you ever seen color like that? Now you know why I named her Jaden!'"

"You were named by a pirate? I am impressed."

Jaden let out an unruly chortle and Zachariah joined in. It felt good to laugh together. Jaden picked up the story again. "As he spoke, I hid behind his leg. The pirate just laughed and pushed me forward. I remember Talla wanting me, probably because she wanted a child so badly, but Teeku wasn't convinced. He said, 'But she's a girl. Who will rule when we are gone? A girl?' He sounded disgusted.

"Talla didn't give up and I remember them talking about dragons, though I didn't know what a dragon was, and the worth of an egg versus a young dragon, and a female dragon versus a male, and what I was worth compared to them all. Teeku seemed angry about everything and so did the captain."

"I can't believe you were brought to Yamis by pirates. Was the captain nice to you?"

"I only have vague memories on the ship, but I do remember that when Talla finally bought and paid for me and her servants were going to take me away, I looked back at the pirate and wanted to cry. I didn't want him to leave. I remember seeing tenderness in his eyes, and I ran back to him.

"I hugged him, and he dropped to my level and spoke kindly to me. I remember him saying 'You are my Jaden, huh? You be a good pirate, like I taught you.' He looked up at the royal couple. 'I always told my men she was special. You have one that I haven't been able to give up easily. Take care of her!' He tossed my hair then pushed me away, wrinkling his nose, but then he never looked back. The servants pulled me away and I cried."

"So you never learned to like it in Yamis?"

"I loved the beauty in Yamis, though the jaguars always scared me. I loved being by the sea. I loved Justine, and when you came along, I loved you. But I always felt displaced there, like I did not belong. I always wanted to know where I was from. In fact, when I was about five, I remember my maidservant chastening me, 'Jaden, you must not ask your mother those questions again. You hurt her.'

"I pressed, 'But I want to know why my hair is red and everyone else's is black. Why is my skin like cream, and yours is like coco?'"

"You asked Talla that? I never worried about what color my skin was," Zachariah said.

"Of course. You had a mother and father who looked just like you. I didn't know it was wrong or how offensive it was, like I do now. I was only told, 'Those are the kinds of questions you can't ask.'

"Generally, Talla would defend my right to ask questions because she wanted me to be an intelligent queen, but not those questions. I remember a day when I was especially persistent in asking why I was different, and she said sternly, 'I like that you ask questions, but when it comes to who you are, all that matters is that you are a princess of Yamis, nothing else.'

"Yet I persisted. 'But where did the pirates bring me from?'

"I remember Talla looking down at me. She always kept her distance as she would with one of her servants. 'Let me tell you something.' Talla took my hand so that I would keep up with her long strides and led me outside.

"I vividly remember walking through the jungle, into the open sunlight of the beach, and then to the edge of the sea and wishing that I could see where I came from. I asked something like, 'Did I come from out there?'

"All she said was, 'You were sent here to be our next queen and for no other purpose. The only place worth anything in all of Trivar is Yamis. You are lucky the pirates brought you here. We have everything. Food grows by itself. The sea and the jungle provide all our meat. Our warriors protect us from inlanders, and pirates are our friends. You are here to enjoy the splendors of this land and become a queen. Do you understand?'

"I did understand. I wasn't to ask the questions that meant the most to me because Talla didn't have an answer for me or didn't want me to upset her peace. I looked quietly out to sea wishing I could see more and feeling like a lid was shut on my core desires. But I did the only thing a five-year-old has power to do. I looked sadly into Talla's eyes and nodded my head, yes. Talla looked not unkindly upon me. But even as young as I was, I never desired to be close to her again.

"It was shortly after that that Talla became pregnant with Tallu and everything changed. I remember a servant saying sadly to me, 'Well, looks like you will have a little brother or sister in a short time. What will that make you?' I didn't understand at the time, but it became quite clear as the months and years passed."

"How did you stand it?"

"I don't know. I remember a day when Tallu was just learning to roll from his tummy to his back and from his back to his tummy. Everyone sat in the large hut watching him for hours. I got so bored. Luana and Arabetta were bored, as well, and began teasing me about my red hair and freckles. I hated them.

"On days like that I usually asked to go see Justine. No one cared much, and I usually got to go. But that day, they wanted me to stay and be happy about Tallu's milestone. I remember asking to see Justine, and when they wouldn't give me permission, I burst into tears. Talla became upset, and Teeku ordered me to go.

"I ran out of the large hut and turned down the sandy path toward the sea, tears blinding my eyes. When I got to the beach, I stopped to look out beyond the sparkling waters, but the tears kept coming, clouding my view. Running south along the shore on my well-worn trail, I passed cave after cave until I arrived at the large one guarded by huge Yamis warriors.

"Because of my tears, I could barely distinguish the guards from the palm trees and, without saying a word, flew past them into the dark. I couldn't see anything in the cave, but that only slowed me slightly because I knew my way through those passages as if they were a part of me. I rushed past one cove after the next until I heard the familiar grunts of my special dragon.

"In the torchlight I was able to see her dark figure lying on the ground, and I threw myself onto Justine's back and sobbed her name. I remember crying until I felt like I couldn't breathe, and I had to pound my chest and scream to get the air to flow again. I remember a guard saying roughly, 'Jaden, you will wake the other dragons!'

"I tried to slow the pain but couldn't and buried my head in Justine's mane to muffle the sound.

" 'Jaden!' The guard repeated.

"I jerked my head up and glared in his direction, trying to control my breathing. I whispered to Justine between sobs, 'No one...cares about me... I am too...different... I am not...cute...like stupid Tallu...with his dark skin...and black eyes... Oh, Justine...I am so glad...you aren't coco-colored... I needed you to...be different, too... I hate Arabetta and Luana...and Teeku.' I added Teeku in almost a whisper so the guards wouldn't hear me. Then I buried my head in Justine's mane and cried myself to sleep."

Jaden chuckled softly. "What awful memories. I am sorry. Although that was one of the worst nights, it was also one of the best because that was the first night that the man with blue eyes came to me in my dream and said, 'Jaden, you are loved.' "

"That was the first dream you had with him? You were still really young."

"Yes, I was seven."

"What happened in that dream?"

"Not much. I just looked up at him and wanted to run to him but found myself crying instead. Behind him I saw the woman with black hair and green eyes. The blue-eyed man reached his arms out to me. Then the dream faded away."

Jaden sat quietly for a moment before speaking again. "I don't know why they always leave. I want them to stay. I want to understand who they are and what they are saying. When I began having the dreams, I knew I had to be free but didn't know where to go...until Xzavier came.

"He came three years after my first dream, when I was ten, and we were all in the large hut. I was trying to look interested as Tallu received fencing lessons from a Yamis warrior. The king and queen watched proudly. A skeleton of a boy came stumbling into the court. I remember gasping, not because the boy was so emaciated, but because he had skin the color of cream, and he had sandy-colored hair. The servants looked at the royal couple, and when Teeku nodded, they quickly fetched the boy.

"By this time, I felt more like one of the servants than a member of the royal family, though Talla and Teeku still referred to me as a princess. I rushed to the young boy with the rest of the servants. He seemed so beautiful to me. My heart ached for him and wanted more than anything to see him survive. I reached out and touched his face, but as I did, one of the guards picked him up and brought him to the servant's quarters. They had to work quickly to save him.

"I followed the group of servants and guards to their quarters. I knew I didn't fit in at Yamis, but it hadn't crossed my mind, at least not seriously, that there were others like me besides the people from my dream. I wanted to cry and laugh at the same time. He had to live.

"Xzavier was almost twelve when he arrived. He had escaped with his nurse from Xannellion after his father tried to murder him because of a prophecy that Xzavier would someday rise up, kill him, and take his kingdom." Jaden scoffed lightly at the irony and continued, "They traveled for months in the jungles. His nurse died from exposure and starvation, having given everything to Xzavier so he would make it alive to Yamis.

"When Xzavier recovered he was determined to return to Xannellion and overthrow his father. Teeku saw his potential and believed his tale about Cannote trying to murder him. Teeku offered to help supply Xzavier with whatever he needed to overthrow Cannote and take possession of Xannellion.

"Teeku never wanted to leave Yamis but believed that the boy would remember him after Xzavier gained rule over Xannellion. When Xzavier agreed to conspire with Teeku, Teeku promised him any woman in the kingdom. I made myself that woman.

"Teeku and Xzavier worked together for seven years to raise dragons, increase their wealth, and collect the rarest specimens of animal and plant in order to placate Cannote. Xzavier went along with it until one day...Teeku and Talla were dead. After slaying Teeku in his sleep, he sent Tallu into the most southern regions of Yamis alone, confident that the dragons would finish him off. I never saw or heard of him again. Xzavier actually felt somewhat close to Talla and couldn't kill her. But she saved him the trouble by poisoning herself the morning after Xzavier killed Teeku."

"He killed them? How do you stand him? I hate Xzavier more than ever. Why did you tell me this?"

"Don't you want to know what really happened? Don't you want to know why I can no longer falsify my attentions to him? Don't you want to know that Teeku and Talla didn't do the horrible things Xzavier told you they did?"

"Why did you let me believe those terrible things? I loved them."

"Should I have caused you to believe horrible things about your father instead?"

"I don't know if I can hold my tongue any longer!" Zachariah said.

"You have to! All of this is for you. We have handled it this long..."

"You have handled it this long, though I don't know how. I will kill him, mother, if I ever get a chance."

"No! Then you will be just like him. Every time he kills someone he sinks lower in his own filth. I have watched it. Please don't fall as he has, please. For me."

Jaden rose abruptly. She walked quickly to Justine and Danthor, Xzavier's dragon, and unchained them.

"Mother?" Zachariah said.

"Come with me, son," she urged.

"Do you think Phillip will come back into the dungeon tonight?"

"No, he was hiding something. Did you see that glowing thing on his wrist? He knows he would have to explain it to us if he were to run into us again, and there is no fear of Xzavier coming down. He will be hung over for the next two days."

Zachariah snickered. Jaden led Justine to the back door, followed by Zachariah with Danthor. Jaden found the mild night air instantly refreshing.

"We've never flown together before," Zachariah said.

Jaden laughed sardonically. "I hope, once Xzavier finds out we've borrowed his dragon, that we live to do it again."

They mounted the dragons and flew into the darkness, the fresh air fanning their faces. It was quiet for a long time, except for the wind whistling across the wings of the dragons. Jaden led as they flew out over the jungle toward the west ocean. For some time they coasted over the black sea in the moonlight, lulled by rushing wind. Later they soared over the length of the beach as the tide below ebbed and flowed.

Eventually, Jaden reluctantly turned Justine back toward the castle hoping that Zachariah would follow. She felt uncertain that he would because he was so angry. Moments later Zachariah flew over her, swooping down in front and spinning Danthor.

Jaden followed, and she and Justine executed a perfect barrel roll. In a few minutes they were flying around each other and racing back to the castle. Jaden stabilized Justine and let go of her mane, throwing her head and arms back, inhaling the fresh air. For that moment at least, she was free.

4

The Third Daughter Prophecy

Two years passed. Jaden sat on her dark marble throne next to Xzavier, who slumped in his throne with his head in his right hand and pouted about boredom. Zachariah stood at Jaden's right. She watched as an older man guarded by four soldiers walked slowly into the throne room past cold pillars of black and white marble. The man's wrists were tied behind his back, but he didn't appear to be much of a threat.

He passed through the streams of light that entered through long, narrow windows high above them. The man's shoulders were straight and broad. He was dressed in the white robes of the Jeremian knights, a fanatic group of religious zealots who refused to be ruled by Cannote or Xzavier or any of the kings of Xannellion. They believed that Gillantri, the god of Arway, their heaven, was their one and only king. The Jeremian people and their knights called themselves Arwavians. They were a thorn in Xzavier's side.

The prisoner held his head high and stood serene. Jaden was disgusted. Jaden expected Xzavier's demeanor to change once he realized that a Jeremian knight was approaching, and it did. He lifted his head, let his arm drop, and narrowed his eyes. Xzavier scrutinized the man for several minutes. Finally, he stood and walked down the seven stairs to the floor and approached the man, demanding, "What are you doing here?"

"I am here because I believe in Gillantri and the laws of Arway. And because I won't worship you, you have destroyed my village. I was taken prisoner because I would not yield to your demands that we support you just because we live in the shadow of Xannellion. You must stop persecuting our people. You killed my entire family and will no doubt kill me, but I feel compelled to come before you and urge you to stop persecuting the good people of Trivar."

Xzavier looked at him, surprised at his boldness.

"You do this of your own will? What a fool. You will die soon. Our next chariot race needs a pre-game show and our Twin Shaumas love to eat Arwavians. You Arwavians are the only thing that comes between me and obtaining the rest of Trivar."

"Your problem is that you are too lazy to work for what you need and want. If you knew anything about your kingdom, you would respect the people who live here instead of taxing them into poverty so that you can sit on your throne, sleep with your concubines, and abuse your son and his mother..."

Xzavier slapped him with the back of his hand, causing his cheek to bleed and said, "I am through with this conversation. Take him to the dungeon and get him nice and fat for our upcoming games."

Xzavier didn't watch him leave. He turned and walked casually to his throne and sat down.

"Jaden, do you ever get bored of all this?"

"Often."

"Of course, you'd rather be dreaming about some imaginary family or some faraway place. Why do I still talk to you, anyway?"

Zachariah leaned forward. Jaden shot him a warning look.

"Father, I have an idea," Zachariah offered.

"If it has to do with your ridiculous navy, I won't hear it."

"No, it has to do with a plan I have for a massive crossbow that can shoot gigantic arrows or bolts over the highest wall or across the sea to enemy ships. There is the option of having them lit with fire or explosives timed to detonate as they..."

"Zachariah, why do you dream like this? Oh, yes, because you are too much like your mother."

Zachariah ignored his mother's second warning look. "That peasant, though a despicable Arwavian, was right. You are lazy and care only for your concubines and for hurting us. If you would drink and sleep less, you might wake up and realize that with very little creativity and effort, you could rid us of the pirates invading our northern coastline, which would save thousands of pounds of gold that now goes toward paying those pirates to retreat, only to have them return and demand more later.

"You might also realize that there are more effective ways to fight battles, to collect and use taxes, and still get the people behind you. And you might appreciate that my mother is more valuable than you know. You might even see that you have a son with merit as well. I have the plans and the ability to build and run a navy for you if you'd give me the resources I yet lack, but you wave me off like a rebellious child, drink some more, sleep some more, and hurt us some more!"

Zachariah was breathing heavily. He had chastened his father before, but Jaden had never seen him go this far. Xzavier slowly stood to his full height and straightened his broad shoulders. He was shorter than Zachariah by an inch or so, but he outweighed him by fifty pounds, making him look much larger. Jaden sat rigid, trying to control her anger so as not to make the situation worse.

"Son," Xzavier hissed, "you think you are brave to speak so boldly, but you must know that I remember every word of treason in this realm, and it will not go unpunished."

A cold draft made Jaden feel dangerously exposed as Xzavier turned to his guards. "I am done for the day. Send out all the courtiers and loiterers. Close the throne room door, and send in my ladies."

Jaden rose and left immediately, leaving Zachariah standing alone in front of his father's throne.

The next afternoon at the same long table where Cannote was killed two years earlier, Jaden and Zachariah were eating their midday meal. Jaden could feel Zachariah watching her.

"Why did you have to say all that yesterday?"

Zachariah smiled wickedly. "It felt so good."

"But you know you put yourself in danger every time you do that."

"What's he going to do? Kill me? That crazy Arwavian spoke the truth. I could no longer stand there and say nothing when, at peril of his life, an insane man spoke what I have always felt but dared not say."

"No one is safe with Xzavier."

Awkward silence followed.

"So, how did you sleep last night?" Zachariah tried changing the subject.

Jaden ate a bite of fruit and replied slowly, "I had another dream..."

Xzavier interrupted Jaden by entering the hall. Seeing that she stopped speaking, he waved his hands impatiently, "No, go ahead, tell us about your dream. I'd love to hear it."

"Did you sleep with the pigs last night? You look awful," Jaden stated without hiding her disdain. Xzavier was so hung over that he either did not notice or chose to ignore her. Zachariah snickered.

Jaden began in a hushed voice, hoping Xzavier would not hear much, "I was in a foreign land, much like Yamis, green and lush but more lovely, and I saw a beautiful girl..."

"A beautiful girl, you say? Now that is the kind of dream I could get into." Xzavier sat down next to Jaden and gave her a sloppy kiss on the cheek.

Jaden moved away and turned toward Zachariah, trying to ignore Xzavier. "Well, the beautiful girl had two older women with her, perhaps the same women I saw with the baby on the war ship in dreams past. One woman looked old enough to be the girl's mother, and the oldest one could be her grandmother. They were all three pleading for my help, when suddenly, they all transformed into exquisite lilies in the summer sunlight. The youngest became a silvery blue lily, the next oldest a darker blue, and the oldest a midnight blue lily."

Xzavier's face grew dark. "You are filling our son with foolishness. First the sea, and now The Third Daughter Prophecy..."

"The Third Daughter Prophecy?" Zachariah inquired.

Jaden flashed her son a warning look as Xzavier answered him. "It is just some ancient fable perpetuated by dotty old men who try to lead the young astray."

Xzavier turned back to Jaden. "Our son is never going to be the greatest warrior of Xannellion if he believes in fabled dreams and longs for the unsteady sea."

Jaden stood quickly, knocking her chair to the floor. "Our son is the greatest warrior in Xannellion. He has proven that in tournament after tournament, race after race. When will you open your eyes and see?!" Her heart raced.

Xzavier snickered slowly, surprised but amused by Jaden's outburst. "I will believe he is the finest warrior in all Xannellion after the New Moon Festival."

"What?" Jaden dared to ask.

"I have put together a little competition..."

"No! You promised!"

"Jaden, sit down, really! Calm yourself!" Xzavier stood to leave. "This isn't your concern. There has been some question about whether my son is truly undefeatable, and I am determined to find out."

"You promised after the last race that you would never again require him..."

Xzavier sneered as he walked toward the door. Over his shoulder he shot out, "Do you really believe in your stupid dreams, Jaden? If you do, you are a fool. I'm going to get some food in the kitchen and let you talk about these things."

Xzavier opened the door, but before he left, Zachariah pursued the question. "Who would know about this prophecy?"

"My father would..." Xzavier laughed contemptuously as he departed. His voice trailed off as the door closed.

Jaden looked at Zachariah, looked at her food, noticed the dark, wretched stain on the table and threw her bowl across the room, shattering it against the far wall.

****

Later that evening in the dark, rank dungeon crawling with dragons and their offspring and teeming with bats in the rafters, Jaden walked quickly down the cement stairs.

"Xzavier."

"Quiet," he hissed. "You'll wake them!"

Jaden inhaled quickly and plunged in, disregarding his warning. "Are you really planning a race for the New Moon Festival?"

"Just after the Twin Shaumas finish off that dirty Arwavian."

"Do you wish our son to live to see his twentieth birthday?"

The dragons began screeching wildly.

"Look, you woke the dragons. Now they need dinner."

"Xzavier, answer my question." Jaden felt beads of sweat forming on her forehead. "I will stay until you answer me."

"You just don't understand," he spat out the words. "You never did. Power isn't something that someone hands you because you are beautiful. It is something you have to work for. And once you have it, you must work harder to keep it. Zachariah is wrong to accuse me, of all people in this kingdom, of laziness.

"You see, I have not forgotten his words. And work, Jaden, is something you have done so little of in your precious life. But I didn't bring you here for your ability to work. No, putting up with you and the boy was a fair price for obtaining the whole of Teeku's kingdom. And I guess you still have some beauty left, although there used to be more rewards..."

Xzavier came forward and passionately kissed Jaden, who struggled to break free. Xzavier released her, smoothed his robe and laughed.

"You promised he would never race again..."

"He's young and strong. Besides, I have to prove Xannellion's strength. I cannot be seen as weak. We will either have to go to war to prove our strength or it has to be Zachariah. And well, it isn't time for war – yet."

"I will not allow it. It is too dangerous." Jaden felt heat in her face.

Xzavier swung around and began backing her out of the dungeon, speaking slowly and quietly. "Who is in control of Zachariah's training? Who has gotten him this far? Who knows how to keep power in this pathetic kingdom? It is I, not you. You eat the fruits of my bold plans and bask in the glory of my hard work." He spoke the last three words with grave emphasis.

She retreated another step and felt the cold stone wall behind her. "What if Zachariah dies?"

Xzavier leaned in close. She could feel his breath on her face.

"You selfish woman. Do you ever listen to me? This is not about Zachariah."

With that, he turned back to his dragons and, almost as an afterthought, backhanded Jaden into the wall where she wrinkled in a heap to the hard, cold ground. Startled rats and spiders scurried, and bats flew out of their roosting.

She lay there unconscious while he returned to his pet dragons as if nothing had happened.

"Oh, my precious babies," he said to the dragons. "Soon you will be able to fly through the country. The day will come when you will rule the skies, and I will rule the whole of Trivar."

****

Something nibbled Jaden's toes. She tried to sit up, but her head throbbed. She felt as if she were coming out of a dark hole when she tried to open her eyes, which refused to focus. Where was she? She groaned. Her head hurt. She tried to sit up again but fell back against the hard wall. In the dim dungeon, Jaden saw Justine's yellow eyes staring down at her.

"What are you doing here, girl? How did you get out of your nest?" Jaden held Justine's chain to help herself up. Her body felt bruised all over. She heard the squeaking and scurrying of rats and the rustling of bat and dragon wings. Her body throbbed, but a deeper pain surfaced as she remembered the reason why she was on the floor. She returned Justine to her nest. Brewing with anger, she worked her way to the stairs in the darkness.

Emotions boiled inside her as she absently felt her swollen lip and the dried blood that spilled in a thin line down her chin. She paused in her pursuit of the stairs and let out a cry of pain. Angry tears burned the corners of her eyes. Leaving the rats, bats and dragons behind her in an uproar, she climbed the stairs.

She had descended these stairs to confront Xzavier shortly after the evening meal the day before. Now light flooded through a small window at the top of the stairs. Passing the window, she paused to see bright daylight, the source of which seemed directly above her. Could she have been out for that long?

Jaden finished the climb and tried to open the door to the upper castle. The heavy door was difficult for her to open on normal occasions, but she was now too sore and weak to move it. She punched the door and leaned against it with all her weight, when suddenly, it opened. She turned around to hide her face, but there was no way to avoid being seen by her deliverer.

"Mother! What happened? You are filthy and bleeding."

Zachariah picked up Jaden. She winced but gladly sank into her son's arms. Zachariah carried her quickly and quietly through the back hallways and up the servant's stairs toward Jaden's bedroom.

"I have been looking for you since you missed breakfast. When I inquired about you to Xzavier, I mean my father..."

"You can call him Xzavier," Jaden offered with a weak smile.

"Xzavier said that you must have been out late last night, and his snickering told me that something was wrong. I have secret riders looking all over Xannellion for you, but I didn't think until now to look in the dungeon...You need to eat. I saved your afternoon meal for you."

Up to that point, Jaden hadn't thought about food but now realized that she was very hungry.

Zachariah carried her to her chamber and carefully put her in bed. "Are you going to be all right if I leave you for a moment?"

"Yes, yes, of course." Jaden closed her eyes. It felt good to be in her soft bed.

Zachariah returned with a plate of food, which she consumed heartily. After Jaden finished eating and cleaned up, she returned to her bed and Zachariah took a chair in the corner. Jaden fell asleep for the rest of the day.

When she woke, Zachariah jumped to his feet. "Mother, what's wrong?"

Jaden fell back on her pillow. Zachariah stood by, unsure of what to do.

"Go sit down. I'll be fine. My whole body feels bruised, but I will heal."

Zachariah pulled his chair next to Jaden's bed. As they looked at each other, she saw her own eyes in his. She also discerned his anger at his father mixed with compassion for her.

"I will kill him when I am king! I will!" He reached for his mother's hand and buried his face into it.

"Save your anger for another day, my son. You will be king, but you must play the game. Be careful. Do not anger your father. Go along with him. We have upset him enough for a time."

Silence followed for a moment, and she could see Zachariah formulating something in his mind. So she waited.

"Mother," he said somberly, "I have been making some inquiries at the wharf about The Third Daughter Prophecy."

Jaden's eyes brightened and filled with curiosity, and then a wave of concern clouded her countenance. "Does your father know?"

"No. But I am learning some interesting things. I might need to take a trip on a ship to a place northeast of Alexandria called Wallace."

"And when would you be planning this trip, son?"

"After the tournament."

"Xzavier will never let you."

Zachariah shrugged. "I think he won't have much say in the matter. I am not asking him. But that isn't what I am most concerned about. I want you to come with me. You've wanted to escape Xannellion since we came here two years ago. 'Get me out of these dirty, hot streets and back to the fresh air,' you've said. What air is fresher than sea air?"

"You would ask me to enter Arwavian territory? That scares me more than Xzavier."

"Ever since your dream the night before we entered Xannellion, I can't get those haunted green shores out of my mind. I think I will find them in Wallace. I have to sail there...and I have a man who will take me. I know we will find the answers to all of your questions about where you came from. And I need to know more about this Third Daughter that you dream about. She is compelling to me. But I can't leave you here. Not after what Xzavier has done."

Jaden rubbed her head. "I can't talk about this anymore today. Please promise me that you will focus on winning this race first. We'll discuss Wallace after. I need you alive, Zachariah."

"Oh, I'll be living, don't worry about that. I have things to do..."

Jaden closed her eyes.

5

Longing

Jaden woke from a dream. Tears streamed from her eyes. In the darkness, crickets chirped and frogs trilled. As she calmed down, bits and pieces of her dream returned, but nothing fit together. The face of the blue-eyed man lingered. His eyes were gentle but upset...angry. But it was not the hot, vindictive anger she knew from Xzavier. This was different somehow. In the dream she was running from the blue-eyed man. At the end of the dream she turned to him. The sorrow and compassion in those blue eyes softened her stubborn, tortured soul. Then she woke.

She got out of bed, knowing it was fruitless to try to go back to sleep. Her preoccupation turned to Zachariah's race today. It had been a fortnight since Xzavier's assault. Her bruises had faded, but the emotional pain caused by Xzavier's unkindness had not. And today her son would play a pawn in a foolish and dangerous chariot race for the purposes of proving Xannellion's strength and feeding Xzavier's narcissism.

Xannellion chariot races were a regular pastime. They were wasteful, generally, but lucrative for some. So many lives were snuffed out by that one event that people made a living selling pine boxes outside the gates before the race.

Jaden made fists and brought them to her face in anguish. Maybe Zachariah was right, maybe she would go north with him. Anything would be more tolerable than this, maybe even the fanatic Arwavians. Jaden laughed out loud.

For the rest of the night she paced her room. By sunrise with little sleep and no distraction from her fearful thoughts, her apprehension and distress became unbearable. She needed to get out of the castle and fly.

Jaden left her room quickly. She hated Xannellion with all of its stone and so little soil. Yamis was surrounded by exquisite nature. She missed the feeling of cool moss underfoot. She longed for the sand, sea, and jungle. Though it was dangerous to go into the jungle alone, around the Yamis palace and by the sea Jaden could freely roam.

But in Xannellion, because of her position as queen and the growing hatred of their subjects toward Xzavier, it wasn't safe for her outside the castle walls. She grew potted plants on her deck outside her room and loved her view of the jungle, but she found her only real freedom during the early morning hours when she could quietly sneak Justine out the lower exit of the castle by the moat, get on her back, and fly. There was nothing like the power of a dragon, to feel its wings beat the air and hear its cry as creature and rider ascended into the glowing sky.

When Jaden entered the dungeon, Justine jumped to her feet in anticipation. Jaden walked Justine quietly to the lower exit of the dungeon. Jaden slipped onto Justine's back, and they took to the air, which sent a thrill through Jaden's soul. Once Justine was stable, Jaden threw her head back, breathing in the cool fresh air.

Jaden recalled when Teeku gifted the baby dragon, Justine, to her. Hour after hour, day after day, Jaden fed her, held her, played with her, and pretended to be her mother. As Justine grew, a bond formed that Jaden didn't understand for years. In fact, not until Jaden's adoptive parents were dead did she realize that she had attached more to Justine than to them. Justine was her real family. Jaden laid her head down on Justine's neck and hugged her.

It felt so good, so liberating to fly above the dust and dirt, the haté, anger, and power of Xannellion. She was free to feel her own feelings, free to unwind: no worries, no cares, just freedom. Unfortunately, this morning there wasn't a lot of extra time for freedom, and after a few more minutes she reluctantly turned Justine around to head back, facing the sun and the day that was before her.

Above the trees in the pink dawn, they passed bats returning home after their night of mischief. She hated bats. When she reached the moat, Justine tucked her wings and flew straight into the lower hall by Xzavier's lair, landing softly, so as to not be heard.

But as she and Justine walked through the back door, Jaden saw someone waiting for her in the shadows. Someone knew she had gone out this morning. Her heart sank. She knew there would be trouble. The closer she got, the clearer the person became. Xzavier was waiting. Jaden hadn't spoken with him since he left her unconscious and hurt in his lair a fortnight earlier. In the darkness, she couldn't see the expression on his face but feared the worst.

"Xzavier, what are you doing down here? Don't you need to get ready for the festivities?" she asked absently as she led Justine to her nest.

"You are not permitted to ride these creatures in the daylight. You know that," he said in a smooth but threatening tone.

"They need the fresh air as badly as I do. If you would just keep them in Yamis or somewhere besides this old dungeon…"

"I can't have you ruining things," he spat out in disgust, domineering over Jaden as she patted down Justine.

She set up Justine's bedding and gave her a couple rabbits and an opossum. Justine quickly cracked their backs and put them aside for later when she could eat in peace. Often, Jaden came down to watch the skill of the dragons as they seized and ate their prey, but this morning she hardly noticed.

She was trying to think of a way to get out of the dungeon, when she realized that Xzavier was distracted by the dragons, Justine in particular. Normally, she would ask what he was doing, but, presently, she felt grateful clear path to the stairs.

When she reached the door, Xzavier spoke. "I suggest you mind you today, Jaden. It is an important day for my kingdom."

Jaden bit her lip and restrained her red-haired tendencies as she walked up the stairs. But under her breath she said, "Maybe you should mind yourself today, Xzavier!"

****

At the stadium, a servant peeled and sliced a golden mango for Jaden. He set the dish of sliced fruit on the table in front of her. She ate without tasting. The adrenaline surge and knots in her stomach denied her all pleasure. Not even her brushed satin-cushioned seat and servants waving fans to relieve the muggy afternoon heat had the power to relieve her distress.

Jaden shifted her weight. Her son preoccupied her every thought. Even with the artificial breeze, the air felt stuffy, like a storm was coming. Jaden noticed only a few clouds in the west as a man announced something about a pre-game show. Her focus became acute when she saw Justine paraded center-stage in the arena.

She shot a fierce glance at Xzavier, but he ignored her. A steady rage surfaced from her core. He violated her to the center of her soul. He called the shots for her son with complete disregard for Zachariah's life, and now her dragon was on exhibition in front of the whole kingdom without her permission.

Justine and the Jeremian knight whom Jaden had seen in the throne room weeks ago were both in chains. They were led by a man who was even larger than the knight to the center of the stadium. The man whipped Justine vigorously to anger her. Every crack of the whip pained Jaden's soul. She wanted to rush the field, tackle the offender, and ride away on her dragon.

"I will go north with Zachariah," she said under her breath. "Whether you like it or not, I am through with you," she finished through clenched teeth.

Though he didn't hear her, Xzavier deliberately kissed Luana, then Arabetta, as if nothing else mattered. Jaden resolutely dropped her shoulders as she watched the horrible show that she could neither stop nor escape.

"I need another mango over here," she said sharply. The nearest servant quickly peeled and cut a mango, arranged it nicely on a plate, and placed it on a tray near Jaden. Jaden pushed away the plate and waved off the servant.

Justine thrilled the crowd. Even the most reserved subjects roared with approval. The Jeremian knight, stripped down to a loin cloth, had a sword in his hand. It soon became clear, however, that he had no intention of using it. The large man whipped him, but the knight released the sword, wordlessly exclaiming his refusal to fight Justine.

"Fanatics," Jaden whispered. Justine didn't seem interested in eating him, either.

The crowd gasped. Two fierce black gryphons, the Twin Shaumas, entered the arena from the east entrance. The Shaumas stalked the smaller of the two prey with practiced perfection. Ratana, the smaller gryphon, headed directly toward the Arwavian, and the larger of the two, Tyrane, with eyes narrowed, approached the knight from the rear.

The man prayed to the skies, standing still with his head tilted back and arms at his sides, as Ratana crept toward him. Suddenly, the larger gryphon leaped into the air with ebony wings aloft, aimed his monstrous claws and beak at the knight's back, and hit him hard. The knight died without a cry.

But the gryphons weren't in it for the meat. They were killers. Jaden, usually indifferent, felt nauseated. Tyrane removed himself from the knight and immediately began stalking Justine. The large man whipped Justine hard, forcing her to rear up on her hind legs and let out a bloodcurdling screech that energized the bloodthirsty crowd.

Ratana worked to distract Justine while Tyrane again moved in for the attack. Now, barely breathing, the tense and silent crowd watched the Twin Shaumas in terrible suspense. For five years, the famous gryphons had defeated every human and beast they faced. The Shaumas were two of the few things that Xzavier kept of his father's possessions. Xzavier enjoyed feeding Arwavians, Jeremian flying tigers, jaguars, lions, and other creatures to the Shaumas. But today they would see how a dragon fared.

Justine turned around to see the gryphons stalking her from two directions. Jaden let out the breath she had been unconsciously holding and stifled a laugh. The crowd couldn't read Justine's expression, but she could. Jaden pulled the mangos toward her and ate. Justine stood to her full fifty-hand height and screeched. The man with the whip, now fearing for his own life, ran away, forgetting to unchain Justine.

The crowd was near hysteria. She flapped her enormous wings and leaped onto the closest gryphon. Picking it up in her talons, she dropped it, and then picked it up again, cracking its back. In one swift move she lunged at the other, gripped his head in her mouth and flipped him to his back.

Mortally wounded, the second gryphon convulsed on the ground. Justine hopped over, landed on him, and with her sharp mouth quieted his suffering. Too stunned to react, the crowd was silent. Xzavier sat up straight. But shortly, the crowd regained its voice and went wild, stamping, clapping, and screaming their approval.

"Fan closer to me. It is so muggy today," Jaden said to the nearest servant as thick, dark clouds replaced the fluffy white ones in the western sky. The audience cheered as the Shaumas and the knight left the stadium on stretchers and Justine was herded off the field.

Moments after the center ring was cleared, the charioteers entered the arena from the east side of the Xannellion Stadium. Jaden saw Zachariah's wavy golden hair. He took a couple of swift practice laps before he stopped at the starting line. His confidence showed as he waved to the cheering crowd.

Jaden waved at her son, who waved back as he took his place for the race. When the horns blew, he leaped from his starting box and immediately jockeyed for the front position. By the last corner of the first lap, Zachariah only needed to beat Antonio and James for the lead.

Without warning, Antonio's wheel shot into the center ring, and his chariot teetered and spun out of control. Antonio hit the ground hard. The horse ran wildly, finally stopping near the arena wall. Antonio had wrapped his arms in the reins to keep a better grip, though this had often sealed the death of a charioteer upon impact with the wall or ground.

The crowd erupted. This promised to be a good race. The servants ran to Antonio. By the time they reached him, calmed his horse, and untied him, he was dead. The pit in Jaden's stomach deepened, and she pushed her mango away.

When Jaden spotted Zachariah again, he was whipping his horse on at a reckless pace, vying against James for the lead. Jaden unconsciously covered her mouth with her scarf. She stood to better see her son and James rounding the first corner of the second lap.

"No, Zachariah, please, no," Jaden whispered through her scarf. "Not again."

Zachariah gained on James, but as they sped into the corner, Zachariah, who followed James on the outside, tried to pass him. At that moment, James's right wheel flew straight into Zachariah's left side, knocking him off his chariot like a rag doll. The centrifugal force nearly threw him to the arena's wall. But he, too, had tied his arms to the reins and was jerked back toward his chariot. The horse dragged him, battering him against the ground.

James had not tied his arms to his reins, so when the tire sprung, he was catapulted and trampled by the oncoming chariots. Some tried to dodge him and lost control. Zachariah's horse sped off the track dragging the chariot with Zachariah. A servant finally caught hold of the reins and slowed Zachariah's horse. With the momentum, the chariot and Zachariah crashed into the stone wall.

The crowd cheered. This was what they had come for. Jaden implored Xzavier with tears to let her go down to her son. She was not shocked to see smug satisfaction on his face. Justine had performed perfectly and impressively. Jaden's dragon had won him the day. So why should he care about their son dead or dying on the track? He had proven his power. A raw, bitter resentment for years of injustice and abuse intensified Jaden's rage. Without waiting for permission, Jaden moved in the direction of her son.

Xzavier grasped her arm. "Zachariah is dead. Sit down and finish watching the race." His eyes lit up hotly, but he released her. "After the race, come with me. I have a grand feast planned, accompanied by dragons to entertain us and our guests."

Jaden reeled. "My son could be dying and you want me to leave him? Are you that vile, that you could leave your son, your own flesh, to die? Goodbye, Xzavier."

The crowd on its feet let out another roar. Xzavier's face reddened. He snatched Jaden's arm in an iron grip, pulled her near, and hissed in her face, "Your son was becoming too headstrong, like his mother. He defied me openly in front of my advisors. Never, not even in Yamis, did he support me. You filled him with faerietales and dreams and now you are paying the price. He is nothing anymore. See our kingdom! They are entranced. Justine was miraculous, better than I could have imagined. The future holds glorious possibilities."

He loosened his grip and laughed. In his sweetest tone he said, "Jaden, Zachariah's death was no accident…"

"What?" Jaden felt numb with rage.

Xzavier pulled her close. She tried to free herself in vain.

"This is the game we are in," he said. "One of my servants shot an arrow that sent James and Antonio's wheels flying. Perfectly executed, wouldn't you say? This is what you want. Give up the resistance. Let's rule this kingdom together."

His grip tightened.

Jaden glared at him and tried to pull her arm free. He let her struggle to prove he had control before releasing her. He pulled out a rolled parchment paper enclosed with an official seal.

"Do you see that seal? You know it. It is my seal, the king's seal. I know you, Jaden. I figured you might choose your son over me. Now I see that I was wise to take this precaution. It states that no one in this kingdom can help you. Even better, the black gryphons, wolves, and our dragons will be sent to destroy you and those with whom you flee. I trust that you won't be so foolish as to defy your king. Really, there is no choice here."

He executed these last words so menacingly that it chilled her blood. No choice, she restated in her mind.

"Give me leave to care for my son," she said. Shaking with anger, it was all she could do to keep her voice calm.

"I will mercifully give you one last chance to comply, my headstrong Jaden. You have until sunset to choose before the proclamation will be posted throughout the kingdom. If you defy me, neither of you will live through this night. That I assure you."

As he finished his last words, Jaden darted past him.

6

Freedom

Malice burned inside her. How dare he? But there was no time for that now. Revenge would come later. Jaden reached Zachariah and pushed away the servant attending to him.

"Let me see him!" She began assessing the damage. She didn't notice the winning charioteer make his victory lap. She didn't hear the crowd cheering the winner. Her whole soul was in tune with her son only.

The servant had cut the reins from the traumatized horse and laid Zachariah on his back close to the stone wall. The remains of his chariot shaded his mangled body from the intense direct heat of the sun. Jaden dropped to her son's side.

Her heart broke to see his blond hair streaked with red. Skin on his chest, belly, legs, and arms was raw and burned from having been dragged. She gently touched his face. She put her head close to his chest without hurting him. There was a slight rise and fall! She put her hand by his nose and felt air coming from his mouth... He was alive!

Turning to the servant, she commanded, "Help me rearrange this chariot into a sleigh."

Jaden's hands trembled as she untangled his arms from the reins. Dark clouds continued to accumulate and offered slight but welcome relief from the heat. Jaden set her jaw, narrowed her eyes, and worked with the servant to finish removing the chariot's wheels. They carefully placed Zachariah's broken body on the hard makeshift sleigh.

"I will sit next to him. Lead the horse out the west gate."

"I cannot."

"What! You must! I am queen of this land and I order you to lead my son's horse out the gate!"

The fearful servant said, "I will lead the horse to the gate, Queen Jaden, but I will be killed by my master if I go any farther."

Exasperated, Jaden yelled, "If you don't do it, I will kill you!"

Xzavier had threatened to send the gryphons at sunset. There wasn't much time to escape Xannellion. The servant led them to the stadium's outer gate and stopped. Jaden took the horse's reins and fearfully glanced to the north and to the south.

Just as the sun went behind the clouds, an idea sparked in her mind. Her eyes brightened. She said to the servant, "Stay here. I will be right back!"

The servant sighed in relief. Jaden sniffed at him in disgust, set off toward an inner set of stadium stairs, and ran down. Jaden passed guard after guard who immediately recognized her as the queen and let her pass. She entered the bottom level where they kept the animals. In the far corner, Justine lazily chewed on the hind leg of one of the gryphons. Full and content, Justine barely noticed Jaden until she stood right in front of her.

"Hello, girl. I didn't mean for this to happen. Now we have more to do. I need your help."

Jaden turned to the guard over Justine and ordered, "I need my dragon now."

"I'm not supposed to give her to anyone but Xzavier at the end of the day."

"She is my dragon and you will unlock her."

"Sorry. Xzavier has plans for the dragon. I'll lose my position, lady. Or my life."

Jaden felt the panic rise into her throat. Images of Zachariah flashed in her mind. "I don't have time for this. Give me those keys."

"Take them."

The guard waited defiantly.

In desperation, Jaden climbed onto the dragon's back.

"Justine," she said. "Get him."

The guard dropped the keys and ran into his chamber behind a foot-thick door. Jaden darted from Justine to snatch the keys. She unlocked the chains from Justine's legs and the shackles from around her neck. They hurried through the hallways and up the wide, winding staircase back to the main level.

By the time Jaden returned, a crowd of people stood around Zachariah. Two box sellers had brought their most ornate coffins and were searching for kinsmen to claim the body. The servant was nowhere to be seen. Disgusted, Jaden hurried over to her son. The crowd moved clear of Justine. Some ran away, and others watched from a safe distance.

She pointed to the two sturdiest men. "Carefully pick up my son and put him on my dragon after I am seated!"

The men whispered uneasily while Jaden mounted Justine. Justine obediently bent down as the men picked up Zachariah and placed his long broken body in front of Jaden. Jaden steadied him and leaned forward, clenching some scruff on Justine's mane.

"Fly carefully, girl. Let's go!"

With an enormous flap of her wings, Justine lifted and thrust forward through the gates of the stadium into the intermittent sunlight and headed directly south. The air was hot and muggy, and when the sun broke through the clouds, it burned down on them from the west. The streets were filled with people who were startled by the sound of Justine's large wings beating against the air above them. Women screamed. Men dropped their large bundles or carts and stared. Children hid behind their parents. People scattered in every direction.

Justine flew strong and fast. Jaden led her south to the swampy region where she and her son passed through only two years earlier when they entered Xannellion. She hoped she would have enough time to come up with a plan as she flew over the swamps. Before getting close enough to the southern wall to be spotted, she turned Justine eastward, away from Xzavier's guards.

The southern forests were remote and filled with stumps and rotting trees. Moss clung to everything, creating eerie shapes. The air became muggier over the damp ground. Very few people dared travel in this area, and certainly no one lived there.

Jaden's mind raced, "Where can we go, my son? What chance do we have of getting out of Xannellion? We have no friends, no allies, nothing outside of Xzavier's castle." Jaden again checked the skies. Observing fewer breaks in the gathering clouds, her nerves felt raw.

"Stop being a fool, Jaden, you are stronger than this!"

She loosened her hair out of its setting, letting it fly free.

"But where do we go? I know you would choose a sea route, but your father will have those routes covered first. I can't go to Yamis. There is nothing there now, and it is too far away for you. I need to find somewhere safe from Xzavier but close enough to get help quick... Oh, Zachariah, why did you try to get around James on the corner?"

Jaden dropped her head, completely exhausted and trembling. At that moment, the setting sun broke through on the horizon under the threatening clouds that covered the sky. She lifted her head, allowing the power of the sun to fill her with new resolve.

"Oh, it might work. Can I stand it?" Jaden's face twisted as if she had tasted awful medicine. "It is the only option for you...but Arwavians... What will they do to us? Son, we need to go north. That means we need to get over the northern wall to find cover in the thick northern forests." She directed Justine to fly north.

Shortly, they neared the eastern road out of Xannellion. Jaden saw movement to the northwest coming from the center of Xannellion. Soldiers, wolves, and, "No... No, no, no! Black gryphons on the street. He promised – not until sundown! The sun isn't even touching Mount Sol yet."

Immediately, Jaden pulled Justine eastward again. "We've got to leave Xannellion over the eastern wall and go into the open land to the east. I didn't want to do that. There is no cover. But if we try to cross over this road, we'll have to out-fly gryphons all the way to Jeremiah. If we go to the wall we might buy ourselves a few minutes."

"Think, Jaden, think..."

Flying parallel to the eastern road, she studied her son's profile. An aching pain grew inside of her.

"What am I doing?" Jaden closed her eyes and spoke to the sky. "Do not give in to your fears, Jaden, you have to fight. If there is any possible way to succeed, you will! You are no longer a prisoner inside Xzavier's castle. You must stop acting like one!"

Jaden struggled to keep a grip on Zachariah as he began writhing in pain and moaning. A warm raindrop landed on her cheek, sending a chill through her whole body.

"Not now," she said. Another large drop landed on her forehead, and another, and another. After a moment, the heavens let loose and the rain poured down mercilessly.

Jaden worked to get Zachariah into a more comfortable position while keeping him balanced on Justine's back. Jaden realized that it had only been this morning that she was flying over the jungle to the north of Xannellion. Her stomach growled but eating was the least of her concerns.

"We will make it to that cursed Arwavian city. I hope someone will practice their famous charity on us."

Jaden laughed as she imagined the more-likely reception that she and her son would be offered. She sarcastically rehearsed in her mind her ironic plea, "Please take care of me. I am the Queen of Xannellion, your enemy. The king just brutally murdered one of your people. But our son and I need your help..."

Jaden peered through the pouring rain unable to see the eastern wall. Justine flew strong. Soon, the wall loomed just a short distance away. Guards and wolves were gathered near the east gates, along with three or four gryphons.

"Justine, I need you to fly swift, as sure as you have ever flown, my friend. Take us as high over the wall as you can." As she said this, she wrapped her arms around her son and they flew into the clearing between the forest and the wall. Rain was pouring off them as the wolves spotted them and jumped in their chains.

Guards shouted orders to fire. Jaden heard whistles of arrows flying at them. A few whizzed by close enough for her to see them, but Justine persisted upward. As they flew over the wall, wolves howled and men yelled while trying to keep sight of Jaden. Three black gryphons took flight in pursuit, while the fourth stayed closer to the men running north toward the eastern road. It would only be a short time before more followed.

When they flew over the eastern road outside the city gates, she saw dark figures, like a flock of large crows, clearing the eastern wall of the city.

"More gryphons. No! Justine, fly to the forest north of Xannellion. Maybe we can get lost in the shadows."

Every few seconds Jaden checked behind to see the gryphons gaining. Her heart thumped erratically, "Justine, fly faster!"

By the time they neared the northern wall, the gryphons were so close that she could see their glowing eyes. Jaden held back a scream. Zachariah writhed in pain, making it difficult, especially in the rain, to keep a good hold on him. Right then, and for no apparent reason, the gryphons doubled back toward the east gate.

Jaden stared in disbelief as rain pelted her. It didn't make sense. At that moment, Zachariah fell silent and limp.

"No!"

Breathing heavily, near hysteria, she said, "You cannot die! Do you hear me? Hold on!"

Lowering her head to his chest she felt the slight rise and fall of his shallow breathing. Relieved, she laughed. Her laughter began softly and grew louder until she threw her head back and screamed into the darkness as the rain washed over her.

****

The sun reappeared under the thick cloud cover as it lowered behind Mount Sol. Although it still rained, the warmth of the once oppressive sun now gave Jaden some reprieve. Ahead of her to the northeast, the forest canopy ended abruptly before the base of a substantial hill, revealing many tiny points of light.

It's the Arwavian city of Jeremiah, named for their first leader and martyr, Jeremiah the Sure, Jaden thought. She glanced behind her. Jaden wiped her wet face as the rain stopped. She pictured Arwavian families sitting about their hearths, warmed by a cozy fire and never suspecting what was coming. Again she checked behind for pursuers but saw only engulfing darkness as the sun's light began to fade. She hoped the clouds held no more rain.

Jaden grew increasingly concerned about what was ahead. Even if the Jeremian knights did take her and her son in because of their renowned charity, would the knights have the means and ability to protect them from Xzavier and his dragons? Impatiently, she clenched her jaw. It seemed like they would never get to Jeremiah.

With the darkness came the cold. Jaden worked to keep Zachariah close to her.

"We'll be there soon. We will make it. I just hope they will spare us. Us!" The irony evoked a laugh. "But what am I thinking? There is no choice. We need their charity. Let's hope they are as crazy as people say... Help their enemies in need, indeed," she whispered, glancing nervously behind her.

She cringed in terror.

"Oh, Zachariah, dragons, dragons..." Although distant, she recognized the size and form of Xzavier's dragon in the lead, followed closely by the Scorpion's distinctive beast. That is why the gryphons turned back, she thought. Why trust gryphons when you have dragons? And Xzavier wants to take us down himself. Her anger rose again. They were too quickly closing the gap between them and her. She knew that too soon she would be able to make out Xzavier's face.

The glowing hearth fires of Jeremiah were closer but not close enough. Despite the panic she felt, a secondary plan began to form in her mind.

"Justine, give us all you have, my dear friend. We have to get as far as we can, and then you must let us down quickly. I will tell you when." Closer and closer they came to the Arwavian city, and Jaden began to feel more hopeful.

A drop of rain landed on Jaden's hand. She stared incredulously, just as another landed on her other hand. She let out a low moan and glared at the heavens.

"Justine, drop quickly to that patch of ground below us, beyond that stream." As they descended, she held tightly to Zachariah, who began moaning again, causing the dragons behind to let out their screams. They could almost taste their kill. Then the second deluge of the night let loose from the black skies above.

Jaden's tired body drooped.

"How can I do this?" But as her face fell, she saw her son's face, helpless and nearly lifeless. She rallied her spirits as Justine descended into the forest clearing. When they touched the ground something inside her broke free from the bondage she had so long endured, releasing a reservoir of strength.

Justine lowered her body enough for Jaden to slide off with her son. She couldn't hold him while standing and they fell to the ground. Zachariah moaned loudly, sending Xzavier's dragons into another screeching fit, and Jaden saw clearly what she had to do.

Rain mixed with the salty tears as she turned to her dragon, "Justine, I need you to protect us. Stop them, dear friend." Jaden kissed her muzzle, and Justine faithfully lifted her tired wings to protect them. Jaden bowed her head to keep the rain off Zachariah, but her tears still drenched his face.

Jaden searched in the direction of Jeremiah, not knowing how she could get Zachariah there. She tried to lift him and failed, but she was able to pull him under a nearby bush. Blinded by tears and the rain, she sank in her grief, listening to the screeching, ferocious wing beats and gnashing of vicious beasts above her.

She felt hoof beats reverberating through the ground and heard barking dogs approaching rapidly. But before she could respond to the noise with hope or fear, another sound almost stopped Jaden's heart: the mortally wounded scream of Justine. Jaden heard a mighty crash in the forest behind her. Her heart ached. Fresh tears stung her eyes. All she could do was cover her son's body with her own. It wouldn't take long for the dragons to reach them now.

The beating of dragon wings was growing closer, when out of the darkness overhead soared the fierce creatures that all Xannellions feared: the flying tigers of Jeremiah. The dragons began to shriek horribly. Another air battle raged above, while below, Jaden felt more numbness than hope. Zachariah stopped moaning and lay still. Jaden listened and waited until the dogs, horses, and knights came bounding out of the woods. They surrounded her and her son.

"We need your help. My son, he is injured. I am afraid he might die. Please?" The knights didn't hesitate.

"Richard, you and Benjamin help these two back to the city," the leader said.

Richard and Benjamin dismounted as the other knights rode off into the jungle. Jaden watched the two knights work to get Zachariah carefully onto one of their horses. The younger of the two knights helped her onto his horse, sat behind her, and both horses galloped for Jeremiah.

Jaden looked back skyward to watch the flying tigers distracting Xzavier and his dragons. The rain and clouds began dispersing, and in the scattered moonlight, Jaden saw the silhouette of Xzavier as he turned and yelled something at the Scorpion. They managed to dodge their attackers and were charging straight toward her and her rescuers.

"Dragons...Xzavier... They are coming!" Jaden yelled to the knights.

Richard and Benjamin rode harder. Approaching the city wall, the younger one cried, "Open the gates! Open the gates!"

Wings beat fiercely behind them, and if not for the persistent assaults from the flying tigers, the dragons would have caught them. As the knights neared the gates of Jeremiah, the flying tigers were called off, and arrows from the fortress began to fall on Xzavier, the Scorpion, and their dragons. The dragons hovered close for a short time before retreating out of reach of the arrows.

Xzavier yelled to the attacking knights as the arrows rained down, "I am Xzavier, The Serpent Lord! If Jeremiah shelters my son and his mother, Jeremiah will suffer!"

With that, he spun his mighty dragon, Danthor, away from the showering arrows and in the direction of Xannellion.

Jaden slumped onto Benjamin's chest.

7

The City of Jeremiah

The clattering of horse's hooves on the wet stone streets echoed through Jeremiah. Through dissipating clouds, a large moon shined gently upon the passing band as they neared a gate to a spacious courtyard. Beyond the courtyard stood a large but cozy house. Richard waved to a guard at the gate who let the two horses, knights, and wounded pass.

Benjamin stopped in front of the house. He put his large hands on Jaden's arms, gently pushed her forward and easily jumped off his horse, leaving Jaden on the saddle.

"Will you be all right for a minute, my lady? We are a little shorthanded tonight, and I need to help Richard with the young man."

"Yes, yes," she said. The events of the night haunted her.

Jaden saw a petite young woman open the door. She watched as the two knights carefully carried Zachariah into the cottage. Jaden wondered, What kind of knights are they? Probably as crazy as the Arwavian who died earlier today in the stadium. The image of his death sent a shiver through her.

Jaden stretched her neck from side to side. Moonlight illuminated the gardens in front of the house. Around the right side she saw an orchard. The trees looked silvery in the light from above. The warm glow of dancing firelight spilled out the front door as if to invite weary travelers inside.

But would she be safe? Jaden gazed toward the light. A wave of exhaustion rippled through her, leaving her barely able to stay in the saddle. All the physical and emotional pain of the day caught up with her. An image of Zachariah colliding with the west wall of the stadium hurt her again.

She didn't notice Benjamin, who asked, "My lady...are you all right?"

"Of course I am not. Help me down." There was no other choice but to go with him. There was nowhere else to go. Jaden hesitated before taking Benjamin's outstretched hand.

Benjamin gave her a funny smile but helped her down and walked her toward the house. Jaden entered tentatively. She heard a gentle female voice say, "Put that cot over here near the fire... Richard, run up to my chamber and fetch me more blankets... Before you do that, boil another pot of water... Benjamin..."

"Excuse me. I'll be right back, my lady," Benjamin said.

Jaden's legs felt weak as she listened. "Lay that down carefully... Put that on the other side of the hearth... Benjamin, I'll need another cot for the woman and one for me. Looks like I'll be here for awhile."

As Jaden's eyes adjusted to the darkness, she saw more clearly the slight figure standing near the substantial hearth, not ten paces in front of her. The long, narrow hall disappeared into darkness. Jaden could see a long table with benches surrounding it and a sizable family tapestry on the wall next to the table. There was a lot of open space.

"Benjamin, could you please help the lady?"

Benjamin wrapped a warm blanket around Jaden's shoulders and walked her to the cot. "Sit here, my lady. I will bring you something to eat," he said kindly.

Jaden skeptically studied his light green eyes but did what he said. She watched her rescuer while he got food ready. He was young, not much older than Zachariah, robust with short reddish-blond hair. He was handsome, strong, and full of life, but, by all appearances, gentle and kind, although she figured she would see the – other side – of his character eventually.

She turned to Zachariah, who lay still, except for the up-and-down movement of his bruised and bloodied chest. Seeing his handsome face stained and his blonde hair matted in red sent another wave of pain and exhaustion through her, leaving her feeling cold and distressed.

Benjamin handed her a wooden bowl of warm stew, a piece of fresh bread, and a wooden cup of grape juice seasoned with herbs. As she ate, flashes of dragons and flying tigers raced through her mind.

Hoping to distract herself, she watched Zachariah being attended to by the delicate girl. She couldn't be twenty years old but seemed an expert in caring for the injured. Once Zachariah was in a comfortable position, the girl came over to Jaden, propped her up on pillows, and attended to her scrapes. Handing Jaden some warm tea, she asked, "What is your name?"

"Jaden."

"And his?"

"Zachariah."

The dainty girl turned back to Zachariah. Jaden ate slowly, struck by how peacefully this young girl worked. It was like nothing Jaden had ever seen, and if she hadn't felt so safe, she would have attributed it to some dark magic.

As the girl bent down near the fire to get some warm water, Jaden saw her graceful, delicate features. Like a faerie that had grown too big, she had straight, brown, short hair, large black eyes that entirely hid her pupils, and her slender fingers seemed long in proportion to her petite body. Effortlessly, she prepared poultice after poultice, placing them on one wound and the next, covering Zachariah's many bruises and possible internal injuries.

Once his wounds were dressed, she dipped a cloth of soft jacquard into a mixture of goat's milk loaded with crushed berries and herbs and placed it on Zachariah's discolored forehead.

"Benjamin, I might need your help."

"What do you need, Danae?"

"I am going to try and set these bones. I need you to restrain him carefully. He doesn't need any more bruising." She skillfully examined each of the bones in Zachariah's right leg from the hip down, completing the process by nodding in approval. Then she moved to his left leg. When she finished examining the rest of his leg, she returned to his hip.

She carefully, yet firmly, gripped his leg above the knee and pulled swiftly. Jaden heard a loud pop as his hip slipped back into place. Next, Danae felt down his entire right arm, nodding when she found every bone in order. But she softly groaned as she checked the left arm.

Jaden stopped eating and watched. Danae gripped his forearm arm and twisted until it popped, making Jaden's stomach turn. She set her food on the floor and laid down. Danae bound up his lower left arm securely with strong, stiff cloth covered in a sticky substance. The substance allowed her to wind the cloth around the arm tightly, making the cloth stick to itself to keep the bone firmly in place.

Jaden was mesmerized but felt increasingly fatigued. Somewhere between his left shoulder being popped back into its socket and his face being cleaned up, Jaden fell into an exhausted but restless slumber. All night dreams of dragons chasing her woke her periodically. Each time, Danae adjusted her blankets and said calmly, "Go back to sleep. You are safe in Jeremiah." And Jaden would fall back to sleep.

Late the next morning, Jaden came out of a dark dream moaning. Scenes from the previous day greeted her coldly. Her body was stiff and sore. She smelled the fragrance of delicious food and noticed the delicate girl still attending to Zachariah. Sick to her stomach, she sunk quickly back onto the cot and closed her eyes.

"I hope you slept well. Can I get you anything?"

Her sincere concern disarmed Jaden. "Yes, some more of that juice from last night, and do you have something for a headache?" Jaden put her hands on her head.

"I'll be right back." Danae returned shortly with a cup of juice, herbs, and cloths like the ones she placed on Zachariah's head the night before. She allowed Jaden to drink some juice, while placing one rag on the back of her neck and one on her forehead. After Jaden finished the juice, Danae gently laid Jaden back on her pillows.

"Obviously, you have had a difficult time. Don't fight the exhaustion. It is your body's way of healing."

Soon Jaden's headache let up, and she relaxed. She rolled onto her back and stared at the ceiling. The whitewashed walls contrasted sharply with the dark timber rafters. Dark brown wood framed the ceiling, windows, and doors, as well. Jaden watched rays of sun mixing with swirls of smoke from the fireplace until she surrendered to her fatigue again for the better part of the day.

Sun was shining through the west windows in warm reds and pinks when Jaden finally awoke. She got up and walked over to her son. Danae offered her a stool and some warm food. Hour after hour Jaden sat there until the light of day departed. Emotions from the previous two days arrived with the darkness, and for the rest of her second night in Jeremiah, she sat next to Zachariah wrestling with a myriad of thoughts, feelings, and emerging revelations.

Jaden fought this emotional awakening. And the more she resisted, the more overwhelmed with pain and anxiety she grew. Her chest felt inflamed with an intense, raw pain, like a gaping wound that threatened to engulf her heart. There was nothing to distract her from it, no glimmering gown or argument with Xzavier. She couldn't escape it. She no longer had her beloved Justine to fly her into the morning sky.

All she could do was stare at her son's bruised face and feel. For hours she reviewed over and over in her mind the events that occurred since she stood up to Xzavier in the dungeon. She grew increasingly furious as she remembered all that led up to the horrible sound of Justine's final screech and the crash of Justine's body in the jungle. Rage swelled until she stood abruptly and screamed in her mind, "Xzavier! How dare you!"

Unable to contain her anger, she demanded, "Why haven't you healed him?"

Startled, Danae stammered, "My lady, it will take time. You brought him to me nearly dead. Not even my gifts are sure to bring him back."

"It is no excuse. In my kingdom, he would've been healed by now, or the doctors would be hanged for their incompetence..."

At that moment a man entered the room from a hallway behind them and approached Jaden. His dark brown hair dusted with grey fell to his strong jaw in thick waves that parted to reveal a handsome suntanned face with intense black eyes. Jaden knew instantly that this man deserved her silence, if not respect.

He said quietly in a rich, low voice, "Never in my house will you speak to my daughter that way. I will return you to your kingdom if you would like your doctors to try to do better. Though I assure you, even your doctors would have failed to see your son through the last two nights. He owes my daughter his life, and you owe her an apology."

With that, he stood at his full six feet, his thick arms folded across his chest. His dark eyes, which his daughter obviously inherited from him, were blazing as he waited for Jaden's apology. Jaden's green eyes narrowed, wild and fierce, darting from this man to his daughter and back to her son like a wildcat caught in a corner.

"How dare you? You don't even know who I am. I am Jaden, Queen of Xannellion." With her head pounding, she flew out the front door shouting, "Take me back to the forest! I have to find my dragon. Get me a horse, now. Can anyone hear me!"

But she collapsed to her knees, unable to go farther, anger, fear, and exhaustion forbidding her. Against her will, tears fell, first slowly, and then in a torrent. Her shoulders shook as she put her face into her hands.

Danae's father followed, knelt down by her side, and said, "Jaden, your dragon is dead." He picked her up in his arms, carried her back to her cot and gently put her down.

Jaden wiped her tears, her eyes revealing both shame and irritation. Gathering her composure, Jaden demanded, "Who are you that dares chasten the queen?"

Smile lines formed naturally on his handsome face, and out of his soul an amused chuckle arose. Then with somber confidence, he answered, "My name is Gideon. My house shelters you. My daughter heals your son. My knights rescued you and paid the price for your freedom."

Without any further explanation, he turned tenderly to Danae. "Is there anything else that you need, my dear?"

"No, thank you, father."

"I'll place a guard at the front door. If there is any trouble, just yell. Tell Jaden, Queen of Xannellion, that she can roam your garden once she apologizes. I'll be in my chamber if you need me." With that, he disappeared down the hall.

Jaden glared indignantly in his direction with hot tears cascading down her face. How could she be in debt to this arrogant, prideful man? Exhaustion once again forced her to lie down in her cot. She pulled the blanket over her head and quietly sobbed.

8

Heartless Peasants

On the morning of the third day, Jaden woke late. She remembered the incident with Gideon. In her kingdom, she said what she wanted. No one dared to humiliate her, except Xzavier, and even he usually waited until they were alone. Among what sort of people had she fallen?

Danae poured her tea. "Would you like bread, too?"

"Bread would be nice. I'm starving," Jaden grumbled in sharp contrast to Danae's gentleness. Soon she sat eating warm homemade bread and sizing up this young, delicate girl. Who was she? And why did she insist on being so kind?

Without waiting for a "thank you" or more scowling from Jaden, Danae walked over to check Zachariah's wounds. Zachariah lay perfectly still, except for the rhythmic rise and fall of his battered chest. Danae attended to Zachariah gravely, yet carefully. Jaden caught a tender look from Danae as she ran her fingers through his thick, sun-colored curls to check his skull.

"What happened to your son? I have seen many young men scarred in battle but this...this is more like someone barely failed at drawing and quartering him."

Jaden studied Danae's sincere eyes. For an unguarded moment she actually wanted to tell her.

"He was in an accident... That's all," she said. "Who told you he was my son?"

"No one needed to. I knew because you came at great risk to your own life, in pain yourself. You would not leave his side. The most faithful nurse would not sacrifice what you have for her charge. You could only be his mother."

This lanced the festering wound in Jaden's heart. *I do not belong here*, she thought to herself.

"I've got to get out of here!" Jaden said. Danae watched Jaden with fearful eyes. Out of control, Jaden hissed, "I have to go for a ride!"

"Oh, you can't. You have to stay in the house. The guard won't let you."

In her most condescending voice Jaden commanded, "It is your job to keep an eye on my son. I will decide what I am going to do!" She flew out of the room toward the front of the house.

Jaden threw open the door to see Gideon speaking with the guard. Without pausing, she tried to pass by, but Gideon grabbed her arm and stopped her.

"I thought I asked you to stay inside with Danae."

"I will not stay. You can't keep me a prisoner here. I am leaving!"

"I can't let you leave. You are in too much danger. Please go back inside."

"You'll have to drag me, for I will not go back."

Gideon let go of Jaden's arm and said, "I will not force you to accept my help, but where will you go?"

Jaden glared at him not knowing what to say. All she knew at the moment was that she could not bear Danae's goodness a moment longer. "You have left me with nowhere to go and nothing to do!"

"You could explore Danae's garden behind our house. It is enchanting." Gideon smiled slyly. "But you'll have to apologize to her first. Or have you already?"

"You heartless and cruel man! I despise that I have no other choice than to stay and accept your arrogant charity. As soon as we are better, I will find some other place!"

Jaden returned through the open door without closing it and whirled past Danae like a hurricane.

"I will be in the cursed garden if my son needs me! And I have been told to say I am sorry... Sorry!"

Danae looked down to hide her smile. Jaden took little heed as she hurried to the garden. She rushed along the cobblestone past flowering shrubs and trees before halting abruptly in her tracks. In front of her sat the largest, fiercest creature she had seen since her arrival in Jeremiah. Her heart beat frantically as she tried to take a breath.

The animal was the color of medium-orange honey with stark black stripes and dramatic white markings on its face and body. It had dark black eyes and large teeth. But its most glorious feature was its enormous golden-orange feathered wings that boasted great power. Jaden backed up on the cobblestone pathway until she bumped into the door of the house. Reaching behind and fumbling with the handle, she nearly fell onto the floor, slamming the door behind her.

"A flying tiger is out there," she pointed toward the garden.

"He won't harm you. That's Old Trapton. My father found him in a trap on one of his mountain trips and brought him back. I nursed him to health, and he's been my father's companion ever since."

"You and your father told me to go out into that garden! Did you hope I would be eaten?"

"He is well fed and won't attack, unless you attack him. I assure you, you are safe with our tiger, or we wouldn't have let you out there."

"I am well aware of how to handle wild and ferocious animals and delicate ones alike," Jaden smirked. "I'd just like a warning before I am sent into the lion's den next time."

Jaden returned to the garden, more cautiously. She walked around, secretly hoping to see Trapton again, but he must have been as spooked as she was because there was no sign of him.

It was hot, although not as hot as in Xannellion, and the shade of the trees offered some relief. Although Jaden wanted to despise Danae's garden, she found that it reminded her of Yamis. In Xannellion, she had longed to walk outdoors but never could without jeopardizing her safety. Her only occasion to smell clean, fresh outdoor air had been to walk out onto her balcony or fly on Justine.

A feeling of safety stirred inside her as she walked among the bright red and pink flowers, blue and white ones, and the tall ferns and palms. The undergrowth, although not as lush as in Yamis, was a vibrant green. Little birds flitted from bush to bush. Some birds displayed bright yellows and reds. Others were simply black, brown, and white.

In the middle of the garden, under the shade of a star fruit tree between two dwarf palm trees, Jaden found a simple wooden bench carved with flying tigers at each end. She sat down. A few minutes later, the door to the garden opened. Jaden was swinging around ready for a fight, when she saw Benjamin walking toward her.

As he got closer, he said, "You found my bench. I carved that when I first became a knight. It isn't as nice as some, but Danae likes it." Realizing Jaden wasn't impressed, he changed the subject. "How are you, my lady?"

"Fine as can be expected for a queen who is kept prisoner by heartless peasants," Jaden said in a less-than-severe tone to the young man with strawberry blonde hair. He reminded her of her son, whom she missed desperately at the moment.

Benjamin was strong and well proportioned. Jaden guessed that if Zachariah and Benjamin stood side by side they would be similar in stature. She sized him up in his simple, brown homespun outer-robe, ivory under-robe with a plain, dark brown leather sash. His leather sandals were inferior to those made in Xannellion. He walked confidently but with humility that Jaden took for weakness. Jaden stared at him disapprovingly.

Benjamin sat down on the bench near Jaden and began humming.

"What song is that?"

"It is a song my mother used to sing to me as a child about Gillantri and his mighty deeds."

Jaden scoffed at this and changed the subject, asking somewhat disdainfully, "Is Gideon really as powerful as he acts?"

"Gideon is not only powerful, he is good. Better than any man I have known, besides my father, of course. Gideon is my hero and has been since I was a child."

"What do you mean that he is good? No one with power can be good." Jaden was suspicious.

"I've never known a more honest, kind, and giving man than Gideon. He lives in this modest house, although he governs the entire city, including the knights. He wears the same clothes we all wear. He works for his livelihood and does not expect others to do for him what he can do for himself. He has no servants, no hired hands. He humbly worships Gillantri, our God, and lives according to his teachings. He is the reason I became a Jeremian knight. I wanted to become like Gideon. When I was a boy, knights used to come home from fighting and praise not only his strength on the battlefield but also his wisdom, virtue, and goodness."

Jaden sniffed in disbelief, feeling a twinge of jealousy because of Benjamin's sincere loyalty to Gideon. She again changed the subject.

"Where are you from?"

"I grew up in a little village just north of Jeremiah with my brothers and parents. Our village, like many other Arwavian cities, was ravaged by Cannote before he died."

Jaden recalled her first feast in Xannellion but dismissed it quickly from her mind. She asked, "How many brothers do you have, Benjamin?"

"I have seven older brothers. I am the youngest. Each of us followed after my oldest brother by joining the knights of Jeremiah." Benjamin paused and pulled an orange out of a pocket under his brown cape and began to peel it.

"Eight children, I can't imagine how your mother managed. You say your brothers joined the knights. Are they still fighting?"

"Yes, a few of us are still fighting. My oldest brother and Richard and I are still engaged as knights of Jeremiah. Three of my brothers died fighting for Arway. We know they are at peace with Gillantri, though we miss them."

"I thought you were fighting for your city, Jeremiah?" Jaden tested, "Why Arway too?"

Benjamin peeled the orange and gave Jaden a piece. She paused for a moment but accepted it while he answered her question.

"We fight for Jeremiah to protect our Arwavian ways. Consequently, we protect the city of Jeremiah. Jeremiah is the closest large Arwavian city to Xannellion. Only the elvan city of Ononzai is larger between here and Alexandria. We have always felt that Jeremiah must stand firm to protect Arwavians in the south."

Jaden raised an eyebrow, staring at him more closely. She noticed freckles all over his face that made him seem tanner than he was, and his light green eyes were smaller than Zachariah's but were not altogether unattractive.

Jaden tossed her hair. "I am sure folklore about Gillantri brings you comfort. I do not believe such things myself. But I am sorry about your older brothers."

A quiet moment passed between them.

"You said your mother had eight sons?" Jaden resumed. "If three of you are knights, and three have given their lives, where are your two other brothers?"

Bushes rustled in front of them, and Jaden took in a quick breath of air as Old Trapton made his return.

"He won't hurt you. Come here, old fellow." Benjamin began petting the large animal. Then the petting turned into teasing, as Benjamin used both of his large hands to hold Trapton's mouth shut. Trapton good naturedly tossed his head around, giving Benjamin a challenge.

Soon they were wrestling with each other. Jaden's eyes grew wide with concern, and she walked behind the bench undecided about whether this was a friendly match of strength or not. Benjamin let out a loud, happy roar as Trapton flipped him to the ground and put one paw on Benjamin's chest. Trapton proceeded to lick Benjamin's face. Jaden covered her mouth to stop her laughter. Finally, Benjamin pushed Trapton aside, got up, brushed off his clothes, and wiped his face with his shirt sleeves. He sat on the wooden bench again.

"Come here, old boy," he called.

Trapton approached. "See Jaden, you are safe. The only danger here is a good licking." Benjamin chuckled again as he tousled the hair on Trapton's head. He kept Trapton to his left so that Jaden wouldn't be bothered.

"To answer your question, my two remaining brothers live near my mother and father in southern Jeremiah. After several years of fighting, my brothers chose to marry and settle down, and, like my father, to help with the family farm. Nearly all of my parents' children and grandchildren live close by, although mother often tells me, 'If your brothers had lived, I would have many more grandchildren, so don't you disappoint me Benjamin.' The deaths of my three brothers were most grievous to mother."

Benjamin pointed to the orange that he had left on the bench and gestured for her to have some. She took a piece, enjoying the sweet, juicy fruit as he finished his thought. "My brother's sons want to fight for Jeremiah too. They probably will someday."

Jaden swallowed and then paused thoughtfully. "Your mother doesn't need any more sadness than she already has. Why don't they become farmers like your father and two brothers? Increased farming would not only keep you alive and provide food for your family, but if you were very successful, it could provide food for others as well." Jaden lowered her brows, feeling a little irritated that his mother's sadness affected her so much.

"What good would farming do if we are all slain by the Xannellion King's minions? Or if we are spared, what purpose would drive us to live if we could not freely worship and conduct our lives as we please? My brothers died to protect more than just our lives. This is about more than just survival."

He lowered his eyes. "Jaden, I have been less than a gentleman."

"What do you mean? State what you feel. Don't apologize." Jaden checked to see if he was mocking her but realized that she had just missed a social cue. "Tell me more."

"I would be content to be a farmer myself, if I had the assurance that my family would be safe and free. But in the shadow of Xannellion... For centuries, Xannellion has spared no effort to reign over all the free Arwavians of Trivar. If it weren't for brave men like Gideon, we would be slaves to Xannellion, like you were."

"I am not a slave." Jaden's eyes narrowed, but she remembered her own censure to herself as she had fled Xannellion: *You are no longer a prisoner inside Xzavier's castle. You must stop acting like one!* Still, she resisted admitting the truth to this bold youth.

"But neither were you free." Benjamin stated this so gently and unassumingly that Jaden couldn't fire back at him.

She opened her mouth and shut it again. "Go on."

"I chose to become a knight. While my two brothers play equally important roles as farmers, I could never be satisfied myself as a farmer when I know that I have it in me to defend and protect. It is a great honor to fight for Jeremiah."

"You strongly value your Arwavian beliefs," Jaden said.

"As I mentioned, my father fought for many years before settling down as a farmer. During the whole of it, he bore and provided eight more knights for our cause. Most of our retired or injured knights work to support the active knights. We have enough farmers, weavers, and artisans to keep us fed, armed, and clothed. Although, lately we have taken in so many refugees from other cities that Jeremiah's resources are thinning.

"Some of our knights are moving to Alexandria and other villages farther away from Xannellion because life here is more dangerous. Some of the knights believe they would be better help to Arway if they were closer to Alexandria in the north where our culture is freer and stronger. But I think that the closer we stay to Xannellion, the less ground darkness can claim.

"It is definitely more dangerous with Xzavier as king. While it has always been Xannellion protocol, raiding Arwavian villages has increased. Since you came, we hear of nightly raids with Xzavier's men burning whole villages. Entire communities of refugees come seeking help, telling wild tales about his cruelty. There are also many like you who individually flee from Xannellion. If only we could have kings like Gillantri, darkness would not take hold. Maybe then I could be a farmer." Benjamin's voice revealed sadness.

"I am amazed at your passion for Gillantri." Jaden's tone changed as she said,

"But I cannot believe how you do about Gideon, though I see that you believe it as strongly. Such is the way with impressionable youth."

Benjamin kept his eyes down and grinned at this, causing anger to rise in Jaden's soul. "You think what I am saying is funny?" she said.

"I don't believe...I know Gideon is a good man, and I would gladly give my life for him, begging your pardon, my lady. He is my oldest brother."

Jaden's mouth dropped.

"Jaden, I have to take over the watch at the front gate soon. I will tell Gideon that you are doing better."

Her face reddened. Gideon sent you out here to spy on me? She stood.

"You may leave now," she said.

"Gideon was only concerned about you," he said. "You will learn to trust eventually, my lady. We aren't as bad as you've been told."

Jaden took a short breath and exhaled audibly. "You are too much, Benjamin of Jeremiah. Does nothing irritate you?"

He slowly got to his feet and grinned. "I suppose some things irritate me, but you'd have a hard time irritating me. You are just ignorant of our ways. I can forgive you for that. Besides, you'll learn sooner or later – everyone can improve. That's what my mother always taught me."

Jaden flung her red curls back and wanted to say something sharp but could only get out, "Need I remind you that you are speaking to a queen?"

"Yes, 'a queen who is a prisoner to heartless peasants,'" he said with a sparkle in his eye. He added, without the slightest hint of being ruffled, "May I walk you back inside? It will be dark soon."

"I'll be in later. But could you get Old Trapton to go back into the garden? I just don't want..."

"You don't need to explain. Go on, ol' boy! Get going!" Benjamin said with a slap to Trapton's hind quarters. Trapton turned his head, begging with his eyes, hoping for another spar. But seeing Benjamin's serious face, he dropped his tail and disappeared into the foliage.

Jaden sat back down on the bench and said, "Thank you, Benjamin, I appreciate your company today. I really do."

Benjamin waved his hand and returned to the house as pleasantly as he had come.

9

Zachariah

That night, as the sun set in the west, clouds rolled in. The air felt muggy and thick until a wind whistled up the hill through the ancient city of Jeremiah, swirled around in Danae's peaceful garden, and then finished its exhale up the mountains beyond. Jaden walked against the wind back to the cottage. Upon entering, she startled Danae, which immediately irritated Jaden.

"When is my son going to wake?" Jaden snatched a piece of bread and sat down on her cot, waiting impatiently for Danae to answer.

Danae quietly finished putting away her clothes, bowls of water, and ointments.

"I don't know, I just don't…"

Zachariah made a sharp groaning sound, causing Danae and Jaden to jump. Jaden scrambled to his bed. They waited and watched. Shortly, he began moaning once more, a moan marked by both pain and sadness. Jaden retrieved the crushed berries that Danae had made into a paste with other healing agents and began carefully rubbing it on his chest. Danae quickly heated her broth that had kept him alive thus far, when suddenly he let out a horrible cry, as if he were dying.

"Why can't you stop this, Danae?"

"Just a minute," Danae answered while removing the broth from over the fire. She brought it to Zachariah. While busy, she had not missed noticing the volcano erupting in Jaden's eyes. Quietly she said, "Healing isn't an easy process. There isn't any magic balm that stops the Trivarian body from experiencing pain as it recovers from damage such as this." She pointed to Zachariah's broken body.

"Zachariah has been through a great deal of trauma," she continued. "The only way for him to heal is to allow him to revisit the pain to a lesser degree and then release it. It is like working backwards from the point of injury to health again. It will take a lot of work and great faith from all of us."

When Danae said this, it stung Jaden's unraveling heart, although she didn't know why.

"Whatever!" She waved her hands dramatically. "Just make him comfortable!"

Danae gently pulled Jaden away from applying ointment and motioned for her to sit down. She checked Zachariah over carefully, making sure nothing was out of place. Every so often he would let out a yell that made Jaden's nerves tighter.

"Jaden, you never told me how all of this happened."

"A chariot race," Jaden said.

"Oh."

Danae stopped everything she was doing for a long time. She just stared sadly at Zachariah, making Jaden feel uncomfortable

"I'm so sorry. So tragic. Many of my friends, even my twin brother and mother, died in war. But the sorrow I feel for your son is different," she said.

Jaden felt agitated but waited impatiently, as she was curious to hear what Danae would say next.

"My sadness for him is compounded by the frivolity of why he might die. It isn't for a noble cause, to protect innocent lives or to fight a great evil, but for sport. For sport, this strong and handsome young man may never live to have a family, be inspired by a great purpose, and live out his life fighting for it."

"Well, you don't know anything about power and what is required to maintain it," Jaden said indignantly, standing up. She put her hand to her mouth, upset at herself for sounding like Xzavier, but unwilling to apologize.

Both women fell into their own thoughts. While Danae dutifully worked to keep Zachariah comfortable, Jaden paced the floor. Soon rain began to fall, starting with a few drops, becoming steady, and before long pounding on the roof, which drowned out her son's groaning.

Zachariah stirred his broken body at intervals, which resulted in anguished cries. As the hours pressed on, Benjamin and Richard came in to help where they could, but eventually they had to return to their posts. Later, Gideon came down from his chamber.

He walked up behind Danae and whispered, "Go get some rest. I'll watch him for awhile." She wearily bowed her head in agreement. Jaden watched the tender exchange but turned away after he patted his daughter's shoulders and she left.

Zachariah wrestled with pain for the better part of the next twelve hours. At times he writhed, struggling between life and death. Gideon, although not as tender, did all he could to temper the pain, but to no avail. He laid another blanket over Zachariah. Jaden puzzled, Could Benjamin be right about Gideon? Gideon poured some juice in a cup and handed it to her.

She quietly nodded her thanks and drank, unable to put Gideon into a familiar mold. There was no man in her world remotely like him. And then it dawned on her – the blue-eyed man of her dreams. Was he like him? Did he really exist? If so, would she ever find him?

Or was she so desperate for goodness in her life that she created a delusion? The last thought felt so awful that she released it immediately and focused on Gideon. He held Zachariah's hand while Zachariah moaned through another wave of pain. Her heart hurt.

Sometime after that, Jaden fell into an uncomfortable sleep, waking every time Zachariah made a noise. Once she woke to Gideon pulling the blankets up close to her face. His dark brown eyes smoldered in the firelight.

"Sleep. He is finally resting. I won't leave him." The rain pounded furiously on the roof. But something in his face made her feel safe. She closed her eyes and slept.

Jaden did not wake until mid-afternoon the next day. The rain had stopped, and Zachariah slept peacefully. Jaden's emotions were close to the surface, so she lay there silently, watching Danae make Zachariah as comfortable as possible.

Then something new happened. Zachariah grimaced, turned his head to the left, then to the right, opening his left eye briefly, and then he opened both eyes. Jaden had moved next to him beside Danae. He turned his head to the left and took in the unfamiliar environment. Finally, he turned to the right, where he focused on Danae's peaceful face.

"Who are you?" he said in a gruff voice. He tried to clear his throat and nearly faded out again.

Danae took his face in her hands, staring with determination into his green eyes and commanded him, "Zachariah, keep your eyes on me. Do you hear me?"

Jaden worried and wondered if he could hear or see. But his eyes focused on Danae again as she pleaded, "Zachariah, if you can hear me, say something!"

He moaned.

"That's right. I know you are in pain, but now you must stay awake. Keep your eyes open. My name is Danae. You have been badly injured. Your mother brought you to me. She is here."

Jaden leaned closer to Zachariah as Danae began again, "Zachariah, you have to stay awake. Please stay awake!"

Jaden gently moved Danae out of her way and motioned for her to sit down. She took her son's face in her own hands and began where Danae left off, "Son, look into my eyes! You are not a quitter. You must not give in to your pain! Keep your eyes open!"

After a short time, Danae touched Jaden's shoulder, and Jaden stepped aside.

"Zachariah, can you see me? Be still. You are safe in my father's house...far away from Xannellion."

When he heard the word Xannellion, his eyes became wild. "I was racing... catching up with the leader...something hit me... Oooooh," he moaned. "Mother, I am heading for the wall..."

"Son, my son, look at me now!" His focus returned to Jaden's face. She saw the pain, the memories that were now flooding his mind.

"What happened? Who is this girl? Where is Xzavier? Where is my chariot? Why..."

"You are safe in Jeremiah, far away from Xannellion," Danae said, stepping forward again. Jaden's face clouded over with emotion from the trauma, which was still too fresh in her mind, as well.

"You are badly injured. You must calm down. Be still. I am Danae, daughter of Gideon, Captain of the Jeremian knights. Your mother risked her life to get you here so that we could help you. We have been watching over you for the past four days..."

"Four days!" Zachariah tried to sit up.

Jaden gently pressed his shoulders back against his pillows. "No, don't do that! Stay still. Your body is healing." Jaden felt cross again.

Danae motioned for Jaden to sit down on the chair beside Zachariah while she dished up some broth. Zachariah sipped broth and listened to his mother relate what had happened since he had lost consciousness in the stadium. Jaden noticed Danae's shallow breathing as she heard about their escape, black gryphons, wolves, dragons, and Xzavier.

Zachariah listened calmly throughout the tale but began to cry when Jaden told of Justine giving her life for them. Jaden didn't know how to respond, for he hadn't cried since he was young, and it hurt her deeply. Without hesitating, Danae wrapped her gentle arms around him and let him cry. Sadness and anger engulfed him. He cried like he had lost everything.

Tears escaped Jaden's eyes. She wrapped her arms around herself and watched Danae's gift of charity work its magic. After a short time, Zachariah pulled away and said through tears, "Xzavier won... The race had to be rigged... I was going to win that race..."

"It was rigged, son. Xzavier told me with his own mouth. He had a servant shoot an arrow at James and Antonio's wheels. One flew off and hit you."

Zachariah went white with rage and tried to rise from his cot. Danae gently held him down.

"What are we doing in Jeremiah? All I've fought for, all we had... It's gone!" Great waves of pity washed over Jaden as she realized deeply their new position in the world. "Mother, Xzavier must be stopped. We have to avenge ourselves!"

"We will avenge ourselves, but we cannot while you are broken up. You must heal first!" Jaden slumped in her chair. Slowly, weakly, she stood and said, "So rest, son. I am tired. I am going to sleep. Danae, take care of him."

Jaden retreated to her cot. She turned over and over, sometimes waking, but mostly dreaming. In the darkest hour of the night, Danae finally gave in to her exhaustion and fell asleep at Zachariah's side. But Jaden stared into the darkness.

10

The Crazy Arwavian and His People

At dawn there was a quiet knock at the door. Jaden, who had not slept well, glanced around the room. Seeing no one awake, she wrapped her blanket around her shoulders and rose to answer it. When she got within a few feet of the door, she heard quick footsteps behind her. Benjamin put a solid hand on her shoulder and whispered, "I'll get it. You rest."

Jaden stopped but didn't turn back. Benjamin opened the door. Pale light entered with a cool breeze. Jaden sucked in a quick breath of air and moved toward the door. A young man with nothing on but fire-singed rags pointed to a body lying on the ground outside. Benjamin rushed to kneel beside the body. The young man in rags trembled in the cold. Benjamin rose and walked to Jaden, who was pale and upset.

"My lady. This isn't something you should have to see. Please go and rest. I will take care of it."

"I know him. I saw him. He...you know him?"

By that time, Gideon came from behind Jaden and collapsed next to the corpse.

"No," he gasped.

"Do you know him?" Benjamin inquired of Jaden.

"Yes, he was the cr...the Arwavian whom Xzavier saved for the games. I watched him stand up to Xzavier in our throne room. He died in the Xannellion Stadium. He refused to participate. He did not put up a fight."

She could not remove her gaze from the grey, stiff figure on the ground. It had never occurred to Jaden that this man had a family who loved him and comrades who would miss him. Her thoughts drifted to her son lying inside. How could she have been so unfeeling, so heartless? Jaden trembled, but not from the cold. Benjamin put his arm around her and turned her around.

Numb, she followed him to her cot and sat down. He glanced at her as if he wished he could help, but instead he returned to support his brother. Jaden saw nothing more, lost in her own pain. Someone woke Danae and brought her outside. Gideon, Danae, and Benjamin rushed in and out for a couple of hours while Jaden sat there thinking and feeling.

When she was with Xzavier, he was the villain. It was obvious that she was trapped by him, admittedly by her own choice, but only as a means to an end. She never considered herself good or heroic, and she even doubted whether or not there actually was a good or a bad.

But the goodness she felt from the Jeremians since her arrival made clear her own lacking. After being assailed by her thoughts for two lonely hours, the only conclusion she could accept was that she was the villain too. Lying down, she pulled the covers over her head to block out the memory of the peaceful Arwavian being struck dead by the black gryphon's talons and beak.

"Jaden, I need to talk with you," Gideon said, sitting on the cot beside her and gently shaking her. Startled, she sat up and pulled the blankets around her. Sunlight filtered in through the high, small windows of the room, telling her that it was early afternoon.

"I'm sorry to wake you, but Benjamin said that you had seen Les before he died. Is that true?"

Tormented, Jaden stared at him. "You have no reason to keep helping my son and me, especially now. I can never..."

Gideon placed his hand over Jaden's mouth. "Please. I am not here to hurt you. You and your son are safe with us as long as you choose to stay. I have known Les since we fought together as young knights. I love Les. We have always been close. He is the leader of a small village of knights to our south. I just want to know more of what happened to him."

Jaden's face lost all color as the words stabbed her, but she listened silently as Gideon spoke. "A fortnight ago, he went missing when Xzavier ravaged his town. Many escaped. Xzavier typically allows this, knowing the refugees will be a burden on us. But Les never came. We searched for him, but we could not find him anywhere. I just want to know what you know."

Jaden searched Gideon's eyes and cringed. Her dream from last night flashed in her mind: it ended with Gideon comfortably talking with the blue-eyed man. She felt angry and trapped in a foreign world. Her emotions threatened to tear her apart. There was no choice but to relate to him all that had happened to his friend.

She tearfully related everything she knew about Les, beginning in the throne room. It seemed that a lifetime had passed since she sat beside Xzavier in Xannellion. Gideon closed his eyes as if watching the scene play out in his mind. Jaden imagined he also closed his eyes to hide his pain. In the end, she related how, in the Xannellion Stadium, Les refused to fight but stood and prayed to the skies as he died.

Gideon grimaced. "I am glad he died well, though I expected as much. Will you please come with me and share what you know with his people?"

Her face must have betrayed the shock she felt because Gideon said quickly, "You don't have to if it would be too hard for you. I just think they need to hear it from you. Benjamin said he'd bring you to their camp later if you are willing."

"How do you know they won't blame me?"

"You are in Arwavian lands. It is different here."

Conflicting emotions churned inside her. How could she face the people of the man she condemned to die a mere few days ago, a man that she thought was despicable, fanatical, and even crazy? She had made so many mistakes.

"I owe you for all you have done for me and my son. I will speak to them."

"Then Danae will help you get cleaned up, and Benjamin will be here shortly to escort you. I have to help some new arrivals and prepare the people for what they are about to hear." Gideon put his hand kindly on Jaden's hand before departing.

Jaden ran her fingers over her hair and stared at her hands. How did I get so filthy? she thought.

She asked Danae, "Where do you get fresh water for a bath?"

"We have a little pond beyond my garden."

"A little pond?"

"It will be more than sufficient for a bath."

Jaden stood and fingered her silks, filthy and torn beyond repair. Knowing that Danae wouldn't have anything that would fit her, she glanced around the room and saw a bundle of clothes sitting next to her cot that she hadn't noticed earlier.

They weren't silk, but linen, left in the linen's natural light tan color. The floor-length dress was embroidered with muted colored threads around the edges in a simple but striking way. Lifting it to the height of her shoulders, she admired the square neckline and long, open sleeves. A simple sash matching the embroidered hems adorned the waist.

"Where did you get this?" Jaden asked.

"It wasn't me. It was my father."

Jaden absently fingered the embroidery. "Where is your little pond?"

"Walk straight through my garden, out past the back fence, across the north-south path and into the jungle. It is not far. Take your time. They have a lot to do to help the refugees who have come."

"Refugees?"

"Yes, another village burned last night. The people just arrived."

Jaden nodded, unable to take in anymore. She had no room for more pain or guilt. She watched Zachariah sleep and asked, "Is he all right?"

"He is healing. His body is very tired, but he is doing well, considering what he has been through."

As if in a trance, Jaden walked out the back door, through the garden, past Trapton, and out the fence. She hardly noticed the north-south path before she entered the jungle. Shortly, Jaden arrived at a secluded pool of clear water fed by a waterfall.

"Danae was too modest about her little pond," she breathed. She hung her new linen dress on a low palm. Soaking in the nature around her, she removed her slippers and walked to the edge of the pool. Shafts of yellow sunlight dazzled the surface. The trees surrounding were elegantly dipping their branches into the frothy blue water like ladies wetting their feet.

With all of her clothes on, Jaden entered, sinking into its luxurious depths, while her auburn hair spilled all around her. Floating on her back, trying not to think about anything but the renewing water, she watched the lazy clouds pass from one side of the clearing to the other.

Occasionally, scenes from the morning flashed through her mind involuntarily. Every so often, she remembered the man with the blue eyes from her dream talking with Gideon, as well. She struggled to resist these disturbances to her serenity.

She rubbed her face with the sweet water. After wiping the water from her face with her hands, she tried to peer into the thick, vibrant green jungle. Unfortunately, the light revealed but a short distance into it. Birds sang from every direction, helping to calm her.

Diving into the water, Jaden opened her eyes below and saw groupings of rocks interspersed with wavy green and brown plants. She turned to watch the white water stir under the falls. Bubbles surfaced around the edge of the pool. A dark shadow passed over. Jaden jumped. She vigorously swam to the surface and wiped her eyes, relieved to see that it was just a lazy cloud.

But the fear that Xzavier could possibly find her here alone urged her to return to the cottage. She reluctantly left the pool and changed into her new dress, enjoying the feel and scent of clean fabric against her skin.

When she approached the back fence, Trapton was dutifully waiting for her. She tentatively patted his neck and walked through the garden toward Gideon's house when she saw Benjamin, all cleaned up as well, waiting for her on his bench.

Benjamin stood. "You look beautiful, my lady."

Jaden flushed unwillingly, thinking how young and handsome Benjamin was and hoping that soon, it would be Zachariah standing and talking with her. "Is it time?"

"Yes."

"Well, let's get going then."

"The horses are waiting at the front of the house. Danae asked that we walk around so Zachariah can sleep undisturbed. Come this way."

Benjamin put his hand in the middle of Jaden's back and courteously led her toward the house. They followed a short path to the northern corner of the house and opened a gate that revealed the lovely orchard she had noticed in the moonlight the night she arrived.

"Gideon's wife loved this orchard. Danae has cared for it in her memory, but he hardly ever comes here. I'm sure it grieves him in his loss. Watch your step, my lady, the path is crumbling. Danae asked me to repair it before you arrived, but things have been busy." He smiled teasingly.

Jaden glared at him. Benjamin took her hand, steadying her over the uneven ground.

"You should trip me, not help me! How do you smile so easily on a day like today? You are a bunch of crazy Arwavians, just not crazy in the way I used to think."

"I like you, Queen Jaden. You and your son are worthy of help. We don't blame you for the deaths of our people. We blame Xzavier. It is plain to see that you are different. Let us make our own decisions about whom we help and don't help."

Jaden felt tears burning the edges of her eyes and fought to keep them from brimming over. She blinked into the bright sky while Benjamin put his hand on the small of her back again, walking her in and out of the shade of the fruit trees.

"It would be so much easier if you would just be direct with me, Benjamin! Tell me I am the villain that I am. I am not an honored guest! I am the wicked Queen of Xannellion!"

Benjamin laughed softly. "Yes, the wicked queen who escaped from the wicked king to save the life of their wicked son. You are so wicked that Trapton wants to lick you to death. He may seem harmless, but if you had much evil in you, you would definitely be missing vital appendages by now.

"Not to mention, my brother. He may seem kind because he is kind. But naïve he is not. He is a good judge of character and has a keen intuitive gift of discernment. He sized you up in the woods and had us take you to his house. Why? Because he discerned good in you. He even left Danae alone with you. Did you notice that he never sent guards to watch you?"

"Except to keep me trapped inside his house!"

"That was for your own protection. He was afraid you'd try to leave the safety of the city."

"Why does he care?" Jaden pushed Benjamin's hand away from her back and walked angrily toward the front of the house. She got onto her horse before Benjamin could help her and waited arrogantly until he mounted his.

"I wish you could see yourself the way we all see you," he said. "Maybe someday you will."

Benjamin led his horse away from the house and into the street. The horse trod on the cobblestones, making a lonesome echo. Stone houses of the same dirty sand color of the streets lined the winding road that led to the top of the hill in Jeremiah. They walked their horses through street after street.

Through the opened doors of their simple homes, she saw people busily working. She did not see what she considered typical families. There were far more men than women and very few children. Often she saw a lone woman among five or six men and feared the worst for her safety.

But after passing many similar scenes, she noticed the women smiling, laughing, or teasingly slapping the men with dishrags. She saw nothing of yelling or fighting, and things seemed much the way Gideon ran his own household.

There were burlap tents set up next to the houses and in alleyways where space allowed. In them she saw more children and women. Many wore rags, but no one seemed sad. They obviously had no home and no possessions, but she often heard singing and laughter.

"Who are all these people?"

"Oh, you are speaking to me again?"

If Benjamin had been sarcastic, Jaden would have turned around and gone back to his house, but she could hear his kindness, and it had the desired effect. "I can only hold out so long with you crazy Arwavians."

Benjamin laughed. "These are people whose villages were destroyed by the night raids."

"Oh..." she said.

"Xzavier increased his night raids after you and Zachariah arrived here. Nearly every night a village is destroyed by his dragons with their powerful talons or burned by his men. They slay anyone who can't run away. Mercifully, he doesn't chase after the survivors, but we think that is because he wants us to be overwhelmed by refugees so that we are increasingly unable to defend ourselves."

Jaden shuddered. She imagined parents and children peacefully asleep in their homes, alarmed by dragons screeching and... She had never considered what quieting down the resistance really meant, as Xzavier referred to it. Jaden fell silent, lost in painful memories, when Benjamin stopped.

They were half-way up Jeremiah's hill at an open field filled with tents and refugees. In the midst of the tents, Gideon stood surrounded by people who obviously gathered and waited for Jaden and Benjamin. Benjamin offered Jaden his hand. She stared at this innocent, handsome, friendly young man, and although she wanted to take the reins and ride away, she felt safer with him than she had felt with anyone in her life.

Benjamin led her through the camp in a gentlemanly way with his hand on her lower back. Although he showed more courtesy than she had experienced in her life, it ultimately felt suffocating to her.

"Benjamin, you don't need to do that. I promise not to run."

Benjamin chuckled. "Of course, my lady."

As they moved through the camp, Jaden noticed that the provisions were homespun, probably from the Jeremian artisans that must be working day and night to provide for so many refugees pouring into their city.

Iron pots and pans over small fires boiled unattended. Simple rag dolls and little wooden swords lay on bed rolls inside tents. Metal washbasins, pewter spoons, bowls and plates were stacked neatly near the fires, washed and ready for the next meal. These people were unbelievable to Jaden. How was it possible that these crazy Arwavians, mostly knights, were so well prepared and able to handle a crisis of this magnitude?

As they neared the group and Gideon, Jaden's heart raced. There were many people, and she had to tell them that she had sentenced their leader to death. Her legs grew weak. Benjamin noticed and put his arm around her waist and held her arm as she walked. This time she didn't resist.

Gideon moved over to them and whispered, "I am so glad you came. This means so much to these people. They have worried about Les and are grateful to hear from you."

"You didn't let them keep their weapons for this little talk did you?" Jaden asked wryly.

Gideon laughed and spoke softly, "I have shared with them what you went through to get here and what Zachariah is still going through. They are on your side."

Gideon turned to the crowd and said in a loud voice, "This is Jaden, Queen of Xannellion. She has graciously offered to share with you what she knows about our beloved friend, Les, whom we buried with his fathers earlier today. My lady," Gideon motioned for her to begin.

Tears filled Jaden's eyes as she saw the expectant faces before her. She began to relate the things she knew about Les. With every word, she felt condemned by their goodness, and in the end she could barely speak.

When she finished, Gideon said, "Thank you, Queen Jaden. As you see from the wet eyes before you, we all thank you, and we know it must be difficult."

Gideon spoke for a few more minutes about the goodness of Les and the trials their people were going through, but Jaden heard nothing. If it weren't for Benjamin's strong hold on her, she surely would have collapsed.

When Gideon finished, a few of Les's closest friends came over to thank Jaden. Each one thanked her kindly, embraced her, and wished her and her son well. Jaden tried to be gracious, but for the most part, she just cried. When it was over she let Benjamin lead her back to her horse and ride with her. His horse followed hers slowly back to Gideon's house.

"You did a fine job, my lady."

Jaden twisted in her saddle to look at Benjamin.

"None of you understand, do you? When I saw my son dying on the track in our stadium, all I wanted in the world was for him to live. That is all. I somehow got him on my dragon and flew to the first place I could, even though I thought you were all insane. I needed your protection. I had no choice. I only hoped that your famed charity would be as people have said, so that you would not kill me and my son when we arrived.

"If I could have gone somewhere else, anywhere else, I would have. I hated you and your people. I can't say that I enjoyed seeing Les's pain and death, but it would be a lie to say I cared about him or tried to help him. I was disgusted by his weakness against Xzavier and again at his death. I will admit that when he died, it made me feel sick, but that is the most virtuous feeling I had toward him. There is nothing in all my contact with Les that makes me deserve the kindness shown to me back there."

"Do you hate us now?"

"What do you mean? Did you not hear me? I am the villain."

"But now that you know more about us, do you hate us?"

"Of course not. How could anyone hate you? But you should hate me."

"Why?"

Jaden slapped her hands down on her thighs as she turned away from Benjamin. "Stop it! Please stop."

Benjamin rode silently back to the house. When they arrived, he helped Jaden down and then departed to put the horses away. Jaden watched him go. His strong, lean body bowed just a little as he walked the horses toward the stables.

Not knowing what to do next, Jaden walked into the orchard. She walked until she was alone and no one could see her easily from the courtyard or the stables, and she fell to her knees and cried.

11

Dream to Freedom

Jaden began to dream...

As she slept, she passed through images and scenes. First, she saw the blue-eyed man walking into an open field. Gideon approached the blue-eyed man. The two men conversed comfortably together as if they had a strong connection, which she envied, for some reason.

In the next part of the dream, Jaden was in a courtroom charged with energy. Guards escorted her from the back of the room. They appeared to be protecting her from a group of fierce people who were on trial. The enraged people yelled at her, threatened her, and filled her with such fear and pain that she fainted.

The blue-eyed man left his place as the judge and stepped between Jaden and the hostile people. He picked her up in his arms and she leaned against his chest like a child. She felt safe and protected. She never wanted to leave him.

Afterward, the dream swept her away to a garden. A powerful and intelligent man, like Xzavier, accompanied her. At first the man intrigued her and she enjoyed their stimulating conversation. But during their discussion he began to change, and she grew increasingly uncomfortable. Right in front of her, he morphed into someone or something dark, angry, aggressive, and seething with misery. He frightened her. She recognized him as the leader of the group that hated her in the courtroom.

Next, she was in a dark dungeon chained to a wall. Fear overwhelmed her. She felt dazed and lonely. She heard a voice chanting rhythmically in a language she didn't understand but felt she should recognize. After a time, she realized she was hearing her own voice. Her cell door opened. The light from outside blinded her.

Someone walked toward her. She lunged at him, but the chains held her back and ripped at her wrists. She cried out in anger. As her eyes adjusted to the light, she saw the blue-eyed man coming toward her. Peace emanated from him. She wanted his peace, but here she was in darkness, chained to stone.

"Jaden, I am here to help you," he said. "You are loved by so many. Free yourself from the hate that will destroy you."

His hands reached tenderly toward her. Somewhere deep inside and buried by hate, she longed to be free. Her whole soul yearned for his peace. He held her face and, with his healing hands, smoothed away the anger that constricted almost every muscle in her body. As she gave way to the peace, she began to rest and feel relief.

Without time to completely appreciate the feeling of release, great sorrow surfaced, flooding over her in waves. She sobbed with a broken heart. He unlocked the chains with a wave of his hand. Then his eyes bore into Jaden's soul.

She held her breath trying to quiet the sobbing as he spoke again, "You are going to be all right now. It won't be easy. You have much yet to overcome. But it will be all right. Come with me." He put his arm around her. Weakly, she walked toward the light. Jaden awoke sobbing softly. She wiped the tears away. It was still dark, but an unusual peace settled in her heart.

The next morning, in the moments between sleep and consciousness, Jaden thought she saw little faeries flitting around her head. They sang a peaceful melody that pricked one of Jaden's childhood memories. It was sweet and peaceful, but upbeat and hopeful. She listened for awhile, lost in the edges of her memories, when she heard Gideon's voice.

"Jaden," he said, "I am sorry to have to wake you."

Jaden woke up in the orchard with a blanket over her and a small shelter covering her. When she opened her eyes, there were no faeries, and she didn't dare bring it up, for fear that Gideon would laugh. He always seemed to be amused by her. She wiped her eyes and smoothed her hair as she sat up. Gideon peeked under the shelter.

"How did you sleep?"

"Who did this?"

"You fell asleep last night in the garden, and we didn't want to disturb you by returning you to the house. Danae brought you the blanket, and I put the shelter over you. The nights are warmer now, so we thought you would be comfortable, and it really is peaceful out here."

"Benjamin says you don't come out here often."

"It is a peaceful place, nonetheless," Gideon said matter-of-factly. "I apologize for waking you, but I need your help. The danger increases, and I need to learn more of what you know about Xzavier and his dragons so we have the best chance of protecting Jeremiah and the Arwavian villages in the south."

Jaden rubbed her eyes, realizing that they were horribly swollen.

"I can help you," she said.

"I have to return to my chamber. When you have had some breakfast, Danae can help you find me."

Jaden reached for him to stop. "I slept well. Thank you."

Gideon responded with a nod and left.

Danae met Jaden at the door.

"Zachariah had a difficult day and night. He woke with a fever while you were bathing yesterday. He was in a lot of pain. We helped him through it, but it was a long night. He finally settled down near dawn, but I think he will sleep much of today. If you don't mind, I'd like him to remain asleep as much as possible."

She understood better now why Benjamin did not return her to the house. "Yes, I agree. I'll be quiet."

Danae prepared a modest plate of food for Jaden. She ate quickly. When she was finished, Danae led her down the length of the main room to the east corridor. Jaden thought about this gentle girl surrounded by her mighty father and uncles. She followed Danae down a narrow hallway with windows facing Danae's garden to the south.

On the opposite wall hung two sets of bows and quivers of arrows, one shiny and new, and one tarnished and battle-scarred. There were two shields, one shiny and bright, and one dented with hints of rust beginning to eat at the edges. A few paces farther hung two swords and two daggers, the same as before, one shiny and one well worn.

"Who do these weapons belong to?" Jaden asked, distracted for the moment from her concern about meeting with Gideon.

"I had a twin brother. He was the hero. I never took to fighting. I guess it wasn't my nature. My mother always supported me but she was so strong and brave too..." Danae answered Jaden quietly with a sadness that Jaden hadn't observed before.

"I haven't met your mother. Where is she?"

Danae lowered her eyes.

"Oh, you did say something about her... I don't know where Zachariah and I would be if you had been a good warrior instead of a gifted healer." Danae lifted her eyes appreciatively.

At the end of the corridor, they arrived at a large door with an intricately carved relief of men in an ancient battle. There were knights fighting a host of evil creatures. On the knights' side were many creatures that she didn't recognize. She wondered if any of these creatures still existed.

The creatures and people on the other side of the battle were distinguishably dark and evil. The leader of this evil host sent a chill through her body. She turned her focus to the edges of the door where detailed carvings formed weapons, lilies, and flying tigers. Everything about the door was elegant. Too elegant and ornate, in fact. It seemed out of place to Jaden because it didn't fit with the simple decor of the rest of the house.

"Where did this door come from?"

"When the cathedral on the hill was burned the first time by the Xannellion King, Basilius, my father's grandfather saved one of the doors and made it part of our home. For the knights who visit and for my father, it is a reminder of who they are fighting for and what they are fighting against."

"Oh, it is striking."

"Thank you. Would you like me to knock?"

"No, I can do that. Go back and take care of my son – I mean, please take care of him?"

Danae smiled and departed.

"I'll be back soon," Jaden called after Danae with little confidence. But she straightened her shoulders, lifted her regal head and gave a strong knock at the door.

"Yes, come in," Gideon said from inside.

Jaden opened the heavy door and entered a large chamber. Two large skylights revealed the room's contents. There were no windows. Gideon sat at a solid, square table that was intricately carved like the door. Sixteen chairs surrounded the table, four on each side of the square.

At the far end of the room stood ornately carved bookshelves built into the wall from floor to ceiling. The other three walls displayed panoramic scenes of mountains and valleys in Trivar painted in such careful detail that Jaden could almost feel the breeze and smell the fresh air. What kind of men appreciated such beauty?

"Please sit down, my lady. Would you like something to drink?"

"Yes, thank you." Jaden watched Gideon carefully as he poured her a drink. He was a handsome man, tall and strong, but with a calm demeanor that reminded Jaden of her dream. This frightened but intrigued her. When he walked toward her, she stood and nearly knocked over her chair. She caught the chair and took the cup he handed her, almost spilling it as she set it on the table.

"You are not in danger. I only want to discuss security matters with you."

"Don't treat me like a child," Jaden spat. "You Jeremians are so...irritating!" She fussed with her dress but lost the battle and flung the fabric down. She sat down, put her hands on the table, and glared at Gideon.

The amusement on Gideon's face turned serious. "I held off inquiring of you as long as I could. I wanted your son to get better before I troubled you with matters of protecting Jeremiah." He paused to see Jaden's reaction.

She acknowledged him with her eyes.

"I am glad he is recovering," he said. "Danae can raise the dead. I have always said so."

Jaden wanted to add to the compliment, but pride would not let her. The best she could do was nod.

Gideon accepted her nod and continued.

"My first question: how many dragons does Xzavier have?"

Jaden studied Gideon closely, not trusting him entirely, but wanting to. Carefully, she began.

"The king of Yamis started raising dragons before I arrived in Yamis."

"You aren't from Yamis originally?"

"No, I believe I am from the north somewhere, but I don't know for sure." Jaden tried not to sound vulnerable. "The king first found the dragons when they came to the southern borders of Yamis to birth their young in the early spring. People in remote villages whispered rumors about a flying predator, jeweled in color, and frighteningly powerful. Teeku, the king, spared nothing to learn all he could about these dragons.

"We still aren't sure where they come from or where they go from midsummer until spring. All we know is that couples arrived together in early spring to find a nesting spot in a cave or hollow. Many pairs of mates come but spread out to give each other their necessary hunting space. The male keeps the female fed while she lays two eggs and fiercely watches over them. When the baby dragons hatch, one is inevitably larger, and the mother takes special care of it, leaving the smaller one to shrivel and die.

"It took the king years to figure out how to procure a dragon for himself. They are so powerful and territorial. Many of his most able servants lost their lives in this effort. Finally, he decided to seek to obtain the smaller of the two dragons, the discarded one, and nurse it to keep it alive. It was complicated and very dangerous, but eventually he obtained two dragons. By the time I was ten, they produced two offspring. The larger of the two offspring...was...Justine, my dragon."

"The one who protected you on your arrival?"

"Yes." Jaden forced herself to keep eye contact with Gideon.

"The king had two adult dragons and one egg when Xzavier arrived. By the time Xzavier killed Teeku, there were five adults, six young, and four eggs. Originally, Teeku followed the wild dragon's lead and kept only the strong egg, hoping to improve the size and strength of his weaker dragons.

"But when Xzavier took over, he kept the small and large eggs and sent men to hunt for more of the small discarded ones. Instead of helping Xzavier, this severely hampered his efforts. The smaller, weaker dragons contracted diseases that spread to their stronger cousins, killing many. And the smaller dragons birthed more stillborn and deformed dragons, if they could reproduce at all. Even so, by the time we left for Xannellion, he had fourteen adult dragons and one hundred young that were over half a year old. A fitting surprise for Cannote..." Jaden fell silent.

Gideon's eyes widened. "I heard about the welcome feast but didn't realize he used young dragons." Gideon gave a low whistle. "How many dragons do you think he has now?"

"Eggs included, he probably has close to one hundred and fifty."

"How soon can they fight?"

"They are deadly from birth. But it takes four years before they are large enough and trained well enough for battle. The twelve remaining adults are battle-ready, although the one hundred young are now almost two-and-a-half, and Xzavier will begin training them soon. Also, the one hundred young will be able to mate when they are three, and their numbers will grow rapidly at that point."

"One hundred and fifty dragons. What do you suppose Xzavier will do with all those dragons?"

"Zachariah is the only one who knows any of Xzavier's plans. He spent a lot of time in Xzavier's councils. I cared little to know what Xzavier was up to."

Gideon rose. He ran his fingers through his hair. "We know Xzavier won't stop until he gets the two of you. He is determined. There have been dozens of small settlements burned and destroyed throughout Xannellion."

"Of course he is determined. I never doubted he would let us go easily, but I didn't have a lot of choice in the matter. The only way to save Zachariah was to escape." Jaden began to shake.

Gideon picked up a blanket, gently draped it around her, and rested his hands on her shoulders. "I am sorry this is hard for you. I just need to know everything you can tell me so that I can protect you, your son, and my people." Gideon pulled out the chair next to Jaden and sat down.

Jaden softened again because of Gideon's sincerity.

"Xzavier needed me to obtain my father's kingdom. I needed him so that I could leave that kingdom and find out where I was born, where my...origins... really are. He was angry and bitter toward his father for banishing him as a young child. Do you know the story?"

Gideon shook his head no.

"An oracle told Cannote that his son would rise up, kill him, and become king. Consequently, his father attempted to kill Xzavier when he was ten, but his mother covertly interceded in time to spare and send Xzavier into the southern jungles with his nurse.

"Xzavier's nurse was shrewd and careful. It took two years, but somehow they made it to Yamis shortly before the nurse died, probably from exhaustion. From his mother, the nurse, and his father, Xzavier learned to value resourcefulness, power, and, above all, survival.

"Though Xzavier came to the land of Yamis an exiled, broken boy, his sufferings only made him more vengeful and determined to return and conquer Cannote. Teeku quickly saw the advantage of uniting me to a prince of Xannellion and becoming aligned with Xzavier. Teeku brought him into our palace and raised him, but Xzavier never wanted his pity. He had plans."

Jaden grimaced and then stared into Gideon's dark eyes.

"The king was deceived," she said. "I don't know why I am telling you this..."

"I think I understand..." Gideon tried to say.

"How could you ever understand, here in your perfect world? Your world where you can smile without shame, laugh without reproof, and feel joy. No, you could never understand."

Gideon gently asked, "Did you ever find out where you are from?"

Jaden flushed. "Why do you have to ask such questions?"

"I realize this is a personal question."

Something about his genuine concern caused her, for the first time, to want to stay instead of run.

"Before Cannote died, he told me I was probably from somewhere north of Alexandria. I've heard it called the Highlands. Before Zachariah's accident, Zachariah wanted to take me there, but everything fell apart."

"Yes, I could see you in the Highlands. That is quite possible."

Jaden found herself wanting to tell Gideon more but then felt sick to her stomach. Who was he? Gideon, an Arwavian, whom she used to regard as the enemy.

"Is there anything else?" she said curtly.

"Yes, I have one more request, and you may go." Gideon paused. "May I speak with your son? I have more questions about Xzavier's councils..."

"That is out of the question until he is better. He has barely regained consciousness. You must give him time..."

"There is no time, Jaden. Too many lives have been lost already."

"Not until he is better." Jaden stood, folded her blanket, and left it on the chair. She stared at Gideon and leaned toward him as if to say something more, but instead she straightened her shoulders, turned, and walked out the door.

As she walked somberly through the hallway, knights approached and passed her on their way to speak with Gideon in his chamber. She stayed close to the wall but held her chin high. She saw Benjamin grin at her, and the other knights courteously tipped their heads as she passed, but she refused to acknowledge them. Never before had so much respect been given to her. She didn't trust it.

She heard the chamber door close behind her.

12

Danae's World

Danae and Zachariah were talking quietly when Jaden came into the great room, but they stopped when they saw her approach.

"How did it go, mother?"

"I am tired. Don't let me interrupt you." She curled up under her blankets.

"Go on," Zachariah encouraged Danae softly.

Danae lifted her eyes to Zachariah and said, "You were cast out and hunted by your father, the king. You and your mother sought refuge here in Jeremiah. We have taken care of you. You would have died, or even worse, if left to your great Xannellion ruler! The knights of Jeremiah stand for all that is good and saved your life." Danae spoke in a low but firm voice that intrigued Jaden, who couldn't sleep.

Zachariah's eyes were wide at Danae's words. "I owe you my life, and I will repay it someday. I just need to get better, and I will repay it." Zachariah's eyes became dark. "I have more than one debt to repay when I am better." He glanced over at Jaden, who anticipated it and closed her eyes before he saw her.

He turned back to Danae. Jaden opened her eyes again. Zachariah's eyes softened, cloaking the darkness inside him. They were silent for a moment until Zachariah said, "I am sorry for staring, but you are so different from anyone I have met. I don't understand why you helped my mother and me when we obviously weren't your people. I mean...we could've been enemies from Xannellion, sent to spy on you," he snuffed ironically. "Why not kill us or imprison us?"

"Well, I don't think Xzavier would have sent spies to us half dead. But, nevertheless, you were in trouble, and we were in a position to help. That's what we do. We are all children of Gillantri. He taught our people to love each other and to serve those in need."

"You are indeed very different from any girl I've known," Zachariah said in such earnest that Jaden's eyes widened again, then narrowed. She couldn't help but agree as she thought about the shallow ladies Zachariah had known in Xannellion. Not even the courtiers in Yamis would have sacrificed as this young lady had, even if they benefited in some way.

"I have taken too much time talking about this. You are tired." Danae seemed ruffled and began checking his dressings.

Zachariah reached out and took her hand. "Please tell me more."

"No, you need sleep. We will have plenty of time to talk. You need to get better."

Jaden watched Danae take Zachariah's hand and carefully lay it on his chest and squeeze it gently. Danae visually searched the area, making sure all was in order. Zachariah began nodding off when Danae noticed Jaden watching her.

Danae blushed and picked up Jaden's bowl of soup and some bread. She handed them to her. Jaden glanced back sheepishly and accepted the soup and bread. She rose from her cot and walked out into the garden, sleep having left her entirely.

Jaden hoped to distract herself from her thoughts by eating the food. She found Benjamin's flying tiger stone bench and sat down. The sun dropped lower in the western sky for Jaden's fifth night in Jeremiah. But her conversation with Gideon, her son's interchange with Danae, and her dreams filled her with so many emotions that she left her bowl of soup half empty and her bread half eaten on the stone bench.

She began pacing. Old Trapton, smelling the food, wandered toward Jaden. She placed the bowl on the ground for him and resumed pacing. After a minute, she began talking to him as she paced.

"How did I, the Queen of Xannellion, get into this mess?" Trapton peered up at her with soup on his whiskers. He cocked his head to one side. But wanting soup more than conversation, he put his head back into the bowl. He soon finished. His eyes begged for more, but Jaden was too caught up in her thoughts to notice.

"My son is enjoying the company of an Arwavian, and I am helping the leader of the knights of Jeremiah to defend Jeremiah against the king! It is outrageous! It is treasonous."

Jaden put her hand on her stomach. Trapton walked over and licked her other hand. Jaden jumped. She tentatively touched the top of his nose. He nudged her leg with his large head. Jaden observed the black lines on his face in between the rich amber color of his fur.

"You really are an amazing creature, aren't you, Trapton. Better than those old black gryphons with their crow-like features and midnight feathers."

She stood. "I really hate Xzavier. Yes, we feasted and lived high, but I didn't enjoy it. I was trapped, a slave of sorts..." She thought about Benjamin's comment as she absently rubbed the big tiger's head.

Jaden stopped and took Trapton's face in her hands. "Are these people crazy?"

Trapton looked at her innocently but with an almost-human depth in his eyes. "You don't think so do you? How can people be so kind? During all this stress and difficulty, I haven't heard Danae offer a cross word." Jaden let a little sigh escape.

"And Gideon. Well, I am not sure about him. He always seems to be laughing at me. Not to mention that he treated me with disrespect and embarrassed me in front of his daughter." Trapton cocked his head toward her. "I know, old fellow, he was defending his daughter. He does laugh at me, though." Jaden gave Trapton another pat and stood up.

"You know what Trapton? I think Zachariah can help your Gideon. More than I can. Maybe it will help defeat Xzavier and defend this village from the danger we have put it in. But I have to admit to Gideon that I was wrong earlier. How frustrating this new world is, Trapton. Strange new rules! And the worst of it is that Gideon will accept my mistake without hating me for it. I would feel less pressure and embarrassment if I weren't the only one who was contentious."

Jaden patted him again, bent down to pick up the empty soup bowl, and returned to the house. Zachariah rested peacefully on his cot. They were alone in the great room. He turned to see Jaden enter.

"How are you feeling?"

"I'm improving. I am glad you came in. I wanted to see you."

Jaden leaned over to hug him. He wrapped his one good arm around her and squeezed.

"Come and talk with me," Zachariah said. Jaden sat on Danae's stool and took her son's hand.

"What in the world is happening to us?" he said.

"We have been rescued."

"A fortnight ago, I would have been so angry that you brought me to Jeremiah. But I had no idea. Danae is so calm. It makes me feel as if I'm full of fire and venom by comparison. I want what she has. Benjamin is more at ease than any of my lazy palace dogs back in Xannellion, but he isn't the least bit lazy. Gideon is powerful and good. Nothing is as it was. I feel dizzy."

"I agree. I have no bearings in this new place. At first my only desire was for you to recover and for us to avenge ourselves of Xzavier's treachery. Now that you are recovering, my determination to get back at Xzavier is...well, it is changing..."

Zachariah sat up. "Mother, don't talk like that. We will avenge ourselves. I have seen more and more clearly his debauchery as I have watched Gideon and his brothers serve us and protect us. We must defeat him, and I will take his place. I will rule like Gideon and become the greatest king Xannellion has ever known. I will bring peace to Trivar. And I will build a powerful navy, of course."

"Of course," Jaden mused. "Son, Gideon wants to talk with you about Xzavier and his defenses, vulnerabilities, anything you know about Xannellion that could help Jeremiah defend itself and us. We've put them in a difficult position. Do you feel like you will soon be well enough to do that?"

"Do you know if Gideon is here now?"

Jaden rolled her eyes. "Give yourself at least one more night."

"You don't know. I have information that Gideon needs. May I go?"

"No. Don't be foolish. You are barely able to sit, let alone stand. After a good night's sleep, I will consider it."

Zachariah sighed resignedly. "I know, I am fatigued. You'd think after sleeping for days I'd have more energy."

"Danae says that it takes a tremendous amount of energy to heal. It isn't as simple as you might think."

"She is wonderful, isn't she?"

"For a crazy Arwavian, I suppose. I didn't know if you were going to make it."

Zachariah pressed her hand. "I had to make it. Xzavier is the one who won't. Mark my words, mother, he doesn't have much time left here in Trivar."

Sadness crossed Jaden's face. "Be careful. I watched your father kill many people for the sake of revenge, and it only made him darker and less like the Xzavier I knew when he first came to Yamis."

"I know, but I am different. You need to trust me."

"I know you are different. Maybe you should sleep now. It is so good to have you back."

Silence passed between them.

Zachariah resumed, "It wasn't an accident that we came here."

Jaden took in the brilliant colors scattered by the setting sun through the west windows.

"I agree," she said as she tenderly hugged him. She straightened his blankets and tip-toed to her cot to fall asleep.

13

"I Think Jeremiah Suits Me"

The next morning, before the sun rose above the trees that encompassed Danae's garden, Zachariah was awake.

"Mother, I need to stand. Will you help me?"

Through blurry eyes Jaden asked, "What?"

"Remember, I need to talk with Gideon today. So many thoughts are crowding my mind. I have to tell him now."

"You can't sleep a little longer?"

"I slept all night, like you required," Zachariah begged like a puppy that wanted to go for a walk after being cooped up in the house all winter.

"You need to wash up first. And when you go to see him, I will go with you to make sure you don't overdo it. But first things first, let's see how well you can stand."

Zachariah slowly moved his legs to the edge of his cot and let them drop to the floor.

"Oh, that feels good. I was feeling so cramped."

Jaden offered him her hand. Danae, who had been fixing something on the fire, walked over and offered her hand as well. With their support, he slowly stood and walked toward Jaden's cot.

"I am fine. My legs feel a little stiff and sore, but there is no great pain. Well, except in my left hip. But if I use my right hip more, the left one doesn't feel so bad. I'll be running in no time."

Jaden and Danae laughed.

"I am relieved," Jaden said. "I was so worried when I saw that wheel fly at you."

"Don't bring that up again. It makes me angry."

"I'd rather not think about it myself."

"All right, now I am going to see Gideon."

Danae said, "You don't look ready for a meeting." She and Jaden giggled as Zachariah stood in the entry way in a night shirt, his hair standing on end, smiling like a boy who had just won his first chariot race.

"There now, I've been laid up for days. Go easy." Zachariah feigned hurt feelings. "Is there some place for me to wash up? And do you have some extra clothes I could wear?"

"Benjamin left some of his for you next to the fire. And there is a washroom in the back with a basin, fresh water, towels, and everything you should need. I could call Benjamin if you need help getting dressed."

"No, I can manage. Is your father around?"

"You go wash up. I'll check," Danae said as she walked into the eastern corridor.

For the first time since Jaden could remember, her heart felt light. It wasn't entirely free of pain or concern, but it was less distressed. To see her son walk, to hear him laugh again, to know he was going to be all right gave her hope, something she had not felt in some time.

When Danae returned, she said, "Jaden, can I speak with you for a minute?"

"Sure."

They removed to the fireplace and sat on two stools. Danae fidgeted with her dress and bit her lip.

Jaden frowned and said, "Just tell me straight. I can handle whatever you need to say."

"My father is concerned about you coming to the meeting today, but before you get the wrong idea, it is because he knows how difficult it was for you last time, and he doesn't want to cause you more stress. I know it sounds like he doesn't want you there, but he told me to let you know it is only because he wants what is best for you..."

Jaden laughed, "Danae stop. You aren't upsetting me. Yes, I feel uncomfortable, but it isn't the way you think. It just surprises me when any of you show me concern. I don't trust it because I know I don't deserve it. I am beginning to see that your concern is genuine. Still, the only reason I want to go today is to make sure that my son doesn't surpass his limits physically."

"I will go, if you don't mind. I will attend to him. I assure you, we will see that Zachariah is soon resting once more. My father suggested that you go to my pool today. He said you also need much care."

Jaden's eyes widened and softened. "He said that?"

Danae smiled.

Jaden's eyes became wet and emotion threatened her composure. She stood and said, "I don't know how to respond to this."

"Just say thank you and let us help you."

Before Jaden could collect herself, Zachariah appeared from the washroom.

"I think Jeremiah suits me."

"You look nice, son." Jaden glanced at Danae.

Zachariah caught their exchange and turned to Danae, questioning. She answered him, "Your mother is going to go soak in the pond. I am going with you to keep you in line."

"You are leaving me in the hands of a miserable Arwavian, mother?" He winked at Danae.

"She may be gentle, but I know she will do as she says!"

"Well, then, let's get going...we've wasted too much time this morning."

Jaden watched as Zachariah limped and Danae walked toward the eastern corridor.

"Danae, please make sure he doesn't get too worn out. Tell your father I said so. And tell him thank you."

Danae just bobbed her head twice. Jaden gathered up a towel and another change of clothes that Gideon had left at the foot of her cot. Benjamin entered the long room from the eastern corridor wearing his riding clothes and armor.

"Where are you going this morning?" Jaden said.

"I have business in Alexandria, but I'll be back soon. You won't even miss me." Benjamin turned to go out the front door.

"Alexandria? Why that far?"

Benjamin stopped, "Well...I have an assignment."

"Please tell me what is going on."

"Oh, it is nothing."

"A trip to Alexandria doesn't seem like nothing."

Richard opened the front door. He saw Jaden and Benjamin talking and waited. His eyes were exhausted and his clothes and hair were dusty, like he'd been traveling for a long time. Jaden realized that she hadn't seen him since she first arrived and began to see that things were happening that no one was sharing with her.

"Richard, I haven't seen you for awhile."

"Yes, my lady, I have been busy with the refugees. But I'll be around for a time, now that Benjamin..."

"...Now that I'll be covering for him, taking care of the refugees," Benjamin finished. The two brothers exchanged a glance. Richard's darker features more closely resembled Gideon's, but they all had the same strong build.

"Are you going to tell me what is going on, or do I just have to continue to pester everyone about it and worry?" Jaden said in her most motherly tone.

Richard winced toward Benjamin, who said, "Jaden, we are just taking care of the people. Nothing more or less."

"But it is because I have put you in danger that you are doing this. Is it not so?"

Both young men avoided her gaze.

"If it is because of me, then I need to share the burden of it. Please tell me."

Finally Richard said, "Gideon made us promise to not tell you. Please don't make us break our promise."

Furious, Jaden said, "Why? Why do you all do this? I have put you all in so much danger. I am so sorry!"

Benjamin wrapped his young arms around Jaden and hugged her, completely disarming her. She hugged him back and felt like crying. He pulled away and said, "You haven't put us in danger, Xzavier has. But we know what we are doing. This isn't the first time we have had to sacrifice. That is our job. That is what we do. But we are being watched over."

Jaden nodded, "I don't want you to break your promise to Gideon. Please be careful."

Benjamin smiled and gave her another hug. He turned and followed Richard out the front door. Just before the door closed, she said again in her motherly tone, "Please be careful!" It was a challenge for her to disconnect Benjamin from Zachariah.

"Of course. Thank you," he said, and he was gone.

"Alexandria," Jaden mused to herself as she walked out the back door to the garden. She stopped at the bench and called, "Trapton...Trapton!" Some branches began to move and Trapton popped through expectantly. "Trapton, I need an escort to the back of this garden."

Jaden walked over to Trapton and put her hand on his neck. Together they walked through the garden until they arrived at the east gate.

"Trapton, can you stay here for awhile?" She took a backward glance toward the cottage, opened the gate, and walked across the path into the thick palms. Jaden soon arrived again at the turquoise pool and dazzling waterfall. She took in a cleansing breath as if seeing it for the first time. She moved into the water. Sinking into its warmth, its rejuvenating powers began to work on her. She closed her eyes and thought about Alexandria.

****

When dawn broke the next day, Jaden sent Danae for a bath and straightened up the room. She sat next to Zachariah while they ate breakfast.

"I told Gideon everything," he said.

"What exactly is everything?" Jaden asked.

"All about Xzavier's plans to pull down the rebellious knights of Jeremiah because he and Cannote failed miserably at controlling them... That made Gideon laugh. I love his laugh. I hope someday to laugh as freely as he does. I feel so constricted, so oppressed. But here, they are like," Zachariah paused, struggling for the word and then grinned as he said, "like children! Free spirited and innocent, yet they aren't naïve." He mused over that for a moment.

"Anyway, I told him that Xzavier has wanted to destroy Jeremiah from the time he learned about them and that Xzavier has been gathering intelligence from Xannellions known to oppose the Arwavian way of life.

"Gideon said that this was good and bad news. It's good news because those who oppose the Arwavian way of life often have incorrect information about Arwavians. He said that this gives us an advantage. I don't completely understand, but he said something about knowing things that Xzavier can never know without faith.

"On the other hand, it is bad news because many of those whom Xzavier will gather used to be Arwavians, but they chose to reject the Arwavian way. These hate the Arwavians more than those who have never tasted their way of life. I thought that was strange because if they once loved one way of life, I thought they would always feel tenderly toward that way of life at least to some extent, like how I feel about Xannellion.

"I mean, I don't wish to return to things the way they were, of course, although there are parts of our life back with Xzavier that I miss a lot. But Gideon said it is different with Arwavians. He said that once they feel the light of Gillantri, they fall lower into the darkness if they choose to later reject it."

What Zachariah said sent a chill through Jaden.

"I don't completely understand, but I trust Gideon," Zachariah continued. "Mother, Gideon is going to train me as one of his knights."

"What?" Jaden put her hand over her stomach. "You are just barely getting well!"

"If I am going to defeat Xzavier, I have to train with Gideon. He can give me the advantage I need. Listen, Gideon is convinced that Xzavier is gearing up for a large offensive soon. You know I am already well trained, and I know that when I get better, I will be able to spar as well as any knight, and no one can beat me at archery. But with Gideon, I can do more, I'm sure of it. And I need real battle experience..."

"Real battle experience? No! You have just escaped death. You don't know what I have been through the past few days. I just can't let you..."

"Gideon will prepare me well. I have to."

"But your arm. It is not even healed."

"Gideon said it won't be long before I'm ready. He has seen bones that were much worse than mine heal in a fortnight with Danae's special salves and wraps. I'll begin slowly and go from there."

"How is your hip?"

"Well, it is sore when I stand up and achy after a full day, but Danae works magic. It is so much better."

"Do you not see the danger here?"

"The danger is what we left behind. We are in Jeremiah. Everything is going to be fine."

"So you are ready to jump into this world head-first? You know so little about it. What if..."

"Stop fretting," Zachariah stood and wrapped his arms around her. He whispered in her ear, "I know what I am doing."

The back door opened. Both mother and son turned quickly, surprised that it wasn't Danae.

"Hello. You two must be the Xannellion transplants. I am Franklin. Sorry to startle you. I am here to see Gideon."

"Gideon told me a lot about you. It is good to meet you," Zachariah said as he hobbled over to Franklin.

Jaden watched her son shake Franklin's large leathery hand. Franklin was bald and a few inches shorter than Zachariah, but his shoulders were broader, and everything about him seemed larger. He wasn't fat, yet she could barely discern what size his frame was under all his thickness. He wore an off-white toga, more Xannellion in style than Jeremian. She had seen clothes like that only once...

"I'll be in shortly," Zachariah said. Franklin bowed courteously at Jaden and left for the eastern wing of the cottage.

Jaden couldn't wait to ask, "Do you remember the day we went to the market..."

"I thought the same thing, but he is so stout, and the elves are so slender and tall..."

"That is what they were called, elves."

"Isn't he great?"

"I guess so. He made me a little nervous. He walks around like Gideon, too sure of his own power or something."

"It is called confidence, mother. And you walk around the same way."

"But something is different... I don't trust them."

Zachariah paused for a long moment.

"Please give me your blessing," he said. "I have to do this. We have to conquer Xzavier. We have put Jeremiah in tremendous danger. Could you see me with you somewhere safely hidden, while the battle is raging and all these innocent people are fighting Xzavier to protect us? I can't do it."

Jaden wrapped both arms around her stomach. "I know, but visions of you near death assail my mind. I hoped that once we were free from Xzavier, you wouldn't have to do dangerous things again."

Taking a quick breath, she lifted her head to face his pleading green eyes. His eyes were so similar to hers. She sighed and said, "You have my permission."

"I will be careful. I will protect you and destroy Xzavier. Someday I will be King of Xannellion, and you will sit in the palace, and this time no one will harm you! I promise!"

Zachariah kissed his mother on the forehead and followed Franklin down the hallway to Gideon's chamber.

14

Not Benjamin

Near the end of the fortnight, Danae gave Zachariah permission to use a bow and arrow to begin working the muscles in his left arm. He'd pull the bow as far as he could and then slowly release it, over and over again. After a short time, Zachariah was able to shoot arrows at a target, but he wasn't strong yet.

"Back in Xannellion, no one could surpass me at archery. Now look at me!" he said. But soon he was moving the target farther back.

One night, Zachariah stood near the back door of the cottage and aimed to the end of the garden. "Watch this, Danae, I'll hit that target."

"I know you will."

He pulled the string back, aimed, and let the arrow fly. It flew past her flowers and trees and hit the target directly in the middle. Danae jumped and clapped her hands. She threw her arms around his neck. They both laughed.

"See, I told you I was the best, the best in all Xannellion!"

Danae laughed. "I always believed you."

"Thank you for believing in me. Thank you for everything."

He held her for a minute, and then he said, "I'll race you to my arrow."

She laughed and ran, just beating him because his hip still gave him trouble. She turned around as he took his last couple of steps. He retrieved the arrow and trapped her eyes with his. She tried to turn away. But Zachariah lifted her chin, met her gaze, and slowly kissed her, lingering as long as he felt she would let him, and then he backed away.

"I have wanted to do that for some time now," he said.

Danae's eyes were surprised but not unwilling. He leaned in again, but Jaden called, "Danae, Zachariah, it is time for lunch."

He turned, hoping his mother didn't see them. Convinced that she hadn't, he chuckled good-naturedly, put his arm around her shoulder and said, "Would you help this old cripple back to the house?"

"You are too much," Danae whispered as she wrapped her arm around his waist and they returned to the house.

****

"My lord, you are welcome. You surprised me. What brings your Greatness to my humble abode at this hour of the night?"

Xzavier bowed profusely trying to make up for the alarm and anger he felt. Xzavier had been feeding his young dragons and teaching the older ones to fight and kill when Daman arrived.

"Xzavier," Daman said in a low and penetrating voice, "I am very disappointed. You left Jaden and Zachariah behind, in the enemy's camp. What were you thinking, my friend?"

"I am going back for them. I am burning villages and filling Jeremiah with refugees that will distract them…"

"And give them more men to fight for them."

"Even now I am raising an army of men, double the size of my standing army. And in a year my dragons will be ready. My lord, when I saw Gideon and his men and their flying tigers, I decided it would be best to wait."

"Wait? When you had them all within your grasp? Your dragons would have made short order of those knights and their flying kitties! And you could have returned Jaden and Zachariah to Xannellion," Daman hissed. "I have supported you since you defeated your father. I gave you his kingdom, but you must think more like me. You must act when it is time to act! Do not wait for permission. War is not something we fear, especially with little fanatic cities like Jeremiah. I gave you power, more than Cannote. To keep it, you must use it!"

Xzavier nervously fingered his glowing translucent-amber bracelet when Daman motioned for his servant, who waited in the shadows behind Daman. The servant clutched Xzavier's throat and began to squeeze. Xzavier felt the breath inside of him constrict. Shock and anger coursed through his body but he had no means to defend himself.

The dragons were silent, fully aware that their true lord was in their midst. Daman's servant let his grip loosen. Xzavier dropped to his knees, holding his neck and gasping for air. Daman exited, flourishing his black cape. He departed with his men through the hidden tunnel below Xzavier's lair.

As he melted into the darkness, he said, "It is your job to make right what went wrong at the city of Jeremiah. I want Jaden and Zachariah back! Whatever it takes!" Then he was gone.

Still on the floor with his head pounding, Xzavier wondered out loud, "When will we be strong enough to attack Jeremiah?"

Forgetting his dragons, he headed for his chamber. Darkness filled the castle. Only a stream of moonlight shone through the upper windows casting eerie shadows on the opposite wall. His footsteps echoed through the empty halls. When he arrived at his chamber he crawled into his bed and fell asleep.

Not long after, Xzavier was rudely awakened by a loud knock at his chamber door. "Master, please open quickly."

Disoriented, Xzavier pulled himself out of bed, threw on an outer robe, and opened the door.

"What is it?"

His servant cowered before him. "My lord, begging your pardon, but we just received word that a Jeremian knight returning on the road from Alexandria was captured by our men. They flew him here on the back of the raiders' dragon. He is barely alive," he cackled dryly. "If you want to question him, you'd better do so quickly, my lord."

"Had your message been less important I would've had you fed to my dragons."

He flew past the messenger in his night clothes. Adrenaline coursed through him as he ran down long corridors and past fine halls to the holding chambers in the southern dungeon.

"Guards," he said, motioning for them to open the doors to the chamber. A pale, shallow-breathing young man lay on the floor. Life seethed out of the open wounds on his body.

"Who are you?" said Xzavier without wasting time.

The young man stared in defiance. Xzavier got down on his knees and hissed into the boy's face.

"I am Xzavier, The Serpent Lord. Do you want to die peacefully or would you like the rats to nibble at you for a week?"

The boy spat in Xzavier's face. Xzavier recoiled and kicked him. The lad began coughing up blood.

"Stop him from dying this instant!" Xzavier commanded. A servant girl came in to comfort the boy and calm him down.

"Does anyone know his name or anything about him?" Xzavier straightened his robes and calmed his demeanor.

A raider answered, "His comrades called him Benjamin before we killed them, sire." "What else do you know?"

"We attacked them on the northern border of Jeremiah. We were returning from a night raid when we saw a heavily armed brigade of knights. Luckily, we had a dragon."

"Did you find anything on them?"

"There was nothing, sire."

"Were you returning from Alexandria, boy? What were you doing?"

Benjamin closed his eyes.

"We'll heal you and then kill you if we have to. Tell me what you know!"

Benjamin's body became still. Xzavier grabbed his face and shook it but there was no life left in him.

"Weak Arwavians. I hate them." He roughly pushed Benjamin's pale face to the side and stood. "You didn't try hard enough! These knights weren't just making a pleasure run on that road. Gideon isn't stupid."

Xzavier then turned to his highest ranking guard and said, "What do our spies know about Jeremiah, Alexandria, and every city between? I want information about their homes and armories and everything you can find out about Jaden, Zachariah, and communications between the Arwavian cities. I need to know their secrets."

"I'll check with intelligence and get back with you later today."

"If that is the best you can do. Also, have one of your men write a note saying that we know what Gideon is up to. Pin it on this pathetic knight and drop him at the gates of Jeremiah. I want the fear of Xzavier, The Serpent Lord, to engulf that city!"

****

Jaden lingered in bed. Danae rose hours earlier and Jaden smelled inviting aromas wafting up the stairs from the main hall. After the first seven days, Danae offered the other bed in her room to Jaden. Danae was growing on Jaden. She wasn't surprised to see her son spending more and more time with the gentle girl when he was not training.

Reluctantly, Jaden threw off her covers and let her feet fall over the side of the bed. The room was simple and pleasant. Sitting on the window seat, she could see the garden. On evenings after a warm day sweet smells floated through the window.

Last night it had rained. Jaden loved it when it rained at night because the next morning seemed fresher. She breathed in the cool air and got dressed. As she put her slippers on, a horrible screech alarmed her.

"Dragons," she whispered and rushed out the door and down the stairs, as Gideon, Zachariah, and Franklin came running out of the eastern corridor.

"What was that?" Gideon cried.

Zachariah and Jaden said, "Dragons."

Gideon halted, the full weight of the word sinking in.

"Franklin, stay here with Jaden and tell Danae..."

The back door flew open before he could finish, and Danae appeared dripping wet in a towel.

"What was that?"

Without answering her, Gideon said, "Zachariah, come with me. Danae, I love you. Jaden, tell her what is going on." And like a strong gust of wind they were gone.

Jaden began to shake and immediately put her arms around her midsection trying to make it stop. Danae rushed to the washroom with her clean clothes, quickly dressed, and rushed back out.

"Jaden, what in Trivar was that? Please don't tell me it was dragons."

"We've put you in so much danger..." Jaden said while trying to create more space in her chest so she could breathe.

Franklin asked, "Do you remember when you first got here?"

"Yes."

"Has anyone complained about the danger we are in?"

"No, but that still doesn't change the fact that we are the reason you are in danger."

"You are safe," Franklin said. "We are going to be all right. If it hadn't been you, it would have been someone or something else. Cannote would have given anything to destroy Jeremiah, and now Xzavier is picking up where his father left off. More than that, Jeremiah has been a thorn in Daman's side from the beginning. Daman can never truly defeat good. It may seem dark at times, but he is on the losing side."

Jaden remembered when she first met Franklin. She and Zachariah wondered if he was an elf. She softened, thinking of when she asked him, "Are you one of the elves?"

Franklin's grin had started in his eyes and spread over his face. "I'm afraid I like to eat too much to be one of them, but their attire is very comfortable."

Jaden had smiled at his comment and noticed the unique embroidery around the edges of his clothes stitched with soft golden thread. The exquisite patterns were very masculine.

"You could only have gotten those clothes from the elves themselves because I have never seen embroidery so fine."

"Yes, the elves. Though Alexandrian artisans come close."

"Alexandria has embroiderers who can create work like this?"

"I said nearly as well, but, yes, their embroiderers are next only to the elves."

"Your eyes mock me," she had said.

Franklin then sat back letting the amusement spread once again over his face. "You are one of us now," he had said sincerely.

Jaden remembered she had protested but her memory was cut short when Richard flew through the door.

"Franklin, Gideon needs you right away."

Franklin stood.

"Everything will work out, you watch. Danae, Jaden needs some of that tea you are making, sooner rather than later." Franklin winked at Danae, who quickly turned and poured tea for Jaden.

The front door slammed shut and in a second flew opened again. Zachariah entered and stopped halfway between the door and his cot. Tenderly, he walked over to Danae and put his hand on her petite shoulder.

"Danae, I am so sorry. It is Benjamin... They found him at the southwest gate..." Jaden watched the shock register in Danae's dark eyes.

"But he was in the north...are you sure...the southwest gate?"

"Yes, I was there. Your father believes he came from Xannellion. They are taking him to the temple and need your help preparing his body. Your father wants me to escort you and Jaden there."

Danae's eyebrows knitted together, her long thick eyelashes blinking back the tears.

"Not Benjamin," she said. She leaned forward into Zachariah. He pulled her close and held her while she cried.

15

Dragons

"I will destroy Xzavier. And as king, I will bring peace to this land," Zachariah said to Danae as he held her and let her cry. "You will not have to watch more of your family die to protect this city against the darkness in Xannellion. I promise you, I will avenge this wrong."

Danae's eyes were filled with tears and cautious hope.

"Thank you. I long for that day."

Zachariah took her hand. He motioned to Jaden.

In response, Jaden followed Zachariah and Danae out the front door where two horses waited. Zachariah helped Jaden mount a chestnut, and he helped Danae onto a black stallion. He climbed up in front of her. Jaden watched Danae bury her head into Zachariah's back. The horse's hooves clopped loudly over the cobblestones.

Distracting herself, Jaden watched stone cottages pass. Besides the irregular height of the cottages, they appeared very much the same: neat rows of cottages with no decoration except late blooming summer flowers in pots by the front door and curtains hung neatly in the windows.

Only a fraction of the men remained in the refugee camps but no women or children. She remembered her earlier conversation with Benjamin and Richard. Pieces of the puzzle were finally fitting together. The refugees must have been smuggled into Alexandria. Only the refugee men who were able to fight were left. Benjamin died protecting her. Her heart ached painfully in her chest.

They passed the field where Les's people had camped. It reminded Jaden how she had treated Benjamin that day, and she wondered that he wasn't frustrated with her. What she wouldn't give to hear him laugh his casual laugh or grin his contented grin again. She had grown very fond of him in a short time and would miss him.

In the middle of her thoughts, she looked around and realized this was the farthest she had traveled in Jeremiah. She thought how ironic it was that she had wanted freedom from Gideon's house the first day there, but since then she had not even wondered about the rest of the city. It said a lot about how comfortable she had become with him and his household. Then she thought of Benjamin again, gentle Benjamin. How could someone kill such a good young man?

Up and up the horses climbed the switchback streets through Jeremiah past rows of cottages, flying tiger fields, and artisan shops to the top of the hill. Jaden immediately loved the flying tiger fields. The tigers were so free. They roamed together, flying at will toward the East Mountains, while others returned from there. She longed to get on one of them and fly away. Closing her eyes, she imagined flying with the wind on her face.

As they rounded the last bend, Jaden got a clear view of the temple. Most things in Jeremiah were plain and understated, but the temple, where it was said that Jeremiah the Sure had been martyred and buried, was exquisite. It was a fitting resting place for Jeremiah's first knight, martyr, and namesake.

The exterior walls of the grand structure sparkled, as if crushed crystals of different colors had been mixed into the plaster. Trees, flowers, and sculptures unfamiliar to Jaden filled the immaculate grounds. It was like she had entered another world. The contrast to Xannellion was stark. It felt like an extension of the natural world instead of manmade.

All of the sculptures – images of happy families, heroic knights, Arwavian creatures with wings, and flying tigers – were fluid and graceful. Well manicured trees pointed upward, mirroring the temple spires. They stopped in front of the temple. Zachariah climbed down from his horse and helped Danae and Jaden dismount. Danae led them inside.

Jaden's eyes struggled to adjust. The room was lit only by sunlight pouring through skylights and tall, colorful stained-glass windows that adorned the east and west walls, which captured best the first and last rays of sunlight each day. As objects became clearer, she noticed that, as with the garden outside, everything inside pointed upward, including high arches that formed the main and sub-support systems of the structure.

Zachariah put his arm around Danae's shoulders. Jaden followed them. They passed corridors leading to the left and right. As they neared an alter that stood below a stained-glass window at the far end of the temple, Jaden examined pictures around the border of the window that depicted the ancient leaders of the Jeremian knights teaching their people. The main body of the window portrayed Gillantri flying on a magnificent eagle toward a white glistening city that must have symbolized Arway.

Jaden frowned. "How can Gillantri be so great and let Benjamin die?" She stood and glared at the stained-glass, trembling with sorrow, anger, and fear. Her insides wrenched. She turned away from Gillantri and looked back into the dimly lit temple, finding herself alone. She heard voices trailing down a corridor to her left, which she followed until she came to a door with light spilling out beneath it.

She entered the room and saw a hearth at the far end with a roaring fire. A table to her left was neatly arranged with a pitcher, herbs, and folded cloths. Gideon and Richard ripped the cloths into specific sizes and then handed them to Danae, who gently wrapped Benjamin's broken body. Jaden turned away, feeling nauseated.

Zachariah crossed the room and gave Jaden's arm a tender squeeze. She admired her boy, so strong and handsome. She turned back to Benjamin. How could a young man filled with so much life and promise lie there, grey and cold? She whispered to Zachariah, "I will never allow you to fight for Gillantri!" She spun away and left the room.

Jaden walked numbly, deliberately avoiding the eastern stained glass window. She tripped out the doors to her chestnut horse. She stood for a moment, dropping her head and shoulders as everything came loose inside of her. Someone touched her shoulder but she didn't want to know who it was. If it was Zachariah, she was too mad to talk with him, and there wasn't anyone else whom she trusted enough to allow seeing her cry.

The hand gently pulled her shoulders around. It didn't completely surprise her that Gideon's face appeared through her tears, but it did surprise her that she welcomed his embrace. It surprised her more that she felt completely safe for the first time in her life. He didn't say anything but let her cry. She cried until she felt uncomfortable.

"Thank you."

Jaden backed up near the horse and wiped her face, and then implored Gideon, "Why?"

Gideon spoke with pain in his eyes, "I am not sure. Here in Jeremiah, we see so much death. It hurts every time. And when it happens to someone as close to you as Benjamin, it hurts more. It feels like Daman wins more than his portion of the battles. I believe that in the end he can't win the war though, not unless we give in."

"But he did win. Benjamin is dead. He was good. He believed in Gillantri and did everything right!" Jaden's throat began to close in but her eyes blazed.

Gideon peered into her soul. "He was ruthlessly killed by Xzavier's men over whom Daman has much control...but did Benjamin give in to their cruelty? From the looks of things, he didn't give an inch. Did he even wish for a moment that he was on their side? No, not Benjamin. No matter what they did to his body, he knew that his soul belonged to good.

"He gained strength by his goodness and now is heading to a joyful reunion with loved ones who have gone on before. He paid the ultimate price of a true follower of Gillantri and his rewards are great."

Gideon paused, emotion showing as moisture at the corners of his eyes. He took a cleansing breath. "He is free to move forward, to become even stronger and better. Don't you see? Daman gains nothing unless we give in to him."

"But what about your mother and father? This will break their hearts."

"It might." Gideon's sad eyes reached out to her. "I know my heart will never be the same. But our job is to choose what side we are on. Are we going to accept our pain and turn to Gillantri for healing or fight him and fall prey to the darkness?"

"Sometimes the darkness feels safer," Jaden said honestly.

Gideon stared thoughtfully at the sky and said, "The love between Benjamin and us will not go away just because we are separated. Some day we will fly to those better lands and be together. With these intense trials we gain knowledge and experience that we can get no other way. Who knows but that when we overcome this pain we will find more peace because of these very trials that right now threaten to crush us?"

Jaden yearned to believe him but her heart felt like it was being squeezed and twisted in her chest. Visions of Zachariah nearly dying intermingled with the fresh images of Benjamin...kind Benjamin.

"I want to believe you, Gideon, but right now my heart hurts too much. Please don't try to convince me to let Zachariah fight... I love him more than ever since all this happened, but it seems too hard right now. A mother shouldn't have to endure these kinds of sorrows. Thank you for your help, but I have to go. Please let me go."

She felt frantic, trapped by his goodness, and full of anger and pain. He helped her get on her horse and reached out and touched her leg.

"I didn't come out here to convince you to let Zachariah fight."

Feeling angrier, she faced the road ahead, gave the chestnut horse a good kick, and rode off, leaving Gideon standing by himself in front of the temple.

****

Jaden arrived at the cottage and flung open the door. She stormed to the back of the house and entered the garden. Trapton looked up from his nap, but Jaden didn't even glance at him as she ran out the gate and into the forest. She didn't slow down until the friction of the water forced her.

As she swam, her anger cooled. Images of the blue-eyed man from her dreams speaking with Gideon irritated her. She swam deep into the cool waters, trying to avoid the feeling of peace being offered to her. When she surfaced she asked, "What am I doing in Jeremiah?"

After a time, she stopped swimming and rolled onto her back.

"Why?" she cried to the woods around her. "Why did you take Benjamin? This is crazy."

From the north edge of the pool, Jaden noticed a movement. Her head shot up but she only caught a glimpse of a human form.

"Who's there?" Jaden asked.

She couldn't see anything and put her hands into the water to wash her face. When she opened her eyes she saw something again.

"This isn't funny. Show yourself."

In a moment, she saw long shadows moving among the trees. Jaden was afraid to swim closer. Even if she wanted to, the north side of the pool had a steep ledge that would prevent her from easily climbing it. Fear drove her from the pool to the cottage. No one was home yet, but she felt safer inside. After she dried off, she fell asleep upstairs on Danae's bed.

Sometime later, a noise from downstairs woke her. The light was dimming and through the window she could see reds and gold mixing in the eastern sky. Jaden went downstairs. Danae was fixing lunch. Jaden didn't know what to say. She felt sad and guilty.

She was no use to Danae, so she stood in the middle of the great room watching the smoke rise and disappear into the rafters, when, to her horror, a red flame disintegrated the roof above her. She ran to Danae and pushed her toward the back door just as more glowing red holes appeared in the ceiling. It felt like a dream. Jaden's mind raced to find answers as to why this could be happening. The holes weren't coming from the fire in the chimney.

"Danae, where is your father?"

"I don't know..."

As they left the cottage they watched Trapton fly into the sky and let out a warning cry. Jaden had never heard a flying tiger's roar so close. It pierced the air with raw majesty. Her gaze tracked him in the darkening sky, when everything painfully came into view.

Two dragons passed directly above them carrying Xannellion riders who were rapidly shooting flaming arrows. Jaden observed that the arrow tips were wrapped in cloth that had probably been dipped in kerosene or another flammable fluid, which the riders lit before shooting. They attacked Gideon's house and barn, even as flying tigers from all parts of the city flew near to help.

Jaden pulled Danae into the shadows of her garden to wait out the attack. They huddled together unable to stop staring.

"Why?" Danae asked.

"I don't know. Maybe Xzavier is testing out the defenses of the city or trying to frighten Jeremiah into letting us go."

"We will never let you go."

The rider of the smaller beast seemed determined to destroy Gideon's house. The tigers impeded his efforts. Finally, Trapton made a hard assault upon the dragon, broadsiding it. The rider was ejected and fell to his death, and the massive dragon dove toward the front wall of Gideon's cottage and crashed through the flames, disappearing in the vicinity of the fireplace in the large room.

The larger dragon flew in the direction of the houses that lined the streets up the hill toward the temple. The rider burned everything he could, but the tigers were out in full force. Every turn found him face to face with ten more tigers. The dragon fled toward the southern jungles, but one tiger managed to latch onto the dragon, and they spiraled in a dive to the forest floor.

It appeared that the dragon riders had done the worst of their work long before attacking Gideon's house. Knights were yelling to one another, coordinating the water brigade, and putting out fires all over the city. Even with few refugees left, there were plenty of men to contain it. But in the lower city fires burned through the night.

Late into the night, fears of where Gideon, Zachariah, Franklin, and Richard were kept sleep from Jaden. Images of Benjamin's cold and lifeless body tormented her. Guilt in the form of a sharp pain in her side plagued her.

Danae wept, unable to handle all the death and destruction. Jaden held her close and wished she could stop the pain. She watched the skies constantly, hoping that Trapton would return. The longer Trapton failed to return, the sadder she felt. Sometime during the middle of the night, Danae finally gave in to fatigue, but Jaden never did. They remained huddled together in the garden until morning.

****

Gideon opened the gate from the orchard on the south side of what remained of his house. Early morning light illuminated the concern on his face. Jaden felt a rush of joy when she saw him and shook Danae awake.

"Your father is here. Wake up."

With wide, horrified eyes Danae stared at Jaden and then at her house.

"I know," Jaden said, trying to soothe her. "They have been putting out fires all night. I am so sorry."

Unable to respond, Danae got up and ran to her father who embraced her. Gideon approached Jaden.

"Zachariah is fine," he said. "He'll be here shortly."

Jaden trembled. "How is everyone else?"

"Franklin and Richard are fine. Trapton is healing. He fought well for an old tiger. The dragons came under cover of night, low to the jungle. By the time we knew, well, it just wasn't soon enough." He looked ragged, older than before.

"Jaden, I need you and Danae to come with me. I have a place set up for you in the temple. We cannot stay here."

"Father, what is it?" Danae asked, noticing something Jaden didn't.

"I'll explain later. Is there any way you two could find some food for us? The men are exhausted and hungry. Knights are clearing the way to the cellar for you now. Have some of them help you get the food so we can go to the temple."

"Yes, father." And as an afterthought, Danae said, "I am glad you are all right."

"I'm glad you are, too," he said.

Later that afternoon in a hallway of the temple, Gideon took Jaden's hand and walked her toward an inner chamber. She could hear men discussing things, as the sounds echoed off the walls inside the temple. As they walked, Gideon said, "It is now obvious that you are not safe here. But the dragon attack is only part of your danger. We are leaving tomorrow morning before first light."

Gideon handed her a blood-stained note. "It was pinned to Benjamin when the guards found him."

The note said, "Return Jaden and Zachariah to Xzavier or great darkness will descend upon your city! This boy told all! Xzavier, The Serpent Lord."

Jaden's trembling increased and everything spun around her. Gideon put his arm around her shoulders to support her. She folded into his chest and he held her.

"Gideon...I really liked Benjamin...your house...Trapton...I am so sorry...I am so sorry..."

Gideon sat down on the floor of the hallway with her and let her sob softly. Jaden didn't fight it this time. No sleep along with the trauma broke down all her barriers and she let him comfort her.

Finally, Gideon said, "You have lost everything for your son. If we can help you, we will. Xzavier is only using you to get to us. He and all the Xannellion kings before him have sought a reason to destroy us. This isn't something you did. You are just the excuse. But you are in very real danger. I have a plan, but I need you to trust me."

Jaden wiped her face with her sleeve and peeked up into his brown, kind eyes.

"I want to trust you, Gideon, and I will do anything you say."

"That is good enough. We need to get to the council room and prepare. Can you handle that?"

Jaden nodded. He helped her stand, and together they walked to the chamber door. Gideon opened it and followed Jaden inside. Jaden sat at a large square table that was similar to the one in Gideon's home chamber. Lining the room were statues of men and woman whom Jaden didn't recognize.

There was a large window facing the East Mountains. It looked so peaceful out there. No fires burned. Everything was still. Jaden remembered the day she envisioned flying on the back of a flying tiger into those mountains. That desire screamed from deep within her soul today. She could almost feel the wind on her face and the freedom from her pain.

Richard and Franklin were discussing something with Zachariah, and Jaden reluctantly returned from her daydream. All three men were covered in soot and exhausted. Gideon helped Jaden find her seat and started the meeting.

"Thank you for gathering this group, Richard. Please, everyone take a seat. We don't have much time."

Jaden noted the absence of Benjamin and wilted inside.

"Our tigers that patrol the perimeter were easily taken out by the two dragons and the archers riding them, Richard. We need to add more tigers to our patrols. Of all the buildings in the city, I am grateful this one was miraculously spared. The city is being cleaned up. I sent a messenger to mother and father and the rest of the knights' families, and funeral preparations are being arranged.

"As we have discussed, we are leaving for Alexandria first thing tomorrow morning. We had considered doing this after the last group of refugees was safely away from here but had no idea our hand would be forced so suddenly. Though none of us believed for a moment that it would be simple, it is now more dangerous."

Zachariah stood. "I thought I was going to stay and help defend Jeremiah?"

"Let me explain, son." Gideon had no energy. "I need to train you first..."

"Begging your pardon, Gideon, but I will no longer allow that," Jaden interrupted. "It is out of the question."

"I have to do this!" Zachariah leaned toward Jaden.

Gideon motioned for Zachariah to sit down. "I made my decision and it cannot be changed. There is more." Gideon paused to let his words sink in. Everyone but Franklin seemed surprised. "I got a report last night that one of our men heard noises under the south tower."

Franklin noticed Jaden's confusion and said, "The south tower is one of Jeremiah's main arsenals."

"But who would be under it?" Jaden asked.

Franklin answered, "I have suspected for some time that the kings of Xannellion were influenced by ancient evil writings, and possibly by Daman himself. Daman, of course, is a fallen son of Gillantri."

"What are you saying?" Jaden asked.

Gideon stood up, went to the back of the room and removed an old leather-bound book from one of the bookshelves. He gave it to Franklin and returned wearily to his chair. Franklin turned to one of its pages and began to read.

"When Alexander was at the end of his reign in the second century of Trivar, it reads, 'Alexander began to wax old and he gathered his children around him. He told them of the wonders to be seen in Arway and the joy to be had if they would follow Gillantri's teachings. He shared with them his love for them and his desire to be with them forever in Arway.'

"Then he warned them of Daman's desire to destroy them. 'My children, we spent many years in Arway with Gillantri and Daman before we came here to Trivar. Gillantri knows us and loves us. But Daman also knows us. We fought against him for the right to come here to Trivar and gain knowledge and experience for ourselves. He lost that battle and desires now to destroy us.'

"Daman was deported out of Arway, a planet not far from here, to the center of this world of Trivar, trapped in never-ending darkness. Gillantri, in his wisdom, knew that Daman would find a way to the surface and provide challenges for us to overcome. Even now he tunnels under Trivar. Perhaps he has already begun surfacing to recruit Trivarians to follow him. As we have seen, our only defense is to follow Gillantri and his teachings...'"

"Tunnels...under the ground?" Jaden couldn't contain her shock. It made the hair on her neck stand on end. She stared at the ground half expecting someone to burst out of the floor. She rolled her eyes. "This is ridiculous." Jaden stood.

"Please sit. Whether you believe this or not, you agreed to hear me out." Gideon rose and walked over to her, and he put his hands on her shoulders.

"We're all worn out," he said. "But as we have seen time and again in Jeremiah, when we are the least able, the most is required of us. There is real danger, more than we had feared." Gideon pulled her chair out for her, and she reluctantly sat down.

As Gideon went back to his chair, Jaden watched, her eyes softening.

"How did they know about these tunnels at the beginning of Trivar, yet we don't know about them now?" Zachariah said. He was still skeptical.

Franklin's eyes sparkled as he answered, "Daman covered his tracks very well. When the knights were strongest, they did all they could to fill in the tunnels. Some even went into the tunnels, though few returned. The ones who returned told stories of dark and wicked things. This fueled more searches and many tunnels were caved in or covered up. Sometime after the martyrdom of Jeremiah the Sure, Daman must have realized that it worked against him for people to know where his comings and goings were. He became more covert. Over time he was forgotten. There are few in Trivar who remember that he is doing this. I personally believe that he wants people to think he doesn't exist so that we let down our guard."

Zachariah had his head in his hands. Lifting it, he said, "In Xannellion, I believed that Daman was a faerietale. For that matter, Gillantri was folklore, too. But while you spoke of Daman, I remembered that after Cannote was murdered and things got worse with Xzavier, he began wearing this amber bracelet and spending more and more time in the dungeon.

"He told me there were glowing amber tunnels accessible from the dungeon where they were mining this unusual stone. I didn't think much about it. Besides, I knew the dragons needed a lot of attention and Xzavier is obsessive about how they are trained. He may be sloppy with other parts of his kingdom, but not the dragons. I wonder if he is closer to Daman than we know."

Jaden agreed, "Yes, as difficult a person as Xzavier was before he killed Cannote, he sunk to new lows after that. I just thought it was the added power of Xannellion. I can't believe we are talking about these things as if they are real."

Gideon said empathetically, "That supports our suspicions, thank you. Richard, as I said earlier, I am going to need you to keep our men on alert. Gather in our volunteer forces from the outlying areas of Jeremiah and the remaining refugees who are fighting with us. Intensify their training according to the new information we have received from Jaden and Zachariah about the tunnels. I wish I had more time to discuss it with you, but I trust that you and Franklin can handle things. I only regret that I won't be with you for the funeral. Please tell mother and father I love them and I am sorry."

Gideon lowered his eyes, collected himself, and then raised them. "I believe it will be better for us to get a head start before spies tell Xzavier that I am missing from the funeral. I have arranged a small travel party so that we will be nearly invisible. This morning, I sent decoys west up the coast and on the eastern trail toward Vikland. We must go by the inland western road. The jungle will provide cover for us in the daytime and easy shelter for the nights.

"Once we reach the canyon lands we will have to hurry before the first flood hits, but my hope is that Xzavier will focus his remaining dragon power on patrols of the west coast and the eastern trail toward Vikland. The river itself should be our only threat in The Zikong River Valley. It is a beautiful but dangerous place this time of the year. I am hoping that Xzavier will determine that we would not be foolish enough to travel the gorge during the flood season."

"I don't want to go into that canyon now," Jaden said, feeling overwhelmed at the idea of traveling anywhere, let alone into the Zikong during flood season.

"If we go to the West Ocean and buy a boat with enough men to sail it, we would be spotted immediately. Xzavier knows Zachariah's love for sailing, as well as his connections with sailors on that ocean. He will expect you to take that route. And with pirates in the south and Vikings in the north, no one is safe traveling the East Sea these days. The eastern road to the north is where Benjamin..."

Gideon's throat seemed to close on him, but he pushed through it. "Benjamin and nine of my men were attacked and killed on their way home. Xzavier may expect us to use that familiar route and will guard it. The canyon ridge is a straight route but there is little fresh water or cover.

"That leaves the western passage. The danger of the flooding is our ally. I have friends midway where we can regroup, if necessary, before we push on to Alexandria. I believe the western passage is the last place anyone else will be traveling and the last place Xzavier will search for us. I hope these benefits give us enough time to reach Alexandria before he finds us. I sent for provisions. They should be here shortly."

Gideon nodded toward Zachariah. "I know you want to defend Jeremiah and, if you were able, to kill Xzavier, but I support your mother. Jaden, I believe that you will find more answers to your questions about your origins and The Third Daughters as we travel north. I have never had the leisure to learn much about them, but in the north there is more peace."

Jaden glanced at Zachariah, who must have mentioned something about the prophecy, but she only said, "Gideon, thank you for your support. I can't live with him dying again."

"You are welcome, my lady, but I ask permission to train him while we travel. I believe he could be of great use to us in the future."

"I cannot deny either of you this." Jaden's stomach wrenched and she moved her arms around her midsection slowly, so as to not alert anyone. But Franklin caught her eye.

As it lowered in the western sky, the sun fell on the East Mountains creating an inviting light on the ridges and grassy hills while the meeting closed. Jaden wandered the hills in her mind until she was the only one left in the room with Gideon.

"It's beautiful out there," Gideon offered, startling Jaden out of her escape from reality.

"Yes."

"And the temple is peaceful, isn't it?"

"Yes, it is."

"Often leaders of the Jeremian knights have come to this room for solace when darkness and pain threatened to take them. I have sat heavy-hearted in this room more times than I wish to relate, but I always leave feeling more at peace and believing that there is a better world that I am fighting for."

"I would be happy just traversing those hills today."

Gideon put his hand on Jaden's shoulder sending a surge of energy through her that her heart tried to resist. She stood and faced him, "I don't know that I believe as you do, but if the people in Arway are half as good as you, I'd love to see it, maybe someday."

"You will."

"We'll see."

"Get your belongings together and then help Danae. There is a lot to do before we sleep tonight." Jaden nodded and departed feeling lighter than when she arrived.

That evening, Jaden and Danae organized their belongings and prepared for the journey. Afterward, they returned to Danae's home to dig through the rubble and reclaim some of her belongings. Remains of the dragon nauseated Jaden and reminded her of Justine and all the death that she faced lately.

Jaden placed a folded scarf over nose and mouth and tied it at the back of her neck to reduce breathing in the ash and the wretched smell of scorched debris. Her heart squeezed tightly in her chest as she walked through Gideon's home. She remembered her first glimpse of Danae as she directed Benjamin and Richard to prepare a place for Jaden and Zachariah. She thought of the luxurious pool of crystal water. She almost laughed as she remembered Trapton wrestling with Benjamin.

Warm feelings came as she recalled Zachariah and Danae shooting arrows out in Danae's lovely garden. She remembered her first sight of Gideon with his arms folded across his chest trying to get her to be kind to Danae. She smiled.

Stepping on a soft piece of dragon flesh startled her back to her awful reality. After searching as best they could at Gideon's ruined house, they returned to the temple and finished the food preparations for dinner. Jaden felt more tired than hungry, but the smells of dinner kept her from going straight to bed.

Danae pulled bread from the fire. The heavenly smell was comforting. Everyone sat around a table in the main hall of the temple near the enormous stained glass window. Jaden looked again at Gillantri flying back to Arway and cringed. I don't know if I can ever buy a story like that, she thought. How could there be a world so good when I am stuck in a world like this?

Everyone ate silently, lost in their thoughts. Jaden ate her bread heartily and enjoyed drinking the spiced apple juice but couldn't eat anything else. Zachariah ignored Jaden, upset that he couldn't stay and defend Jeremiah. Gideon didn't eat anything but spent his time explaining to Danae what the new plans were.

Jaden couldn't tell how Danae felt about the plans because she was so quiet and somber. She never complained. All she asked was, "Are we traveling through Ononzai?"

Gideon responded, "We will be traveling past there but not stopping." Jaden wondered if Ononzai was the midway stop Gideon had mentioned earlier.

As they finished their meal, a knock came at the main temple door. Gideon rose, walked to the door, cracked it open, and whispered to someone before returning to the table.

"Our supplies have arrived and we can leave first thing in the morning. If you need to sleep, I suggest you do so now."

Then Gideon turned to Danae and said quietly, "Danae, Arran couldn't come right away, but he will meet us in a few days."

Jaden watched the exchange. Gideon seemed indifferent but Danae's countenance fell as she turned to clean up dinner. Everyone left, leaving Jaden and Zachariah alone as the darkness settled in.

Every muscle in Jaden's body felt weak.

"I am going to turn in," she said. "I'll see you in the morning, son."

Zachariah wouldn't acknowledge her. Jaden dropped her head and left him. As she settled in for the night, she thought of the shadows in the forest earlier. Then an image of Benjamin's broken body entered her mind. Her stomach wrenched. More images from the day flooded in... Gideon's kindness and his destroyed home, Zachariah's anger, Danae's pain, Franklin's incessant knowing.

She slipped under her covers hoping that sleep would remove the tumult of her emotions.

16

To Alexandria

Jaden drifted into a restless sleep. As her mind lost consciousness, the blue-eyed man entered her dream. He reached his arms out to her, and she finally ran into them instead of away from them.
"Why do you grieve so?" he asked gently.
"It is so hard. I feel so much pain."
"The pain and sorrow will pass if you accept them and let them go." The reproof was gentle, but true, and it stung her heart.
"You don't understand my pain..." but even as she said the words she felt she was somehow wrong.
"You have many cares and challenges. You must not expect yourself to be free from them all at once. It is impossible. Even for the most determined, it takes time. Remember my peace. Receive it. Rely on it."
"There is no peace. It is so hard here in Jeremiah... I am so different from them..." Jaden began crying and felt ashamed.
"Things will get more difficult. But if you trust me, as it gets more difficult your goodness will also increase, and with your goodness, your peace."
"I can't handle it getting worse... Please don't make me go through more." Jaden felt angry and frustrated, not wanting to leave, but not wanting to stay.
He was silent for a time and Jaden felt him fading. "Please don't go. I'm sorry, I will listen..."
She waited, crying, silently pleading until she was again securely in his embrace.
"Part of learning and growing is experiencing pain," he said. "The pain allows the darkness in you to surface. If you allow your pain and darkness to rise, accept and release both, then replace your pain and darkness with my peace, you can return to live in Arway someday."
Jaden lost her temper and pushed him away.
"I don't have darkness in me, I am Jaden the Great..." as she said it, he faded away and didn't return.
Her dream continued. Images of Xzavier and dragons terrorizing villages

kept her adrenaline surging through the rest of the night. Jaden ran from them. Another man, darker and more evil than Xzavier, came toward Jaden as if to embrace her. There was a part of her that felt compelled to allow him to take her, but she resisted. She remembered the blue-eyed man and suddenly didn't want anything to do with this dark one. With her rejection, he departed, along with all his darkness. But she was left alone, crying.

She felt someone shaking her awake, but she couldn't leave her dream. She searched desperately, hoping for one last interaction with the blue-eyed man. She longed for his presence, peace, and love to warm her melancholy soul. But someone kept shaking her gently. Like coming out of a sticky fog, she finally opened her eyes. Another shake and she pushed back her covers to see Gideon kneeling beside her.

"What is wrong?" he said. "We need to leave."

Jaden looked up into Gideon's brown eyes and felt the sharp contrast between his peace and her pain. She rubbed her eyes and sat up.

"Everything in Jeremiah mocks my lack of peace. How do you all come to be so peaceful? Benjamin just died, your city is in great danger, you are caring for your enemies and leaving your home, and you are calm as day! I don't deserve this!"

"Please. We need to be going. Besides, Trapton wanted to say goodbye."

Jaden's eyes softened as she thought of the old tiger.

"We need to go."

A short time later, Gideon and Jaden stood by Benjamin's flying tiger bench with the ruins of Gideon's home in the background. Trapton cocked his head to the side and Jaden melted.

"I'm going to miss you, old boy..." Jaden hugged Trapton. "So much goodness that I don't deserve. But thank you, Trapton. I hope I'll see you again." She gave him another big hug then sat back down.

"You do deserve this. I hope you can trust that sooner than later. You are an amazing woman. Gillantri must be so pleased with you."

Jaden stared at the burnt cottage that, in almost one full moon, had become more comfortable, safe, and friendly than any home in which she had ever lived. Next she thought of Benjamin.

"You have sacrificed too much for me. That's all."

Gideon ignored her comments and asked, "Are you ready? I think everyone else is."

"Yes, I am."

"I gathered a few things for you." He motioned to a pack that he had set at the foot of her rolled bedding.

She lowered her eyes and said quietly, "Thank you. Thank you for my clothes and...your kindness."

Gideon bent his head to see her eyes. Jaden couldn't help but meet his eyes as he said, "You are welcome, Jaden of Xannellion."

Gideon searched her eyes for a moment. He said, "We need to go before our cover of darkness lifts."

Jaden and Gideon met his family at the back of his crumbled house. Gideon said to Richard, "Brother, I will miss you. Take care of yourself and our dear city. Tell mother and father I love them and I wish I didn't have to miss the funeral. Let our men know that I appreciate their sacrifice. Tell the families of the fallen knights that I feel their loss keenly. I will be back soon. If you need anything, you have Franklin." Then he embraced his brother and comrade-in-arms.

Next he spoke to his trusted adviser. "Franklin, thank you for being here. I don't know what we'd do without you." Gideon gave him a strong hug.

Pulling himself through the emotions of the night and with a faint sparkle in his eye, Gideon told Jaden and Zachariah, "I have arranged for three capable guides to lead us to Alexandria. I will introduce you to them when we are out of the city. Be quiet. We want as few people to know we have left as possible." Zachariah hugged Richard and Franklin, as did Danae and Jaden.

"All right, Zachariah, Danae, and Jaden, let's go."

The small group walked toward the back garden gate. Fortunately, the moon was still out, though it was beginning to descend toward the western horizon. Danae's garden glowed sadly. Jaden walked past small flowers dancing like silver faeries in the pale streams of moonlight. Trapton came and licked Gideon's hand. He patted Trapton's head, knelt down, and hugged him.

"We'll be back soon, old boy. Keep an eye on the place, all right?"

Jaden felt sorrow catch in her throat. When she passed Trapton, she gave him a hug but couldn't say anything as she patted his head and walked on. Trapton faithfully followed behind.

Shortly, they passed the bench with the little star fruit tree standing primly behind it and dwarf palms on both sides. Her eyes lingered for a moment. Then she followed Gideon soberly through the garden and out the back gate, leaving Richard and Franklin by the remains of the cottage and Trapton just inside the gate whining softly.

They followed Gideon down an alley behind the garden, heading north on the overgrown path. Up ahead, three men in elvan clothing and one graceful mare waited for Gideon and his three companions to approach. When Gideon approached, the elves waved and turned to lead the way out of the city.

They followed the overgrown path until they reached the northern city gate. They passed through without anyone seeing them but the night guards of that gate. Under cover of darkness, they traveled west toward the trees. Once they were far enough into the forest, Gideon called for the elves to stop. He gathered the whole group together.

"Come closer. Here, I am not worried about our men from the gate hearing us, but Xzavier's spies could be anywhere."

Gideon didn't have to say it but Jaden glanced down, wondering if there were any tunnels under them.

"Not just below us, Jaden, there have been more bats and spiders around since Benjamin's return."

Jaden stared above her and shuddered.

"I hate bats."

As if on cue, a huge spider dropped on Gideon, who swatted it to the ground and struck his sword through its center.

"The sun will rise soon. I have a light and will take up the rear. The elves have another light that they will shine in front. Danae and Jaden, you will walk between us and should be able to see well enough. But stay alert. These trails aren't maintained anymore. We will travel west until we get to The Eagle's Glade, where we will stop for breakfast before moving north.

"I want to introduce you to our guides. They have been dear friends of my family for generations. Etheltread is our lead guide. He knows these woods better than anyone."

Etheltread stepped forward. He was slender but fairer and taller than the other two elves. His hair was blond and pulled away from his face in a braid. His ears were thin and long and graceful like the rest of his face. In the dark his eyes seemed silvery blue and wise. He also had smile marks at the corners of his eyes. He bowed elegantly without saying a word.

Gideon then motioned to another elf and said, "This is Meadthel, Etheltread's next younger brother. He is the best tracker in the whole elvan kingdom. His services will be invaluable."

Meadthel stepped forward with a friendly grin. He was the handsomest elf by far. He had dark blue eyes that danced with delight and dark brown hair pulled back with small braids. Jaden liked him instantly. He bowed jovially, winking at Danae, and stepped back with Etheltread.

"Meadthel provides us with endless entertainment, as well," Gideon said with a chuckle. "Our final guide comes not from Ononzai, but from the south sea island of Petra. Porter is our defense. He may seem friendly, but don't cross him. Zachariah, he will be your trainer. There is no one more masterful in all Trivar."

Porter stepped forward and coarsely bowed. His body, though long and thin, was thicker than the other two elves. From his strong jaw line to his exposed calves, muscles rippled. His hair was long and jet black. His eyes, eyebrows, and small goatee matched his hair, and his skin was a rich brown, like the natives back in Yamis. Jaden could tell he was fierce and in ideal physical condition from the methodical way he moved. He soberly tipped his head to Danae, who returned the gesture.

"We should meet with Etheltread and Meadthel's youngest brother Arran, along with some other elves, in a few days."

Jaden noticed Zachariah tense up at the mention of Arran, but Danae's face glowed. Jaden returned her focus to Gideon.

"They were delayed but will come as soon as they can. I have briefed our guides on who you are. They know everything that is going on in Jeremiah and are keenly aware of our danger. Heed everything they say. Don't pause in your obedience, for that pause could mean your life. We will keep a medium pace so as not to wear out the women too soon."

"We'll be fine, thank you," Jaden said.

Everyone stiffened as they heard the satiny sound of bat wings. The bats began to cry out in high-pitched squeaks, causing everyone in the party to search above for them. The elves shined their lights upwards, as did Gideon, while Meadthel and Porter got out their arrows and shot four bats dead in two smooth motions. All became quiet and still again.

Gideon said specifically to the elves, "We will need to be on guard constantly."

"We better get going," Gideon addressed the whole group. "Any questions? ...Good, let's go."

The birds and monkeys chattered back and forth to one another as if they were reporting the sun's whereabouts. It gave the jungle a less forbidding feeling. They walked slowly and carefully through the darkness. Jaden felt somber, still hung over from her troubling dreams.

She remembered that this forest was the one that protected her and Zachariah the night of their escape from Xannellion. Recollections of Justine lifting off into the rainy sky haunted her. It felt like a lifetime ago.

"How are you, Jaden?" Danae asked.

"It is dark and you are traveling in front of me... I think you are an elf, too!"

"You were so quiet."

"I miss my dragon..."

"These woods remind me of many things, too. When I was a child we used to play out here before Cannote began patrolling our borders. It became too dangerous. Before long, my only refuge was my garden and the pool behind our cottage."

"Your garden and pool are a refuge, indeed," Jaden said longingly.

"Yes, but I love the glades and hiding places out here, as well. My mother used to bring me to find herbs and flowers and watch the birds and monkeys. After lunch we'd hike through the woods. I've missed that."

They walked along, each in their own thoughts.

Jaden slowed and whispered, "What was that?!"

"You can see them?"

"Yes. I saw them yesterday too when I swam in your pool."

"Were you upset then, too?"

"What do you mean?"

"I am not trying to pry…it is just…the wood nymphs only come when we need them. They are more Arwavian than Trivarian. Some say they were sent by Gillantri to help heal and comfort us through our time here in Trivar."

"They seem to glow…"

"Yes, the elves say their purity lights them from within."

Jaden changed the subject. "I am sorry you and your father will miss Benjamin's funeral."

Danae didn't respond right away because she was enchanted by the nymphs dancing in a free-flowing ballet around them.

"We don't much like funerals anyway. But we handled it better before my mother died." Danae turned her attention back to the nymphs.

The wood nymphs faded away with the shadows of the night, and somehow Jaden felt better because the nymphs had been there.

17

Wood Nymphs

"Two years ago I walked down that same road from the northwest gate to this glade," Danae began again as everyone proceeded north after breakfast.

"I thought you said you couldn't come into the forest after Cannote began patrolling it?" Jaden asked, preoccupied because Zachariah still wouldn't talk with her. At breakfast she had tried to make light conversation with him, and he ignored her.

Gideon had intervened with a look that told Jaden he was working on Zachariah. She reluctantly let it go, daring to trust Gideon's influence over her son. Zachariah had eaten his breakfast quickly. He and Porter sparred for a time while everyone else finished eating.

Though troubled by Zachariah's anger, Jaden had been enchanted by what everyone reverently called The Eagle's Glade. It was an opening in the thick jungle, as if the jungle paused its intertwining for a moment just to introduce a little tranquility into its chaos.

Dark green moss covered the relatively even ground. A well-behaved little stream wound around one of the edges of the glade, filling the air with soothing babblings. If they weren't so close to Jeremiah still, Jaden believed she would lie down in the morning sunlight and never want to leave.

Danae's voice brought Jaden out of her thoughts. "Four years ago, my twin, Daniel, was killed in a battle by a javelin. He died instantly. Richard found him, removed the javelin, and brought him home. My mother and I dressed his wounds and prepared him for burial. I felt like half my soul withered and died with him. I was only sixteen. I didn't know how to go on.

"My mother, who had faced death all her life, made her peace with it. She was a daughter of a Jeremian knight, able to fight and face dying, like most of the women in our culture. But I guess I am too sensitive. It was more than I could bear.

"Daniel and I had a special connection that neither of us understood. He played my faerie games with me in the herb garden for hours. He would often laugh and say, 'Danae you must be an elf.' I tried to play sword-fighting with him and made a poor partner, but he never made fun of me.

"Even when we were older and I felt different and misunderstood, he would play war with me gently, letting me win and telling me I was a good warrior. He was more like an older brother than a twin. Then he was gone. I limped along in life for the next two years, when out of nowhere my mother was also killed in a minor skirmish. I had always felt my mother's love, even though she didn't really understand me."

Danae paused. "It was funny. She often came to me for advice about feelings and emotions and things more feminine in nature, especially after a trip we took to visit the elves. Ozella, queen of the elves and mother to Etheltread, Meadthel, and Arran…you haven't met Arran, but he is very dear to me…anyway, they made a big deal about my elvish gift of healing.

"That trip changed my mother, or maybe it changed me. I felt more confident in my gifts and unique abilities. I felt less ashamed of my weaknesses, and my mother seemed to see and respect me more for who I am. But coming back to Jeremiah, all my old insecurities resurfaced."

Danae grew quiet and thoughtful. Jaden was shocked. She never would have guessed that under all that peace and calm, Danae could have felt so much insecurity and pain. She didn't know what to say.

"When my mother died, I committed myself to bed and wished with all my heart that I could die too. I prayed many times a day that the Great King Gillantri would take me to him so that I could stop feeling so miserable.

"After a moon passed, without telling me, my father sent word to Ononzai, the city of the cliff-dwelling elves. He asked for Ozella to come right away. Before half of a fortnight was up, Ozella and Arran arrived, ascended the stairs to my room with my father, and knocked at my door. 'Leave me,' was all I could say, but they came in anyway. Then I saw my father and, behind him, Ozella and her son Arran. Without quite knowing why, I began to cry.

"Ozella and Arran walked around father and sat next to my bed. Arran said, 'Danae, please don't cry. Your days of mourning are at an end. I have something to help you.' He held my hand gently. Just his touch softened the edges of my sorrow and I stopped crying. He said, 'Typically, you would not be quite old enough to experience this, but because of the many losses and the grief you bear, I have been given permission to share it with you. Have you ever heard of Nightflights?' I answered, 'No.'

"Ozella sat beside Arran and said, 'Life is a funny thing here in Trivar. We face tragedy and trials that makes no sense to our hearts. Answers that console us are difficult to find. Early in the history of Trivar after the teachings of Gillantri were revealed, one of your great-grandfathers recognized a thread that ran through all of his teachings: 'Come to me.'"

Jaden felt a tingle all the way through her as she remembered her dream. She felt dizzy and nearly tripped over a large root.

"Ozella said it puzzled my predecessor, and he and his good wife made it their life-long work to understand the directive, 'Come to me.' They were the ones who finally commissioned the great temple on the hill and spent their lives building it. Though it wasn't finished before they passed on to Arway, they had spent many years praying to understand the meaning of 'Come to me.'

"She said many people mocked them and were angry because my great-grandfather and his family focused less on training and fighting with the knights than understanding Gillantri's teachings, especially the admonition, 'Come to me.' Well, they prayed and prayed and worked and worked on the temple, and when he could, my great-grandfather fought, as well.

"Some of their sons died in battle and many grandchildren dreamed of following their fathers to war. Things felt dark in Jeremiah, as they might feel to you right now, but over time, something about their prayers changed. It wasn't until their most trying moments that they prayed with the best kind of prayer, the kind that is so sincere and heartfelt that there was no deceit in them, no fear, no doubt. Just a pure desire to be helped by the Great King Gillantri.

"As they knelt in what is now known as The Eagle's Glade, they heard the flapping of great wings, and two enormous monarch eagles approached from the sky. My great-grandparents were frightened at first and wanted to run, but they were riveted by the magnificence and power of these creatures. When Ozella told me this, I felt that inside my heart was an imprint of these birds, as if I had known them before, and it made me shiver all over.

"Ozella implored me, 'That isn't all, my dear, we don't have much time to discuss this before it gets dark, so listen carefully. The eagles landed on either side of your great-grandparents, who were still on their knees. They both felt as if the eagles intended for them to climb on their backs and ride.'

"Surely it was more than they ever imagined would come of a prayer. They boarded the great birds not knowing what might happen. In an instant the great wings flapped with thrilling power, and up they went into the night sky. They huddled close to the great birds and felt warm and safe for the first time in a great while. They flew to Arway..."

"Arway? It is impossible. You can't mean it! Did they die?" Jaden's voice rose in pitch as she spoke.

"That was my same question, and Arran answered, 'No, they didn't die. They only went to the first level in Arway, not all the way to Mt. Arway and the White City.' Once my grandparents learned about Arwavian ways, they returned to Jeremiah on the eagles, feeling renewed. Their dedication to the temple was fired to a new level. As Arran and Ozella opened this part of Jeremian history to me, I felt like I finally connected to someone in my extended family and truly did belong, even though I wasn't a born fighter.

"My father said later that while Ozella spoke he noticed faint color returning to my cheeks. For the first time since Daniel died, I felt there was some hope for me. I wanted to see those eagles and fly with them more than anything..."

"So did you go?" Jaden didn't want to hear more narrative. She just wanted to know if this faerie-like girl actually flew on an eagle to Arway.

"I did."

There was no lie in her voice, no stuttering, no wavering in her answer.

"Really? You flew with eagles?" Zachariah asked.

"I did, but it was more difficult for me than I first thought it would be. After the conversation with Ozella and Arran, I felt better. My depression had dissipated and I felt more energy than I had since Daniel died. But that night, it was really cold. Earlier that week it had snowed. From my bed looking out the window, I had seen it coming down, but it gave me no joy, and the darkness of the storm had only added to my depression and sadness.

"Ozella and Arran's visit changed things. Something was different. The cool air added to the excitement I felt. I put on my rabbit skin hat and muffler. The soft fur felt warm and safe. I descended the stairs and smelled the evergreen garland that had been strung for the winter festivities, which I had almost missed.

"I remember saying, 'I'm ready father. Where are we going?' His answer couldn't have surprised me more: 'Just outside the northwest gate. Stay close to me. Observe all that I do and remember it so that you can do it again later. I am sure that for a time you will want to go more than I can afford to take you.'"

"I said, 'Yes, father, but I am suddenly afraid.' Do you remember that father?"

Gideon chuckled good-naturedly. "Yes. I wasn't sure what to do then. I remember shrugging my shoulders toward the elves. Arran said, 'Danae, we have been friends since you were born. Your father, my mother, and I will be with you until you leave with the eagles and you will be perfectly safe. Do you trust us?' I was grateful for our friends that night. I was so worried about you."

"Do you remember what I said to his question?"

Gideon chuckled again. "Yes, something like... 'I trust all of you. I just don't trust what is outside the walls of our city.'"

Everyone laughed at that. But Danae sobered and said, "Yes, but you see, mother was much stronger and much braver than I am, and she was killed by an ambush just outside the walls of our city."

Gideon became somber at that remark. Danae continued, "For years I had been forbidden to leave the city, except under heavy guard to visit Ononzai. Even the eagles that had so excited me minutes before were suddenly frightening to me. What if they took me to Arway and never let me return? What if I fell? What if they killed me? With all the excitement of learning about Nightflights, I hadn't realized my intense fear. My depression threatened to descend again.

"I said, 'I am sorry, but I don't know if I can do it.' Father said, 'Well, you have to want this in a real and determined way or it cannot happen for you. If you are not ready, we can try again some other time.'

"Just the thought of not going was enough to strengthen my determination. It was obvious to me at that moment that I didn't want to go backward. There was nothing for me if I went back to my bed, except more sorrow and pain with no relief. The path was clear. I had to face my fears. Not only was there nothing for me to go back to, I saw plainly the disappointment on my father's face and knew that my weakness worried him greatly."

"Danae...really," Gideon said.

"No, father, don't. I know that none of the rest of our family would have thought twice about a Nightflight. Oh, how I wanted to stand up fearlessly and run out the door, but something inside me was pulling me back to my safe bedroom. I remember hushing my fears, deliberately standing up, and facing the front door as if it were Daman himself. Arran offered me his arm and together we put one foot in front of the other until I was outside in the cold night air."

Jaden had had enough. "Danae, I am sorry, I just don't buy all this about your beliefs...monarch eagles...I've been all over the south of Trivar and never saw a monarch eagle. Black gryphons, dragons, bats, and even flying tigers, but I have never heard of a monarch eagle. It is too much. I am sorry about your losses, truly, but I can't deal with the rest of it."

With that, Jaden fell behind.

****

Jaden made sure she wasn't too far behind to hear, but she felt suffocated by the talk of eagles and Arway. It was getting hotter, and her feet were killing her. She didn't know how she was going to be able to walk for the rest of the day, let alone for days on end.

Gideon stepped beside her. "How are you?"

"Don't ask me that again," Jaden said. She was only mildly upset, finding it harder and harder to be angry at a man who never got angry at her.

Up ahead, she heard her son say to Danae, "Tell me more about the eagles. I would do anything to fly one!"

Distracting herself from her son's enthusiasm, she focused on how the jungle trees leaned in and out over the trail like a misshapen fence intertwined around itself. Palm trees and palm fronds reached up toward the light shining through the canopy. Red flowers on large green bushes filled the spaces between palm trees, ferns, and undergrowth.

Small flowers littered the forest floor where they could find enough light to grow. Saplings fought for their own space in the light. The trees were covered with moss of all colors: bright yellow, dark green, orange, and brown. The moss formed in a variety of shapes, from grass-like green to little dots of orange that covered branches.

Jaden saw Zachariah watching Danae, as was his habit since he first opened his eyes in Jeremiah. Danae blushed and quickly began again. This time, against her better judgment, Jaden was drawn back into the story.

"The wind that night felt cool and invigorating, renewing my strength and determination. Every step took focus, but with Arran, my father, and Ozella, we made it quickly to the west gate. We walked for some time in the early darkness of the night, when the sky began to glow silvery blue. It was enchanting. As we exited through the gates outside the city, I remember my stomach swirling. That is when I first saw wood nymphs.

"They only show themselves to those who need comfort. But once you have seen them, they're easier to spot the next time," Danae explained. "All around me faint silhouettes danced in and out among the trees. I could barely see the details of their shimmering garments at first and wished that I could get closer.

"Soon my wish was granted. As we traveled, more and more nymphs waltzed through the woods while many more lined the pathway ahead. These nymphs danced nimbly from one place to another like ballerinas with strong partners in a well-rehearsed performance, graceful and slender. They glowed full of light from somewhere deep within them.

"Each one was unique in appearance. They were taller and thinner than elves, but most of them had short hair and petite features. The nymphs' hair and eyes came in every shade imaginable: flowing red, blond, brown, or black hair with every color in between, and eyes of the darkest black to the lightest silver blue, with shades of violet, jade, and frothy green. Their long thick eyelashes matched the color of their hair.

"One instant they were dancing, and the next they were posing in such a way as to become a part of the jungle scenery. I've been told that they actually morph into trees. They truly are the most elegant creatures."

"Except for Ozella's sons, of course," Meadthel piped in.

"Do I have permission to consider you creatures, Meadthel?" Danae shot back.

"Only if we are the most elegant ones," he said, bowing toward Danae as he walked, dodging branches and roots, and smoothly turning forward without missing a step. Jaden laughed out loud for the first time since Benjamin died. It felt good.

"So, as I was saying," Danae continued, "they are the second most elegant creatures next to Ozella's elegant sons."

Everyone laughed and Jaden forgot her pain as Danae continued to tell her tale. "What impressed me the most about the wood nymphs was how free they were, not laden with grief and sadness, like I was. I longed to dance like they did and feel free. I envied them."

Jaden cringed, her pain descending heavily again.

"With nymphs lining our path, we came to the entrance to The Eagle's Glade, which was guarded by a male nymph. My father said, 'Danae, we are here. Be still. Watch carefully. This is what you will need to remember.' He stopped in front of the male nymph. Male nymphs were very masculine in contrast to the females. This one was dressed in clothes you would expect on an overgrown faerie of the woods. His forest green shirt accentuated his muscles and the strength of his upper body. His khaki pants hung loosely to the ground around his bare feet.

"He stood silently as if waiting for something. Gideon addressed him, 'We are here, for the Nightflight, good Zyphus of the Wood.' With that the Nymph bowed his head, acknowledging him. Gideon finished, 'I have brought my daughter, Danae, of whom you have been told. She has special permission to enter this glade.' Again Zyphus bowed his head. 'We have come bearing no ill will. May we enter?'

"Zyphus answered in a whisper that sounded like the deep rushing of wind through the trees, 'Gideon, you and your daughter may enter, and your escorts may follow.' We thanked him and my father took my hand and walked toward Zyphus with Arran and Ozella following close behind. Once we passed him, Zyphus fell in line with the other nymphs that were lining the edges of the glade shoulder to shoulder.

"The light from within each of the nymphs united, making the glade seem like it was on fire. Amazed at the glory surrounding me, I almost forgot why I had come, until I saw my father get down on his knees and motion for me to do the same. My father's words were simple but sincere: 'Dear Gillantri, King of all Arway and Trivar, may my daughter Danae come to Arway this night?'"

Jaden envisioned the enchanted glade where she ate breakfast earlier that morning with nymphs lining the edges. Shivers raced up and down her spine and bubbled in her stomach.

"My heart pounded and my palms were clammy. Questions flooded my mind. What is going to happen? Where exactly is Arway? Can I really handle all this? But before I thought of another question, I heard a great rush of air above me. An enormous winged creature dove straight out of the sky. It fell faster and faster when at the last possible second, it opened its wings and slowed to a gentle stop on my right side.

"My father gently touched my shoulder and said, 'Here you go, my child. When you return, the nymphs will see you safely to the west gate. Arran will wait to return you to our home from there.' I remember I couldn't breathe to answer him. All the pain and sorrow, the fear, anxiety, and desire to run coursed through my body. I told him I couldn't go without him. I felt ashamed and frustrated.

"My father said, 'Of course you can go without me.' His belief in me empowered me. I trusted him. He helped me onto the eagle's back and took a step away. He said, 'Tell the bird that you are ready to travel to Arway, and on your return tell the bird to take you back to the glade near the city of Jeremiah. That is all you must remember. Take care, I will see you shortly.'

"The eagle was motionless until I said, 'Please take me to Arway.' At the word Arway, the great bird lunged forward, lifted his huge wings, and gave one great beat, then another and another. I took one last look at the glowing nymphs, my dear father, Arran, and Ozella, as the glade grew very small and faded from view.

"We flew so high that I could see the whole city of my childhood with its cottages, tall towers, and, of course, the breathtaking temple. It surprised me to see how large this forest is. It seemed to stretch all the way to Xannellion and nearly to the Zikong Valley. Above me, the night sky sparkled with stars, so many more than I could see from the ground.

"I leaned in close to the giant eagle and felt as cozy as when I was snuggled up in my bed beneath a down comforter. I felt the eagle's power and, yet, there was something peaceful about this huge creature. That was the most incredible thing about that night, the peace and safety I felt."

Danae glanced at Zachariah. She suddenly felt embarrassed. "I am sorry. I am afraid I have been talking too much."

"Please don't be sorry. I love to hear you talk about these things. Besides, it makes the hours go by quicker. It is almost time for our midday meal."

Danae looked up, and Jaden followed her gaze into the tangle of vines and tree tops above them and saw that the sun was directly overhead. Even Jaden was surprised at how quickly time had flown.

18

Spiders

For five days they traveled, camping off the trail to avoid being detected. Thick underbrush popped back into place after everyone tramped through it. Only the most astute tracker could have detected their presence. At night, one of the elves stood guard for four hours and then traded with another elf.

One day just after lunch as Zachariah sparred with Porter, he glanced at his mother. Jaden massaged her feet, as she did on every break. He hadn't forgiven her for making him come. More than anything, he wanted to be in Jeremiah. Any day Xzavier would attack the city. But rather than avenging himself, he'd be sparring with Porter in the jungle.

It was so infuriating that he despised to be near his mother. This time when he glanced at her, however, he noticed how worn she was. He was beginning to soften toward her, when suddenly Porter kicked Zachariah's legs out from under him. From the ground he glared at his mother, blaming her for his lack of focus.

She stared sadly at him while she finished massaging her feet and put her boots back on. He hadn't spoken to her since they were preparing to leave. Zachariah stood and began fighting harder than before, backing Porter up to a tree. Porter grinned.

"That's more like it, boy." In a blink, Porter escaped being pinned and twisted up Zachariah again, holding Zachariah's hands behind his back and pushing his face up against the same tree.

"But you haven't conquered the master yet."

"I hate it when you do that," Zachariah yelled.

"When I do what? Beat you?"

"Yes! It makes me mad."

"Then get better."

Zachariah tried to get free. Porter held him for a few more seconds and then let him go. Zachariah dusted himself off and said, "We need to move on. I don't like Porter right now."

Gideon laughed and said, "All right everybody, let's get going. Zachariah's had enough."

Zachariah saw his mother's empathy and turned away, picked up his pack, and hiked harder than he had before. After traveling a short time, it began to rain. Zachariah's heart sank. He hated walking in the rain, but at least it gave him a reprieve from the bugs. He checked on his mother and Danae as quickly as he could without them noticing. Their heads were down, and they walked slowly through the puddles. Water dripped from their faces and arms. For a minute, Zachariah wished he could walk back and talk with them but decided against it, turning to face the muddy road ahead.

Moments later, Jaden let out a yell. Zachariah spun around as she fell to the ground in the middle of the trail. She fell face first into a mud puddle and did not move. Gideon grabbed her shoulders and lifted her limp body. Zachariah watched Gideon examine her. He found a bright red, swollen lump on her right collarbone.

"It is hot," Gideon said as he quickly cleaned off the area, revealing red lines shooting out from the center in every direction. He removed his dagger from its sheath and cut two little slits into the redness. Puss oozed out.

"Danae, get me a poultice of something that will draw out the poison. Hurry."

Danae opened her knapsack, removed some herbs, rubbed them into a paste with the rain, and placed it on the open wound.

"That should help, but I don't think we have caught it in time. The poison is far beyond the bite."

"Sir," Etheltread spoke. He had a strong and almost musical voice, one that could lure you to sleep or lead you through danger safely.

"What is it?"

"We have a means to draw poison. Danae is correct that it has gone too completely into her blood for the poultice alone to save her. Time is short. May we help her?"

"It is for Zachariah to decide."

"I know nothing about this. Please save her life." Recollections of his rudeness mercilessly flooded his mind. Anger swelled inside him as he stared at his pale mother. Gideon picked her up in his arms and walked into the jungle with the elves.

Danae and Zachariah were left by the road with the extra provisions and horse. The rain poured over them. Zachariah stood in the middle of the path while Danae moved their supplies and horse under the branches of a nearby tree.

Why have I been so unforgiving? Zachariah thought. He had saved his mother from his father's wrath many times but had never been as scared for her as he was at that moment. His mother's ashen face pierced his thoughts.

"What is going to happen?" he asked.

"I don't know," Danae said.

"If I hadn't been so awful to her, I would have known something was wrong."

"The poison is deadly, but if anyone can heal her, the elves can. I just wish Arran were here. He is the real healer."

Zachariah flinched, irritated to have Arran's name mentioned. Danae put her hand on his arm and a little surge went through him.

"It is going to be all right."

Zachariah's distress wavered simply because of her faith.

Gideon ran back toward them through the forest. "Zachariah, your mother needs you, come quickly. Danae, you too." He turned and ran back toward Jaden and the elves.

Danae and Zachariah followed as quickly as they could through the thick underbrush and pouring rain. Zachariah didn't know what to expect and didn't dare hope. Shortly, they arrived at his mother's side. Jaden lay on the ground at the base of a large tree with low branches reaching out over her head. Before they got to her, Etheltread spoke.

"Your mother is not dead, but she is not well, either. The poison traveled throughout her body. We are doing all we can for her until Arran and the others get here. It is as if she has given in to the poison. She doesn't seem to be trying. Please talk with her."

He realized at that moment how badly he needed his mother. She could not leave him now. He sat under the tree that shaded her.

"It's me, Zachariah... Please, mother. I need you with me. We cannot avenge ourselves if we are apart. I need your strength. You cannot leave me. Please don't leave me."

Zachariah rubbed her hands between his. Her coloring was bad and she scarcely breathed. "Mother, please. Do not give up. The Great Jaden never gives up. Listen to your son, who needs you." He laid his head on Jaden's left shoulder and closed his eyes. Jaden didn't stir.

He lifted his head, "Etheltread, I don't have power to help her. What can I do?" Zachariah was shaking.

"It is up to Jaden and Gillantri now. She heard you, but she must choose. It will be a long night for all of us."

Etheltread turned to Gideon and the other elves. "We should make camp for the night. Porter, scout ahead. Find Arran and bring him back as soon as you can."

****

Zachariah stayed by his mother's side. Emotions stormed through him like the waves of rain that were pouring over head. During the middle of the afternoon, a whisper came from behind him.

"Zachariah."

He scanned the tree above his head and all around him. "Who's there?"

"I am Daman, your friend..."

"I have no friend by that name."

"Oh, but you are mistaken. I am your friend. I have a gift. Your mother's dragon, Justine. And I will give her to you..."

"Justine died."

"I saved her...for you. You need her to avenge yourself of Xzavier, claim his throne, and save Jeremiah."

"I can avenge myself without a dragon. I don't need any help from you."

"Oh, I think you do."

"Go away."

"But you could be a hero. Save Trivar."

"Just like my father is a hero, huh? I don't want to hear anymore. Leave me, Daman." Adrenaline coursed through him.

"I will return. Think about it." There was a rustle in the woods, but Zachariah could see nothing. Soon Gideon came over, put another blanket over Zachariah's shoulders, and sat down beside him.

"How are you?"

Zachariah smiled weakly. He felt alone.

"How is she?"

Zachariah noticed how differently Gideon's peace felt in contrast to Daman's anger. He welcomed that peace, but something about the power Daman wielded lingered.

"About the same as before, I can't tell really."

"How are you?"

"Could be better," Zachariah said.

"I know the feeling."

They sat silently for a time. Zachariah listened to the rain falling on the leaves all around them.

"Tell me about your life in Xannellion, how you were raised, what you saw, and what life is like there."

Zachariah sighed, "I've told you all I know about Xzavier, sir."

"No, I want to know about you and your mother and your life."

"There isn't much to tell. We lived in a grand palace that belonged to Xzavier. I dined on the best food, wore fashionable robes, trained for chariot races, and learned the skills of war for sport. I was waited on day and night. I loved every moment of it, or so I thought..."

"Or so you thought... What do you mean?"

"Well, up until the chariot race I thought my life was all I wanted. I was going to be king. I had power, wealth... Much has changed. Now I want to kill the man who once gave me everything."

Zachariah's face went dark. Then he thought of something and asked, "If I could get a dragon...would you be interested?"

Gideon jerked his head toward Zachariah, "Why would you want a dragon?"

"For defending Jeremiah."

"We have the resources we need to defend our own. No, our flying tigers will do fine."

Zachariah laid his head back next to Jaden's and felt disappointed.

"I appreciate what you are trying to do for me and for Jeremiah, but I need you to respect your mother's wishes. There will be many years for you to fight with us. Let us defend Jeremiah this time. Your mother will come around. After all that has happened, I don't blame her for wanting to keep you alive a little longer."

Zachariah didn't respond.

"Porter said you are learning your drills quickly and well," Gideon said.

"Porter exaggerates. He toys with me when I am giving my best effort. I have never seen a warrior as able as Porter."

"If you can keep up with him, there isn't anyone in Trivar who can best you."

"I believe that."

Gideon tenderly felt Jaden's forehead. Zachariah watched and said, "Thank you."

"You get some sleep. We don't need two of you down." Gideon patted Zachariah on the arm, stood, and walked into the rain.

Every so often Zachariah woke to check on his mother. Nothing seemed to change. He felt miserable. The harder he tried to sleep, the less sleep came. Thoughts of flying on Justine, killing Xzavier, protecting Jeremiah, and becoming king energized his mind. But by nightfall, he was crankier and more miserable.

Danae brought some food. "Here is your dinner," she said.

"Thank you," he said, trying to sound pleasant. But when he saw the salted pork and piece of old bread, he made an angry face and pushed it aside.

"You have to eat. You need your strength." Danae gently pushed the plate toward him again and asked, "How is she?"

"The same, I think."

Danae broke off a piece of the bread and put it into Zachariah's hand, "How are you?"

"Fine, I guess." Zachariah took the bread but didn't eat it.

"If you need anything, let me know." Danae stood to go, but Zachariah reached out for her hand.

"Please don't go. I need your company."

"If you eat, I'll stay," Danae said timidly.

Zachariah's eyes twinkled, "You may seem innocent..." He put the piece of bread in his mouth and chewed. Satisfied, Danae sat back down.

"Have you noticed the nymphs since Jaden got the spider bite?" Danae asked.

"All I notice is your sadness and beauty," Zachariah said matter-of-factly. He had no energy to hide his feelings.

Danae turned pink. "Zachariah."

"No, I haven't seen the nymphs."

"They have been here, trying to comfort you. The nymphs bring peace with them to share with those who need it. You have needed it, and, Zachariah, please don't look at me that way." Danae stood again, "I need to get back and clean up dinner."

He stared up at her with his troubled green eyes. "You bring peace with you, too. Thank you."

Zachariah was sincere, but it upset her.

"You are welcome, Zachariah of Xannellion," she said and returned to where she had been cleaning up.

Zachariah of Xannellion... It was like being reminded that he was from a different world, and a lesser one at that. In the middle of his thought, he heard Etheltread call out to elves running from the north on the trail. When they reached him, they embraced.

"Arran, my brother, how are you?" Etheltread said. "Gregors, Roneem, my friends, welcome. We have some food ready for you. Arran, we need your assistance."

Danae heard the commotion and ran quickly to her childhood friend, Arran, who picked her up in his arms and gently kissed her on the cheek.

"How are you, my dear? I was away when the call came for us to escort you. I hear you have been busy for the past moon."

"Oh, Arran, I have missed you so much. Jaden needs you now. She is under the tree with her son, Zachariah."

Danae was glowing, and even through the rain Zachariah could see she was smitten with this elf. Zachariah couldn't see anything special about him. He was about Zachariah's height, but slimmer and fair with medium blond hair worn in the elvan fashion. But something about him brought a light to Danae's eyes. Zachariah's countenance was dark when the new elf and Danae arrived.

"Zachariah, this is Arran, my dear friend. He is a great healer and will help your mother."

"We don't need his help. She is getting better and will be fine. You have all done enough."

"She needs more help and you know it. He can help you..." Danae sounded betrayed.

"Danae, I can't accept any more help. I have been at your mercy for too long, but since he's an elf and so good, I can't stop him from helping others, so do as you wish."

Zachariah stood, glared at Arran then walked into the dark rain. He only went far enough to not be seen and then shamelessly sat down below a tree branch and eavesdropped.

"Arran, please help her. Zachariah doesn't mean it. He hasn't slept and is under a great deal of stress. I am sorry for his behavior," Danae pleaded.

"Danae, you don't need to apologize for him. I am here for you."

Zachariah watched as Arran took Danae's careworn face in his hands and wiped away the worry lines and distress.

"Let's go to Jaden. I have a few things that might help her."

Danae seemed energized as they departed together.

How could she have considered me when there was Arran? Zachariah thought. He felt foolish. It was obvious that she missed Arran. Zachariah began to think dark thoughts about avenging himself of Xzavier and becoming King of Xannellion.

That will show Danae who is worthy of her. While he thought more about dragons and revenge, he saw Arran place his hands with open palms facing down about one or two inches above Jaden's body. He began sweeping her energy field to drain the bad energy. Then suddenly he stopped.

Danae stared at Arran curiously. "What did you find? Is something wrong?"

Zachariah strained to hear what Arran would say next.

"I have felt something like her energy before... I don't know what it is..." Arran drifted off into his thoughts as he finished with Jaden.

"You are amazing. Even now her color has improved."

As if I did nothing, Zachariah thought.

Gideon approached with Etheltread.

"Arran, Etheltread said you were here. Welcome. Where is Zachariah?"

"He left some time ago. He seemed pretty upset." Danae said. She backed away from Arran.

Gideon turned to Etheltread, "Etheltread, please go find Zachariah. Take your light and return quickly. Danae, stay with me. Arran, get unpacked. We have work to do tonight. We are glad to have you here."

Gideon helped Arran to his feet. Arran bowed his head. Turning to Danae, he winked at her and returned to camp. Zachariah slipped deeper into the forest so that Etheltread would find him farther away.

19

Explosion in Xannellion

    Etheltread returned Zachariah to Jaden's side where Danae sat faithfully watching. Etheltread said, "I am going to spend a little time with my brothers and kinsmen. Will you two stay with Jaden?"
    Zachariah and Danae looked at each other and then back at Etheltread. Zachariah answered first, "Yeah, go be with your family."
    Etheltread waited for Danae to nod. Satisfied, he disappeared into the dark evening rain. There was silence for some time. Neither Zachariah nor Danae knew what to say. Finally Zachariah spoke.
    "Why didn't you tell me?"
    "About what?"
    "Don't play games, Danae. About Arran."
    "You never asked."
    "Why did you let me believe I could mean something to you?" He lay down beside his mother.
    "You do mean something to me."
    "Yeah, Zachariah of Xannellion. A curiosity from another world, not someone you could really care for."
    Danae's eyes penetrated Zachariah's as she said, "I do care for you. That is all I have done since you came to Jeremiah…"
    "Yes, you have been charitable. I don't need your pity. Arran is charitable too."
    "He is one of my dearest friends."
    "That's right, defend Arran. I know you love him. I am sorry I ever dared hope."
    Danae lay down on the other side of Jaden. He could hear her softly crying but was too hurt by her obvious lack of love for him to say anything else.
    All night long it rained. Sometimes it rained so hard that the water made it through the thick foliage above them. By first light, they were quite wet. No one had spoken. Zachariah had not slept very well and he could hear Danae stirring.

As the sun rose, Zachariah slipped into a short but deep sleep. When he woke, Danae was gone. He sat up, soaked and uncomfortable. He stretched and hit a branch above him that sent a small shower of water on him and his mother. Jaden began to stir. She opened her eyes.

"Where are we?"

"Oh, mother!" Zachariah fell onto her chest.

"What in Trivar are you doing?" Jaden fairly yelled, alerting the entire camp to come see.

Zachariah lifted his head and said, "You were bit by a poisonous spider...but you are alive!" Zachariah took in a quick breath and let it out slowly.

"Welcome back, Jaden." Gideon said bowing low. "Danae, bring this lady some food, if you please."

Danae returned with cold tea and bread. "Eat slowly. Your body hasn't been working very well the last day or so."

"Do you mean to tell me that I have been out for a whole day?"

"Yes, a whole day and part of a night, but thanks to our friends here, especially Arran, you will have more days to make up for the one you lost." Gideon pointed to Arran and the rest of the elves. Arran seemed to see something inside of Jaden that made her uncomfortable. It reminded her of the way Franklin seemed able to see into her soul at times.

Jaden searched all the concerned faces and felt overwhelmed.

"I don't know how to thank you..." Her voice gave way to emotion. She regained her composure. "I never thought that people could care like this... I don't understand...but I am grateful." She turned to Gideon and asked, "How can I thank you?"

Gideon just waved it away. "It is what we do. You are worth it."

Zachariah noticed his mother's face rise in color.

Then Arran stepped forward. "My lady," he said, "we have helped some, but it was your son who saved you. You would have given up, had it not been for Zachariah talking you through your worst moments and staying by your side all night in the rain."

Zachariah glanced sharply at Arran, wondering what motivated him to be so generous. But as he saw his mother's eyes moisten in response, he softened.

"Thank you, son."

"You are welcome." He gave her a hug. It was a relief to be close to her again.

****

Four days later, they were camping by a small tributary leading to the Mother of All Waters in the Zikong Valley. They were nearly out of the jungle.

Jaden said to Etheltread, "Before we move this morning, I have to wash in the stream."

Etheltread waved at her, and Jaden walked off through the woods. Her mind happily wandered, reflecting on everything and nothing. Since waking from the spider bite, she and Zachariah had gotten along better, though something was different about him and he wouldn't talk about it.

She could see clearly that Arran and Danae upset him. But Danae still spent time with Zachariah, and when she did, they enjoyed one another. She took a breath, savored it for a moment, and let it out slowly. The cheerful stream danced along in the speckled morning sunlight, lapping the mossy stones at its edges. Jaden bent down to wash her face in the tepid water.

As she cleaned up and put her boots back on, she heard something. She stood and turned toward the road. There was a horse and rider, a knight from Jeremiah, on the main trail coming from the south. She ran toward him. The horse's coat dripped with foamy sweat and was limping. The rider leaned forward in the saddle, exhausted. Soon every person in camp was running toward the rider and his horse. Gideon spoke first.

"Young man, what news do you have from Jeremiah?"

"I am afraid it is not good news," the young man said and then nearly fell off his horse. Gideon caught him and set him on the ground. Jaden held him up while Gideon tried to loosen his clothing.

"I'm fine. I'm fine," the boy complained and tried to stand up but fell back.

"Just sit now. We'll worry about walking later," Jaden said.

"Zachariah, get some water," Gideon ordered. "Danae, we need some food, as well. Arran and Etheltread, this horse is in need of care. Meadthel, please unpack. We may be here another day. Porter, once Zachariah is done with the water, begin sparring practice. Jaden, please stay with me and the boy."

He asked the young knight, "Do you think you can make it into the jungle a ways?"

"Yes, of course."

Jaden and Gideon linked arms with the knight and together helped him to stand. The three of them walked slowly toward camp.

"So, what is your name, boy?"

"I am Jed, sir. My mother and I came from Xannellion and I joined up with your knights when we arrived, three moons ago. Since then, I have spent much of my time in Xannellion keeping an eye on things."

The young man was strong and tall, though the lack of hair on his face gave away his youth. Jaden remembered when Zachariah was fifteen or sixteen and growing stronger and beginning to fill out. It was not so long ago. She discerned and recognized a familiar undercurrent of anger in the boy and wondered what his life had been like in Xannellion.

Gideon must have noticed it, as well. He asked, "What inspired you to become a knight?"

"Xzavier killed my father, sir, when my father tried to leave Xannellion with our family for Jeremiah. My mother and I escaped." Color in the boy's face darkened as his rage surfaced.

Jaden felt her throat close up.

Gideon said, "I am truly sorry."

Jed clenched his fists trying to regain control and said evenly, "Franklin asked me to find you. He wanted me to tell you personally what I have seen."

Gideon said very seriously, "Come sit next to me and tell me every detail."

They sat down under the branches of a tree near camp. Jaden sat next to Gideon, pulled her legs to her chest, and wrapped her arms around them. She stared into the filtered light above her, trying to breathe in a full breath, but failing as the boy related more.

"I was in the streets of Xannellion, not five days ago. It had just rained and everything seemed cleaner and fresher. People were going about their business, when a man yelled for people to make way and two litters broke through the crowd. It was Xzavier and the Scorpion."

Jed spit like he had tasted something foul. "They were in a rush, more than usual. They were heading for the races at the stadium...but you know how they do...four men carrying each litter, acting like they are the only people in the world, knocking women and children out of the way without a thought. What I don't understand is, after that, the people are grateful that they were close to the king!"

Jed let out a little snort. "Everyone waves at Xzavier and the Scorpion like they are gods, even if they have to wave from the ground."

"Yes, go on," Gideon gently prodded.

"Anyway, I went over to help a lady up who had been knocked over and had spilled her basket of laundry all over the street, when a huge explosion rocked the stadium."

"An explosion?"

Danae came over with some warm soup and bread, interrupting Jed's story.

"I hope this is all right," she said. "We are down to minimal provisions, but it is warm."

Enjoying Danae's beauty, Jed said, "Thank you. It's fine."

Gideon's eyes found Jaden and seemed to ask, Are you all right? He knew that the conversation about the king must be difficult for her. Jaden chuckled, and Gideon laughed, realizing his mistake. Still, Gideon didn't break his gaze until she grew red and turned away.

Jed ate his food quickly, barely breathing between bites. When he finished, he began again, "After I helped the lady, I ran toward the stadium along with everyone else in the city. It became more and more chaotic as I got close. Dust was thick in the air. I removed my shirt to cover my nose and mouth, but my eyes burned, limiting my visibility more.

"Disoriented people emerged through the smoke, running away from the scene, screaming. Many had blood on them, and all were covered in dust. As I broke through the stadium entrance, there were dead and wounded people lying amidst the rubble. Others were being carried, and some just sat by the remaining pillars in a daze. It was horrible.

"Then from inside the stadium I heard a voice calling to the people. I followed the voice, though I could barely hear it. Others heard, too, and began filling back into the stadium. I sat close to the west entrance and couldn't see the person speaking but knew his voice...it was Xzavier.

" '...This was an obvious plot to kill me. Don't they know they are nothing? A small band of foolish, rebellious peasants. They will be crushed! The knights of Jeremiah must pay for the deaths and sorrow they so recklessly caused.' Xzavier riled up the people until he couldn't speak anymore, and then the Scorpion took over until the dust choked him, and then Xzavier went on again. Eventually the dust settled some, and I saw Xzavier and his men. The crowd filling the stadium had become violently angry, and Xzavier had men signing up by the thousands for service in their army.

"My contacts in Xannellion tell me that this was all planned by Xzavier and, possibly, Daman, too. Strange rumors have been circulated by some of Xzavier's servants of a dark lord who talks with Xzavier in the night. Most people in Xannellion dismiss this as ridiculous, but I think there is truth to it. His head servant was killed recently and left dead in the street near the palace. Some say it was because he knew too much about Daman and Xzavier's secret meetings."

Jaden exchanged glances with Gideon. Jaden figured it was best that Jed didn't know how much she knew about these people he was talking about. But it made her sick.

Jed ate another bite and said, "Strange things have been found in Jeremiah, as well. After the explosion at the stadium, I stayed long enough to gather the information I have told you and then rode as hard as I could to Jeremiah. I found Richard and Franklin at your house. They had just finished the funeral for Benjamin and our other comrades earlier that day and seemed worn out. Your garden was full of knights and family.

"Richard and Franklin listened carefully to my report. Franklin calmly turned to Richard and said, 'We have work to do.' Then he thanked me and asked Richard to alert all the guard stations to learn if any of our knights were involved with this explosion. He asked me to sleep for the night and return to them in the morning.

"Exhausted, I agreed. When I awoke the next morning, I reported to your house where Richard and Franklin briefed me on what they found. They searched every possible place in Jeremiah, homes included, and some suspicious things came to light. At least a dozen knights were missing – and had been missing for about two days. Also, explosives were missing from the south tower arsenal.

"Tracks from inside the arsenal disappeared not ten feet outside the arsenal. They were thick and round. Some knights speculated that dragons had landed there, but Franklin confirmed they were not dragon prints. Unfortunately, he didn't exactly know what they were, or maybe he didn't want to share. He said that they came from 'below, not above,' and that you would know what he meant."

Gideon simply said, "I do understand. Go on."

Jaden again felt the hair on the back of her neck stand on end and couldn't help looking at the ground around her.

"Sir, they found the same type of tracks outside each of the missing knight's homes and guard stations. The tracks disappeared after a few feet..."

At that moment, Etheltread came quickly toward them and interrupted, "Sir, I need your help, immediately."

Gideon dismissed himself. "Thank you for your report, Jed. There is more that we will talk about. It is time that you rest now. Jaden, please see to it that he gets the things he needs. I will be back shortly."

20

Attack

The young man gladly reclined, closed his eyes, and allowed sleep to take over. Before Jaden returned with his blanket and spread it over him, he was snoring. She felt grateful for the boy's courage and determination to get them this message so quickly.

She looked for Gideon. He was behind her only a few yards away. She sat down with her back against the other side of the tree where Jed slept. The boy's horse was lying on the jungle floor while Etheltread felt its leg. Etheltread's serious expression alerted Jaden that he had found something wrong with the horse beyond exhaustion.

"Spiders," said Etheltread.

Jaden felt the sore on her collarbone. It was still red and scabbed. She kept her hand there while she watched Etheltread motion for Gideon to be quiet.

"I have given this horse something to help it rest."

Gideon watched as the sedated horse closed its eyes. It gave a little jerk, and then it was still. Etheltread checked its pulse and Gideon bowed his head. Etheltread pulled out a small dagger and pressed it into the horse's leg.

Jaden was straining to see around Gideon, when what looked like a pocket of infection opened, and immediately a pack of dark, filthy spiders darted out in every direction. Skillfully, Etheltread, Arran, and Gideon stabbed every one of the spiders before they got away.

Jaden turned away, nauseated. She held her stomach and listened to Etheltread.

"Gideon, Daman sent his spies inside the horse's leg. Fortunately, they weren't able to return to tell him what they found, at least not these. They have been growing inside this horse's leg long before he left Jeremiah, possibly before he left Xannellion."

Jaden shivered, not from cold, for it was getting hotter as the sun rose to its zenith.

"I hope we make it to Alexandria before his spies tell him where we are," Gideon said, without much hope.

"I agree," Etheltread said. "We tried to save the horse, but with all the exercise required to get here, the poor thing pumped her entire body full of venom. The venom in these little spiders is not as powerful as older spiders. But there were so many of them feeding off the horse's hind leg that it didn't have a chance."

"I understand. You did all you could. In all my years as a soldier, you'd think I'd feel less sorrow over time. But I grieve more now when a person or an animal dies."

She thought of Benjamin and Gideon's men who so recently died. Gideon grew quiet. His eyes held so much pain. She wished she could make it go away, a thought that surprised her.

"It would be a good idea to bury this horse far from the road, and then we all need to get some rest. I will finish my conversation with Jed first thing in the morning. After that, we will begin our descent into the gorge. I hope we're not too late. We don't stand a chance once Mother starts to swell. Unfortunately, we have bigger problems now than even the mighty Zikong."

Gideon grew quiet again. "Etheltread," he said. "I am not sure how long I am going to be able to stay with you."

"What exactly do you mean?"

Jaden lifted her head to hear his answer, concerned by the graveness in Gideon's voice.

"Jeremiah is facing a fight sooner than I expected. After listening to Jed, I feel that I need to return before we arrive in Alexandria."

"I understand," Etheltread said.

"But I am also concerned about Danae. She seems unusually tired, and we haven't even faced the extreme heat of the canyon lands. Once we get past Ononzai, we will be within a fortnight of the northern forests and I will breathe a little easier. The weather is more forgiving there, but...she just wasn't cut out for this."

"We will protect her, sir, if you feel you need to leave."

"It isn't just Danae's comfort. She is all I have..."

"We will support you with whatever decision you choose."

"Thank you for listening to my concerns. I don't think I am ready to leave yet. Maybe after Ononzai. I will probably turn back after that. Could I take Jed and Porter with me?"

"Of course. Besides, once we are home, we will have more comrades to replace them. You do what you need to do. You know we are committed to help you in any way we can."

"I rely on it. Thank you, Etheltread."

Jaden felt her heart racing. How could her life be so upside down in so short a time? Not only was she in the Arwavian world she once despised, but now she had feelings for one of their most powerful men. She put her head in her arms.

****

Jaden rose before the sun and started breakfast. After hearing Gideon's concerns for his daughter's stamina, she had instructed Danae to get some extra sleep.

Gideon stirred. He sat near the fire with a blanket still wrapped around him.

"Good morning," Jaden said quietly. "How did you sleep?"

"I'm afraid it was a long night for me."

"Here's something warm for you to drink," Jaden said, handing him a steaming cup and waiting for him to say more.

Gideon opened the blanket on his right side and motioned for Jaden to sit down. She hesitated but sat, feeling calmer than she expected. Gideon shifted uncomfortably.

"I think you heard me talking with Etheltread last night."

"Yes?"

"I know Jeremiah needs me, but I don't want to leave Danae."

She wondered if he was asking for her advice.

"You will do the right thing."

"Well, that is the problem, both decisions are right. I need to know which is more right."

"You are too good, Gideon. I have never known a better father. Danae knows you have responsibilities in Jeremiah. She will understand."

Gideon struggled to respond while probing Jaden's green eyes.

"I know she will understand," Gideon said. He paused. "That's the problem. She never complains, but I see the betrayal in her eyes every time I have had to leave her in a tough situation, especially since her mother died."

Gideon paused again. Jaden let him find the words. "It is just that after Benjamin died...it has been so hard on her. She seems to be slipping again. Then with all this walking...I don't know."

"First of all, Gideon, the walking is saving her life. She can't completely slip into depression when she has to move forward like we are. Second, I think that you are suffering every bit as much as she is."

Gideon flinched and turned away. "That is unacceptable..."

With knit brows, Jaden turned away, as well. What had she said? She knew she shouldn't give advice to this man. Now she had hurt him...again.

"That's what you get for asking my advice," Jaden said. "Next time figure it out yourself." She flung the blanket off her and busily finished breakfast and cleaned up the camp.

She didn't want to see Gideon's reaction, but as she was throwing a rag into the pot of boiling water, she felt a hand on her back. She turned to see Gideon's dark, sad eyes too close. She felt breathless. He wrapped his arms around her and put his head on her shoulder.

This surprised her so much that she almost forgot to hug him back, but after a moment, she put her arms around him and said, "I meant to say...your only weaknesses are not taking care of yourself and pushing too hard... I didn't mean to make you feel bad... I was trying to help."

Gideon pulled back and stared at Jaden. Her stomach fluttered, though she wasn't about to move. He brushed her auburn hair out of her face and smiled.

"I meant to say that it is unacceptable for me to be unable to do more. Thank you for caring enough to tell me the truth." He leaned forward and kissed her on the forehead. She couldn't breathe. Then he gently pulled back and walked into the jungle.

Jaden watched him disappear. She felt disoriented, stunned, and sat down near the fire. The flames lapped at the pots, dancing in the gathering light of morning. Absently, she stirred the coals, causing them to leap higher.

A short time later, Gideon returned and said, "Thank you. I feel better."

"You are welcome. Anytime you need to be offended, just ask."

They both laughed quietly, and then Gideon turned to address the members of the camp.

"I need everyone to wake up," he said. "We have much to do today! Out of bed!"

Everyone rolled out of their blankets, slipped on their clothes, and started packing.

Once everyone was ready, they gathered around Gideon and Jed, awaiting the report. "For those of you who don't know him, this is Jed. He is one of my knights from Jeremiah. As you know, he arrived yesterday morning bearing difficult news. Someone set off an explosion at the Xannellion Stadium, presumably to kill Xzavier and the Scorpion. My knights have been blamed."

A low murmur of disgust rose collectively from the group.

"We know it isn't true. Nevertheless, Xzavier is seeking revenge on the knights of Jeremiah. All the common people are gathering behind Xzavier to avenge the deaths of their people. Thousands are gathering to Xzavier's banner from the outlying villages around Xannellion. I feel that I need to be in Jeremiah to help protect our city."

Danae swallowed hard, tears falling from her eyes. Jaden put her arm around her. There was silence. No one wanted to speak.

"Danae, I will be with you until we pass Ononzai. After that, you should find safer roads and a cooler climate on the way to Alexandria. You will be safe with the elves. And I will worry about you less."

"Of course. I understand." Danae tried to smile.

In a passion, Zachariah blurted out, "Gideon, I must go back with you!"

"That is out of the question. I need you to protect Danae and your mother."

"I must go. I know Xzavier better than anyone. I know his strengths and his weaknesses. I can read his very thoughts. You cannot defeat him without me. Arran can take care of your daughter, and the elves can defend this group better than I can. You must take me!"

"Zachariah, I appreciate your pain..."

"You know nothing about my pain."

"My mind is made up. You are staying," Gideon's eyes were determined.

"You are making the wrong decision, Gideon!" Zachariah said and stormed into the woods.

Gideon watched him leave before finishing his address.

"Once we pass Ononzai, Porter, Jed, and I will need to head back to Jeremiah. Etheltread will lead you through to Alexandria with a group of ten extra elves."

Etheltread spoke. "Sir, we must get our company through the gorge to Alexandria immediately. We are tempting the Zikong. Every minute is precious."

"I agree. Etheltread, find Zachariah, and then we will go."

Moments later, Etheltread returned running back through the jungle with Zachariah close behind him, fear in their eyes.

"Bulbanes...hundreds of them... Protect the women."

The horse neighed and stamped the ground, then unexpectedly charged in the opposite direction from which they came with the supplies loaded on her back.

Gideon yelled orders. "Danae, you and Jaden stay by the fires and keep them burning. You'll be safe by the fires. Roneem, collect some more dry logs and stay with the women. Porter, you, Zachariah, Etheltread, and I are going to set a wide perimeter around the camp. Arran, you, Jed, and Gregors set up an inside perimeter. Don't let anyone through to the women! Do you understand?"

Jaden shook out of anger and fear. She walked over to Danae and put her hand on her arm. After a few minutes of anxious silence, Jaden heard dark noises coming from the jungle, rough, raucous, heavy noises, and shuffling like a rainstorm underground. Jaden was searching the jungle, when a voice cackled in the darkness.

As if the jungle itself came to life, hundreds of bulbanes threw themselves at the men in the outer ring. Fortunately, Etheltread, Porter, Zachariah, and Gideon were well trained, for not one bulbane got past them for the first few minutes.

The four of them moved as one body, each with two swords, leveling the ugly creatures. Jaden couldn't see their features well, though she could see that they were shorter than Danae and stocky. Their dark greenish brown skin blended into the jungle perfectly.

Gideon yelled, "Arran, fire arrows over our heads."

Arran, Gregors, Jed, and Roneem shot arrows into the air, many falling on their marks. Bulbanes squealed and yelled like dying hogs. It made Jaden's skin crawl. Jaden and Danae held each other tightly, but Jaden noticed the fire was dying. She detached Danae and fed the fire with some wood, but right then Etheltread was hit with one of the bulbane's clubs and went down. Swarms of bulbanes covered him, and though Gregors tried to fill the hole, it was too late.

Bulbanes ran into the camp and got as near to the fire as they dared, leaving Danae and Jaden no place to run. Jaden took the cold end of a burning log from the fire and waved it at them. A bulbane snarled at her, his long ugly teeth glowing in the firelight. She saw every feature on his awful face, from the long bulbous nose, mole-like eyes, and elephant ears to his large hairy feet and ragged loin cloth.

His breath smelled of rotten meat, making her nauseous. Danae fainted behind her next to the fire. A bulbane lunged toward Danae, but Jaden dexterously positioned herself in front of Danae, waving the log. Three other bulbanes surrounded them and knocked Jaden's log away from her. One threw Jaden over its shoulder, and another did the same to Danae. Both ran into the forbidding jungle.

Jaden screamed as the firelight quickly faded behind them. All she had worked for and been through seemed wasted. Why would she be allowed to survive until now just to fall prey to bulbanes? She let out another loud scream.

When she did, the bulbane pounded on the back of her thigh with his rock-like fist, making her cry out in pain. He hit her again in the same spot, and she tried to stop but let out a whimper. She stared at Danae wishing there was something she could do.

At that moment, a white light lit up the jungle and the bulbane carrying Danae fell to the ground, writhing in pain. The bulbane absconding with Jaden went down, as well. She scrambled over to Danae and tried to wake her. Jaden attempted to pick up Danae, but the charley horse in her leg wouldn't let her stand up all the way. Jaden cried as she laid Danae back down on the ground near the stinky, writhing bulbanes.

Jaden was searching the jungle in the direction of the fire, when Gideon, Etheltread, and Zachariah appeared. Zachariah picked up Danae and Etheltread picked up Jaden, who surrendered willingly. They hurried back toward the dying fire.

"We have found a place to hide. It is going to be all right," Gideon said. "Up ahead."

Jaden saw an ancient tree that Arran and others of the group were climbing.

All around the tree were gathered a dark host of bulbanes. Gregors and Roneem protected the others so they could climb. But Jaden puzzled how Gideon could possibly get all five of their group to the tree?

She was learning to trust him, she realized, because she knew in her gut that he must have a plan. She kept her mouth shut until some of the bulbanes spotted Gideon's group and rushed toward them. When Gideon did nothing, Jaden cried, "Don't you have a plan?"

As soon as she spoke, Arran, from his place in the tree, shot a light at the pack of bulbanes and sent them flying toward her group. They easily dodged the bulbanes and followed the path that the light cleared to the tree. When Gideon stopped, Zachariah quickly lifted Danae up the tree, and Meadthel helped Jaden up. Gregors and Roneem held off the remaining bulbanes with their swords until everyone was in the tree. They followed last.

The elves shot light and the men shot arrows until the last bulbane fell. It was over. The elves could barely stay in the tree because of exhaustion.

Jaden glared at Etheltread, whose eyelids kept falling and asked, "Why in all of Trivar did you wait so long for the light show?"

"We were doing well until one bit my arm. We are only allowed to use our power in our extremity."

"A mob of bulbanes is extremity!" she cried.

"We only have a few shots before we are good for naught and must have time to regain our strength."

"What about Danae?" she asked.

Etheltread glanced at Zachariah, who was trying to revive Danae.

"She'll be fine."

"Next time, do it sooner!" Jaden said and settled into the crook of a branch.

21

Zikong River Valley

They spent the remainder of the day and slept that night in the tree with no signs of more bulbanes. No one slept very well, but at least they were off the ground. In the morning, the mare returned with all their supplies. The elves recouped their strength, and by mid-morning they were ready to go. Etheltread looked the worst with his bandages from bites and many bruises. Zachariah watched as Jaden walked over to Etheltread and gave him a gentle hug.

"Sorry about last night," she said.

"No worries. I learned to not mess with the queen." Etheltread laughed.

"The queen was grouchy and doesn't like bulbanes!"

"The elegant elf doesn't much like bulbanes either." Etheltread tried to wink but, because of swelling, couldn't do it very well.

"It hurts me when you wink. Please don't," she chided.

They both laughed. Etheltread caught up with his brothers, and the elves led the way, followed by Gideon, Danae, Jaden, Zachariah, and Jed, who was leading the horse.

Zachariah noticed the trees growing farther apart as the sound of the Mother of All Waters grew louder. It sounded like a demon to him. But when they walked over the crest of the last forested hill into the Zikong Gorge, Jaden gasped in delight. All the elves breathed in the air as if it were a part of them.

"Let's get going. I fear this beauty comes with a price," Zachariah said rather gruffly. He kept searching the forest for Daman. Though the hairs on his neck stood on end, he didn't see anything.

"What are you looking for?" Jaden asked.

"Nothing. I won't miss that jungle." His answer seemed to satisfy her.

He heard Danae say to his mother, "Every time I travel to Ononzai, the beauty here overwhelms my senses."

"I now know why," Jaden said reverently.

Through Zachariah's sullen eyes, the fresh green foliage near the riverbed seemed like a never-ending extension of the jungle, even surrounded as it was by the reds, browns, oranges, and yellows of the canyon. And although the river glowed with morning light reflecting off its surface, all Zachariah could think was how blinding the light was. The various shades of brown and red layered up the sides of the canyon seemed dull and uninteresting to him. His thoughts were consumed with convincing Gideon that he must go with him.

He overheard Danae say, "It's like I can see all the way to Alexandria."

Zachariah saw a circling osprey suddenly dive straight down, tucking its wings and hitting the water with a small splash. Then just as quickly, it rose out of the water, wings beating furiously, struggling to carry a large fish in its mouth. Flying low to the river, its wings touched the water repeatedly as it tried to reach the shore, dropping in a heap once it got there. The osprey ate its fish until a grey eagle came and tried to steal a free breakfast. The osprey chased off the eagle and went back to eating.

The women couldn't stop talking about the spectacular beauty of the canyon and the osprey. Zachariah was trying to shut out their voices, when Danae tripped over a large, sharp rock. Before she hit the unforgiving ground, Zachariah caught her around the waist and held her until she got her footing and then gently let go.

"Thank you," she said.

"You are welcome." Zachariah sincerely meant it.

The landscape changed dramatically as they descended toward the canyon floor. Rocks jutted out everywhere. Only the hardest rocks remained after centuries of erosion from wind and flooding. Little grew except a few tough plants that clung to the soil trapped in crevices. Where there wasn't any soil left, little cactus-like plants wrapped their roots around the rocks themselves.

Nothing bloomed now, since it was the end of summer. Except for the green undergrowth immediately surrounding the river, everything seemed mercilessly baked. Dry sagebrush skeletons blew around in the slight morning breeze. The moving air felt good, but Zachariah knew it would get much hotter today. He hoped that when they reached the gorge floor, the water would provide some respite from the heat and from his troubled thoughts.

They walked on as the sun rose higher and higher. It became uncomfortably hot. At midday, Zachariah pulled Etheltread aside.

"Does it get cooler by the water?" he asked. "My lips feel parched. There is no saliva in my mouth and no water in my canister." Zachariah opened the canister to make sure by tipping his head back and waiting for a drop to come out. But nothing did.

"I'm sorry to disappoint you, but it gets hotter. There is slightly more moisture in the air down there that makes it feel hotter, and the reflection off the water is severe. The one thing that will save us is that there aren't many days like this left. Summer is drawing quickly to its end. You see the leaves on the bushes by the river? They are turning color. Things will cool down." Etheltread's last sentence was laced with foreboding.

"You say that as if cool air is worse? You can't possibly like this heat?" Zachariah asked concerned.

"You will see. As the days grow colder there is less to eat. Less food in the river, sky, and brush. Berries and fruit become scarce. It gets cold even during the day, and you will long for this wonderful dry heat. But worse than that, any day the river could rise up and swallow you. Enjoy the heat, my friend, it's not that bad." Etheltread patted Zachariah on his shoulder then turned to address the rest of the group.

"Porter and Meadthel will run ahead and refill everyone's water canisters at the river and keep them filled as we travel. But in addition to plenty of water, we have something else we want everyone to start using as it gets hotter." Arran approached a large cactus plant, took out his curved elvan blade, and cut off pieces of the meat while everyone gathered around.

"I need everyone to suck the moisture out of this Sutac plant to prevent overheating and dehydration," Etheltread said. He took a piece of the meat from Arran and showed everyone how.

Zachariah stepped up to try it first. He swallowed and immediately spit it out on the ground. "I'd rather shrivel and die!"

"I know it is bitter, but you don't understand what we are facing today." Etheltread was in earnest, so Zachariah dutifully took some more, making an awful face.

Jaden followed Zachariah and tried to act like it didn't bother her. Jed swallowed it down easily, but when it came Danae's turn, she politely said, "Arran, may I try to go without it? After the bulbane attack, I am not feeling so well. I have such a weak stomach."

Arran said, "Danae, it is for your own good. We need all the help we can get against the heat in this country, you especially."

"Thank you, but I am going to try a day without it. I am sure I will be able to handle it with my own herbs." Danae got into her pack, dumped some herbs into her water canister, shook it up, and drank it.

"If I see any signs of dehydration, I will insist you have some," Arran said.

Danae touched his face and said, "Thank you for your concern, dear friend."

Irritated, Zachariah walked to the head of the trail.

By nightfall they had wound down switchback after switchback until Zachariah was dizzy and crankier. His mother expressed his exact sentiment when she said, "When will we ever get down to that Mother of Rivers?"

"Mother of All Waters?" Meadthel corrected. Meadthel enjoyed egging Jaden on.

"That's what I said, you arrogant elf!"

Everyone laughed, but Jaden glared at Meadthel with a twinkle in her tired eyes.

"I've fallen in with a heartless bunch!" she said.

"Only another mile or so before we can make camp for the night," Gideon said.

That night they set up camp quickly, preparing simple food. Everyone retired without so much as another argument. Zachariah heard calls of coyotes, bats and owls swooping overhead, and other smaller creatures scurrying through the brush. He pulled his blankets around him tight and fell asleep.

In the middle of the night, something woke him, but by the time he was fully aware, the only thing out of place was Danae. She was getting back into her blankets. Zachariah was surprised at how cold it was without the insulation of the jungle.

He asked, "How are you?"

She just smiled faintly then closed her eyes. Without thinking more about it, Zachariah fell back into a deep sleep.

****

Everyone else was up and dressed when Jaden finally woke Danae. "Wake up. You need to eat before we clean up breakfast."

"I didn't sleep well last night. I threw up, and I don't feel well."
Danae's face was pale and damp.

"Gideon, please come here." Jaden motioned for him to come and nodded toward Danae.

Gideon took one glance at her and said, "Arran."

Arran came and knelt beside Danae.

"Had a rough night?" he asked tenderly. He felt her forehead, motioning for Jaden. "Please get me a lukewarm rag."

Jaden poured some water out of her canister onto a clean rag and returned it to Arran, who wiped Danae's forehead and face. Next, he had her bring her arms out of her covers and wiped them down as well.

"I feel cold," Danae said quietly.

Arran put his healing hand on her face, "Of course. You have sunstroke. Your body is dehydrated and completely exhausted. You have a fever and I am trying to bring it down. You will feel better soon, I promise."

Jaden saw goose bumps on her arms as she shivered. Arran motioned to Jaden that he needed another rag. He placed it gently on her forehead while continuing to wipe down her arms, hands, legs, and feet. Jaden glanced at her son who was as miserable as Danae but for obviously different reasons. He stood in the back of the camp glaring at Arran's back.

Arran spoke tenderly. "Danae, I know you don't want it, but I need you to drink some of the Sutac juice. It is the only thing with the power to rehydrate you as quickly as we need to today. Your herbs didn't work. I need you rehydrated before the sun comes up and we have to face that battle again."

Danae winced. Her face was so pale and her big brown eyes surrounded by thick lashes implored Arran to reconsider. But she only said, "If you think I should, Arran."

Arran motioned to Etheltread who brought a small piece of the Sutac plant to him. With his left arm, he gently cradled Danae and helped her sit up. She took a small drink and gagged, but Arran encouraged her to keep drinking. She alternated between gagging and drinking, but to Jaden's surprise, she never vomited.

Arran stood. "Everyone, this is what could happen to any of you. It is required from now until the weather cools to drink the Sutac juice three times a day. If you do, than we will have no more sunstroke on our journey. Meadthel and I will keep enough on hand for everyone. Danae you need to have some every couple of miles until you feel better."

Danae grimaced.

Gideon said, "Whether you feel better or not you will be riding the horse until we get to Alexandria. Everyone pack up. We need to go before it gets later."

To Danae he said, "Please take care. Rest as best you can."

Arran sat next to Danae. "Your father's right. My mother wants to see you healthy and strong when we get there." Arran gave Danae a hug. "You are very special to her, you know."

"She is like a second mother to me. I only wish we lived closer. Thank you for your peace. I have needed it lately." Danae gazed into Arran's eyes, giving Jaden a sinking feeling. Out of the corner of her eye she noticed Zachariah hadn't moved when Gideon asked everyone to pack.

Jaden thought about how Zachariah spent more time with Porter lately, training every spare moment. Though the spider incident allowed them to talk again and gave them some feeling of reconciliation, he continued to grow more distant, as if he were sinking into himself. A couple nights before, Jaden confronted him, and he flatly denied feeling disconnected from her but wouldn't talk about it, and before long he was sparring with Porter again.

Gideon rubbed Jaden's back. "Are you ready?"

"Oh...Yes. Actually, I am. Sorry. I guess I was far away..."

"Are you feeling well?"

"I am always feeling well. Thank you."

Gideon offered her his hand and she accepted. Her legs had fallen asleep while she squatted there and she could barely stand. She reached for Gideon's shoulder to steady herself. He put his large hand around her waist.

"Oh, that feels awful. I mean my legs," she said. As she said it, she couldn't help noticing how solid his arms felt.

As the prickly sensation subsided, she saw someone peering at them from her peripheral. She made a nonchalant glance in that direction and caught Zachariah watching. He turned away quickly, but not before she saw the disgust on his face. She responded to Gideon.

"Once again, thank you for saving me. I guess I am not always feeling well. Who knows what embarrassment I might have caused myself if I had stood up without you there?"

Gideon laughed his rich laugh. "Anytime, Queen Jaden."

"Are you mocking me, sir?"

"I wouldn't."

Though Jaden believed him, overwhelming emotions that she had been fighting since she arrived in Jeremiah surged through her. She smiled and lamely walked away with the tingly feeling in her legs still slightly there.

Everyone hiked in the heat next to the Mother of All Waters day after day for nearly a fortnight. Jaden loved best the beautiful twilight when the changing colors of the flora seemed to glow and the breeze picked up from the north, fanning their hot, tired faces. The blessing of a late summer didn't give Etheltread any comfort. He kept his keen eyes peering far ahead, knowing well that their good fortune could be spoiled at any time.

Day after day, Jaden watched Gideon grow more restless. After Danae's brush with sunstroke, he expressed to Jaden his gratitude that he didn't leave for Jeremiah earlier. At times Jaden felt him split in two with concern for both his city and his daughter. Danae didn't recover fully from her heat exhaustion, being continually exposed to the hot weather coupled with the physical exertion required by constant travel.

Arran kept close watch over her, to Zachariah's chagrin. On the other hand, Zachariah was thriving in this environment of physical challenge, and Gideon took advantage of every moment to train and teach the willful young man.

But he became more distant to Jaden and no matter what she did, she failed, until one day, just after dinner when Jaden took a walk by the river during her favorite time of the day. Everything glowed in the waning light of day. She was watching an osprey try for one last morsel before the light completely vanished, when she heard something rustling behind her.

"Mother?"

Without moving her gaze from the osprey, she motioned for him to come close. Zachariah came up behind her and stood to her left.

"Have you dreamed lately about your three ladies and the forsaken green lands?"

"I haven't had any dreams lately. I guess I have been too tired. I hope that as we get closer to the Highlands, I will find more answers." She turned to him, put her hands on his shoulders and interrogated him with her eyes. "Son, I have missed you."

Zachariah looked down. Jaden pulled him into her arms and gave him a long hug. "We have been through a lot since we left Xannellion."

Zachariah pulled away, picked up a rock, and tried to skip it. The rock flew perfectly level across the river's surface, and then was sucked into the middle of the current. Jaden sat down, pulled off her boots and stretched her legs, letting her feet soak in the water at the edge of the river. Zachariah stood, throwing stones. Jaden let him for a time, as she enjoyed the coolness on her tired feet.

Absently, she massaged her right foot as she watched the osprey flutter for a moment, dive into the swift flowing water, and emerge ten yards downstream with a healthy-sized fish. The bird flew away toward the canyon wall on the east side of the river.

Zachariah had grown strong again. His skin was golden brown and his hair was bleached blond and longer around his strong face. He often pulled it back in a braid like Porter, and with his Jeremian clothing, he emanated a mix of cultures.

"Never could I have imagined the change we have seen in ourselves since we left Xannellion."

Zachariah stopped for a minute and said, "So you like what we are becoming, huh?"

Jaden wasn't sure what he meant. "It is still unnerving at times, but yes, I like it."

"It's because of Gideon, huh?"

"What?" Jaden didn't think she wanted to go there. "I like what I see in you, and, yes, Gideon has something to do with how well you are doing."

"You know mother, I have been thinking. I like you and Gideon. It has a strange sort of balance to it. I thought for a time that you would come back with me to avenge ourselves of Xzavier, but I like it better that you become mistress of the leader of the Jeremian knights and I become King of Xannellion. We will still be two of the most powerful people in Trivar, and I won't have to worry about you so much, growing old and being alone..."

"I don't like the tone of your voice, Zachariah. You don't sound like yourself." There was something lifeless in his voice that scared her.

"I thought you liked what I am becoming, mother?"

"Well, I do, but I don't like how you are talking right now. You..." Jaden couldn't put a finger on it, but it troubled her.

"Let's talk about something more pleasant then," Zachariah said. "How about the cute couple, Danae and Arran? Now they are something special."

"Zachariah...come on. They have been friends her whole life. Besides, Arran is a healer. He is taking care of Danae. That is his job. He took care of me and I healed quickly, even while we traveled. It is his gift."

"Yes, yes, his gift. Was there anything else you wanted to talk about, mother? I am feeling tired." Zachariah gave her a dull look.

"Actually, would you come and sit down for a minute?"

Zachariah glanced toward camp and back at his mother, took a deliberate breath, and reluctantly sat down.

"I need to apologize to you," she said. "I haven't been a good mother... No... don't interrupt, let me finish. One of the things I hated about Jeremiah when we first got there was all the guilt I felt while watching these good people. I was so wrapped up in fleeing Yamis with Xzavier that I couldn't see that I was leading you on a path that could destroy you..."

"I am not like that. I am being trained as a Jeremian knight. I will be like Gideon. You don't need to worry about me, really. And you have been a great mother."

"No, I haven't. I spent most of your life jockeying for my freedom. It didn't leave me time for your needs."

Jaden watched the expression on Zachariah's face darken. She felt a lonely sadness engulf her and stared toward the cliffs where the osprey had flown. She searched for the words to express her feelings. She remembered how Gideon had expressed his love and concern for Danae just the other morning, and Jaden decided to try something she had never tried before.

"Zachariah, I love you and I am sorry."

His eyes widened, truly shocked by her words. An old tenderness surfaced in his eyes, for a moment. Jaden watched him wrestle with his emotions and then defeat them. He sniffed and turned away, saying, "Well, that's a new one."

Jaden found herself choking on more of her own emotion. "I really do love you, son."

"If you really do love me, then let me go back with Gideon."

Zachariah stood and skipped another rock. Shocked by the turn in their conversation, she ran her hand over her hair and tried to compose herself.

"I can't," she said simply.

"What kind of love is that?"

"It is my love that asks you to stay. I fought Xzavier for years to keep you from harm, until he nearly took your life. I sacrificed everything I had to save you... I can't let you return to that danger again. Don't you understand?"

"Yes, I see what you want, you want a daughter that can be your nursemaid as you grow old. But I am a son! I was born to be king, mother, and I can't be king and a nursemaid!"

Zachariah picked up a rock and tried to skip it, but it made one long bounce and fell in into the rushing waters. Without another word, he disappeared down the shore of the river into the falling darkness.

22

Sunstroke

Jaden returned to camp and noticed Gideon and Arran talking quietly together.

"What can we do about Danae? Even on horseback, she gets fatigued so easily."

Gideon motioned to Jaden to come closer. "We have a long way to go, and I know of no other way than to keep her on the horse and feed her the Sutac juice," Arran said. "I am worried too. I suggest we get her to Ononzai. She can recover there."

"As much as I'd love to stop there, we don't have the time."

Etheltread sat down next to Arran and added, "Gideon is right. We are taking far too long. The river simply won't hold. We need to speed up and get to the safety of Alexandria."

Arran turned to his brother. "Etheltread, I know how you feel, but Danae can't even handle the pace we're going now. If we speed up…"

"If we don't speed up, the river will wash us away, you know this. In all my life, the river hasn't waited for its first wash for more than a fortnight from now, and it rarely waits that long. If we continue to travel at our current pace it will be just under a fortnight to Alexandria. It is four or five days before we get to Ononzai.

"If we wait in Ononzai for any amount of time, we'll never make it to the northern mouth of the gorge before the first flood. I don't want to take the plateau trails out of Ononzai where there isn't as much cover. Our best option is to pass Ononzai completely, and if we hurry we might make it through. Danae may be uncomfortable for a fortnight, but at least she will be alive."

"If we rest at Ononzai for a few days, giving Danae a chance to regain her strength," Arran said, "we could take the plateau trails out of Ononzai. We could enlist more elves. We'd be safe. I just don't see Danae handling a quickened pace."

"I don't like the idea of putting Ononzai in danger," Gideon said. "I'd rather that Xzavier make no connection to that city." Gideon's troubled eyes searched Etheltread's.

"It's less ideal than just getting through the gorge," Etheltread said.

"I agree with Etheltread, we won't stop unless we have to," Gideon said. "Let's keep to the original plan and push past Ononzai. One or two of you could go ahead and gather reinforcements when we get close. Once I know you have extra help, I will head south. Let's try to make Danae as comfortable as we can and pray we make good time. But Arran, if she gets weaker, I need to know. We will stop only if we have to..."

Zachariah emerged from the brush having just returned to camp. Jaden listened to Gideon while she watched her son lay out his bedding, remove his boots, and go to bed. Her heart ached, feeling completely removed from him. In Yamis and Xannellion they had each other to lean on, no matter how tough it was. It was so different now. Their relationship felt bare, so weak compared to the relationships around them.

Etheltread presented his plan. "Gideon, I know we need to sleep soon, so I will be brief. I have a plan that will speed up our trip. We leave before dawn tomorrow. Meadthel and I will stay ahead of the group to gather and catch food. We'll get camps set up for midday meal and evening meal. We need to keep a steady pace all day. If we travel slightly faster than we did through the jungle and lengthen the time we travel by two hours in the morning and two hours in the evening, we will greatly increase our chances of making it through the gorge safely. With Danae on the horse, the only one I worry about is Jaden. Do you think you can handle it?"

"Of course I can," Jaden said, though she felt extraordinarily weary and didn't sound too convincing.

Gideon questioned her with his eyes. Etheltread accepted her word. "I insist that everyone keeps up on the Sutac juice. We don't have time for people to get sick."

"Etheltread, this is going to be dangerous for our women. If it were just soldiers... Do you think this is wise?"

"This is life and death," Etheltread said. "I can't tell this to you with enough emphasis. Most years we would have been swept to sea by now!"

"All right, our lives are in your hands. We leave tomorrow before dawn."

Arran and Etheltread stood and bowed to Jaden and then Gideon. Jaden could feel Gideon needed more support tonight. "I often wondered, growing up in Yamis, how a place so peaceful could be so deadly. Now I have seen it in the jungle outside of Jeremiah and here in the gorge, as well."

"Yes, that is how nature is, isn't it?" he said distracted.

"So are you Gideon, the worried father, or Gideon, the leader of the knights of Jeremiah, tonight?"

"Yes," he said, coming to himself. "I noticed you and Zachariah leaving camp earlier."

"I had a talk with him by the river."

"Oh. Any better this time?"

"We at least talked longer." Jaden went over the conversation in her mind again. "He's so angry. He is angry about not being able to go back to Jeremiah with you."

"Do you still feel he can't?"

Jaden realized the question came of concern and not pressure. She felt a growing trust for Gideon. "All I know is that I can't give him permission if it means his life."

"Then I support you. He will figure it out in time. There are many years left in his life to defeat Xzavier."

"Was I that angry when we first arrived?"

Gideon wisely dodged the question. "You have come a long way, Jaden of Xannellion."

"It makes me sick to hear you say that. Jaden of Xannellion. Xannellion seems worlds away... I feel so different... But I didn't mean to stay here and talk about myself, I wanted to know how you are."

"I'm always fine. When are you going to get that into your head?" Gideon laughed quietly.

Jaden didn't let it go. "Really."

"I am weary. I am worried about Danae and you..." He put his arm around her shoulders and gave her a side hug. She touched his hand without thinking. Their friendship was deepening, but he would be gone soon.

"I don't want you to leave."

"I don't want to, either," Gideon said. He pulled her close.

****

It was still dark the next morning when Gideon woke his daughter. Jaden stood nearby, cleaning up breakfast. Not far away, Zachariah packed the horse, and she realized he was listening to Gideon, as well.

"Danae," Gideon said. "It is time to get going. Everyone's packed. I let you sleep longer. How are you feeling?"

Jaden could hear the worry in Gideon's voice but could barely hear Danae answer, "Fine, thank you." Jaden knew she was lying.

"Well, I'll send Arran over to help you finish getting ready."

"Gideon, may I help her? Arran has enough to do," Jaden heard Zachariah say. She finished cleaning the last dish and put it in its pack.

"Thank you, Zachariah." Gideon hugged his daughter gently and shot a glance over to Jaden that expressed surprise. She shrugged her shoulders, not knowing what had changed in Zachariah. She hoped that something she said last night had helped.

Zachariah asked Danae, "How are you this morning, fair lady?"

She smiled wearily. "Fine, thanks. Could you bring me some water?" Jaden was surprised again to see him happily hurry off and get water.

"Here you go. Enough of this damsel in distress stuff, all right?" He smiled a cocky grin, but Jaden saw in his eyes his deeper fear that something might happen to her.

Danae looked at the sky. "I'll be all right. It was stupid of me to think I, of all people, could get along without the Sutac juice. All the moisture is sucked into that river. I can't seem to drink enough to make up for the moisture I lose every minute." When she finished speaking, she slumped back on her pillow.

"Can I get you something else?"

"No, I just feel so tired." She tried to prop herself up on her elbow as if to prove she was fine, but her arm trembled.

"Lie down. I'll get your things packed."

She obeyed, appearing close to tears, and closed her eyes. Zachariah got everything ready. When he returned, she had fallen back to sleep. Even as wiped out as she was with color gone from her soft cheeks, her gentle beauty must have struck him because he stood there, just watching her. He knelt down and touched Danae's hair.

"I'm sorry to have to wake you, but we need to go."

Danae woke and looked into Zachariah's eyes. He said, "Let's see if I can get you up on your horse." He easily lifted her into his arms and placed her on her horse.

"I don't even have my shoes on."

"You won't need shoes today. I packed them. If you do, I'll get them for you."

She touched his arm. "Thank you."

Jaden smiled. He nodded to Danae. Then he finished rolling up her sleeping blankets.

Arran approached them. "Thanks for the help, Zachariah," he said. "This morning was busier than usual with two of us going ahead."

Zachariah barely acknowledged him with a tip of his head and turned to Danae. "Are you comfortable?"

"Yes, thank you for your help." Danae watched Zachariah, even as Arran took the reins to lead her horse to the trail.

Jaden fell in next to Zachariah, hoping to see more of him today. "I'll take up the rear," Zachariah called to Gideon, who turned and nodded in agreement.

All day Zachariah kept a close eye on Danae, as did Arran and Jaden. But she didn't seem any better. The heat was taking everything out of her. She fell asleep in the saddle and Zachariah rushed forward to steady her. Arran watched, satisfied that Zachariah had her and kept going. Zachariah walked beside the horse trying to keep Danae centered for awhile before he said, "Arran, stop. This isn't working. I need to sit with her."

Arran stopped while Zachariah carefully got on the horse behind Danae.

"What's going on?" Danae said.

"I can't keep you from falling while I walk beside the horse. Let me help you get comfortable."

He held her cradled against his left shoulder with her legs hanging over the side of the horse on the right. She sank into his arms comfortably and whispered, "Thank you. I feel so awful."

"I know. Just sleep."

Arran mouthed, "How is she?"

Zachariah shook his head in the negative. Gideon came back to see what was going on. Arran quietly filled him in. "Her sunstroke is worse. Zachariah had to sit with her because she couldn't keep herself in the saddle. There is no place to get shade around here unless we set up camp. Etheltread says we can't stop. Fortunately, we are only two days from Ononzai. I suggest we take her there."

Gideon struggled with his emotions. "Arran, please tell me she is going to be all right."

"Sir, if we get her to Ononzai, she will recover. But Alexandria is too far."

"Then we have no choice but to go to Ononzai."

Gideon ran ahead before returning to speak to everyone. "I sent Meadthel and Etheltread to Ononzai. They'll bring back Ononzai's quickest men with something to carry her in. Until then, we will keep up a quick pace so they don't have to come back so far."

For the rest of the day, they marched full speed toward Ononzai. No one spoke unless they had to. By midday, Jaden's feet were burning, but she hardly cared. No one complained. With the sun's last effort, red, orange, and gold splashed across the western sky. When the last rays disappeared, Jaden fell to the ground.

"I'm sorry, my legs won't move anymore..." She buried her head in her hands and the evening wind tossed her hair.

"Gideon, I think we are done today," Jaden heard Zachariah yell ahead.

Gideon came quickly to Jaden's side. "Just rest. When camp is set up, I'll return."

To the rest of the group, he said, "Thank you for giving so much today. I am grateful." His concerned brown eyes glanced at Danae, whose head was down on Zachariah's chest. She didn't move.

Jaden watched Zachariah motion that she was asleep to relieve some of Gideon's worry. Gideon kept everyone unpacking and organizing camp and missed Zachariah's bluff, but Arran caught it and went to him.

"I'd like to see her," Arran said.

"Place the bedroll down, and I'll bring her over."

Zachariah carefully lifted Danae off the horse. She was limp. Zachariah said to Arran, "She is so weak, I don't even know if she is conscious."

Zachariah laid her down on her bedroll and covered her with a light blanket. Using his healing work, Arran cleared as much of the distress from Danae as he could. He focused most of his time on her midsection and head. After a few long minutes, he rocked back on his feet in a crouching position. Zachariah knelt beside him.

"How is she?"

"You were right. She lost consciousness. I believe that I have relieved some of her pain but... She will be all right. We just need to get her to Ononzai."

"You believe she will be all right?"

"There is nothing more I can do for her. She needs rest, so this is probably her body's way of getting the rest it needs." He clasped Zachariah's forearm in a friendly manner, turned, and was gone.

Zachariah finished setting up his bed and gear. Gideon came over to talk with Jaden.

"Your bed is ready and there is food next to it. Don't wait too long or the ants will clean your plate."

"I am sorry I couldn't go farther today."

Gideon gave her a hug and said into her hair, "You gave everything. That is all anyone can ask. Get some rest."

Arwavian kindness still surprised her. She hugged him back. She ate a few bits of her food, went to bed, and slept soundly.

In the morning, Jaden woke feeling grumpy but didn't complain as she pulled out cold food for breakfast. She could tell Zachariah, Arran, and Gideon hadn't slept much, either. No one woke Danae. Zachariah got into the saddle and Gideon handed Danae to him.

The group moved quickly through the low-lying underbrush along the shores of the great river, covering as much ground as possible. By midmorning, Danae opened her eyes. Zachariah hugged her gently.

"I am so glad to see your eyes open."

"How long did I sleep?"

"Longer than I did." Jaden heard Zachariah try to laugh. Danae laughed weakly, as well. Everyone walked briskly until halfway through the day, when Jaden heard a faint sound.

"It sounds like men singing," she said.

The singing grew louder and louder, echoing through the canyon walls. Everyone searched the valley trying to catch the first sight of whoever was creating the music. Before long, Porter, who was out in front, ran back to report.

"Meadthel is coming with a company of our brothers from Ononzai. Prepare Danae to go on ahead."

Gideon rushed back to Zachariah and Danae.

"The elves are here for you. We will meet you in a couple of days. All is well."

"Don't worry about me, father. Ozella will take care of me." She put on a brave show but was so weak that Jaden worried they may have waited too long. Gideon picked up his daughter.

"Do you want her to take any of her supplies?" Zachariah said, heading for the packs on the horses.

"No, no, they need to travel light. Ozella will have everything Danae needs when they get there."

Shortly the elves came into view. They were a splendid sight: twelve of them with Etheltread and Meadthel, all dressed in light tan traveling attire that blended in with the landscape like deer in a forest. They were so nimble that they fairly floated.

"Mother is waiting for Danae," Meadthel said. "They are ready for her."

Gideon carried her to the elves, who held a long, sleek litter with a sunshade over the top. She would travel comfortably the rest of the way to Ononzai. They placed silk blankets over her to protect her from the elements and keep her cool.

Etheltread, Meadthel, and four of the new elves joined Gideon's party to help hunt and prepare camps. The other eight elves raced away, four of them carrying Danae and four jogging along behind, ready to trade in shifts with the first four when they tired. Within minutes they were out of sight. Only their songs could be heard echoing off the canyon walls as Gideon's group got under way again without Danae.

23

Ononzai

Two days later, as the setting sun shone warmly on the eastern canyon wall, Jaden heard ethereal music, like angelic trumpets mixed with magical wooden wind chimes. The elves in Gideon's group sang in response. The music and elvan voices blended with echoes through the canyon in an intoxicating, soul-energizing melody. Through weary eyes, Jaden saw a glowing city built into the canyon, and at the very top, the elvan palace, Onair.

"Ononzai, city of the Zikong River," Etheltread announced.

As they drew near, Jaden observed the city walls. They were made of the clay from the canyon but had been mixed with whole jewels so that the setting sun illuminated the jewels, scattering colors in every direction.

Many elves came to observe the new arrivals. The women were tall and slender with straight, long flowing hair of all shades, from the whitest blond to the richest black. No one wrapped their hair up, but left it down. Occasionally, Jaden saw some who wore small braids, flowers, or leaves woven elegantly into their long tresses.

Their dresses were made of silk dyed in all the canyon colors, from clay reds and browns to the gentle greens and blues of the river and its shrubs. The men wore robes of silk that accentuated their tall frames and made them look more Arwavian than Trivarian. Their children were peaceful and watched with large, intelligent eyes.

Jaden wondered longingly if she would see the blue-eyed man or the woman with the black hair and her husband among the crowd. Maybe this was where she and her family of origin hailed. Though everyone said she was from the Highlands, something about the elves of Ononzai made her wish she belonged here. The city entranced Jaden, and for a time she forgot her sore muscles, burning feet, and exhausted body. Gideon put his arm around her waist.

"Let me help you, my lady. We have a little hike to the palace."

"Thank you, but I don't deserve it. I am sorry for how awful I have been. The last couple of days have been difficult."

"None of us has been our best. No harm done." Gideon tried to hide his obvious hurt, and it made Jaden feel worse. She painfully recalled the day Danae left.

"How are you doing?" he had asked her that day. "Would you like to ride the horse now?"

"Gideon, don't ask me how I am doing ever again... I am fine!!! I don't need your charity or your stupid horse."

The pain on his face hurt her even now. It had been constantly before her mind over the last day and a half. Gideon had obeyed and left her alone with her anger and pain. Stubbornly, Jaden hiked the whole way to Ononzai to prove she didn't need to ride the "stupid horse."

And to her further irritation, Zachariah was happier and more content than he had been since she forbade him to fight in Jeremiah. He had extra energy to take in a few lessons from Porter on their short food breaks, as well as before they started in the morning and before they went to bed at night. But he knew better than to help Jaden after the way she responded to Gideon. So Jaden had been left alone.

Now she walked meekly beside Gideon, grateful for his strength.

"I had another dream last night."

"Really? Was it the blue-eyed man again?" Gideon asked.

"Yes, it is always the same feeling, and the circumstances are always similar. I am trapped somewhere and he liberates me. He is the most peaceful being I have ever known. But then I become angry and his sad blue eyes penetrate my soul. I cry like a child but don't know how to reach him. The elves' peace reminds me of him. You are often talking with this man in my dreams."

"Why do you become angry?" Gideon tentatively asked.

"I don't know. Every time I ask that question, I lose my train of thought. I... think it frightens me for some reason."

"Anger can be scary," Gideon said with a wink.

Jaden cocked her head, ready for a fight, but she simmered down when she saw his sincere eyes. She changed the subject.

"The elves are beautiful. Everything here is so...elegant."

"Yes, I love Ononzai," Gideon said. "Now that we are here, I will only stay until Danae recovers. Jeremiah needs me."

Jaden stared at the individual stones on the ground. They were randomly broken flat clay pavers the size of a foot that were placed together like the mosaics in Xannellion. The smooth clay felt good to walk on after the uneven, stony ground of the canyon.

"Gideon, I don't want you to leave."

Gideon gave Jaden a little squeeze. Jaden observed the buildings. They were tall and grand, like the elves. Every so often one of the elvan guides who had traveled with them would shout to a relative or friend, embrace them, toss the hair of their children, kiss the wife on the cheek, and then return to the line.

As the last rays of sun fell beyond the western canyon wall, Jaden heard the sound of heavenly trumpets once again and realized they were nearing the palace. She leaned heavily on Gideon's arm. Jaden gazed down into the canyon from where they had come. She was shocked to see how far it was. The road leading to the palace wasn't too steep, only because it wound back and forth many times.

"We are nearly there, Jaden. Well done."

Jaden glared at him, unable to accept the compliment but unable to spend any energy arguing.

Gideon was about to say something, when a horrible rumbling sound echoed through the canyon. It started out soft and crescendoed in fury. They all stared wide-eyed toward the river to see a wall of water filling the gorge. Debris was swept away before the merciless flood.

As the waters rushed through the Zikong River Valley, Gideon said, "If Danae hadn't needed help...we would have all been down there..."

They all stood in wonder. Overwhelmed with exhaustion, Jaden's legs grew weak. Gideon quickly tightened his arm around her waist.

"Etheltread, will you make sure Jaden finds a comfortable place to sleep tonight? I have some things I need to take care of."

Jaden's eyes pleaded with Gideon not to return to Jeremiah. He placed his large, warm hand on her cheek.

"You will feel better after a night in Ononzai. I will see you in the morning."

He kissed her forehead, lingering for a moment, then gently handed her over to Etheltread, who lifted her into his strong arms and carried her across a courtyard and through the palace doors.

****

Sunlight poured into Jaden's bedroom. She hadn't noticed anything but the softness of her bed the night before. Her bed frame looked like polished ivory with flowing silks draped over the top canopy frame. Her sheets and curtains were yellow and gold. The room was accented in gentle greens, making her feel like she was in a sea of spring daisies. Besides the exquisite beauty, it was peaceful.

Jaden rose from her bed, drawn to the window. She opened it, breathing in the sumptuous breeze as it entered. She leaned over the windowsill and took in the scene around her. Immediately below her window, lush terraced gardens covered with vines, bushes, flowers, and dwarf trees unfamiliar to Jaden swayed with the breeze from the canyon.

A decorative stone wall surrounded the garden. The wall was made up of short pillars spaced every few feet apart with a low brick-like wall connecting the pillars. Each pillar was carved into a statue of some kind that Jaden couldn't see clearly, as she was too far away. Below the wall stood the houses Jaden passed the night before that lined the winding road almost to the floor of the canyon.

Seeing the engorged river brought back travel pains. Idly, she ran her fingers through her stiff hair, leaned her head back, and was about to stretch, but at that moment a graceful, silver-haired lady knocked briefly and entered the room. She had the air of a queen.

"Good morning, Jaden, Queen of Xannellion. It is good to have you safely here in Ononzai."

Her voice matched her grace in every particular. It floated like petals dropping from a rose in mid-summer. She walked over to Jaden and sat down in a chair next to the window.

"How are you feeling?"

"Besides a slight headache and sore muscles, I am feeling much better."

"How would you like a warm bath to start your day?"

"A warm bath is tempting, but I would like some breakfast first, please?"

"Of course. It is coming as we speak. Breakfast first, breakfast first. Then we will get you into the bath and some fresh clothes. You'll feel like a new woman."

As she spoke, there was a knock at the door. The elf glided to the door and opened it. An elegant young girl walked in with a tray full of food. Tentatively, Jaden nibbled the delicate green fruit shaped like stars. By her third bite, Jaden forgot her manners and inhaled it, unashamed.

"Now, slow down, or you will make yourself sick, dear."

Jaden ate slower. The older lady patiently waited. When Jaden finished the food, the woman said, "The bath is all drawn and ready for you."

Jaden wiped her mouth and followed the beautiful lady across the hall into a great wash room with high ceilings and open skylights that revealed blue skies littered with fluffy white clouds. There were windows set in archways that presented a sweeping view of the western canyon wall.

"I'll be back later. Take your time. I put some oils and special salts in the water. Enjoy." With that, the graceful woman left.

The fragrance of the bath oils alone worked their magic. As she sank into the warm bath, all of her remaining distress melted away. Her mind was restful while rehydrating her body after days of dust and dryness. Jaden soaked until she felt like a full sponge.

Then she got out of the bath and wrapped a long, thick towel around her. Near the door she found a gown hung and a matching pair of shoes. The gown was made of deliciously soft red silk. The simple style and embroidered edges were truly elegant. She caressed the material between her fingers, enjoying its smoothness.

After drying off, Jaden slipped on the silky gown. It smelled like spring.

"Only in Ononzai," Jaden whispered.

She twirled around and giggled, unable to stop herself, when there was a knock on her door.

"Come in," she said over her shoulder.

As the door opened, she took in a quick breath. Her eyes grew wide and tender as she took in the visage of the man who stood before her clean shaven and handsome in his elvan robes that accentuated his suntanned skin, strong physique, and gentle, dark eyes. Why must she feel this way, torn between her darkness and his light?

"I didn't expect you. I thought the lady would come back." She couldn't get her words out right and felt frustrated, but he closed the distance between them and wrapped her in his mighty arms.

"Gideon, please don't kiss me. I haven't done anything to deserve your love. In fact, if we were to count, I have hurt you more times than you have helped me."

"You don't know how much you have helped me. You are a good woman, Jaden."

Jaden pulled away. "No I'm not. You don't know me, Gideon. You don't know what I have been all my life. You have your perfect world, with your perfect people. You don't know the darkness like I do."

"But you fled the darkness. You are becoming what Gillantri always hoped you'd become."

"What Gillantri always hoped I'd become? Since when have you been talking with Gillantri?" Jaden sat down on a stool facing the large window.

"In your dreams."

"Be serious."

"My mother used to tell us that Gillantri expected us to be the best people we could be because we were like the elves before we came to Trivar, spectacular creatures with gifts and abilities. These Trivarian bodies impose limits, but Gillantri knew we could overcome the weakness of Trivar and rise to the heights of Arway. That is what I see you doing, even though you never had a mother tell you that. That is what I love about you, Jaden. Despite the darkness you have faced, you are full of determination to be better. It inspires me."

Jaden's head dropped and Gideon walked in front of her and knelt down. He lifted her chin and brushed her hair away from her face.

"Let me love you?"

Jaden paused, vacillating between her need and her self-punishment. At that moment, the graceful lady walked in carrying a hair brush and some more sumptuous oils that scented the air. Jaden stood quickly and Gideon reluctantly followed.

"Queen Ozella, good morning," Gideon said and went forward to hug her.

"Gideon, you look wonderful. Jaden, I have brought you some things for your lovely hair."

"My lady, I am sorry. I didn't know you were the queen." Jaden rose and bowed slightly, but Ozella stopped her and hugged her.

"There is no need to apologize. I wanted to meet you as a person, not as a queen, and that is how I expect you to see me. I am a person first and a queen second."

Jaden didn't know how to respond to this. "I have never known a queen so…"

"So real?" Gideon answered.

"I have only seen the worst in royal mismanagement, but Arwavians are so different."

"Let me do your hair, please. I am truly enchanted with it."

"But you are the queen. It is one thing to be real, but another to be the servant." Jaden noticed a slight frown on Ozella's face. "I speak too boldly."

"Oh, I am not offended by your boldness. It is refreshing. It's only that I'll be disappointed if I can't do your hair."

"You'd better do as the queen says, Jaden. You never know what an elf queen will do to you in your sleep if you disappoint her." Gideon laughed good-naturedly.

Jaden's eyes widened, but she realized he was kidding and turned to Ozella. "Of course you may do my hair, if that is your wish."

"It is my wish. I have never seen such thick, perfect curls, except north of Alexandria in the Highlands. Our elvish hair is so very straight."

"The Highlands? I have been told that before." Cannote's words flashed through her mind, and she instinctively leaned closer to Gideon.

Gideon touched Jaden's arm.

"I'll be in the gardens when you two are done. Is Danae still there?"

Ozella smiled. "Yes, and you'll find she is doing quite well, considering the condition she arrived in."

"I can't thank you enough. I knew if anyone could help her, you could." Gideon's eyes were full of emotion. He took a quick breath and asked, "Will we be able to tour Ononzai this afternoon?"

"Yes, it is all arranged." Ozella took Gideon's arm. "And we have prepared something even better for tonight after dinner."

"Not a celebration?"

"Yes, an elvish celebration. We thought you could all use a little elvan therapy." Ozella laughed a silvery laugh.

"You are too good to us. Thank you, my lady." Gideon bowed and kissed her hand, winked at Jaden, and left.

When Gideon was gone, Ozella set Jaden in front of a long, wide mirror and brushed out her wet hair. Tenderly she applied light oils.

"What is that?" Jaden said. "It smells like honeysuckle, but it is so intense."

"It is honeysuckle mixed with a small amount of lemon, rose, and jasmine. When we tour our gardens, I'll show you the plants from which the oils were derived. They aren't quite like you might be used to."

"Nothing here is what I am used to."

Jaden fell silent enjoying the aroma and Ozella's peacefulness. When she finished, Jaden's long auburn hair was pulled away from her face gently with sprigs of some twisty vine littered with sparkling white flowers that fell with her curls down her back in several rows from one side of her face to the other.

Jaden said honestly, "My hair has never looked so beautiful."

"It is easy to make your hair look beautiful."

Jaden looked down. "Please tell me about the Highlands."

"Oh, you would love the Highlands. Everyone loves the Highlands. They are the greenest part of Trivar, besides the jungles of Yamis where you are from. El-kirin inhabit the forests with their cousins, the deer and elk. I love the peacefulness of el-kirin."

"What's an el-kirin?"

"You've never heard of el-kirin?"

"No, what are they?"

"They are magical creatures. During the early days of Trivar, el-kirin were common, but after the expulsion of the knights and Arwavians out of the southern part of Trivar, many of the el-kirin migrated north. There are no large cities in the north like Xannellion. Alexandria is much smaller. In the Highlands, only pockets of people live here and there. So the el-kirin roam free."

"Please tell me more. I'm not sure where I was born, but even the name Highlands calls to me. I have had dreams about places as green as Yamis, but the landscapes in my dreams felt so forsaken and barren compared to the jungle."

"Yes, I guess they could seem forsaken. However, they are anything but barren. They are filled with little glen critters, lake creatures, forest animals, and other beings that are filled with Arwavian magic. Have you ever seen a faerie?"

"When I was a child in Yamis I thought I saw a faerie once, but my adopted mother Talla, had me fan her for a week for suggesting I saw anything so ridiculous. And when I first arrived in Jeremiah, I thought I saw faeries as I woke one morning."

"Oh, that woman was very wrong. Faeries are real. It makes sense that you would see a faerie as you awoke because faeries are dream weavers. They help us face our emotions through dreams, but only if we are ready. You must be on the right path to have seen faeries. And Danae mentioned that you saw the wood nymphs. Very similar creatures. Very similar."

"How are nymphs and faeries similar? Nymphs are so grand, larger than any human I know, or elf, for that matter, and faeries, well, they are so small, fragile almost."

"I will tell you their secret if you keep it protected."

"I promise."

"Faeries and nymphs can morph."

"Morph?"

"Nymphs take on the form of trees when impure hearts are near, but when your heart is pure, they take on their Trivarian forms and dance."

"Faeries turn into trees too?"

"No, they turn into flowers and small vines or plants. It is how they keep from being harmed by Daman or his servants. If someone kills one of their plants, they have a short window of time when they can actually remove their spirits to another, safer plant. I can't wait to show you our kingdom. You will be most pleased."

Ozella smiled kindly and said, "I don't know where you came from, but your clear complexion, your thick, curly auburn hair, and your above-average height points to ancestry from the Highlands."

Jaden turned to see Ozella. "Thank you," Jaden said. "Thank you for your kindness. In less than a day you have shown me more motherly love and affection than I have known in my life-time."

Ozella gave her another hug and then said, "Jaden you are a special woman."

Jaden pulled away. "Why did you say that?"

"Look who you found. One of the best families in Trivar. Do you think all families are as good as Gideon's?"

"I am sure I have never known people so good, but what does that have to do with me? I left Xannellion with Zachariah nearly dead. I only knew one place to go. That doesn't make me special. I was desperate."

"Nothing happens by accident."

"I certainly didn't plan the events since I left Xannellion."

"Yes. But look how events have unfolded. You found your way to the home of Gideon of Jeremiah. You earned his family's love and trust, you met Franklin, who obviously thinks highly of you, you loved Benjamin before he died and he respected you, you have seen faeries and nymphs. My sons would protect you with their lives and Danae loves you. You don't accomplish all that in so short a time without being someone special."

Jaden gazed out the window and rehearsed memories of her time since fleeing Xannellion. The sun glittered off the riverbed.

"Ozella, may I share something with you?"

Ozella touched Jaden's shoulder but said nothing.

"I don't believe that I deserve their love and trust. I have lived a dark life, focusing only on my selfish needs. I have not adjusted easily to these good people and their higher, peaceful ways. They have taken me in and loved me without just cause." Jaden laughed tenderly. "I don't feel they love me because I am special. They love me because they are so good."

"I believe they would serve you without cause. They might even sacrifice what they have to protect you without cause, but I am sure they wouldn't love you like they do if you weren't special."

Jaden fell silent.

Ozella sighed. "You will see in time what you fear to see now. What I say is true. Don't ever forget you were a daughter of Gillantri before you were a daughter of Trivar."

24

El-Kirin

Ozella and Jaden caught up with Danae and Zachariah in the gardens. Immediately, Jaden noticed the brightness in Danae's eyes and the glow in her cheeks. She embraced her.

"I am glad to see you up and around," Jaden said. "The elves do work magic, don't they? How are you feeling?"

"I am feeling better, thank you."

Danae didn't offer any more explanation. Jaden realized that she had grown to care for this little nymph of a girl. She felt joy in seeing her doing well. That was still a new emotion for Jaden. Her joy doubled to see her son smiling and enjoying Danae. Jaden noticed that Danae wore a dress of light green silk that accentuated her petite figure, and Zachariah was stunning in his flowing white outfit that offset his tanned skin and brilliant green eyes.

"Well, I'd like to officially welcome you to Ononzai!" Queen Ozella said in her lilting voice. "Let your hearts be light, soak up the healing sun and fresh breezes that blow out of the canyon, and let's explore."

Gideon took Jaden's hand, Zachariah took Danae's, and they followed Ozella. Jaden reveled in the warm smell of baked earth, sage, and clean water. The sun felt pleasantly warm on her skin. She tried to maintain her calm as she held Gideon's hand. It was the comfort she felt that upset her.

She recalled her earlier conversation with Ozella. "...They wouldn't love you like they do if you weren't special," Ozella had said. "You will see in time what you fear to see now."

Part of her enjoyed the security she felt with Gideon, yet in part of her soul something didn't set right with her. She couldn't understand it, let alone try to explain it. As they walked out of the gardens she saw the stone fence that she had spied from her window earlier in the morning.

"Ozella, are those images of faeries carved into that fence? Whoever carved them didn't have a vague memory of them, I'd say."

"Each carving is an image of a real faerie whom we saved from Trivar when someone killed the flower form of the faerie and the faerie wasn't able to find a safe place to reestablish himself or herself. We welcome good creatures here and heal them if we can. Sometimes we receive them too late, but if we get them in time, there isn't a good creature we can't restore. Once they are well, we release them back into a safer region of Trivar to do the good Gillantri sent them here to do."

Jaden let go of Gideon's hand, crossed to the fence, and gently brushed her fingers over the first stone statue she approached.

"Not only is the carving perfect, but the colors are brilliant." Jaden admired how the sun played off the sparkling paints. She turned to Ozella who stood radiant in the fall sun. Ozella seemed pleased with Jaden's joy in the faerie wall. Jaden approached Gideon, feeling more comfortable when he took her hand for the second time.

"I have arranged for us to be transported to some of my favorite sights," Ozella said. Her eyes squinted mischievously.

"What are you up to?" Gideon asked.

Gideon and Danae smiled like two children waiting for the next surprise on their birthday. Ozella sang five clear notes. Moments later, through the garden came five majestic creatures. They were shaped like elk but had soft flowing manes.

"Jaden, you asked about the el-kirin."

Breathless, Jaden watched the el-kirin gallop toward her. The largest one, a male, took the lead. Each one was a slightly different shade of green, all brilliantly sparkling. As they drew nearer, she saw small, soft scales covering their skin like soap bubbles or crystals refracting the sunlight into tiny rainbows that illuminated the magnificent green all over their body.

Their silky manes flowed in perfect harmony with their muscular bodies. Gentle intelligence emanated from their eyes. Each el-kirin had unique face markings and a lightning-like horn in the middle of their forehead made of an ethereal material that Jaden could only compare to delicate frosted crystal.

Ozella spoke to the largest one in a language unknown to Jaden. The large el-kirin then looked at Zachariah and walked regally toward him. Zachariah took a step back, but Ozella said, "Zachariah, you will ride Rastanian."

"How can I ride him? He is so huge and has no saddle."

"Here in Ononzai we don't use saddles. We find that animals respond better when we leave them free."

Again, Ozella spoke in her elvan tongue and Rastanian bent down on one knee so that Zachariah could easily mount.

"Gently hold a handful of his mane, and you will be secure."

Three more times, Ozella spoke to each of the el-kirin individually. One walked toward Danae, another walked to Gideon, and another approached Jaden. Jaden boarded her el-kirin and filled her hand with its mane.

"How wonderful you are," she said under her breath. The el-kirin turned its head toward her as if it understood and then followed Ozella, who led out on her el-kirin.

"They are so comfortable to ride," Jaden mused. "I thought for sure they would be too firm, but they are not."

"El-kirin are my favorite," Danae said. "When I was a girl, I used to beg Ozella to take me for hikes on the el-kirin. I could ride all day without getting tired or sore. In fact, it might sound strange, but I actually felt better after riding them than before."

"Yes, years ago, I tried to convince Ozella to give us some el-kirin for war horses, but obviously I lost that argument," Gideon said.

Jaden spun around to see if Gideon was serious.

"No, these are not war animals," Jaden said. "Though they are strong, they are far too gentle." Gideon smiled at her, and she realized that he had been teasing.

The el-kirin loped through the clean streets of Ononzai. Jaden admired the simple but elegant streetlamps and bright, fresh houses with silk shades in the windows. There were murals on the walls painted with such realism that she wanted to jump into them and swim through their rivers, hike through their mountains, play with their children, and explore their magical hiding places.

"Who paints these marvelous pictures?" Jaden finally asked.

"Everyone has at least one dominant talent, often exhibited when they are young children, when they seem consumed with one or two things. They might love numbers and work figures all the day long, or perhaps they love to dance or sing.

"Or they might draw on everything, to their parents' chagrin, or take things apart to try to figure out how they work. Others love socializing or want to philosophize about many things. Some find they are natural leaders.

"In Ononzai when we, as parents, see these behaviors, we fill our children's lives with a little more of what they love, according to the children's requests, and maybe a little slower than they want it. We do this so their desires increase, which causes them to become proficient in their talents. They get to control how much or how little of their favorite activity they receive. It helps them take ownership and enjoy it and want more until they have developed their gifts well.

"Then we work to balance their personalities by teaching them diverse things, like how to read, write, sing, dance, draw, cultivate the land, perfect the skills of war, work with animals, govern people justly, and perform every other practical or enjoyable skill that they desire and that is necessary to live a responsible and fulfilling life.

"We teach them our history and the history of Trivar, math, science, magic, healing, and how to reverence the world around them. Of course they gravitate toward the things at which they are most gifted, and we give them plenty of time each day to focus on those things.

"By the time they reach adulthood, they are competent in their special gifts to the point where they are very useful in our society but also have a genuine respect for others' gifts. So the long answer to your simple question is that the elves who painted those murals are our gifted painters."

As Jaden watched the paintings go by, she remembered wishing to dance as a little girl. She envisioned herself as the best dancer in Trivar. Luana and Arabetta often caught her dancing and mocked her. At some point before Xzavier arrived at Yamis, she had given up dancing altogether.

They rose higher and higher through the city of Ononzai.

"Where are all your markets? I don't see any venders or foods or wares anywhere," Zachariah asked Ozella.

"Oh, you will see shortly where all the action is, young man. We do things a bit differently here in Ononzai."

As Ozella finished her sentence, they turned a corner. At the end of the street, the houses yielded to an open space filled with elves carrying baskets full of fruits and vegetables, as well as earthenware filled with fresh water, milk, or juice. Many were humming or singing as they went from one stand to the next getting the things they needed.

"Our people come early in the morning to prepare and serve according to their unique roles. Some set up their fruit or vegetable stands, while others set up their painting or dance classes. All the children go where they are drawn most, while the parents collect the food and things they need.

"We don't buy or sell. We just trade. Our dance teachers teach children in exchange for food and clothes. Our weavers trade clothes for their children's dance lessons and food. Our agriculturalists grow food for their children's lessons, and so on. Everyone works hard and gives something, and we all live abundantly.

"By the middle of the day, everyone heads down the hill to their homes where they teach their children to be well-rounded, as I spoke of earlier. Those who are without children prepare their wares for the following day."

"Do the mothers teach their children?" Jaden asked.

"Both the mother and father take an active role in teaching their children. You see, both the mother and father were raised in Ononzai and have unique talents, so it makes sense that each parent would share their special knowledge with the children. Often they work together and everyone in the family helps where needed. While one parent works with the children, the other parent may attend to other necessities.

"If the father is an agriculturalist, he might need to focus on growing for a month or two at a time, but when he is between seasons, he takes over at home while his wife focuses on her gifts. Every family is unique, but they all work it out. Some of the families have only a mother or father, and they are helped out by their extended families or by the older members of our society. No one is left alone. Everyone has a role."

"It all sounds a little too – perfect. Don't some people get sick of it?" Zachariah asked.

Ozella smiled kindly, but Jaden noticed her eyes were sad.

"Well, yes. There are some who need to leave. They usually do so willingly and find a place more to their liking, but the elvan people in general love the peace, collaboration, and consistency that allows them to become all they came here to become."

Ozella led them beyond the marketplace to an open field. Upon reaching the field, she stopped her el-kirin and dismounted.

"We will leave our el-kirin friends here. The rest of the things I have to show you we will see on foot. Follow me closely."

****

Jaden and the others followed Ozella into the open field. Right before her eyes, Jaden saw the field unveil itself. It was as if a magic blanket were slowly being lifted from the field. As they walked she saw more and more elves.

"Arway couldn't be more wonderful than this," she said in awe.

"Actually, nothing here in Trivar can compare to Arway. The material here is as different from that in Arway as dirt is to perfectly cut crystal, but we have the aid of magic to make the materials of Trivar magnify to their fullest potential." Ozella spoke with reverence that inspired Jaden.

Jaden gazed around. There were elves, male and female, tending gardens of elegant purple iris, glowing white roses, and flaming orange and delicate pink orchids. As far as Jaden could see there were gardens of one color or another that glowed brighter and brighter.

Walkways led to garden patches with arbors overhung with vines of flowers and fruits, from indigo to vibrant burgundy clematis, to honeysuckle, rose, and jasmine, all filling the air with intoxicating aromas.

After walking a ways, Danae broke free from the group and headed toward an herb garden. Danae embraced the female elf in charge of this garden. They exchanged pleasantries. The group approached them, and Danae introduced everyone.

"This is my father, Gideon, whom I believe you've met?"

"Yes, Gideon, it is good to see you again."

"And you, Lazuli. Your garden is more beautiful than I remembered."

"This is Zachariah and his mother, Jaden," Danae continued. "They are friends of ours."

"Friends of Danae are always welcome in my garden."

"May I stay with Lazuli until you get back?" Danae said. "I am getting tired, and I have missed her and her garden so much."

"Of course, dear, rest as much as you need," Gideon said.

Jaden saw the disappointment in Zachariah's eyes. Gideon saw it, too, and said, "Zachariah, you won't believe what Ozella has yet to show us."

Zachariah seemed antsy. "I am sure it is amazing. Everything here is."

Ozella led them through the gardens to the left.

"If we were to go straight to the end of this garden, we would run into a distillery where we process our most aromatic and healing plants into oils, flower waters, soaps, healing balms, and many other important products for babies, animals, and our older elves, as well as aromatic massage oils, home fresheners, skin cures, and a thousand other things for our people.

"If we were to go right instead of left back there, we would have ended up in one of my favorite places where these same plants are dried and pressed to create decorations and other items, from floral arrangements to sentiment cards. Also, through a special process they create threads from some of our plants to make our finest and most delicate clothing. Oh, I wish I could show you everything today, but we simply don't have enough time."

Soon they came to another field where they again experienced the effect of an invisible, magical blanket being lifted to reveal another unusual place.

"This is our rehabilitation center. I was telling you about this earlier, Jaden."

Jaden looked up to see faeries flying. They were so similar to the statues back in the castle garden fence that Jaden's respect for the artisans in Ononzai increased. They looked like long, thin, tiny Trivarians with wings, about the size of birds. They came in every shade of the rainbow, though some were more muted than others. All shimmered in the Ononzai sunlight.

They were busy, flying from one elf to another, taking things this way and that. Their wings and simple faerie clothing captivated Jaden. Everything about them seemed foreign. They reminded her of miniature elves or wood nymphs. Their delicate clothing flowed easily as they flew. The male faeries were sturdier than the females and, unlike many bird species, the males had the less-dramatic coloring.

One male faerie flew straight to Jaden and gave her a lovely orchid. "I heard these were your favorite, Queen Jaden."

Jaden took the flower from him, flattered. "And what is your name?"

"They call me Little Porter because I am the strongest and bravest faerie in Ononzai." He flexed his arms in front of him to show his bronzed muscles.

Jaden tried to hide her amusement and said graciously, "Thank you for the flower. I feel safer, now that you are near."

Zachariah sniffed at Little Porter.

"You don't think I am strong, Xannellion man?" Little Porter said, getting right up in Zachariah's face.

"Little Porter," Gideon said, "Zachariah is recovering from a rough journey. Maybe he'll spar with you later."

"How are things in our rehabilitation center today?" Ozella asked Little Porter.

"My queen, things are well. The seven water nymphs are improving nicely." Porter pointed to his right, where Jaden saw green-skinned water nymphs being attended to by elves. The nymphs were lying in a shallow pool of water. She wondered what happened to them, but Porter kept talking, and she did not get the opportunity to ask.

"The el-kirin," Little Porter said, "from the mountains southeast of Jeremiah are ready to be discharged to the Mountain Elves for safe return. The elves are waiting for your permission. The faeries and wood nymphs from outside of Xannellion are healing quickly.

"But we are concerned about returning them to the Xannellion woods. Xzavier seems to be burning parts of the forest near Xannellion to create more space for his army. Many magical and non-magical creatures are finding refuge and healing here. Maybe tomorrow you can check on them when you get time?"

"Yes, Porter, that will be fine. Thank you for your report."

"You are welcome, my magnificent Queen." Porter flew to her and kissed her hand before leaving. After a second, he returned and flew at Zachariah.

"I'll deal with you later!" Little Porter said.

Zachariah put his chin down toward his shoulder and glared up at Little Porter, but before he could say anything, the faerie flew away.

Ozella laughed her wind chime laugh.

"Don't pay any attention to him, Zachariah. His poor mother, Rosy, tries to balance him out, but he insists on being the protector of Ononzai. Please forgive his rudeness."

Zachariah rolled his eyes. "No harm done."

Ozella came to a small area where there didn't seem to be anything at all until the magical blanket effect revealed three translucent creatures. They were smaller than faeries, with wings like dragonflies and long thin bodies like sea horses, but they refracted the sun's light through their crystal-like bodies. They flew to greet Ozella who held out her arm, and they landed in a row.

"Oh, Ozella," Jaden breathed.

"These are my special creatures, seraquils. When they are healed, they will live with me in the palace. Listen to their beautiful music."

As she said that, the creatures let out three gentle but intense sounds that harmonized, causing great peace to flow into Jaden's heart. Enchanting sounds of the wind circling, water rippling, birds laughing, and whales conversing, all combined into one peaceful melody.

"They were too damaged to be safely returned to the wilds of the southern jungles. Say hello to the most powerful creatures in Trivar."

For a second, Jaden thought Ozella was kidding, but as soon as her thought materialized, they grew larger than dragons before everyone's eyes. Their wings morphed into powerful wings with fierce claws at the end. Their bodies grew long and thin, like a snake's, but rippled with muscle. Their songs were mesmerizing, and everyone covered their ears, except Zachariah who was spellbound. But just as suddenly, they shrank back to faerie-sized creatures and flew to Ozella.

"That is all they can do for now, but they were once able to breathe fire and death, or light and healing, depending on the goodness of the person or thing with whom they were present. They are weak now and will be for some time, even with our magic."

"When do you think they will be healed?" Zachariah seemed interested.

"I don't believe they will be back to normal ever, but I think they will be as good as we can get them in a year or so. Well, that was the finale. We'd better be getting back so that we can freshen up and be ready for our celebration this evening. Thank you for indulging me."

"Thank you, Ozella," Gideon said. "I don't know what your kingdom would do without you. I don't know what we would do without you, for that matter." He gave her a side hug.

"Gideon, you and your daughter are always welcome in Ononzai, as well as your friends."

Jaden and Zachariah bowed to Ozella.

25

Elvan Celebration

Jaden gazed out her window and breathed in the fresh air as she watched the raging Zikong. A little shiver ran through her as she remembered being on the canyon floor just over a day ago. She ran her hands down her fresh gown, unable to get enough of the fine material.

Ozella knew colors well. When they returned that afternoon from touring the kingdom, Jaden found a rich purple dress with gold accents hung in the room with a pair of simple slippers of the same color. A breeze from the open window blew through the elvan silk of her dress, caressing her body and making Jaden feel more like a queen than she felt when she was one.

There was a knock at the door. Jaden reluctantly crossed her room to the door. When she opened it, Danae stood before her in a simple cream silk dress that was equally flattering on her. "What a great color on you, Jaden. Are you ready?"

"Yes, I was just enjoying the view from my room." They left, and Jaden shut the door behind them.

"I know. I have been begging Ozella to let me stay."

"Beg her for me, too," Jaden said as they walked down the hall.

"I am serious, Jaden. I don't think I can go any farther. I am going to talk to my father about it tonight. I am afraid I have to admit defeat."

Jaden stopped and faced Danae. "You have to be kidding."

"No. I am not going any farther. I just hold everyone back. I realized that if it hadn't been for me, we would have been nearly to Alexandria by now. I just can't travel like all of you can."

"Oh, yes. I am such a hardy traveler. And by the way, if you hadn't gotten sick, we would have been down in the canyon when it flooded. Let's go to the party. You just need a few more days of rest and you'll be fine."

Danae didn't move. "I am not going to be fine."

"Danae, I have to go north. I can't stop here, as much as I'd like to. I have to find out about The Third Daughter Prophecy and if my dreams are leading me to the people up there."

"My father told Etheltread that he needs to go back to Jeremiah. You and Zachariah can go north with the elves, and when my father has made it safe for us to return, you can pick me up on your way home. Of course you must go north to find out where you are from. What's more, my father would never leave you and Zachariah here and put Ononzai in further danger. The elves fight only when it is their time to return to Arway. Had I not gotten sick, we never would have come here or stayed this long. Of course, Ozella won't tell us to leave. But Ononzai is as close to Arway as we have in Trivar. It is more sacred to us than our temple. Ozella isn't just queen of the cliff-dwelling elves of Ononzai, she is queen of all the elves in Trivar. There are other elvan settlements, but none like this."

"I have grown to rely on you," Jaden said. "I don't want to go without you. But what I am more upset about is that you are quitting. I know you can do this. I think you have real strength that you haven't tapped into yet. Now, please don't ruin the rest of my night with more of this talk. Unlike you, I have never been to a real elvan celebration, and I can hardly wait!"

"I am sorry. Let's have fun, but please understand that I have to stay here."

"Well, we'll see. Let's go to the celebration!"

Jaden turned to go and Danae followed, but a heavy feeling settled between them. They walked through the sparkling halls of Onair, following the jovial music that grew louder as they approached the main hall, simply called Joy Hall.

Jaden looked around her in wonder as they neared the hall, her mood elevating at every turn. There were so many exquisite decorations: garlands with many of the bright flowers they had seen earlier and tapestries of the same silk she was wearing, but dyed in all the many colors of Ononzai. Nothing was gaudy or overdone, and everything was exquisite.

At the entrance, Ozella stood radiant in her white sheer dress that made her white hair seem more heavenly than Jaden thought possible.

"Ozella, you are radiant."

"And so are you. Oh, what striking hair you have. Can I touch it?"

"Yes, of course. I'd hate to have something happen to me in my sleep!"

Ozella felt her hair, infusing peace into Jaden as she did. Jaden was wearing her hair down with only a bit from the front twisted and pulled to the back of her head where she tied it with the sprigs of dried flowers Ozella had used earlier.

"Well, enough of this! You have to go in and enjoy yourself!"

"Thank you, Ozella...for everything." Jaden hugged the queen and realized her concerns about Danae had disappeared.

Danae stayed behind with Ozella and Jaden entered Joy Hall. She scanned the large room for people she knew. Elves dressed in every color sang, danced, or swayed to the music. Crystal lights glowed in a bright, jovial way, casting delicate rainbows around the room. An elvan band sat on rugs on top of a platform by the back wall playing music with swing. They played in a happy, peaceful way that stirred Jaden's soul, making her want to dance.

At least ten of the elves played instruments that looked like lutes with extra-long, ornate handles. Others played long flutes carved out of ivory that sounded like song birds calling. A semi-circle of elves with harps made of the same ivory completed the band and elevated the music to what surely must be Arwavian levels. Jaden felt privileged to partake of the experience.

Female and male elves created the music while a band leader perched on a pedestal above the band's platform kept them in sync. The musicians seemed to enjoy the festivity as much as those listening. They swayed to the music and smiled and laughed with each other from time to time. It made Jaden wish she had musical skill.

Silken tapestries hung on the walls between gigantic mirrors. The mirrors' edges were etched and painted a clear color that made the etching sparkle. The etched glass seemed slightly darker than the glass around it, making it stand out. She walked over to the mirror to admire the etching more closely, when she saw in the mirror someone following her.

"You are so beautiful," Gideon said, putting his hands on her shoulders. They stared at each other in the mirror. "Every time I think you can't look more striking, you surprise me."

"In this faerieland, anything can happen."

"It is true. What have you found?"

"I love the etching on this mirror. Everything here is perfect."

"That is for sure. Would you like to dance?"

"I'd love to."

Together they walked to the middle of the room and turned to face each other. Jaden lowered her head and blushed. "It has been so long since I have danced."

"Then follow me."

"I can do that."

Gideon led her in a dance that she had never danced before. "This must be an elvan one."

"Yes. I learned it from the elves. You follow well."

"It must be the elvan magic."

They glided across the floor. Gideon's dark brown eyes peered into hers, making her insides come undone, but she did not turn away. The music slowed. Zachariah and Danae followed them into the middle of the room. Jaden waved at her son, who smiled back. Both couples held each other close as the peaceful music filled the room.

The lights grew dim and Jaden felt her heart beating against Gideon's chest. She wondered if he could feel it too but dared not ask. Zachariah and Danae faded into the distance and all the elves became a blurry background to Jaden's living dream. When the music stopped, Gideon didn't let go.

"Let's get some of the delicious smelling food. I'm hungry," Jaden finally said.

"Yes, let's eat on the balcony, though. It is cooler out there."

Jaden followed Gideon over to the tables overflowing with fragrant, exotic foods. Faeries were in charge of this part of the event. They filled small plates full of fruit and pastries. A faerie filled both of their cups full of sparkling pink juice and made sure each of them had a napkin and fork. Jaden watched joyfully as the faeries delicately flitted from one serving plate to another, waiting for Jaden and Gideon to say yes or no.

"Thank you," Gideon said kindly.

The faeries giggled. Once Gideon and Jaden had all the food they could carry, they headed for the balcony. The fresh air smelled sweet. The moon unveiled itself from behind some rogue clouds and seemed to cast a spell on the already dream-like evening.

They ate in silence, each caught up in their own thoughts. Then Jaden asked, "You never told me anything about your wife."

Gideon looked sideways at her, "You really want to discuss that tonight?"

"Well, it needs to be talked about sometime."

"How about we talk about your husband?"

"I was never actually married to him."

"What? But I thought..."

"In Yamis, no one really gets married. I was given to him, more his property than a wife. We promised each other we'd help the other accomplish our goals... I wish my life was as simple as yours." Jaden turned away.

Gideon got up and faced Jaden. "We don't have to talk about this."

"No, that's not what I mean. I must seem like such an awful person to you."

"Jaden, what were your choices?"

Jaden reveled in his caring eyes.

"I had none," she said. "He was my only way out of Yamis, and then Zachariah came along. I needed Xzavier's protection. I only stayed with him because I hoped Zachariah could take over someday and then I'd be free...safe."

"You are safe now and free. You don't ever have to go back."

Jaden put her head on his shoulder and stared out over the star-filled gorge trying to feel what free felt like. Gideon put his arm gently around her, making her stomach feel unsteady.

So she lifted her head and nodded toward him. "Now that you know about Xzavier, tell me about the wife from your simple world."

"I loved my wife. She was practical, beautiful, spunky, a true daughter of Jeremian knights. Her skills as a warrior kept me on my toes when we would spar."

"You sparred with your wife?"

"All in fun but she was tough, quick, and wiry. When it came to fighting, it was good to have her backing me up. Once the children were born, we agreed that we wouldn't fight in battle at the same time, so that if one of us went, the other would be there for them.

"When Daniel died, I didn't think any of us would recover, but when Shanae died, well, I buried myself in the flying tigers and my knights. I never thought I would dance again."

"I am sorry for your loss, Gideon. You have suffered so many losses."

"You have helped me. I don't know how I could ever have handled Benjamin's death without you."

"I didn't do anything. I made things worse."

"No, you gave me hope."

"Gideon, I want to return your love. Please be patient with me."

He put his plate down on the edge of the balcony and walked fifteen feet away from her, and then he turned toward Jaden.

"What are you doing?"

"Love me."

Jaden looked around hoping no one was listening. She whispered loudly, "You are embarrassing me."

"Love me."

"What?"

"I will stay at arm's length if you insist on keeping me here."

"Don't go so far away."

Gideon stepped toward her and then stopped a few feet away and said again, "Love me."

"This is like my dreams."

"How do you mean?"

"When Gillantri comes to me, I push him away. He won't come closer. And then he fades away. I want him to come to me, even though I push him away."

"Are you familiar with the concept of agency?"

"No. Do you mean power? I am familiar with power."

"All right, agency is like personal power. Its misuse is the reason for all the contention that ever existed in Arway or here in Trivar."

"Tell me more."

"Gillantri taught his children that agency, or our right to choose for ourselves, is more powerful than even he is. He refuses to interfere with our ability to choose, even if we, like Daman, choose to follow after darkness. So if you push Gillantri away, he will accept that as your choice. If you want him to come to you, come to him. You choose."

Jaden became quiet, thinking intently, far away.

"I like that," she said at last. "For so long I have rebelled against coercion. But after many years of having little choice, I find it difficult to avoid becoming forceful and controlling, ironically enough. It is very confusing."

"Do I cause you confusion?"

"Not you." Jaden smiled. "No, you are simple and pure. I haven't felt worthy of you."

"You are so honest that sometimes it is painful to hear you say things."

Jaden stared at this beautiful man and finally realized clearly her feelings for him.

"Gideon, come sit by me."

Gideon appeared disappointed and reticent but did as she requested. Jaden reached over and took his strong, war-seasoned hands in hers and looked into his gentle, dark eyes.

"Gideon, you are the most wonderful man I have ever met. I didn't feel worthy of you, until now. After a few short days in Ononzai, I am finally accepting that there is good in me."

Gideon looked up at the moon clearly upset.

"Gideon, please look at me. I love you like I have never loved anyone before, but every time I think of you and your dear wife, I feel as if I am trespassing. It is nothing you have done, it is just..." Jaden stopped, realizing that she was hurting him again and looked down at the ground.

Gideon gently pulled his hands free, stood, and looked out over the river. Jaden felt like crying and wanted to leave but remembered all the compassion Gideon had shown her since she arrived in Jeremiah. She forced herself to stand and put her arm around Gideon's waist. He wrapped his arm around her shoulders and they stood for a time in silence.

"Gideon."

"Jaden."

They spoke at the same time and laughed. Jaden spoke again, "I would do anything not to hurt you. But I can only be honest with you. You have taught me more about trusting and loving than I have ever known. I couldn't help but fall in love with you. You are everything I want but..."

"But it isn't right."

"No."

"Jaden, you are painfully honest and it does hurt. But you are right. I have been alone for so long, and, well, you deserve for things to be right for you. You are beautiful, strong, and amazing. But you need to find where you are from, and I need to be in Jeremiah."

"Gideon, you will always be one of my dearest companions, and I will forever be grateful to you for saving my son and me from something much worse than death. You saved me from darkness. And from myself. I can never repay you."

A tear escaped Jaden's eye and she leaned into Gideon's shoulder.
"I will be leaving in two days for Jeremiah."
Jaden put her right hand over her stomach.
"Let's not talk about that now, please. If it isn't too difficult, can we just enjoy the rest of the evening together?"
"I would be honored," Gideon answered.
Danae and Zachariah approached behind them.
"It is a lovely night," Danae said.
"Well, hello, you two," Jaden said, trying to conceal the emotion in her voice.
"Can you believe that less than two days ago, we were worn down and weary on the trail in the canyon?" Zachariah asked.
"It has been quite a journey," Gideon answered.
"Gideon, Danae wants to talk to you," Zachariah said. "And I would like to dance with my mother."
"I guess I could share her, and I would love to talk to my daughter."
Jaden glanced at Danae who averted her eyes. Zachariah took his mother's hand and they left together for the dance floor. Jaden noticed Gideon watching her leave.
"Don't worry about them, mother. Tonight is a night to celebrate."
"Yes, thank you, I am trying to remember that. Did Danae tell you what she was thinking about?"
"I think it is a great idea, but let's not talk about it now."
"All right. I will try to be jovial as an elf, though I am sure I will fail."
"I believe you have some elf in you."
Jaden laughed. She loved her son.
"This life suits you," she said.
"No. Not the life of an elf. It is a little too perfect. Although, being here has given me a lot of ideas about how I want to run Xannellion when I am king."
"You will be the best king."
Zachariah clouded over, "If I could just kill Xzavier."
"How can I be jovial as an elf if we have to talk about that?"
"All right, I will pretend like it doesn't exist, but you are forcing my hand."
"What do you mean?"
"Nothing, I am just being jovial."
"Funny," she said.
Jaden was worried but didn't push. Everything around her became a blur. She had just rejected Gideon's love. Danae wasn't going on to Alexandria. Gideon was returning to Jeremiah, and Zachariah wanted to go with him, but every part of her soul longed to go north.
Gideon tapped Zachariah on the shoulder to cut in.
"May I?"
"If I can have your daughter."
"That sounds serious."
"To dance with." Zachariah chuckled.
"She is with Arran at the moment, but I am sure she will be available soon."
Zachariah darkened. "Then I'll go get some more punch."
Jaden watched him go to the refreshment table and sighed. "Love isn't easy, is it?" she said.
"No."
"Are you all right?"
"Tonight, we are together."

"May I have this dance?" Jaden asked.

Gideon smiled.

"I would love to dance with a queen. Can she accept dancing with a heartless peasant?"

"I have been so wrong. You have the best heart I have known," she said as she allowed him to hold her close. She laid her head on his shoulder.

26

Nightflight

Jaden slept peacefully and dreamed of elvan things and Gideon. As she came to full consciousness, she remembered painfully that she had rejected him. How could she reject the man who had given her so much? But she had to be honest. She could not pretend.

There were no cheerful birds to serenade her as she woke. The cooler air that precipitated winter breathed through her open window. It seemed as if the flooding of the Zikong changed the weather, or maybe because of the changing weather the Zikong flooded. She couldn't say which. Jaden was thinking that she should get up, when someone knocked on her door.

"Jaden, are you awake? I need to talk with you."

Jaden barely distinguished Danae's soft voice as she rose, put her robe on, and went to the door.

"Just a minute," Jaden said. She felt lightheaded as she fumbled with the door knob.

Danae stood there with tears ready to brim over.

"Come in, Danae."

Danae entered and sat down by the window.

"Etheltread sent me...to give you this," she said.

It was a note written to Jaden in Zachariah's handwriting. Jaden ripped open the envelope.

"Mother," it began, "I have gone back to Jeremiah to help Gideon. He doesn't know what he's about to face. I have something that will save many lives. I know Gideon will understand once he sees. Please trust me. You will be safe with Etheltread and his kin. They will not let anything happen to you or Danae. Let Danae and Arran know that I have come to terms with them. Love, Zachariah."

"He's gone back to Jeremiah."

Danae cried softly. "I feared that. Last night, I danced with Zachariah one more time after my father and I returned from the balcony. He seemed emotionally detached and far away. He said he loved me but needed to do what he needed to do and hoped I understood. Now I know what he meant. I think it bothered him that I danced with Arran. But it was our favorite song."

Jaden put the note into her robe pocket. It felt like a bad dream. She wished she could wake up and find Zachariah near, but the pit of fear in her stomach confirmed to her that the only way out of this meant passing through more sorrow and heartache. The words of the blue-eyed man from her most recent dream came to her mind: "Things will get more difficult before you are through. But if you trust me, as it gets more difficult and you let go of your darkness, your goodness will increase and, with your goodness, your peace."

Jaden tried to hold onto what joy remained from the night before. But the tighter she held on, the sooner it flitted away. Jaden's mind filled with questions that no one but Zachariah could answer.

Danae gave her a timid hug and said, "Jaden, I will go north with you. You shouldn't go alone." She abruptly departed.

At dinner, Gideon, Jaden, and Danae ate in silence. As the sun was setting, everyone gathered in the garden to hear Gideon's address. Jaden felt sick. Zachariah was gone and Gideon was leaving.

"Etheltread," Gideon said, "when you reach Alexandria in the next fortnight, give this message to King Alfred. Hand it to him personally, and he will know what to do." Gideon handed him the note with the seal of Jeremiah on it. Etheltread placed it in the breast of his robe and nodded.

Gideon said to the rest of the group, "I will be leaving at first light with Jed and Porter on horseback so that our travel will be as speedy as possible. By Ozella's authority a battalion of elvan warriors will follow a day or so after us. These are the Ancients and best warriors in all of Trivar. They are ready to return to Arway. We are deeply grateful." He bowed to Ozella, who nodded in return.

Gideon continued, "The rest of you will be given horses, as well, and an escort of ten of Ononzai's best men. Danae, I am glad you are going north. You will ride with Arran. Please rest all you can and take care of your health. When I see you again, I want to find you strong and well." His gaze momentarily lingered upon his dear daughter.

"Etheltread," he went on, "You shouldn't have much trouble between here and Alexandria on the west road, but keep alert for prairie raiders. You will cross those lands quickly with the eye of Gillantri watching over you."

Gideon looked down. Jaden saw his struggle. He was torn in two.

"I must say goodbye tonight," he said to Jaden. "Please take care and watch over my Danae. Once things quiet down, we will send word. We will reunite soon." He gave Jaden a tender hug, embraced the elves and Ozella, and then he turned back to Danae.

"My daughter... You will never know how conflicted I have been with this decision to separate from you, but please know this – I love you."

Tears welled up in Danae's eyes. Gideon lifted her in his arms and held her close. Setting her down, he kissed her forehead. Their eyes connected. No words were needed between them. Then he walked toward the castle, and everyone besides Jaden and Danae returned to their rooms in silence.

Jaden and Danae watched the river rush and swirl away to the south. The last light of the day emanated from behind the canyon wall, casting dreadful shadows. The coolness of the evening was settling in, and Jaden pulled her scarf snugly around her. After a moment, Danae asked, "Can I share a special experience with you?"

"Of course."

"When you first saw me here in Ononzai, you asked why I looked so healthy after so short a time. The answer is twofold. First, Ozella carefully watched after me and gave me what I needed to physically heal, but even so, my spirits were low. I felt overwhelmed with all that has happened since you and Zachariah arrived in Jeremiah and didn't know how I was going to make it to Alexandria. Ozella suggested a Nightflight."

Danae paused to gauge Jaden's reaction before cautiously proceeding. "You remember me talking about that when we first entered the jungle?"

Jaden grimaced slightly as she remembered her rudeness that day, but she felt more intrigued by the subject now. For a moment her mind wandered to Gideon and how she missed him. She felt sad that she couldn't return his love but felt at peace with her decision. She refocused on his daughter.

"So, when I first arrived, I went for a Nightflight," Danae said. "It was rejuvenating but my body could only handle a short trip. Ozella suggested I go again when I felt better. I agreed. So after the party last night, I met Ozella in the library."

Jaden's eyes widened, but she motioned to Danae to continue. "We walked out the door, down the hallway, into these gardens, and we kept going until we reached an open, grassy area surrounded by desert flowers just over there." Danae pointed north. "I sat in the middle of the open area and called to the eagle. As always, it came swooping down. Ozella promised to be there when I returned."

Jaden sat down on a bench as the full moon appeared behind them and poured its gentle, healing light on them. Danae sat next to Jaden.

"Once I was on the eagle, I didn't feel frail any more. The moon wasn't as full as tonight's moon, but it was equally serene, and with the cleansing night breeze and the powerful eagle lifting me, everything came clearly into perspective. The flight is long but always seems too short when the enormous eagle finally lands gently on a patch of Arwavian grass."

"Is Arwavian grass different than Trivarian grass?" Jaden said, slightly amused by the way Danae said it, as if it were some form of precious treasure.

Danae stared intently into Jaden's eyes and became so serious that Jaden had to smile. "Oh, Jaden, it isn't like anything you have ever known. Not only is it the most glorious green, but it feels like a soft rug. It's like the grass loves to be grass! It grows like no grass is able to grow here in Trivar because light in Arway is exquisite, as if prisms were placed everywhere fragmenting sunlight into all colors of the rainbow so that the plush green grass shows all its depth and range of color."

Jaden felt intrigued.

"Anyway," Danae said, "I got down from the eagle and took off my shoes. I love to walk in Arway without my shoes. I always leave them where I land.

"There were three elves to greet me. A female elf, my guide, and two males who stayed to care for the eagle until my guide and I returned. I followed her to the sparkling green waters of the mountain springs at the base of Mt. Arway where everyone has to wash themselves clean of the dirt and grime of Trivar. I love these springs. They seemed to clean more than the outside dirt. They make me feel alive from inside. When I finished, my guide led me beyond the springs up an embankment next to a stream where she left me. I love sitting by this stream. It is one of my special places."

Danae spoke reverently about this place. Jaden sensed how sacred it was to her and listened more carefully.

"I sat on the ground and watched the sparkling rivulet run by. A water nymph swam near and poked her head out of the stream. She said, 'I am Lily. How are you this day, sweet Danae? What can I do for you?'

" 'I am seeking refreshment,' I told her, 'and I'm just grateful for the gentle sounds and the clean air. Thank you, friend. I can hardly wait to learn more about this wonderful world and travel higher. Maybe someday I will make it all the way to Gillantri's castle on the top of the mountain, but today I just need to refresh.'

" 'I send you peace, sweet Danae. Enjoy, and return soon. We have missed you.' Lily dove back into the stream and somehow, the peace was greater. How Lily did it, I have no idea.

"Soon a flower faerie poked its head out of a water lily that danced on the shore of the stream. 'Danae, we have seen your struggles. How do you feel?'

" 'I am much better, thank you, especially now that I am here,' I said.

" 'What can I do for you?' the flower faerie asked.

" 'I am just seeking peace, and your flowers are providing that nicely, thank you,' I said. I enjoyed the conversation as I sat by my stream. I love the friendly creatures of Arway. The faerie flitted from lily to lily and disappeared into the middle one again. After some time, I got up and my elvan escort appeared. 'Are you ready to go on, Danae?' she said.

" 'I think I should be getting back. It would probably be best if I got some sleep tonight, though it is tempting to stay longer.' "

"As I stood, the elf said, 'Danae, there is more here for you tonight.' I looked at my guide questioningly and she explained, 'Gillantri needs to talk with you.'

" 'With me?' I said. I was nervous. I knew things like this happened, but what in the world could he want with me...tonight?"

Jaden blanched at the thought of Danae speaking to Gillantri. It was hard to believe what she was hearing, but she didn't dare interrupt, partly because of Danae's reverent manner and partly because of a curiosity growing inside of her.

" 'I will take you there,' my guide told me. I followed her in tranquil silence through a manicured garden that followed the stream. We crossed gentle meadows, over stone bridges, and by colorful fruit trees. Iridescent butterflies fluttered through the garden with silky wings that sparkled in the sunlight as they danced from flower to flower.

"I noticed a flower that looked like the common daisy, but there was nothing common about it. Glittering daisies of every shade of the rainbow covered the landscape. I had a funny impulse to eat one, and it made me giggle. To my surprise my guide perceived my thoughts and said, 'I've wanted to eat those myself and tried once when I was a child. They don't taste very good, even here!'

"My guide slowed as we passed translucent crystal statues that illuminated the area around them. These statues, some of which were fountains, were carved into wondrous creatures that appeared to be animated: a pair of winged horses at the entrance, lifelike rabbits ready to spring, lions with manes that seemed to be tousled by the breeze, and many more remarkable creatures I had never seen before.

"Then we emerged from the crystal statue garden into an open field of brilliant green framed by a stone wall. A stone pathway led to a pavilion on the other side. A serene stream wound around through the field creating bubbling sounds..." Danae paused for a moment, embarrassed at her own rapture. She composed herself.

"I'll do my best to describe what I saw next. Until then, I had been among trees, meadows, and gardens with streams, but beyond this field opened a view of Mount Arway. Flanked by lesser mountains and foothills, it rose in grandeur against a sunrise sky of glowing reds and yellows.

"There were three great waterfalls in the foothills. I was longing to go there someday, when something entered my left peripheral view. I turned to see a monarch eagle soaring over the pavilion at the far edge of the field toward me. I had never seen one of these birds in its natural environment, and it overwhelmed me. I walked toward it, mesmerized by its strength, grace, and beauty, but it passed over me, and when I turned, I noticed my guide had remained in the garden of crystal statues. She waved me forward toward the pavilion in the direction from which the eagle had come.

"Tentatively, I walked to another stone bridge that crossed the stream. There were white lilies at both ends of the bridge that filled the air with rich aroma. I found myself again gazing toward the waterfalls as I walked. The path curved toward them so that I could see them without turning my head. They stirred my soul and seemed to heal me as they washed down the mountainsides.

"I wondered if they filtered into a great mountain lake. A mist rose from amidst the trees below the falls. I mused that the little stream behind me must come from that lake. I looked at the stream, tempted to run across the grass and soak in its waters and feel connected to it all, but I kept walking despite my desire. Distracted by the paradise around me, I ended up in front of the pavilion without realizing it.

"It was then that I felt something different, some presence familiar to me but forgotten. My heart pounded and my palms sweat. I felt I was being watched and looked back over the field but couldn't see my guide. I scanned toward the mountains and at the pavilion and my heart jumped.

"Jaden, a man looked down at me with the bluest eyes you have ever seen. I felt my heart pounding a bruise on the inside of my ribs but lost my ability to flee."

Jaden was holding her breath.

"At once, I realized who he was and said, feeling rather embarrassed, 'I am sorry, your Majesty,' and I bowed before him in the most reverent way I knew how.

"He simply said, 'How are you, my precious Danae?' His tenderness made me cry. It didn't make sense at the time, but on my return flight I realized that, though I was loved in Trivar, Gillantri's love was so much purer. My heart longed to accept his love.

"When I found my voice I said, 'I am well, thank you.' I didn't know what else to say. I looked up into his strong, handsome face, wishing that I never had to leave.

" 'Come and sit with me, my dear, we have much to discuss...' "

"Danae, thank you," Jaden interrupted. "I appreciate your story... I see why you must feel so much better. All of a sudden I don't feel well. I need to go back and get some rest before tonight. Can you tell me the rest later?"

Danae seemed to understand. "That was practically the end anyway. Can I return with you?"

"No. I mean, no, thank you, I can find my way back... I just need some time to think and rest..."

She rose and left Danae in the garden. Heading for the palace, her heart was pounding and her hands were sweaty. She trembled. She couldn't get the blue-eyed man's face out of her mind. Her legs felt weak, but they did not fail her. So she started to run.

27

Faerietale

Jaden sat in her room, alone and lonely. Danae's story upset her tremendously, though she didn't know why. She knew Gillantri was troubling to her and that her heart hurt when she thought of the blue-eyed man in her dreams, but fear blocked her from examining her emotions further. She went to the window. The moon was high now, and across the river's surface the dancing light revealed rapids, rivulets, and currents moving together in a magnificent display of nature's power.

A knock at the door surprised her. She pulled herself away from the window and cautiously walked toward the door. Hesitant, she forced herself to open it. A soothing voice dispelled all concern.

"Ozella, come in. I did not expect you."

"Of course you didn't." Ozella laughed. "That is when you need me the most."

"Need you?"

"Yes, that is the way with Arwavian creatures of all kinds. We come when least expected but needed the most. I have a story to share with you."

Jaden felt clammy and nervous at once. "Did Danae send you? Because I don't want to hear the rest of her story tonight."

"You will come to Gillantri in your own time. My story is about who you are and what you came here to become. To be honest, coming to Gillantri and finding out who you truly are and will become is one in the same. Children of Gillantri are complex beings of power who must learn about their unique facets and how to unite these elements in order to become whole someday."

Jaden wasn't sure she understood but dared not interrupt because of the calming effect Ozella had on her. She didn't want to disturb the peace she was beginning to feel. Ozella crossed to the sofa in the sitting area of Jaden's spacious room and bade Jaden to sit beside her. Jaden gladly obliged. Ozella gently placed a hand on the other woman's hand as she spoke.

"There is a faerietale we teach our children here in Ononzai. It is one that came to us from Arway at the beginning of Trivar. I am going to tell you the simplified version for lack of time. I love this faerietale."

Jaden closed her eyes and envisioned herself as a child in the lap of a nurturing mother. She felt safe and loved. She drifted away to a safe and serene place as Ozella told the story "...of a faerie who emerged from a blackberry blossom one spring near a strawberry field. In the strawberry field dwelled many playful strawberry faeries whom the blackberry faeries loved and adored. In the faerie kingdom, there was one critical rule. To stay alive, the faeries had to stay away from any body of water.

"They lived by a great loch. But no faerie ever flew near the shore. This never bothered our story's blackberry faerie, as everything she needed was right around her little blackberry bush and in the strawberry fields nearby.

"One day a horn blew from a far away hill. It called all the faeries away from their bushes and fields to the great stone circle and palace of the blueberry faeries. The blackberry faerie had never been away from her bush and was frightened and excited by the call. She flew with her strawberry faerie friends until all the faeries and faes of the land began to form lines leading to the great stone circle.

"The little blackberry faerie had never seen so many different faeries from all varieties of plants around the kingdom. And the large faes bewildered her with their beauty and grace. The faeries and faes traveled slowly, reverently toward the great palace.

"The blackberry faerie tip-toed on the edge of a stone bridge that spanned an inlet of the great loch. She was pondering why it was unlawful to approach the water, when an iridescent flying fish with silvery blue, green, and purple scales leaped into the air near her and swallowed a lightening bug before diving back into the depths of the inlet.

"Her heart fluttered. But she felt no fear. In fact, the little blackberry faerie wanted with all her soul to jump in after the fish. Her strawberry faerie friends saw the allure and impulse in her eyes and pulled her away from the edge of the bridge and back into line with the other faes and faeries.

"As the strawberry faeries approached the great stone circle palace, they grew quiet and fearful. An eerie blue light emanated from the entrance causing everyone and everything to appear cold and unnatural. The water consumed the blackberry faerie's thoughts, as did her longing to enter into it. Without this preoccupation she would have been frightened by the eerie new environment, too.

"As everyone moved into the palace, she found herself close to the front where tall candelabras towered with sapphire blue candles. Next to the candelabras, a platform rose high above their heads.

"On the platform were two gaudy golden thrones where two blueberry faes sat. They might have been considered handsome if their makeup, clothing, and jewelry were not so garish and tawdry. The blueberry fae king rose and began to speak of power and greatness and how unity would bring greater things to come for the kingdom.

"Looking about, the blackberry faerie discovered that, during the orderly procession into the palace, she was separated from her friends. She searched to find them. An aged male fae caught her eye. Something about him disquieted her, and yet she felt a strong connection to him.

"No sooner did she turn her focus to the blueberry fae king than a hand touched her shoulder. Spinning around, she found the old fae looking kindly upon her with his finger to his lips to request her silence. He handed a neatly folded note to her. With a questioning look, she took it. He knelt beside her and whispered, 'I see greatness in you.'

" 'What do you mean?' she whispered.

" 'The supposed greatness this blueberry king speaks of is servitude to him. The greatness I see in you is true greatness. If you follow the instructions in my note, I will show you your greatness.'

"She opened the note, but she did not know how to read. Turning pink, and appearing more purple than pink in the blue light, she stared at the characters on the page. The aged fae observed her shame and explained, 'It says that I am the true king of this land and am come to reclaim my kingdom. I need one faerie of virtue who is willing to risk all, and we can succeed.

" 'If you are the faerie I believe you to be, follow the road next to the loch toward the great forest later this day. I will send a being of light to guide you to where I live. I will teach you my ways and together we will make this kingdom truly great again.'

"The little faerie shuddered. 'But you can see all who are following the blueberry king. How can you ever succeed with only me?'

" 'It will take courage and virtue,' said the aged fae, 'but I see that in you. Will you follow me?'

"By then, the strawberry faeries had found their way through the crowd to their friend. Having disturbed many faes and faeries en route, the blueberry king glared down from his high platform to quiet the crowd.

"The blackberry faerie shied away from the old fae and allowed her friends to surround her. Things settled down as the blueberry king continued to speak of grandeur and greatness and the sacrifice needed to make this kingdom greater."

Jaden began to feel uneasy again, with that same emotion that overwhelmed her in the garden listening to Danae. She didn't want to offend Ozella, so she fought the compelling urge to run and hide. She turned her head away and tried to be still, but her efforts were in vain.

Ozella must have realized this because she stopped speaking and began singing a lullaby, soft and low. Her voice was inherently melodious, and singing a simple lullaby had an enthralling, lulling, heavenly effect. Jaden fell into a light sleep.

Sometime later, she opened her eyes. Ozella was gone and she was alone again. Jaden couldn't sleep any longer. Her heart ached that her son was gone and Gideon would be leaving early the next morning. She blocked out everything Danae said about Arway, as well as Ozella's faerietale, and if any of it found its way into her mind, she quickly thought of something else.

She went to the window. She opened it and drank in the night air. Outside, the moon had set behind the canyon walls and stars peeked through wispy clouds. She longed to roam the gardens, so she put on a robe and left her room. Finding her way through the dimly lit halls, she escaped to the garden.

It refreshed her instantly to walk among the flowers and well-manicured landscaping. It was nothing like Xannellion's stone, wrought iron, and cement. She recalled with sadness Danae's burned garden in Jeremiah and hoped it would grow back again. She wondered if Trapton was recovering well. Benjamin's image as he wrestled with that overgrown cat made her smile.

Then the memory of his broken body in the temple made her cringe. She looked to the skies that were almost completely clear now and took a deep cleansing breath to regain control of her thoughts. The sweet and spicy scent of Corsican mint wafted from the cracks in the walkway where the minty-smelling moss grew.

How the elves grew moss in this dry climate momentarily perplexed her, until she remembered Ozella's tour of the kingdom and masterful gardening elves. Of course elves could grow moss in the desert! She was digging her toes into the mint and smiling, when someone bumped into her. Fear surged through her, but Gideon's familiar, gentle touch relieved her panic.

"Jaden, you are safe."

"Oh. Gideon. What are you doing up?"

"I might ask the same of you."

"I couldn't sleep."

"Walk with me then. I haven't been successful in that regard either." Gideon took her hand and walked with her under a trellis of late honeysuckle vines that still smelled sweet after the warmth of the day.

"I'm sorry about Zachariah. You have done so much to help us." Jaden couldn't find words to convey her pain.

Gideon gave her hand a gentle squeeze and kept walking. Jaden's emotions surfaced. She cried silent tears that wouldn't stop. She tried to hide them by looking away, but her heart wanted to share the pain, though she knew his pain must be equally difficult to bear and she had already been too much of a burden to him. Back and forth, she argued with herself until it became difficult to breathe evenly, and she realized she must either go back to her room or admit her pain. She released his hand and turned to go.

Gideon put his hand on her shoulder. She remembered the time he had stopped her outside the temple in Jeremiah. Here again he was facing excruciating pain but was ready to help her face hers instead.

"Gideon, I want to help you. You must be struggling, and yet...all I can do is cry for my own selfish heartache. I am sorry."

He turned her to face him and enveloped her in his arms. She gave in to the comforting feeling of safety. "I want to help and not always be in need of help myself," she tried to say as a sob caught in her throat.

Gideon looked into her eyes. She noticed tears in his, as well.

"You don't know how much you help just by being here," he said. "I felt so alone. I am so glad you couldn't sleep. It was a tender mercy of Gillantri that you came out when I needed you. Thank you."

Jaden gently caressed his handsome, sad face and then melted once again into his arms, trying to give more than take. Gideon pulled back, but keeping one arm around Jaden's shoulders, he led her to a patch of grass where he had brought his sleeping bundle and unfolded it.

"Come, let's look at the stars and we'll talk."

Jaden wiped her face and gladly sat down next to Gideon in the starlight that was growing brighter as the night wore on.

"What can I do for you?" she said.

Gideon smiled and looked away. "It is enough that you're here."

"What is on your mind?"

"You are stubborn, aren't you?"

Jaden waited. Gideon chuckled. "All right. Tell me Danae's body will handle traveling to Alexandria well."

"She is her father's daughter. She is resilient."

Gideon laughed. It sounded so pleasant. Why couldn't she love this man?

"What else is bothering you?" Jaden said.

"How are we supposed to face a dragon army?"

She fell silent, gazing up at the sky full of stars. A thought surfaced that she had never considered before. "Gillantri wants you to succeed. He will help you."

Gideon lay back on his elbows. "Do you really believe that?"

"I know I would never be where I am now without your faith in him and your faith in me."

"Yes, that is what I have to rely on. Gillantri. But it is going to take more than faith."

Jaden didn't know how Gideon could win against Xzavier and could not offer more suggestions in advance of the battles he faced.

"I don't know what to tell you more than I have already about Xzavier and his dragons. But there is something else worrying you, Gideon of Jeremiah."

"You see in me more than I wish to reveal. So I am finally resigned to return, but..."

"But you miss her already."

"Yes, I miss Danae. But I also miss you."

Silence followed. In the dark she could hear her heart pounding. Gideon reclined and put his hands behind his head.

"I will miss you, too."

"So now that you know what is on my mind, tell me what is on yours."

Jaden paused and then laid her head down next to him.

"I miss Zachariah. I am sad he chose to leave. I don't want him to fight, but he feels he needs to, and I don't want to think about the battles you both face. I won't think of you being gone tomorrow. But I do feel better being with you tonight."

Clusters of stars shined brightly in the darkness, taking Jaden's thoughts far away. For a time, while Gideon, who was finally able to sleep, breathed deeply, she lay next to him. But sleep wouldn't come for Jaden. Just when the eastern sky brightened ever so slightly, Jaden said, "You had better get ready. Dawn is about to break."

"Did you stay here all night?"

"It was peaceful, and I didn't want to leave you."

"Thank you." Gideon sat up on his elbow and looked at Jaden.

"It is the least I could do. I wish I could do more..." Jaden felt a lump forming in her throat.

"Everything will be right soon," Gideon said. He smiled. "You are dear to me and will always be, but you are right. I will never be over my wife, and it would be unfair to any other woman in my life. But thank you for being there for me during this time. I have truly needed you. Please know you always have a friend in Gideon of Jeremiah!"

Jaden leaned over and hugged Gideon, not wanting to let go. Through her thick, curls Gideon said, "Everything is going to be all right."

"I know. Just...please be careful."

"We will send for you and Danae once it is safe."

She looked away.

"Jaden."

"What?"

"I hope you find what you are looking for in Alexandria."

"Oh, Gideon." Jaden faced him. "Please..."

"We'll be fine."

Gideon helped her to stand. She hugged him one last time before walking up the garden path to the palace. She only looked back once. Gideon was still watching.

28

Moving On

Two days later, Danae silently gazed out the window while Jaden packed. When Jaden finished, she headed out of her room nodding for Danae to follow. As Danae stood, she wondered out loud, "Why did he do it? I don't understand."

Jaden stopped and faced Danae. "Who?"

"Zachariah."

Jaden answered, "He must avenge himself of his father's deceit and treachery. It is in his blood. I spent all my life working to achieve and maintain power and glory under the evil counsel of Xzavier, and we taught our son the same. Being with you and your father has changed us more than we like to admit, but we both have a long way to go."

"He should have listened. It isn't right. I fear for him. I miss him." Danae dropped her head.

Surprised that Danae was so affected by Zachariah's disappearance, Jaden smiled kindly. "If anyone can take care of himself, Zachariah can."

Danae's eyes softened with gratitude for Jaden's reassurance. She gazed out the window at the canyon and took a deep breath.

"I am glad you decided to come north."

"I don't know how I can do it, but at the celebration before my father left, we talked," Danae said as she followed Jaden out of the room. "He understood my concerns, but he told me something that wouldn't leave me at peace until I changed my mind."

Jaden remembered the night of the celebration. "That was the best night of my life."

"Aren't elvan celebrations wonderful?"

"I have never experienced anything like it."

"That night as I stood on the balcony with my father, he told me a story. I'll spare you the entire story, but he told me about how I nearly died when I was a young girl because of a lung infection. I was so sick that no one but the elves could help me. After a full moon of being delirious with fever and near to death, something changed. He asked me what changed and did I remember?"

Danae paused, deep in thought. After a moment, she continued, "I did remember, but it is so simple that I didn't realize how significant it was. I remember hallucinating because of my high fever. I could feel my spirit trying to return to Arway, torn between the difficulties of Trivar and the peace that I wanted to return to. Even as a child I felt weak and out of place here. Then I remembered my family: my brother, mother, and father, and my dreams of doing some good here... I could feel Gillantri urging me to stay and finish my work, but I was afraid. After a short time, it was clear that I truly wanted to stay.

"After I told him this, my father said, 'Danae, I think you are trying to stay in Ononzai now for the same reason you wanted to go to Arway then: to avoid inevitable growing pains and fears instead of facing them.'"

Danae stopped speaking, emotion holding her back. The tears quietly cascaded down her cheeks. "He was right. I am scared. I don't want to go forward. I want Ozella to protect me and Arran to love me. I don't want to go back to my life and feel pain, fear, and weakness. But if I never face those things, I am dooming myself to always live with them. You and my father are right. I need to face my fears and go forward, and that is what I will do."

Jaden gave her a hug. "Well done, Danae."

They reached the stables to find Arran, Meadthel, and Etheltread organizing horses for everyone and fitting the horses with saddles, gear, and provisions. All that was left for Danae and Jaden was to tie their own knapsacks to the backs of their horses.

Jaden nudged Meadthel. "I thought no one used saddles here in Ononzai?"

He laughed. "Are you teasing me, Queen Jaden? Being around elves brings out good things in you. When we leave Ononzai, we usually use saddles, but only on our horses, never the el-kirin. It helps us to be more comfortable during long, difficult travel and allows us to carry more provisions. Etheltread, you need to keep an eye on this one, she is becoming more elvish every day!"

Etheltread and Meadthel laughed, making Jaden feel lighter. Arran motioned for Danae to come to him.

"Mother gave me strict instructions to make sure that you don't get too worn out again," Arran said. "We have placed her special saddle on Salvador, her favorite horse, so that you can be as comfortable as possible. You must stay warm. Now that the days are cooler, dehydration isn't going to be such a threat, but you will get cold if you don't wrap up and keep enough food in your body. I put an extra blanket on your saddle and an extra helping of breads and dried meats in the pouch by your knapsack. Don't ever get too hungry. My mother also sent your green and cream dresses along, as well as some of her favorite flower essence. She said, 'A woman needs these things.'"

Arran smiled and added, "Since Zachariah isn't here, I will ride with you, okay?"

Danae smiled. "Of course. Please tell your mother how grateful I am for her. I don't know how I can ever repay her." Their eyes met and unspoken gratitude and fondness passed between them.

"She thinks of you as a daughter and would be pleased to see you anytime. You are always welcome in Ononzai. Hopefully, next time it won't be under such dangerous circumstances. But now we must get you safely north. Do you remember her instructions?"

"Yes, I will stay warm by wrapping in blankets and keeping food in me, though I fear I won't fit into my lovely dresses if I eat all that is in that pack." Danae winked.

Etheltread addressed the rest of the company. "All right, I need everyone's attention."

Everyone finished up their last knots, got onto their horses, and listened. "We will be traveling through the high desert above the canyon. The terrain is flatter than in the gorge, but windier. There isn't fruit to pick, and very little water can be found. Fortunately, we don't have long to go before we reach the prairie lands. Still, try to conserve water as much as possible.

"We need to travel quickly. Time is very important to Gideon and his troops in Jeremiah. We must get word to the King of Alexandria that his troops are dearly needed to stand against Xzavier and his dragons. We will be traveling like we did after Danae got sick, from before sunlight until dark."

Everyone groaned. "I know how you feel," he responded, "but we will be on horseback, and it really is most practical. Does everyone understand? I will lead out. Gregors, I need you and Roneem to take up the rear. All right, let's go."

Danae settled into her saddle, wrapped the extra blanket around her, and leaned back against Arran. It felt cold as soon as they left the stable, and they weren't even out on the open plateau yet. They rode two by two, Jaden next to Danae and Arran, behind Etheltread and Meadthel, and in front of Gregors and Roneem. Six more of their kinsmen followed at the rear of the company.

****

Jaden was amazed at the change of scenery between Ononzai and Alexandria. They traveled through high plateau desert with its cold nights and hot days, sparse shrubbery and few animals, to the Plains of Wheelen blanketed with dried grass hiding snakes, rabbits, and coyotes, while above soared hawks and vultures.

After hearing about the raiders in the plains, Jaden felt relieved when they had reached the edge of the plains with no trouble. The last part of their journey commenced at the Great Northern Forest, which was presently a dark line on the horizon. A full day before they would reach the safety of the forest, Jaden noticed that the air smelled different. Instead of the sage and grassy fragrance of the plains, the wind carried a sweet, spicy aroma from the forest.

"What is that wonderful smell?" Jaden asked.

"That is the smell of damp pine needles warmed on the forest floor," Arran said. "Most of this forest consists of evergreen trees, although there are patches of deciduous trees, Alders, Big Leaf and Vine Maples, some Aspens, and other trees. The shrubbery will be thick but not as thick as in the south." Arran smiled as Jaden inhaled deeply.

That night they slept on the open plains. Etheltread announced that by next evening they would enter the Great Northern Forest. Late into the night, a breeze stirred Jaden and disturbed her slumber. She recognized the smells the wind carried, though she had never been to these woods before. The unnerving mix of emotions that the fragrances evoked surprised her.

Jaden opened her eyes and sat bolt upright, shaking her thick auburn hair and looking around, her heart and mind racing. Up in the northern sky a cold fire seemed to be burning. Bright, cool colors flowing like an ethereal luminescent ribbon filled the sky. Jaden held her breath. Arran came and sat beside her. He put his hand on her shoulder.

"Time for a changing of the guards?" she stammered.

"Yes, it's time for me to get some sleep," Arran said with a yawn.

Jaden pointed to the sky. "Is this a dream? I've dreamed of lights like this before."

Arran laughed quietly. "No, you are not asleep. That is called the Aurora Borealis, or more commonly, the Northern Lights. The elves named them years ago for one of their queens, Aurora. Those lights in the sky only become more dazzling as you travel north. This pales by comparison."

Jaden stared in wonder as the colored lights floated up and down across the entire northern sky.

"It is like they are a part of my soul. The smells of the Great Northern Forest and these lights...so familiar..."

Arran looked at Jaden intensely, causing Jaden to turn away from the lights and look at him.

"It is because you are from the north," he said.

"Before Cannote died, he told me he thought I was from the north and your mother thinks so, too. I am told I can learn more about The Third Daughter Prophecy in the north, but I wonder how in the world could I have come from the north? Not until I had my Third Daughter dream had I ever given any thought to the north at all. Don't you think that as a child with all my longing to find my real home I would have considered the north?"

"What did the people of Yamis believe about the north?"

Jaden laughed. "They were proudly ignorant of anything outside of Yamis. When we got to Xannellion, opinions of the north were even more negative. There hasn't been open trade between the north and south for centuries...not since Xannellion has been in control. Trivar has been cut in two for hundreds of years."

"What does your heart say?"

She felt stretched and challenged by his question. "I don't know that I want to consult my heart. It hasn't been exactly stable lately."

Arran laughed again. "I'll tell you this. You look a lot more like the people from the north than the people of Yamis."

Jaden laughed bitterly. "You could say that about any major city north of Yamis. In fact, most of Trivar looks more like me compared to people in Yamis."

Arran said, "When I first met you, I had a strange feeling that I knew you or knew of you. I have thought a lot about it during our adventures together. May I share with you some thoughts I have had?"

Jaden hesitated. "I am not sure, but I can't say no."

"Years ago, our brothers from north of the Highlands, the Silver Elves from the land of snow, were asked to help with a delicate situation. I have hesitated to tell you these things because I am afraid it will only give you more clues with no real answers. One time, I found one of the Silver Elves when I was sailing to Rosehannah on other business."

"Rosehannah? Where is that?"

"In the northern Highlands. Rosehannah is now called Wallace and is an ancient sister city to Alexandria. Anyway, I found the Silver Elf half dead on the sea shore where we stopped for water. He had been beaten and left for dead by bulbanes and the fallen lord Daman. Nothing the elf said made sense at the time. He said that a baby had been taken from him by pirates. A special Highland baby. That's all the Silver Elf said before he died. I buried him and sent word to his people.

"When I got to Rosehannah, only four people remained, a village elder and three children. All the villages in the area were in an uproar about bulbanes and

Daman raiding multiple cities looking for The Third Daughter. No one knew if The Third Daughter had for sure been born, but anyone who had a baby girl sought protection from the elves. The elves could only help so many. Many babies were killed but some escaped. I know that at least one baby, probably a female, for Daman left the males alone, ended up with pirates. The elf gave his life for that baby."

Jaden was somewhere far away and lost in thought.

"I hope I haven't upset you, Queen Jaden?"

"No. But a coincidence sends shivers through my soul. Have I ever told you about my pirate protectors? The ones who brought me to Yamis?"

"No."

The last time Jaden had told the story was to her son, Zachariah, the night Xzavier made a fool of himself at his own party. After explaining it to Arran, she asked, "Do you think I could have been that baby you heard about all those years ago? Do you think..."

"Like I said, I don't have any answers for you. But if you were that baby, you are probably from one of the noble families in the Highlands, considering that the family was able to obtain an elf protector. You certainly wouldn't have been an ordinary lass from the Highlands."

"Do you think I am one of The Third Daughters?"

Arran got very serious. "I can't say for sure, but in Ononzai we believe that The Third Daughter was kept hidden from Daman and returned safely to the Highlands."

"I want more than ever to find answers about where I am from and how I am connected to The Third Daughter Prophecy. If I am not a Third Daughter, why did I have that dream? If I am that same child who ended up with pirates, did my parents perish with the rest of Rosehannah? Were they of royal blood? Where are they from? What did they look like? Are they the people in my dreams?"

Arran remained silent.

"You are right, Arran, now I have more questions, but I also have another piece to the puzzle. I hope that the people of Alexandria have more clues for me. I wonder if I could get all the way to the Highlands during our stay? The Aurora...what do you call them?"

"Aurora Borealis."

"They are incredible, aren't they?"

"Yes they are." Arran watched the sky with Jaden for a moment before saying, "Jaden, I told you I had a couple thoughts for you. I shared one of those thoughts, my story of the Silver Elf. I have another thought, one that Ozella made me promise I would share with you. It is a faerietale we tell our children..."

Jaden turned quickly to look into Arran's eyes to make sure he wasn't teasing her like his brothers often did. But Arran's eyes were somber.

"I loved the faerietale you speak of but couldn't finish it the other night with your mother."

"Yes, she told me. She instructed me to tell you the shorter version. She also told me that her intuition led her to believe that you need to hear the rest of this faerietale. She said she believes it was revealed here to Trivar specifically for you."

"What did she mean? That scares me." Jaden felt herself become clammy and uncomfortable all over again.

"Ozella is my mother and I love her dearly, but I don't always understand what she says until time goes by and I live more of life. I believe it will be the same for you. But when the day comes that you understand, it will be the right time."

Jaden couldn't argue with Arran. Of all the elves, he was the most unassuming and disarming. "Then tell me the rest of the faerietale, if you must."

Arran smiled and continued exactly where Ozella had left off. "The blueberry king finished his grand speech and the little blackberry faerie carefully folded her note and slid it behind her waist belt. She argued with herself as if she were arguing with the aged fae. 'The blueberry king talks of true greatness, a great and strong kingdom with all of us working together toward that greatness. That is what I want to be a part of.'

"A voice from within her responded, 'No, true greatness can't come if you are all slaves to the blueberry faes and faeries. You will see, my young friend, that I offer the only path to joy, freedom, and true greatness through learning and exercising virtue and courage.'

"She could see his kind eyes in her mind but discarded the vision and departed from the blueberry palace that brimmed over with faes and faeries. Her strawberry faerie friends accompanied her back to her blackberry bush near the strawberry fields.

"Days, even moons, went by until the leaves on her blackberry bush turned red and orange. But she never went to the forest. In fact, the blackberry faerie forgot about the old fae... Until one day, as the sun was setting over the great loch, she found herself drawn to its shoreline.

"The urge inside of her to be near the water was so great that she flew over the shoreline. She was enthralled by her image reflected back to her. She broadened her gaze and stared across the expanse of water. It enticed her until she almost convinced herself to dive below the surface, but at that instant the old fae's sad and disappointed countenance appeared in her mind, causing her to retreat.

"This was fortuitous because, not a moment later, a large fish with thin, sharp incisors jumped into the air and nearly caught her in its teeth. Scrambling through the air to get to the shore, she tumbled and landed near a patch of grass. During her tumble, she lost the note from the old fae that she had carefully placed inside her waist belt all those moons ago."

Jaden couldn't help thinking of the blue-eyed man's sorrowful eyes. To Jaden, he had seemed disappointed in her.

"This story makes me sad."

Arran paused in his narrative. "Missed opportunities are sad. But this faerie isn't your average creature. She was destined for more than frolicking in the strawberry fields. Relax while you watch the Aurora Borealis and enjoy the aromas carried on the breeze from the forest, and let me finish this faerietale. I think you will like it in the end."

Jaden took in the sights and smells as Arran's voice soothed her.

"Walking slowly back toward the water where the paper ruffled in the evening breeze, the image of the aged fae came clearly to her mind again. Why had she been so afraid? Truly the blueberry king was more frightening. And why did the old fae look so sad? She picked up the letter and placed it in her belt, and without another thought left her friends and her bush and flew toward the forest at the edge of the loch."

"As she neared the forest, fear gripped her little faerie heart again. What if there was no being of light there to show her the way to the old fae? She slowed down and began searching the woods with her eyes as she approached. The sun's last rays of light were blazing into the loch, displaying the final moments of its power, and this allowed her to see farther into the forest than usual, but there was no sign of any being, great or small, not even a mourning dove or squirrels gathering their last nuts for the day. And then the sun faded and the forest became dark and fearsome.

"What should she do? It would not be safe for her to go into the forest alone with owls and other nighttime predators on the hunt. But she couldn't give up and go back now. Yet, all was dark and no one was coming for her.

"The little blackberry faerie stopped fluttering and landed on the ground between the loch and the forest and focused all her faerie energy on the old fae's face and the feeling of his soul in an attempt to connect with him. 'Please, dear old fae! I am here. I am sorry I am so late, but I want you to teach me. I want to learn. Please help me find you!'

"With eyes closed, she concentrated on her yearnings until she felt shaky and tired. When she opened her eyes again, it was almost pitch dark. Midnight blue with nuances of turquoise settled upon the horizon. As darkness consumed the land, the faerie's soul grew darker, as well. Hope faded, and she considered giving up and returning to her bush.

"Then a single point of light from the forest penetrated the black night. The faerie's heart fluttered. Was this an answer to her deepest desire, or was it danger? She remembered the old fae's words about sending her a being of light to help her find him. Could it be?"

Jaden wondered why Arran stopped. He smiled kindly.

"I don't mean to be impolite," he said, "but I can hardly keep my eyes open. Can I finish this story once we arrive at Alexandria?"

While she could hardly endure listening to Danae's and Ozella's disconcerting stories earlier, Jaden now wanted terribly to hear this story to the end. But she understood how tired Arran must be.

"If you need sleep, I understand. But I look forward to the remainder of this faerietale."

"You need sleep, as well."

Jaden laughed. "I am afraid I won't sleep much tonight. The sights and smells and new thoughts are too stimulating, but I will be fine."

Arran nodded and left with a promise to finish the tale soon.

Jaden watched the sky shift and roll, and she inhaled the delicious smells and pondered over the little blackberry faerie and her plight until early in the morning when she finally had to close her heavy eyes and sleep.

29

Alexandria

At the end of the next day, they entered the forest between boughs of pine, cedar, and hemlock. It was so calm in the twilight that Jaden felt protected and safe amidst the trees. The Maples, especially the smaller Vine Maples, were dressed for autumn in brilliant reds, bright oranges, and dazzling yellows with a few remaining smatterings of green. In the direct light of the setting sun, the colored trees glowed against the backdrop of evergreen trees and green flora.

They camped three nights in the forest. Most of the birds had flown to warm southern places, and Jaden saw abandoned nests. Occasionally, an owl hooted, giving the forest an empty and forsaken feeling.

Jaden loved watching the grey squirrels running through the tops of the trees gathering nuts at a frantic and comical pace. Sometimes a chipmunk or squirrel on the forest floor became so intent on his chores that he neglected to notice the party until they were fairly upon him and he was startled, causing him to jump and run into the nearest tree, where he would sit on a limb scolding the travelers for interrupting his winter preparations.

Jaden kept a close eye on Danae. She could see the strain of the journey on her, even though she was doing much better. They didn't talk about Zachariah or Gideon. They tried to keep their conversations light. Arran and the other elves sensed the need for levity and kept everyone in good spirits, as much as they could.

On the evening of the fourth day in the Great Northern Forest, it grew cold, and Jaden wished for a soft bed as she shifted uncomfortably in the saddle. Etheltread suddenly announced, "Behold, the city of Alexandria!"

As Jaden rode out of the forest, a fresh, clean, and inviting fragrance filled her nostrils. It smelled like the ocean, though it was different from the damp, salty aroma of the Western Ocean and sandy beach near Xannellion because here the air was cold and mixed with the spicy scent of pine trees and rich dirt. She thought there had to be an ocean nearby, nonetheless.

"I smell the ocean. Arran, is the ocean close?"

"The ocean lies behind the northwest walls of Alexandria, my lady." Arran nodded at her astuteness.

Guards from Alexandria rode out to meet the company of elves and women crossing the clearing between the forest and the walls of Alexandria. The guards were an impressive sight with their red and white robes and shiny silver helmets. As they sped toward the travelers, Jaden wondered whether or not they were going to be friendly, but upon approach they slowed to a stop and removed their helmets, and she saw plainly that they were welcoming and intended no harm.

The leader, a man of medium but strong build and handsome to look at, said in a pleasantly deep voice, "Welcome, friends of Ononzai. I am William, captain of the guards."

Etheltread spoke immediately. "We have traveled from Jeremiah on a secret mission to bring these two women to the safety of Alexandria. Gideon, leader of the Jeremian knights was with us, but he was required to return because of impending danger. Xzavier, King of Xanellion, is imposing on them. Will you protect these women until Gideon calls for them to return to Jeremiah? This is the Queen of Xanellion, Jaden, and Gideon's daughter, Danae."

William looked at Jaden for a time, as if he knew her, but then smoothly averted his eyes to Danae. His gaze softened as if he were looking at his own daughter and said, "Alexandria has ever been a friend to those in need, especially Gideon of Jeremiah. Is there anything else?"

"I need to speak with King Alfred right away. I have urgent news from Gideon that cannot wait," Etheltread said.

William asked, "What is your name, friend?"

"I am Etheltread, son of Ozella, Queen of Ononzai. These are my two brothers and kinfolk." Etheltread motioned toward the elves. "We will need refreshment, as well, but first I need to speak with the King."

William turned to his closest associate and said, "Lead Etheltread, son of Ozella, to King Alfred right away." Then he turned to the rest of his guards and said, "You are free to return to your quarters. I will escort these women and the entourage to the castle. My Betty will tend to the ladies' needs."

William's man turned toward the castle and galloped away with Etheltread immediately behind him. Jaden, Danae, Arran, Meadthel, and the others were also led to the castle but at a slower pace. A well-weathered, ancient stone wall surrounded Alexandria. A much less ostentatious gate than Xanellion's great archway opened to the city. Above the arch was a carved relief of three lilies that caught Jaden's attention.

"What do those lilies stand for?"

"They are the symbol of Alexandria," William said curtly.

"But what do they mean?"

He neither responded nor acknowledged her question with as much as a glance. Jaden quieted but felt disappointed. As they rode under the arch of the entrance gate, Jaden was amazed by how old it seemed.

"How long ago was Alexandria established?"

"Alexandria was founded by Alexander, the earliest known inhabitant of Trivar, sent by Gillantri."

Jaden fell silent in disbelief, "You mean this city has been standing since the beginning of Trivar?"

Without looking at her, William answered, "Of course not. It was the first city, but we aren't sure how long Trivar had been here prior, and most of these stones were placed here over time."

"Do you have a navy?" Jaden knew Zachariah would want to know.

"Yes, and I can set up a tour for you later," William said dryly. Jaden decided those were all the questions he could tolerate, although it was difficult to remain silent when she began to see symbols of three lilies everywhere.

The stonework kept her mind occupied with the age of the city and its history. It was as if the city had always been there with its ancient stone walls, buildings worn by rain and wind, and gnarled but dignified trees covered partially with moss.

Everything was well manicured and maintained. The streets were clean and the people were pleasantly going about their labors. Neat houses and shops lined the way, and children under the watch of their mothers played on front porches or in pretty yards. It felt safe.

A monument in the center of town caused Jaden to sit upright and stare. It was a bronzed sculpture of three graceful women: a grandmother, mother, and child. Each held a lily. The plaque read, "To Our Women of Alexandria."

She had to ask, "What do the statues and plaque mean?"

William said, "Why so many questions?"

"I am fascinated with your city," Jaden answered. She became conscious of her weariness. It was cold, there were clouds gathering, and she didn't like this man's attitude. "These three women with lilies remind me of The Third Daughter Prophecy. Have you heard of it?"

"Yes, of course. But that isn't what the statue represents. This statue was commissioned because Alexander believed in valuing and respecting women, all of whom deserve honor and protection."

His tone betrayed the sentiment. But then, maybe she was reading into things.

"I have to go to the Highlands before I leave. Is it possible to have your protection to go there?"

"No," William said firmly.

"I don't know when I will ever be back here again."

"If another party is heading north, I will inform you. But that is the best I can do, my lady."

Danae whispered to Jaden, "Are you sure you need to do this now? You are recovering and need to rest. You don't know when we will need to go south again, and you don't want to be worn out for that trip..."

"Danae! I appreciate your concern, but I have to go. I have to know if I am from the north or not. As a child, Talla always told me to put my origins out of my mind. It wasn't until Xzavier came to Yamis that I realized I belonged somewhere else. I never felt comfortable with my parents in Yamis, and though I tried to feel like I belonged with Xzavier, well, once I met your father and Benjamin, I realized it had all been a façade. No, I am Jaden, Jaden from somewhere in the north."

"But you're part of the family of Gillantri. Isn't that enough?"

"I am not ready to go there. I have felt many things about Gillantri, but Arway seems so far away. No, I need something I can touch." Jaden grew quiet but let out a trailing thought, "...even a gravestone or story about who I really am. I have to go."

Danae bowed her head. "I just have to say one more thing. No matter what you find there, I hope someday you realize that you are not just a daughter of Trivar. You belong to Gillantri. I know this because there have been so many times when, even though I knew I was the daughter of Gideon and from Jeremiah, I didn't feel like I belonged. I was different and felt it keenly my whole life. You have seen how frail I am."

Danae paused. Jaden fidgeted uncomfortably.

"It is embarrassing," she resumed, "to be the daughter of Gideon and unable to handle the heat of the sun, not to mention any type of real battle, but I have always felt belonging and connection as Gillantri's daughter. Nightflights..."

"Danae, I don't mean to be rude, but I can't handle talking about Nightflights again. I am glad you find meaning in your connection to Arway, but I can't. Not yet. Please respect that. I can barely accept the feeling of love Gillantri is trying to share with me. I want to feel as you do, but I am afraid it is going to take more time, and I need to honor my pace. I can't explain how desperately I need to find out about my real parents and family. I have to do one thing at a time, and right now, I need to find out if the Highlands is where I am from here in Trivar. I'll work on Arway when Trivar makes more sense."

Danae forced a smile. "I love you, Jaden. If going to the Highlands is what you want, then I want that for you, too."

"Thank you," Jaden said, feeling mild relief.

As they approached the castle, the gathering clouds grew heavy, lowered in the sky, and slowly began releasing their moisture. It wasn't the sort of rain Jaden had ever seen. It lightly sprinkled and increased timidly, settling at a constant but firm drizzle. The clouds filled the sky as far as she could see, which didn't seem very far because the trees and hills in every direction obstructed clear sight to the horizon.

"When clouds looked like this in the jungles of the south, we were in for a thunderstorm that strips limbs off palm trees, but here it's just a constant drip, like a form of torture!" Jaden said.

Danae chuckled, but William seemed more irritated. Danae tried to smooth it over.

"I apologize for our impatience. We have had a long and difficult journey. Our bodies and minds are fatigued, and rest is so near that we can't help but feel anxious. If you could show us to our rooms, we would be very grateful." She looked over at Jaden and smiled. Jaden nodded her thanks to Danae as William called for the head attendant of the house to come.

The lady they called Miss Betty came out the front door and Jaden started. She was homely, tall, and skinny with a simple dress of grey with a white apron. She had long, thick dark brown hair streaked with grey tied on top of her head. Her limbs and fingers were thin and long but not ungraceful, and her face was long like the elves' faces but thinner.

Her skin was fair and freckled. She had a nice but long nose and large eyes with thin lips. She looked so serious. William didn't even dismount and said without enthusiasm, "Hi Betty. This is a group of weary travelers. They need our help." He nodded toward Jaden. "This one has too many questions. Put them to bed somewhere comfortable."

Jaden was confused but dared not ask why William had called her 'my Betty' earlier, like he might call a wife, and then sit there so casually ordering her around. She decided she didn't like him. But she was curious all the same. Nothing he did or said fit with the feeling of power and peace that he exuded.

"Welcome, to Alexandria, friends," Betty said. Her voice was gentle and kind, softening any awkwardness that her appearance caused. "My name is Miss Betty. I hear you have had quite an adventure."

Arran got off the horse and spoke first.

"Thank you. We are so grateful for your hospitality. I am Arran, leading healer of Ononzai. Danae," he nodded toward her, "is the daughter of Gideon, who is the leader of the Jeremian knights. He has left her in my care. Though she is recovering, she has suffered heat stroke and exhaustion during our journey and is frail. I feel it would be best that she get something light to eat and some sleep right away."

"Thank you, Arran. I will see to it immediately." With that, the head attendant motioned for William to take the horses and told the rest of the group, "Please step in out of the rain. Follow me."

****

Arran motioned to Meadthel to follow the horses.

"Meet up with me inside the front door of the castle, when you are done," Arran said. Meadthel nodded, waved at Danae and Jaden, and turned to leave.

"Wait," Danae said. "I cannot thank you all enough for everything you have done for me." The elves bowed each one in turn to Danae before walking toward the stables. William led the way but looked behind as if to keep an eye on Jaden. Jaden turned away, too spent to respond graciously to his attitude.

"Danae, please come in out of the rain. You need rest," Arran said, putting his arm around Danae's shoulders and leading her to the castle door. Jaden looked at the door in amazement.

"Someone with extraordinary talent carved that door," she said under her breath. It was substantial and made of a dark, heavy wood. The stain preserved its natural color. Most impressive, though, was the engraved design that must have taken years to complete. Yet, it wasn't gaudy or overdone. It was elegant.

Miss Betty heard her and nodded. "Yes, that door was created almost 600 years ago. Actually, the king of Alexandria at the time had a son who was a wood carver. The son loved Alexandria. This is his tribute to his land. He had four older brothers, so he never became king of Alexandria but married a maiden from the north and became king of the Highlands. He ruled well and left this gift to Alexandria. Years ago his last descendant was killed by Daman. A group of knights descended from the knights of Jeremiah have been Stewards of the Highlands ever since. Samuel of Wallace now rules as Steward."

"It is definitely carved by a gifted hand." Jaden slowed as she passed the doors and looked carefully at the scenes that were carved on it. The people appeared happy and carefree. One panel displayed the three women with lilies again, but Jaden kept her mouth shut, too tired to find out if it would upset Miss Betty, as well.

Other panels showed fathers and mothers with their children, coronations of kings, marriages, deaths, joy, and sorrow, but in the center was an image of the blue-eyed man from her dream. Jaden felt her pulse race. With difficulty, she found her voice.

"Who is this?"

Everyone stopped and seemed surprised that Jaden didn't know. Danae stepped close to Jaden and wrapped her arm around her. "That is Gillantri."

Jaden looked at the intricate detail of the carving and felt a lump in her throat. The rendering of the picture was so similar to the figure in her dreams that it left her speechless. She remembered the dream she had when she first arrived in Jeremiah in which she was being led out of a dark cell. She felt her heart beat harder. It hurt. She turned toward Danae looking for confirmation. Danae smiled and nodded. Jaden's legs trembled.

After noticing Arran's discomfort with having Danae still in the cold and observing Jaden's fatigue, Miss Betty herded everyone into the house.

"We have many more pictures of Gillantri and Alexander, as well. I will show you them after you have rested."

Jaden quickly unraveled. She felt agitated and nervous. All she wanted was to be alone. Too many events from the past fortnight played over in her head. She longed to see Gideon and Zachariah.

"Where is my room?" she asked more abruptly than she wanted to.

The head attendant, who was speaking with Arran and some maids about Danae, turned to Jaden. "Are you all right?"

"Yes, yes. I am just tired and need to rest." Jaden tried to hide the edge in her voice with a weak smile but failed completely.

Miss Betty nodded politely, not at all convinced. But Jaden didn't care. She just wanted sleep. She took a deep breath, put her head back, and groaned softly as the lady continued. "Arran, I have arranged for Ralph to take care of you and your men. He will bring Etheltread back when he is finished. When the others return from the stables, Ralph will bring you to your quarters. Make sure you get some dinner and anything else you may need.

"My ladies, I will lead you to your rooms. We hope that you will be comfortable. If there is anything we can do for you, just ring the bell next to your beds."

Jaden tried to smile but only managed a grimace. They followed Miss Betty around a corner and up a small flight of stairs into a long elegant hallway filled with paintings. Long thin tables next to the wall held vases of branches with autumn leaves and stems with small, shiny red berries. They left footprints in the plush runner rug as they traveled over it. After passing many doors, they arrived at Jaden's room.

"Here you are, Jaden. This is one of my favorite rooms, I hope you enjoy it. You can open the windows, see the ocean, hear the waves crash against the beach, and feel the cool salt air when you are covered in your warm bed. It is very refreshing. If there is anything I can do for you, please let me know. King Alfred and Queen MaryAnne will want to meet with you and Danae tomorrow after you have rested sufficiently. Let me know when it is convenient for you. Do you have clothes that you can wear to meet them?"

Danae answered, "Most of our clothes are getting worn out, but we each have two new dresses."

Jaden leaned against the bedpost in her room wishing she could lie down.

"That will be fine. I will have someone bring you more clothes in the next couple of days. Dinner will be ready shortly. I will have them hold it for you. Rest and enjoy the sea. It is healing. Ring when you want to eat. Danae, let's get you to your room before I am in trouble with Arran."

Jaden shut her door and looked around the room. Centered on the far wall was a large bed made of dark wood similar to the castle's front door. It was draped with yards of rich, shimmering velvet the color of dried red roses. There was a quaint ornately carved dark wood nightstand topped with a lace doily underneath a candlestick. A plush rug covered the floor. Jaden walked over to the window, opened it, and breathed in the sweet, fresh sea air.

She looked out over the angry sea. Though it was a grey day with heavy clouds, the air was electric, as if the waves were stirring up energy all around her. Memories of Yamis by the ocean caused her to wonder if that was why she loved the sea, but she realized immediately that she loved this sea more, more than any other sea she had been near. It stirred feelings in her that she desperately wanted to understand, feelings similar to those she felt when smelling the Northern Forest and watching the Aurora Borealis.

A soft covered chair and a wash basin with fresh water sat on a small vanity against the wall opposite to the bed. Jaden sat down, washed her face and arms, removed her shoes, and washed the dust from her sore feet. She was so tired that, after sitting in the chair, she didn't want to stand up again. But she forced herself to cross the room to the rug where she let her feet sink into its plush, heavenly pile. She opened the velvet curtains and fell onto the soft bed. Curling up under the covers, she fell sound asleep.

Jaden dreamed about the front door of the castle. She stood examining it, when suddenly it came to life. All the stories engraved around the edges remained unanimated, but the middle image of Gillantri moved toward Jaden. She backed up and began to run. As she ran, she looked behind her to see Gillantri standing still with his arms outstretched.

In a flash, the gates of Xannellion stood before her, and she was in the middle of an angry crowd of people who were jeering and tearing at her. She fell to the ground. But Xzavier parted the crowd, approached, and offered her his hand. She reached to take it, but darkness and fear began to consume and overcome her.

She recoiled and found herself next in Yamis as a young girl. She felt alone and scared. The mocking face of Talla appeared. Part of Jaden wanted to reach out to her and the other part wanted to run. Teeku came into view behind Talla, but he didn't reach out to Jaden. He didn't beckon to her or offer help or relief. Jaden realized he wasn't what she needed or wanted.

Then Justine appeared as a young dragon, and Jaden felt safe at last. Images of hours spent with her dragon made her feel good, but then Justine melted away like wax over a hot fire. Jaden was alone again. Zachariah appeared as a young child, and Jaden cried as she held him. Then, to her alarm, he rapidly grew up and shriveled in feature and form.

Jaden screamed and looked frantically for Gillantri again, and behind her a man gradually came into focus. She felt herself flying back through space and time, passing Yamis and Xannellion, finally falling at the feet of Gillantri by the wood door in Alexandria.

On her knees and with tears flowing down her cheeks, she hugged Gillantri's legs. He reached down and gently helped her stand. He walked with her through the castle door to the nearest hallway bench where they sat together.

Then he did something that surprised Jaden. He placed his right hand on the middle of her back and his left hand just below her collarbone and quietly said, "Take a deep breath." Just the touch of his hands calmed her. Trying to take a deep breath, she became aware of how shallow her breathing had been, but then she immediately felt light-headed.

"You are all right. You are safe. Release the fear and anxiety that is crippling you. Everything will be all right."

His peacefulness began to settle upon her, and she shut her eyes and focused on breathing. Gillantri removed his hands, brushing away the distress from her shoulders, neck, and head. "You are loved, Jaden."

Jaden opened her eyes slowly.

"What did you say?"

"You are loved," he said again.

That was too much. Jaden started to stand. Gillantri reached up and touched her shoulder. She looked down into his kind eyes and felt gently compelled to sit back down.

"It is okay to accept love."

"Why are you saying these things?" Jaden felt irritated.

"Because you are resisting love."

"No, I am not." But even as the words were forming, Jaden knew they were a lie. "I don't think I know what love is," she admitted.

"But you have felt it," Gillantri said.

She felt the truth of his words but struggled to understand. "I never knew love as a child. My parents bought me from a pirate. They made me their slave."

Gillantri smiled knowingly.

"They never loved me. They made me feel there was something wrong with me. I was different. My parents were dark skinned and uncommonly handsome people. I felt ugly with my red hair and freckled skin. It wasn't until Xzavier came along, another half-grown orphan, that I realized how appealing light skin could be. He was beautiful to me...but he never loved me, either.

"I thought I loved Zachariah but realized in Jeremiah that I didn't know how to show him or be sure that he felt my love for him." Jaden paused, looking at the backside of the delicately carved door. "I felt more love in Jeremiah than I had ever known prior. It is hard to accept. It is like feasting after fasting a long time. You want to dive in, but your shrunken stomach only lets you nibble, and then you feel sick. I don't know how..."

There was a pleading in her voice that she tried to hide by looking like she didn't care. She felt relieved when Gillantri called her bluff. "Just take one minute of life at a time. If you feel love, receive it. Embrace it. If you have pain, accept it, learn from it, and let it go. Stop running from everything, including me. You will feel much better." He smiled at her and said, "You need some rest. Let's talk about this more later."

Jaden shook her head no but knew he was right. She had so many questions but couldn't find them in her mind. She struggled to remain aware so that Gillantri would stay near with his hand gently on her back, but she couldn't do it and fell into a deep sleep as Gillantri disappeared.

30

Reconnaissance

In the early morning after the elvan party, Zachariah left Ononzai. He was furious. Danae was in love with Arran. He would be foolish to think otherwise. He rode hard in the dark along the top of the canyon wall on stony and unfamiliar ground. This early in the morning, only starlight illuminated his way along the trail elves used for tracking food. He heard coyotes howl and noticed an overabundance of bats in the area. He wondered if they were Xzavier's spies.

Zachariah's objective was to avenge himself, and nothing – not even his mother – would get in the way now. He convinced himself that he was doing this for Gideon and that Gideon would be grateful for his help in the end. He told himself that in the end his mother would be proud of him when he rid Trivar of Xzavier and restored peace to their war-torn land. Everything would be made right.

He just had to get to the forest and find Daman. Daman would give him Justine, and then nothing could get in his way. As he rode, he recalled the dark, cloaked man who had spoken to him on the shores of the Zikong River the night he fought with his mother. Zachariah was full of rage when he had left Jaden that night. He remembered it all vividly.

"How can she keep me from what is rightfully mine?" he had said out loud.

"She can't," a voice answered from the shadows.

He had recognized the voice, which was pleasant, though it evoked an unsettling feeling. Even recalling it now made him shudder.

"Daman...is that you? Show yourself, man!" Zachariah had said, feeling in no mood to deal with Daman's games.

Daman was a handsome man in his thirties or forties, Zachariah guessed, clothed in midnight shades of black, reds, deep blues, and purples. He looked like royalty to Zachariah. He had tremendous presence and an air of dominance and power.

He appeared the exact opposite of Zachariah in every way. Daman had olive skin with short dark black hair, black intense eyes, and a well-trimmed goatee. His shoulders were narrow, but his cape made him look broader than he was. He was a good six inches shorter than Zachariah, but somehow he seemed taller, larger. And dangerous.

Daman played with a large spider that was trying to escape, but Daman repeatedly turned his hand so that the spider kept crawling over the top, and then over the bottom, and over the top again. A bat flew near, startling Zachariah.

"Why do you give your power away to your mother? Are you not old enough to decide for yourself what is right for you?"

"My mother has done everything to help me gain power. Whatever her failings may be, that isn't one of them." Though still raging mad at his mother, Zachariah didn't like anyone speaking of her that way.

"Grow up, Zachariah. You have one chance to defeat Xzavier when he comes to face Jeremiah. If you are here, running to the safety of the north, you will miss your chance. You know that Gideon can never defeat Xzavier without you and Justine."

"Justine is dead."

Daman laughed, "You know so little, young man...so little."

Zachariah almost walked away, when a thought struck him. "Why should I trust you?"

"You shouldn't. But I do have Justine. She is hiding at the edge of the jungle, waiting for you to return to her. She healed up nicely, like you have."

Zachariah felt uncomfortable. Daman knew too much about him, and his assertions about Justine were insane.

"What is holding you here, Zachariah? Danae loves Arran. It is obvious. Your mother will actually benefit by your disobedience to her. Gideon will be grateful in the end, and nothing will be gained by you going north... But you already know this."

"But I have to help my mother find out about The Third Daughters." It was a lame retort, but the only one Zachariah had left.

"The Third Daughters, huh? Well, let me tell you something about them... The only help you can be to them is as King of Xannellion. They'll need your protection."

Zachariah felt surprised and increasingly unsettled. "I thought you supported my father. Why do you want me to destroy him?"

"I only helped Xzavier because I knew you were next in line. You have always been sharper and more powerful than him. Xzavier is just a pawn."

"Just a pawn, huh?"

"Yes, he is a poor king, indeed. You know that. The quicker you defeat him the sooner Xannellion gets cleaned up, and, well, Zachariah, I have been around longer than your old friend Franklin. I remember the days of Alexander and understand those ancient prophecies better than anyone now alive. You don't have to trust me... But who else do you have?"

After a couple minutes of thinking it through, Zachariah knew what he wanted to do. "All right, Daman, I'll meet you at the edge of the forest and get Justine. But after that, I don't want to see you ever again. Do you understand? I am doing this for my mother, Gideon, and because I have to destroy Xzavier... not for you!"

Daman smirked and let Zachariah finish.

"I can't leave everyone now," Zachariah said. "I have to figure out a few more details, but it won't be long, and I'll meet you at the edge of the jungle."

Daman smiled, put the spider on his shoulder, turned, and melted into the darkness.

Zachariah was glad he was gone but also felt victorious. He had set the terms. And he was no longer trapped. He went back to camp and slept better than he had in days.

Zachariah's mind returned to the present, where he was riding on the top of the canyon. He finally reached the edge of the jungle late on the sixth night of his quest. He looked behind him in the moonlight to where he had descended into the gorge less than a moon ago, and it amazed him to see how much water had filled the gorge. They really had been lucky to get to Ononzai without being swept out to sea.

Approaching his destination, Zachariah dismounted. He gathered his few things, turned the horse toward Ononzai, and urged the horse to go. He walked toward the tangled jungle.

"Where would Daman be?" He knew Daman wouldn't come out of the darkness. He had to go in. As he approached the woods, he heard some rustling, but it was too dark to ascertain the source of the noise. Zachariah took a deep breath, walking slowly toward the rustling, and hoped it wasn't more bulbanes. At the edge of the darkness he scanned about him, but he discerned nothing. He stepped over some ferns, over and under some aggressive vines, and found himself in the dark.

He felt something on his shoulder and brushed it off, not taking the time to find out what it was. Insects buzzed around him, some diving at him and hitting him in the face and head. He swatted at them and moved forward, deeper into the woods.

The roots of gigantic trees were big enough to make a small shelter behind, and there were times when he had to climb over them as if he were climbing a stone wall. As he climbed over yet another root, he saw crystal eyes peering at him from the darkness. They were too high to belong to a horse and much too high to be a bulbane.

"It's me, Zachariah," he whispered. "Justine, is it you?" His eyes adjusted to the dark, and as he moved closer, he saw an enormous figure with its gaze fixed upon him. He sensed that she was nervous.

A deep, smooth voice uttered, "I am glad you came, my son."

"I am not your son," Zachariah said. "Just give me the dragon. I have things to do." Zachariah hated the disgust and filth he felt in Daman's presence.

"You can have the dragon. If you need anything else from me, just let me know. I will always be here for you."

Something about the last statement sent shivers down Zachariah's spine. He approached Justine cautiously. Daman's cape rustled as he disappeared into the darkness. Zachariah was again grateful that he was gone. Zachariah gently touched Justine, who licked his face and hands like a very large, happy puppy. He laughed and pushed her away.

"We have a lot of work to do." Zachariah placed his knapsack on her back and climbed up. He stretched his arms over his head and shook his curly hair back and forth trying to rid himself of his sleepiness. He had to keep moving.

Up, up they flew, escaping the canopy of the jungle into the night sky. He grabbed his extra blanket and wrapped it around him. They flew as far as they could before daylight transformed the eastern skies. At dawn, they flew close to the top of the jungle until they came to the southern border of the city of Jeremiah, staying clear of the flying tiger patrol that guarded the air space around Jeremiah.

Zachariah could barely keep his eyes open. He had to pinch himself and loosen his blanket to stay awake. As they reached the ground, Zachariah quickly dismounted and sent Justine to get some dinner while he ate the last of his food. When she returned, looking quite satisfied, they both curled up and fell fast asleep.

****

Zachariah camped outside of Jeremiah and made daily reconnaissance missions to Xannellion. He figured Gideon would return in about seven days and was determined to obtain all the information Gideon would need to defeat Xzavier. Daman's spies were everywhere, but Justine and Zachariah were able to keep their camp clear of bats and spiders.

The first two days he watched Xzavier's army. He happily discovered they were mostly undisciplined peasants. Even so, there were close to 65,000 of them, if Zachariah's figures were correct. The only group besides the dragons that worried Zachariah was the force Xzavier brought with him from Yamis. They were fierce. Xzavier had trained them well in Yamis and, after arriving at Xannellion over two years ago, he added Xannellion tactics to their knowledge of warfare and strategy. There were nearly 1,500 Yamis warriors.

On his third and fourth day, Zachariah stole into Jeremiah and was relieved to see Gideon's men training from early in the morning until dark, except on the first day of the week when they rested and worshiped in the church for most of the morning and finished the day with their families.

But they were looking good, perhaps as efficient as Xzavier's Yamis troops. Zachariah guessed that when he left Jeremiah the knights numbered somewhere around 10,000. But now he had counted nearly 25,000 strong, including elves who had joined to train and lead them, and the Ononzai elves hadn't even arrived yet. They would be a great asset to Gideon's army.

The new elves didn't look like Ononzai elves. They also didn't look like South Sea elves. Zachariah couldn't place where they were from. They were thicker and slightly shorter than the other elves Zachariah knew. He didn't think they were rougher but maybe more earthy, like the wood nymphs, but they wore delicately woven woolen cloth decorated in the elvan fashion. Franklin seemed to know them well. He hoped he could ask Franklin about them soon.

Once Zachariah felt confident about the Jeremian forces, he returned to Xannellion and focused his energy on learning about Xzavier's strengths and weaknesses. He didn't want to make his presence known to Gideon until he had all the information he could possibly gather.

Zachariah hid in the forest beyond the Yamis warriors' training grounds. On the fifth day, he watched from his tree perch for several hours. The Yamis men and women were like animals. When they saw blood, they acted like frenzied sharks and were nearly uncontrollable, which was a significant weakness. But Xzavier drilled them twelve hours a day, from before sunrise until after sunset, often exposing them to each other's blood and the blood of victims in effort to teach them to control their bloodlust. It sometimes worked.

Zachariah grew tired. Often during the long hours of reconnaissance he remembered those days walking through the Zikong. He thought of Danae's kindness and beauty and longed for her companionship. He recalled the night of the party, which was wonderful at first, until the image of Danae and Arran dancing caused him to shut down his memory of her again. Then he'd think of his mother whom he missed deeply.

From his tree perch toward the end of the sixth day, Zachariah heard Xzavier bark at his men, "No drills tonight. Eat and prepare for the presentation!"

The men roared in support and retreated for dinner. Xzavier stood in the courtyard basking in his power. But something awakened him from his internal gloating, and he scanned the area. He looked straight at Zachariah, whose heart jumped into his throat. Zachariah knew he was well hidden, but he held his breath. Xzavier averted his gaze and returned to the training building. Zachariah bolted out of the tree.

Looks like I need to go into Xannellion tonight, he thought.

That evening, dressed in Xannellion apparel, Zachariah stole through the northern gate unnoticed. He blended into the thronging crowd that stood anxiously facing Xzavier's castle. Before long, Xzavier appeared on the front balcony.

"People of this great city, no other king in Xannellion history has demonstrated the foresight, the brilliance, the power that I have! Because no other king has accomplished what I dared to do! No king in Xannellion's past – ever – raised an army of such terror and formidable strength as mine!"

From behind the castle, ten wildly screeching enormous dragons shot over the audience like arrows. The crowd gasped and then cheered uncontrollably. Troops from Xzavier's massive army marched from behind the castle and surrounded the crowd. They raised their swords into the air, exciting the audience even more.

Zachariah remained stoic. He knew what he had to do. He pushed his way through the crowd toward the castle.

31

The Sea Shore

Jaden woke the next morning feeling better than she had since she left Ononzai. She remembered the ocean outside her window and scrambled out of bed. The early morning fog, heavy over the water, revealed brushstrokes of blue sky. Shortly after Jaden dressed, she heard a knock at the door.

"Come in," Jaden said.

Miss Betty peeked in. "Are you ready for breakfast, my lady?"

"Oh, it smells so good. Yes, I am very hungry, now that you mention it."

Betty rolled in a cart full of aromatic morning delicacies, and Jaden couldn't wait to enjoy them.

"I want to explore the beach this morning with Danae," Jaden said while biting into a fluffy muffin topped with fruit preserves. "Would that be all right?"

"Of course you may, but I don't think Danae will be up soon. I just checked on her and she wouldn't be roused. She is very fatigued." Miss Betty said.

"Is she all right?"

"I think she is fine. She just needs sleep."

"Maybe I'll take a bath and do a little exploring before she is up then?" Jaden brightened. "Yes, I will take a bath and look around, if that is all right?"

"That sounds fine." Miss Betty paused. "I mentioned to you last night that the king and queen desire to meet you. Would it be pleasing to you if I arranged for that this evening after the last meal of the day?"

"Oh, yes, that would be fine. Thank you."

Miss Betty pushed the cart out the door.

"I will be near, if you need anything," Betty said. "I have ordered new clothes and shoes for you. They should be here by tomorrow. If you find that you need something for your visit with the king and queen tonight, let me know right away."

"I think I have what I need for tonight, thank you." Jaden gently nodded, and Miss Betty shut the door.

After eating a delicious breakfast, bathing, and getting into her elegant red dress, Jaden's spirits were high. All the foreboding she felt yesterday seemed like a dream. She let her fingertips gently pass over her purple dress hanging at the end of her bed, which whisked her thoughts away to Ononzai and her time with Gideon. She smiled sadly.

At the window, she allowed the sea air to fill her soul. The fog dissipated and the soft clouds separated overhead. Waves calmly lapped at the beach, inviting her to come and play. After taking in the scene, the ocean fragrance, the cool air that chilled her cheeks and tasted both sweet and salty, she left her room.

She noticed how cheerful this castle felt. The hall was well lit and dispelled the dreariness of the cold, stone walls. Tables with vases full of autumn flowers, leaves, and berries, and paintings of the ocean, flowers, or playing children lined the walls. Beyond the decorations, a feeling of peace and security pervaded the atmosphere that Jaden loved about these Arwavian communities.

After exploring, she returned to Danae's door and hesitated. She didn't want to wake her too early, but she also had done all she wanted to do alone. After a short time of indecision, Jaden knocked.

"Who's there?" Danae said in a groggy voice.

"Jaden."

She could hear Danae get out of bed and slowly walk to the door. The door opened, and Jaden peeked in to see that Danae had slept in her traveling clothes.

"Danae, are you all right?"

"Yes."

"Did you sleep well?"

"Oh, yes, I am just tired after all our travels. Come in. Did you sleep well?"

"Oh, I had a pleasant dream and slept very well. Do you want to come with me to the beach this morning? The fog is burning off, and it looks like it's going to be a sunny day."

"I am so tired."

"The fresh, salty air will do you good."

Danae laughed. "I see I cannot turn you away." Danae changed her clothes and made her bed while Jaden stared out the window toward the ocean. Soon they were ready to go. Miss Betty was on her way to Jaden's room to clean up the breakfast trays and passed them in the hallway.

"Off to the beach? It is going to be warm today. I took the liberty of packing a picnic lunch for you both. It is in the kitchen. Arran and his men will be busy until they leave in a few days. Jaden, he asked that I pass on his request that you please keep an eye on Danae, as she needs much rest."

Jaden exchanged glances with Danae, and they laughed.

"I will do my best."

Miss Betty continued, "Oh, and I brought you some wool shawls. Even on the warmest fall day here it will be cooler than what you are used to down south."

Jaden and Danae gratefully accepted the shawls and wrapped them around their shoulders.

"Thank you, Miss Betty. These feel so warm. What is the quickest and easiest route to the beach?" Danae asked.

"Follow this corridor and go down the stairs to the main level. Instead of going left through the door you came in last night, go right and follow the hallway to the stairs on your left that lead down to the scullery chambers and out the back doors on your right. Remember to pick up your lunch before you go outside. If you get lost, there are people everywhere who can get you back on track. Just remember your appointment this afternoon. Enjoy your day!"

"Thank you, Miss Betty, we will."

They went down to the scullery kitchen, grabbed their lunches, and followed the last hallway through the back doors into the fresh sea air. Jaden inhaled deeply, feeling exhilarated. They walked down a boardwalk behind the castle that led to the beach. It was a long but invigorating walk. The slope from the castle to the beach was steep, but the boardwalk was structured in switchbacks to compensate for the declivity. Wild roses with red rosehips danced brightly among the green, yellow, and orange leaves lining the way. Though the fog was gone, the sun emitted only a weak heat.

"Just look at this," Danae said. "It is magnificent!"

They stood momentarily silent, taking in the blue sky and turquoise ocean with its frothy waves that unfolded on the sparkling sand. White cliffs surrounded the beach, and the green, red, and orange of fall was spattered everywhere on the coastline.

"I see all the colors of the rainbow," Danae exulted. "Thank you for bringing me."

Jaden smiled. "It is lovely."

"I'll race you to the water!" Danae said as she reached the bottom of the boardwalk and sprinted to the endlessly rolling waves.

"Wait a minute, that's not fair," Jaden said, laughing and surprised at Danae's sudden burst of energy.

Jaden and Danae ran lightheartedly and dropped to the powdery white sand before the gentle surf. Danae put down a blanket. They sat for a time, mesmerized by the cadenced ebb and flow of the ocean. Seagulls flew overhead, curious about their new guests. The waves retreated farther and farther with the tide. The sun grew warmer, but the breeze kept both ladies wrapped in their thick shawls. Jaden unpacked their lunch and handed Danae her food.

"I wonder how Zachariah is doing," Jaden said.

"I haven't allowed myself to think about him. It hurts too much. I was falling in love with him, and then he left. I don't think I will ever understand it." Danae took in a quick breath and put her head down, exhausted. She had no energy reserves after the sprint across the sand.

"How could you love Zachariah when you have Arran?" Jaden asked.

There was a long silence.

"I don't have Arran. Since I was a child, I have loved him. We have always been close, but I can never have him. He is an elf. He has been alive three times as long as I have and will live three times as long as he has already. He can only ever be my dear friend."

"That is one of the reasons Zachariah left," Jaden said. "He thought he didn't have a chance."

"I don't understand. Why did he feel that way?"

"It seems obvious."

"How can that be? Arran and I have a special connection, but I spent more time with Zachariah. Sure, I was excited when Arran arrived, but he is a dear friend, and I needed his healing. I danced with Arran, but I explained that that was our favorite song. We have danced to that song since I was a child. I guess I didn't have strength to show Zachariah better how I felt. I thought he knew."

Danae fell silent. Jaden could see the turmoil in her face as the pieces fit together painfully. They both looked out to sea. The mood of the day dampened, Danae's exhaustion became enhanced by her grief, making her quiet and pensive. Her thoughts were far away in Jeremiah, Jaden guessed.

Jaden's thoughts were drawn to that city, as well. How were they handling

Xzavier's spies and attacks? How was Gideon? Did he and Zachariah work things out? A swim in the pool behind Danae's garden would be pleasant right now.

In silence they watched the waves and seagulls. A cooler breeze picked up.

"I am getting cold," Danae said.

"We should get back and clean up before we meet the royal couple."

They gathered up their meal remnants and blanket and walked slowly back up the boardwalk. When they reached the top, both gazed back at the sea. Dark clouds were rolling in over the edge of the horizon and the waves grew larger and angrier. The air had cooled noticeably as they returned to the castle. Jaden and Danae walked pensively through the hallways lined with paintings and candles. Danae shook her head.

"I have to think of something else."

"What?"

"I focus on the paintings, but in every one, his deep green eyes stare back at me."

"He is as much to blame. He was too stubborn and prideful to tell you his feelings and his fears about you and Arran…"

"I just wish I had known… I was so dazed…so sick…I could have stopped him. He could be here now… I am sorry."

"I only said that you and Arran were one of the reasons he left. Avenging himself of his father's debauchery drives him."

Danae walked on. After some time, Jaden realized she didn't know where she was. She tried to backtrack. Stopping to get her bearings, she realized she wasn't any closer to her room.

"Where are all the servants? The castle is empty. I think we are lost," Jaden said.

"I'm sorry. I wasn't paying attention."

Jaden saw a room with a light that shone beneath the door. She walked quickly to the door and peeked her head in.

"Hello?"

A young man rose from a table where he and a young lady were getting ready to eat.

"Who might you be?" He smiled, instantly winning Jaden's heart. Something about him made Jaden immediately comfortable. He was young and strong with short, straight, dark hair and soft brown eyes. He was built slender and tall with tanned olive skin and was quite handsome.

"I am Jaden of Xannellion, and this is Danae of Jeremiah. Who are you?"

"I am Jordan. My father is Samuel of Wallace, Steward of the Highlands, and this is my fiancée, Lillian, daughter of King Alfred and Queen MaryAnne."

The graceful, young woman rose beside him and took his hand. Her long, thick, blond curly hair framed her brilliant blue eyes and fell to her waist. It seemed as if the couple was resting from a hard day, but Lillian smiled easily.

For a split second Jaden felt jealous of Lillian. There was something about her confidence. It was a naïve, protected air that upset Jaden.

"Can we help you?" Lillian offered.

"We are lost and can't seem to get our bearings. We need to return to our rooms. We are supposed to meet with Lillian's parents after our evening meal, and we don't want to be late."

"Well, why don't we eat here together? That will save you some time. Come join Lillian while I get some more food and someone to help you find your way back to your rooms." Jordan motioned for them to sit on the couch.

Jaden stiffened. "Oh, no, we wouldn't want to impose on your meal. We'll just stand here, thank you." Danae looked at Jaden questioningly.

Jordan noticed but politely said, "Please think about it. Lillian, excuse me, I will be right back." Lillian nodded her head.

Jordan passed by the two women and shut the door behind him. Lillian asked, "Please come and sit with me? Miss Betty informed us that you were here. I would love to talk with you about your journey, if you wouldn't mind."

Jaden's first reaction was to resist. She had no intention of liking this girl, but to insist on declining would have made her feelings too apparent.

"Well, I guess we could until Jordan returns." The two tentatively walked over to the couch and sat down next to Lillian.

Before long they were talking about their travels and Lillian's wedding plans. Jaden found herself enjoying listening to Lillian talk about Alexandria. A question entered her mind, and before thinking, she asked, "What do you know about The Third Daughter Prophecy?"

Lillian went pale but kept her gaze steady on Jaden's face.

"From the jungles south of Xanellion to here," Jaden attempted to explain, "I have been trying to find out something about which no one seems to have answers."

Lillian tried to smile and said, "Why would a Queen of Xannellion want to know about The Third Daughters of the north?"

"I am not sure, but ever since I first heard about it, I've felt driven to discover more. This northern land has been hidden from me since I was a child, and the more I learn of it and its people, the more intrigued I am with it: the smells, the sights, and the very feel of it stir my soul."

"Well, you'd have to travel farther north to learn more about that prophecy. I don't know anyone who knows the details about it here."

Not wanting to seem pushy or rude on their first visit, Jaden backed down. She accepted that Lillian wasn't going to say any more and tried to change the subject.

"How long have you and Jordan been together?"

"We have known each other since we were children, but he has lived in the Highlands, and I only got to see him once or twice a year during family gatherings. He has always been dear to me and has put up with a lot..." A sad look crossed her face but quickly vanished.

They continued talking, though Jaden noticed that Lillian wasn't as comfortable. She seemed relieved when the door opened and Jordan entered with Miss Betty.

"So you lost your way, my dears? Well, you made some fortunate turns to end up with these two lovebirds."

Lillian blushed and Jordan laughed outright. "Thank you, Betty, we don't need any commentary from a loving but far too open Aunt. I don't think we can handle more embarrassments from you for awhile."

"Whatever do you mean? I only tell the truth. If that is embarrassing, then you need to come to terms with your own feelings." Miss Betty said with a smile.

"You are his aunt? Are you related to his father or his mother?" Danae asked, enjoying the conversation.

"I was never able to have children and have unofficially adopted them both."

"And a more attentive aunt no one could want for!" Jordan said lightheartedly but sincerely.

After a delicious meal and a good long conversation with Jordan and Lillian, Lillian made Jaden and Danae promise to come back soon. Then Betty escorted the ladies to their rooms. Jaden felt better when it was over, though her curiosity had been piqued by Lillian's unwillingness to share about The Third Daughter Prophecy.

32

Amber Caves

Zachariah entered a side door to the castle while everyone's attention was on Xzavier, his dragons, and the Yamis warriors outside. The castle had changed little since he had left, but he noticed more wrought-iron statues cluttering the hallway.

One of his objectives was to see for himself how many more dragons Xzavier had that weren't flying around the castle in Xzavier's display of power. He walked carefully but quickly through the dark halls. Occasionally, the sudden shouts from the people outside made him jump.

When he arrived at the door of the dungeon, he remembered the day, not so long ago, when he found his mother with dried blood on her face, struggling to open this same door. It enraged him all over again.

He opened the door and quickly descended the stairs. At the bottom he slowed down, not wanting to disturb the young dragons. Because of the dim lighting, it was difficult to see, but everything seemed in order. He carefully found his way around the dragons, alarmed at how many were close to fighting age. There were nearly one hundred that Zachariah figured were within a year of readiness. Many more would be ready a year after that, not to mention there were numerous younglings.

He pulled a bottle from under his tunic and removed the lid. He dripped the smelly fluid on the dragon's food, emptying the full contents of the bottle. Immediately, the dragons gorged themselves. Zachariah was silently musing, when he noticed something...something he had never observed in the dungeon: a door in the back, opposite the exit he and Jaden had used. The door was nearly the size of the whole wall and appeared to be cut out of the rock. The thick door had no frame and seemed heavy. And it was open.

Clever, he thought, I wonder what my father hides here.

Without pause, he grabbed a torch from the wall and disappeared behind the door.

****

Zachariah descended into an underground labyrinth of dark and musty tunnels. He felt the walls. They didn't seem to be naturally occurring caves, but dug out by tools of some sort, picks and large chisels, if he were to guess. There was no sign of life anywhere, just bare rock and the sound of an occasional drip of water. He looked behind him. The farther he went, the more concerned he was with getting back. As he felt along the interior of the cave he discovered a thick rope about waist high attached to the wall, obviously for leading occupants back to the dungeon.

"Xzavier has his faults...but he isn't stupid."

Zachariah grabbed the rope loosely and continued. After a time, the tunnel descended steeply, and Zachariah leaned on the rope more to steady himself. Zachariah began to hear a rhythmic sound, like many people pounding stone, and then he heard a scream, then more pounding and another scream. He froze. But after a moment he moved on, realizing the sounds, amplified through the tunnels, were still a ways off.

After traveling for awhile, amber light emanated from farther ahead in the tunnel. The sounds grew louder and a rotten stench surfaced. Zachariah finally discovered the source of the light. Shimmering, glowing amber rocks covered an entire cavern and were magnified by the crystal clear water of a large underground lake.

If the lake had been the only thing Zachariah saw, he would have been mesmerized by its beauty, but standing inside the entrance to the cavern was the largest and ugliest thing he had encountered yet. It must be a cave troll, he thought, though he had only heard of them. One of Cannote's claims that had appeased his people when they were on the verge of uprising because of troll attacks on outlying villages was that he had killed the last of the trolls. That was years before Zachariah arrived in Xannellion.

The troll faced the lake, bare-naked, except for a breast plate covering its front from shoulders to thighs, a helmet, and a spear that was taller than the troll. It smelled awful. Zachariah could see no fewer than three cave trolls in the cavern and was sure, by the stench, that there were more.

The light from the amber stones illuminated the occupants of the great cavern. Zachariah saw two more tunnels leading away from the cavern, one to the right and one to the left. The right tunnel seemed finished, but the one on the left was filled with bulbanes at work digging the new tunnel.

Zachariah had more time to observe these creatures now than when they had attacked in the jungle. Built like miniature Yamis warriors but darker and terribly scarred, they wore only a loin cloth and stood a mere three-quarters of Zachariah's height. Something glowed in the general region where eyes belonged, and their large, bulbous noses hung down below the top lip of their mouths.

Sharp teeth stuck out of their mouths, some up and others down, like a wild boar's mouth. Their ears looked like elephant ears, thin, wrinkly, and draped close to the sides of their ugly heads. Some bulbanes were digging out the walls of the left tunnel. Some stood on scaffolding while harvesting the amber stone from the ceilings. Others dove to the bottom of the lake and brought amber to the surface.

Bats hung from the ceilings. Supervising the bulbanes were creatures that looked almost human, though disfigured. They were pale and sickly, forlorn, and yet animated in an unearthly way. They moved around the cave, keeping the bulbanes in line, and sometimes they spoke to others of their kind.

As he stared in disgust, a man appeared at the opening of the left cave. He held a red hot branding iron. At no regular, or even necessary, intervals he would touch the iron to the back a bulbane's knees, neck, or waist. Each time, the bulbane would let out an agonizing scream and fall to the ground. Then the man would kick them, and they would stand back up grumbling and proceeding with digging. He strained to get a better look at the man.

No! he thought. Zachariah gasped and backed into the tunnel. His entire body shuddered. Gathering his courage, he stepped back to his hidden viewing point and peered harder toward the left entrance where the man stood with the hot iron.

"It is," he whispered in disbelief. Then he turned and ran back up through the tunnel toward the dragon keep. The rope at times burned his hands. But he didn't care.

33

No Answers

After cleaning up and changing clothes, Jaden heard a knock on her door. She opened it and felt a little thrill as Danae stood there in the same dress she wore at the elvan celebration. Memories of that magical evening came flooding back.

"Danae, you are radiant."

Danae colored and returned the compliment, "And you, Jaden."

"Well, you both look radiant, I agree." Miss Betty arrived to escort the two women to see Queen MaryAnne and King Alfred. "Now there are a few things I ought to tell you. Follow me. We'll talk as we walk."

Miss Betty led them down the hall. Distracted, all Jaden could think about was The Third Daughter Prophecy and what it could mean in connection with her dreams. So many questions raced in her mind that as soon as one formulated, another replaced it. Jaden was straightening her dress and trying to collect herself, when she heard Miss Betty say, "Lillian and Jordan enjoyed their dinner with you."

Danae responded, "Lillian is a dear. I hope we see her soon."

"Well, it is funny you should say so. That was the same thing Lillian said about you, and she has asked that you meet with her tomorrow. She is working on a project with her mother for her upcoming wedding. Lillian said to me after you left, 'I don't know how long the two of them will be around, but I don't want to miss any time getting to know them. They know things about Trivar that I want to learn.'"

Danae laughed. "Well, if that makes her happy," she said.

"Yes, that would be good." Jaden wondered if Lillian mentioned her question about The Third Daughters to Miss Betty. She also wondered what Miss Betty knew.

Before more questions surfaced, Miss Betty said, "We are almost there. Slow down and take a deep breath. These people are kind. No need to be nervous. Now remember, no bowing. Here in Alexandria, no one bows to anyone but Gillantri!"

Earlier, Betty had taught them a few manners that were expected in Alexandria, like looking at the royal couple when walking toward their thrones. The idea to bow to no one but Gillantri appealed to Jaden, but she wondered if she could stop that ingrained habit. They slowed behind Miss Betty, stopping in front of a large door illuminated by a skylight. The door, made of quartz, was clear enough for light to filter through, but it was not transparent.

Two guards stood at attention in front of the doors. Their ornate armor shining in the light added to the drama of the moment. Nervousness suddenly overtook Jaden, who laughed at herself. Had she not been Queen of Xannellion and Yamis? How many people had come to see her and felt as she did at that moment? She shook her thick hair back, straightened her shoulders, and followed Miss Betty through the doors into a spacious hall filled with light.

Great white, translucent quartz columns stood every thirty feet in two parallel lines from the door to the thrones. Light entered the room through dazzling, large diamond-faceted glass windows built into the vaulted ceilings. Yards of white silk swags were fastened at the tops of the columns, draping down in the middle between the pillars. The fabric waved in a gentle breeze that found its way into the hall.

Ancient gold-trimmed tapestries with highly detailed, colorful embroidered images were understated, yet majestic. Jaden struggled to keep her eyes on the royal couple because of her strong impulse to examine the tapestries. Even from a distance, she could discern their superior quality. She remembered what Franklin had said about Alexandrian embroidery being almost as good as elvan craftwork.

One thing that struck Jaden as odd was the lack of courtiers filling the hall. There weren't even servants fussing around the royal couple. There were only the two guards at the door and two more at the base of the platform where the thrones sat. But the silence and uncluttered space lent to the peace and grandeur of the room.

King Alfred stood when they had crossed the room half-way, and when they covered half of the remaining space, Queen MaryAnne stood also. Jaden was struck by their grace and beauty. Both were probably in their forties. King Alfred was slim, tall, and handsome but not strikingly attractive. He looked kind to Jaden, almost gentle, but worn.

MaryAnne had a rounder figure and was pleasant looking and unpretentious with her brown hair tied up around her head. Her eyes expressed a sadness, even though the queen smiled. MaryAnne was the first to speak.

"Welcome, Queen of Xannellion and daughter of our friend Gideon of Jeremiah."

King Alfred took his wife's hand as they descended to the main floor. It felt strange to not bow, but Jaden stood respectfully, as Miss Betty instructed. Miss Betty gave MaryAnne and Alfred a hug and said, "I have business to attend to. Is there anything else that you need of me?"

"Actually, Betty, would you mind returning shortly?" MaryAnn said. "I have some things to discuss with you after this visit."

"Of course. How long until you need me?"

"No more than an hour, thank you."

Miss Betty smiled at Jaden and Danae and took her leave.

At the side of the main aisle stood a roughhewn stone table surrounded by similar stone benches covered with soft cushions. King Alfred motioned toward them. "Would you please sit with us?"

The four of them headed to the table.

"I have never known a monarch to be so informal with visitors to their kingdom," Jaden commented.

King Alfred smiled invitingly. "Xannellion is not a place for quaint customs, I am aware. So much upheaval in that kingdom, so much strife and change. Each new monarch has a new way of doing things. Even the statues, buildings, and people are swapped out every hundred years or so."

They each took their seats. King Alfred continued, "Here in Alexandria, I stand on the shoulders of my father and his fathers before him. This custom of sitting here below the throne started hundreds...well, no, actually thousands of years ago. Originally, the king and queen greeted their guests at a simple stone table with stone benches under the shade of an old oak tree. We held on to the humble ideals of those first people of Alexandria to remind us that true greatness comes from remembering that we are not superior to anyone. We are servants to the people."

"That sounds like Ozella's philosophy," Jaden commented.

"It was Gillantri's philosophy first. The elves practice it and we try our best," Alfred said.

"That is true," Queen MaryAnne said, smiling at her husband. "I am glad to meet both of you. I am MaryAnne, and this is my husband, Alfred. We are sorry to hear about the troubles you both faced recently and hope your stay here will be pleasant. If we can do anything for you, please ask."

Jaden hesitated and MaryAnne noticed, but Alfred said, "I would like to hear about your travels. Tell me about Xannellion, Jeremiah, and Ononzai, and anything important to our safety in Alexandria."

For the next half an hour, Jaden spoke of Xannellion as she had with Gideon. Danae spoke of Jeremiah and Ononzai. Together they spoke of their journey. As they were winding down, MaryAnne looked at Jaden and asked, "Is there something we can do for you? What is it you need?"

Jaden glanced at Danae, took a breath, and plunged in. "A question has haunted me since I arrived in the north. I had a dream, some years back." She paused, looking at the faces of the king and queen, trying to discern if she should continue. But she had to ask.

"I saw a great fleet of the finest ships pulling into a narrow inlet between vibrant green lands. The men in the ships were intelligent and good and fleeing from darkness. There were three women on the ship, an elderly one, a young maiden, and a baby."

Jaden paused noticing that MaryAnne had gone pale and Alfred had put his hand on hers. But no one tried to stop Jaden, so she went on. "Since then, I have had more dreams about these three women and lilies symbolizing them. I feel a strong need to know more about them. The only thing I can believe is that they must have something to do with The Third Daughter Prophecy... I know this sounds crazy, but it is connected to my quest to know where I come from.

"I was an orphan when my adoptive parents bought me from pirates in Yamis. Somehow these women are a piece to my life's puzzle. I feel a connection to them, and in my dreams I even resemble them. Some have suspected that I am from the Highlands. I have seen many statues and lily motifs here in Alexandria. I feel like I am so close, but no one seems to know anything."

Jaden paused again, worried she might have shared too much. The King and Queen fixed their gazes intensely on Jaden, which made her wonder if she offended them. "I have been too bold... I just..."

"No, no, no...those are fair questions." Alfred shifted, trying to act calm. "It is just that I cannot answer them for you, and, unfortunately, I have to ask that you keep your inquiries on the subject of The Third Daughters to yourself while in Alexandria."

Jaden frowned but realized that he wasn't making an idle request. All the same, it felt like he was putting a lid on a violently boiling pot. She didn't know if she could agree to keep the lid on.

"I will tell you honestly," she said, "that I don't know if I can keep silent on this matter because I feel so compelled to find out the truth of my origins and have come so far. But I will try, for I am deeply grateful for your service and hospitality."

"Thank you, Jaden. I hope that you find out more about where you came from. I hope in some other way that we can help."

MaryAnne didn't speak again after Jaden asked about the prophecy. Jaden felt very uncomfortable, but Danae and Alfred filled the time with conversation, giving relief to the queen and Jaden somewhat.

For the remainder of the evening, Jaden fell quiet and thoughtful. Both she and Danae retired early after their long day, but Jaden didn't sleep well. She tossed and turned with disjointed dreams, none of which made any sense.

34

Revealed

In the middle of the seventh day of reconnaissance, two major developments occurred. Xzavier began moving his ground troops in the direction of Jeremiah, and Zachariah noticed a small number of horses and riders approaching from the north. When the horses and riders from the north arrived at the gates of Jeremiah, he recognized Porter in the front with Jed and Gideon.

Zachariah knew where they were headed. He climbed onto Justine's back, flew far north past Jeremiah, and headed east to avoid the patrols of flying tigers. He turned Justine south again to the waterfall behind Gideon's house and landed just south of the pool of water.

"Stay here, girl. I have some work to do."

He ran toward Danae's garden, opened the gate, and headed toward Gideon's east corridor chamber from the outside. The main room of the house was still caved in from the fallen dragon and burned out with ashes, like scars, from the attack. But the east corridor chamber had been renovated remarkably like the original with the exception of an added room and a chimney. Zachariah concluded that the chamber must serve as living quarters for Richard and Gideon until the rest of the house could be rebuilt.

Old Trapton rushed up behind Zachariah, who turned to greet him. Trapton licked him until he laughed. Zachariah petted him and climbed up onto the roof of Gideon's chamber. Crouched near the skylights, he watched and listened. The room lacked the former book shelves, though piles of books lay neatly in the corner. None of the walls were painted and the table looked makeshift. But the original door hung in its proper place.

Gideon entered the chamber and approached Richard and Franklin. Though sounds were subdued because of the glass, Zachariah could still hear what was being said inside the chamber.

"Gideon, it is so good to have you here again."

"It is good to be home. The rebuild is looking nice. It is amazing that you have had time for that with everything else going on."

"Our carpenters and other artisans were freed up with the refugees gone, so they have made great strides in cleaning up the mess the dragons left. Now, of course, they are focused on preparing for war."

Gideon shifted his weight uncomfortably. "How was the funeral?"

"Good. Very good. Mother and father and the rest of the family send their love. They all missed you. But Benjamin's body, along with the rest of our men, are resting in the temple yard now."

"Thank you for taking care of everything." Gideon took a deep breath and plunged into more urgent matters. "There is much to discuss."

Richard began his report. "Daman's spies in the form of bats and spiders infest our city. Bats swarm even during the day. Spiders are everywhere. You can't open your bed without one crawling out. We're able to kill many of them, and we think few make it out of the city, but they are in our food supplies and in every corner and crevice."

As if to make his point, a large spider crawled out of the corner. With his sword, Richard cut it in half and swept it toward the corner again.

"Since the explosion in Xannellion, our men have become suspicious of each other. They question one another's motives about everything. For instance, the other morning during roll call in a routine quarters inspection at the north guard station, the lead guard Vince accused his next-in-command, Jason, of not telling me his real name. Vince knows Jason. We both knew Jason was who he said he was, so it was very odd behavior for Vince. I can't explain it. Well, Jason became upset, and they were nose to nose, ready to take each other down."

"We put Vince in the stocks for questioning," Franklin said, "but he's a good soldier. We hoped to quell the distrust, but our stock yard soon became overflowing with soldiers whom I would have trusted implicitly not a fortnight ago."

"Fortunately, Franklin observed that many of the men in stocks were suffering from spider or bat bites. So we changed tactics and have kept soldiers with bites in confinement for 48 to 72 hours. With a good dose of herbs from Danae's garden on the bite site, they recover and become sane again.

"We drill every day on fighting dragons according to the information Jaden and Zachariah provided before they left. And Franklin has learned much about dragon anatomy from the downed dragon that we salvaged at Jaden and Zachariah's arrival and the two that were killed before you left.

"He cataloged the fleshy parts of the dragon, from the scales to their blood vessels. Then he fed the remaining bones to beetles to clean. He placed the bones in acid to clear off any excess soft tissue and let the bones dry in the sun. Franklin took careful note of their bone structure. Every knight now knows the weaknesses inherent in a dragon.

"Though we still have much to do, I believe our men are ready. Our flying tigers are stationed in the fields to the south of Jeremiah and will be our first line of defense. Foot soldiers and horsemen from all over Trivar arrive daily and are living in tents near the flying tigers.

"Even with the reinforcements, my main concern is our numbers. I am worried about how we are going to face an army of men and dragons. We have the skills to outfight any army of Xannellion, even greatly outnumbered, but... Honestly, Gideon, we are going to need all the blessings of Gillantri in order to defeat an army of dragons." He paused.

Gideon nodded for Richard to go on. "I am frustrated with King Lenox. He refuses to send his knights. In a message to me he wrote, 'I must preach the word. Don't talk to me about fighting. The word has always been mightier than the sword.'

"He has some of the most able men in all of Trivar – if they would be allowed to fight. Porter's brother, Leon, tried to persuade Lenox differently but to no avail. They are protected on those heavenly South Sea Islands and can live lives free of war. Someday they won't have that luxury if they don't engage. The darkness will grow."

Franklin interjected, "Lenox grows old. Petra will soon be king, and he'll change their ideas about contributing to the protection of Trivar, I've no doubt. But it looks like we're out of luck until then."

Richard continued, "Our strategies committee has formed tactics to surround and conquer a dragon with the least amount of men and casualties. First thing tomorrow, I will show you their findings and plans. But today I need to share with you the evidence presented against our men in the attempted assassination of Xannellion's King. This has been disturbing."

"Certainly no one really believes that our men did it?" Gideon said. "Not you or Franklin?"

"Of course we don't believe any of our men would have done it willingly, but given the effects of spider and bat bites... Well, some things just aren't right."

"This is unbelievable. None of our men would do this."

"I know how you feel, but wait until you see what we found."

Richard led Gideon and Franklin out of the house to the stable. Zachariah jumped down from the roof, hurried through the garden to the back of the stable, and peeked in through a knothole. Gideon scowled, obviously upset.

Richard continued, "Here are the clues we've found surrounding the accused men. Each of their quarters were swarming with spiders, no bats. They left all their weapons, changes of clothing, armor, horses, food, anything that would have aided them. We found strange tracks outside their quarters that discontinued after only a few yards. Someone broke into our armory and stole explosives. Outside the armory, the same tracks that we found outside the men's quarters were everywhere, and again they just stopped after some yards. This is the report we gave to Jed to give to you."

"Yes, Jed told me most of that, except about the spiders."

"At first we thought dragons carried the men away, accounting for the disappearing tracks. But there was no sign of struggle or fighting. Also, Franklin pointed out that the tracks were not dragon tracks. They were thicker and rounder. We know these men, some of our very best. They would never go rogue and aggravate the already hostile situation with Xzavier.

"We don't have any proof, but Franklin and I believe these men didn't disappear into the air – but into the ground. We believe they were taken and used as scapegoats. We have men digging, trying to find the tunnels, but we haven't found them yet." Richard finished. He was clearly tired and worn down, ready to concede the responsibility back to Gideon.

"Richard, you and Franklin have done well. I do have one question..." Gideon was interrupted by a knock at the back door of the stables. Gideon looked at Franklin and Richard, and then turned toward the door. "Enter," he said.

The door swung open. "Sir, I must speak with you. I have some very important information," Zachariah said.

35

William

Jaden preferred to leave her bedroom window cracked open to let in the sea breezes, even though she had to stay tucked deep in her covers. The air tasted and smelled of autumn when Jaden woke. Danae felt tired, so Jaden spent the morning at the beach by herself. By early afternoon, fluffy clouds began gathering overhead and a cool breeze chilled her. She put on her shawl and wrapped her knees into her chest while sitting on the shore.

She was pondering The Third Daughter Prophecy and what more she wanted to learn, when she heard a faint cry from behind her. She stood and turned around. It looked like Arran and William. She thought it strange. She headed back toward the boardwalk. The men approached her.

Ever since she arrived, she wondered about William. He was married to Miss Betty, but she rarely saw them together. A few days back, Jaden saw them talking together near King Alfred's study. William was leaving and Miss Betty was coming. They discussed something quietly, nodded courteously at one another, and left without even the slightest sign of endearment. It was the most unusual relationship Jaden had seen. And William made her nervous. He seemed so serious and guarded. Why did both he and Arran come to the beach today? What did he want?

"Hello, Arran. It is so good to see you. And William, hello," Jaden said as she approached them. Jaden looked questioningly at them.

"William and I need to talk with you," Arran said. "Some trouble is broiling, and you are at the center of it. I spoke with William this morning about The Third Daughter Prophecy, and he disclosed to me some disturbing news about your first visit with the king and queen. You apparently upset them. Queen MaryAnne wanted you banished from Alexandria that very day to prevent you stirring up trouble here, but King Alfred wouldn't hear of it, as he gave his word to watch over you."

"But she has been so kind to me." Jaden was shocked. Her stomach tightened up and she felt afraid.

"She is refined and is honoring King Alfred's wishes. But she is still upset and it's hard to tell how long she will exercise restraint in using her authority. Fortunately, William opened up to me, and we agreed that we needed to speak with you immediately. We don't have much time to talk, for William will be missed shortly, as will I. We decided if we sit here by the boardwalk we wouldn't draw attention to ourselves from the castle."

"I don't know what to say. William, will you convey my apology for upsetting the king and queen? It truly wasn't my intention. I just feel these things so deeply and they trouble me. I had no idea that they would cause any harm to Alexandria or any of you."

"I realize that," William said. "From the day you arrived, I could see your pain. I will convey your apology to the royal couple myself."

Is William being kind, even compassionate? Jaden wondered. She wouldn't have been more stunned if Arran had suddenly become cold and withdrawn!

"Thank you," she stammered.

Arran said, "Let's find a seat."

Jaden walked quietly with Arran and William, noticing that her peace was not so threatened by this elf's peace anymore. She reflected back to her first moon in Jeremiah and colored at the thought of her emotional swings and lack of peace. Today, as the soft sunlight played along the tops of waves and warmed her shoulders, so much had changed. She tried not to worry about William and what he might have to say.

Arran spread a large blanket next to the boardwalk. The three sat down, Jaden in the middle with her legs curled up to her chest. She wanted to just listen, and she tried not to enjoy sitting next to William.

"You know my mother would never forgive me if I didn't finish the story."

Jaden laughed, thinking of Ozella and her twinkling voice. "I miss her."

"Well, think of her as I finish the faerietale. William is familiar with this tale and already knows the beginning. The ending of this story will have to be severely condensed, for our time is short. I'll distill it down to its most important parts."

"Wait, you came here to tell me the rest of the faerietale? Arran, I am wondering about you two."

"Just hear us out, William said gently. "It will make sense when we are through. There is no way to prepare you for what we have to say, and we don't have the luxury of time." The kindness in his tone again disarmed Jaden. How could William know this faerietale? Who was this man and what was his purpose here?

Arran's voice calmed her as he began the story. "Our little blackberry faerie was found by the being of light that the old fae promised would be there in the forest. This being of light was a tall and graceful woman who brought our little faerie back to the old fae's enchanted castle in the woods. There she was taught the history of her people and the old ways. Over the winter she learned reading, writing, and many other disciplines.

"She was also taught to better understand virtue and how to do things that were hard because they were right. The blackberry faerie became referred to as The Virtuous One because the old fae had seen virtue in her and believed that she would have the power to change the course of slavery and destruction of their society.

"Now, the old fae had not been present since her arrival, and she wished she could see him again. A handsome picture of him on the wall of his castle brought her comfort. In the portrait he was young and charming. Seeing his kind face in the painting helped her feel close to him.

"Meanwhile, the strawberry faeries had been compelled to work at the blueberry palace all winter. Eventually, they were forced to tell the blueberry guards that the blackberry faerie had been absent from laboring with the other faeries. So when the blackberry faerie returned to her blackberry bush in the spring, blueberry guards arrested her.

"They placed her in a boat. A moat around the blueberry palace connected to waterways that led to an underground dungeon, where they took her. She was thrown into a cell with a weak and dying cellmate, and in the adjacent cell, her strawberry friends were being held captive.

"She knew there was no way to escape and feared that all was lost. She could not save her kingdom and help restore it to the way it was when the old fae was king. As she sat in her cell despairing, her cell companion motioned to her. He was so old and near death that the faerie feared for him greatly. She approached him with pity.

"To her surprise, it was the old fae king whom she had met at the blueberry palace! She recoiled in disbelief at first, but when she got closer, his eyes gave him away. The old fae helped her see that not all was lost and asked her to look around her cell to find what blessings were there. She appreciated nothing about her cell, which looked the same in all directions – except for a round grate in the floor that covered a pipe that went out to the waterway.

"The old fae king reminded her that one of her blessings was that he and her strawberry faerie friends were there with her. Gratitude swelled within the little blackberry faerie and dispelled her despair. Then the old fae told her that her training as The Virtuous One was complete. Now there was one thing that she must do to save her kingdom: jump into the water.

"This, of course, went against everything she had been taught earlier in her life. She knew if she did, she would die. But if the old fae was right, she knew if she didn't obey him, her whole society would die. Remembering the day she felt the urge to follow the silvery fish into the water and again later at the loch, she realized that she had long been prepared to make this sacrifice for her people.

"With a heavy heart, yet with great determination, she made her choice. She was opening the grate, when the blueberry guards began yelling at her to stop and opened her cell door. But before they could get to her, she jumped.

"She didn't die. She discovered she could breathe under water! A silver light led her out of the dungeon, into the moat, into the loch, and out to sea. As the sea water replaced the fresh water, she felt a new surge of energy.

"After traveling all day and into the night by moonlight, she ended up far out to sea where the silver light dove to depths she could not go. She fought and pushed herself, but the pressure of the sea became so great, she was unable to pursue any farther.

"She wondered why she had been brought all this way just to die in the sea for nothing. She felt torn between continuing the fight and giving up. When all seemed dark and lost at last, a third alternative occurred to her – to surrender. Not to give up, but to submit her will with trust in the old fae's words, come what may.

"At the moment of her surrender, the old fae appeared to her and told her not to be afraid. All was well. She felt a great stretching sensation from within herself, and a blast of light went out from her and spanned the whole kingdom. It illuminated the forests, the meadows, the loch, the homes, and the hearts of every living faerie and fae. And with that light, transformation began.

"The faerie regained her strength and swam to the surface, bursting upon the sea as a glorious fae. The silver light led her back to the enchanted castle where she was reunited with the old fae, who was restored to his youth. She had broken the spell over the kingdom. Faeries would be freed from slavery and taught about goodness and light, as in the ancient days. She became queen with the fae king, and they reigned forever in peace, love, joy, and light."

Jaden was confused. "Arran, as much as I have enjoyed this faerietale, I do not understand how it pertains to me?"

William, who had been staring out to sea, looked over at her with tears in his eyes. "You are that faerie, and you need to become a fae."

Jaden could hardly breathe. It was as if the wind had been knocked out of her. This once cold, unfriendly man now had tears in his eyes and genuine tenderness and feeling toward her. She felt moved and began to believe he was revealing to her a truth she could not deny, though she did not understand.

Her whole soul came unraveled and threatened to be her undoing. She wanted to run, hide, bury her head in her hands and cry or scream, but she could not move. Virtually paralyzed, she stared into the eyes of this mysterious and confusing man. All the feelings she felt about how far she had come escaped her, as she admitted to herself at that moment that she wasn't peaceful at all.

Arran spoke quietly. "Jaden, he is right. I brought William with me because he needs to share with you some important things at great risk to the security of Alexandria and against the wishes of the royal couple."

Jaden's mind was spinning. What was happening?

"I am one of six remaining villagers of Rosehannah in the Highlands," William began.

"Rosehannah? Arran?" Jaden asked breathlessly.

"Just listen, there is more." Arran nodded toward William to continue.

"When I was only five years old, my village was attacked by rank, black, bulbous-nosed..."

"Bulbanes." Jaden finished his sentence.

"Yes. So you are familiar with them?"

"We had a run-in with them on our way here. Vile creatures!"

William laughed outright, releasing some of the tension they all felt, and Arran and Jaden joined in. When the laughter subsided, William stared into Jaden's soul as if trying to discern something. Jaden wanted to look away but couldn't because, as uncomfortable as it was, she realized she wanted him to see into her soul. Checking herself in her thought, she remembered Miss Betty and tore her eyes away, hoping he didn't discern her feelings.

He continued, "When I was five, my village was attacked. After the bulbanes destroyed everything and departed, my younger brother, my sister, and I were discovered and rescued by the last remaining village elder under a pile of rubble that was once our home. Everyone else in my village was dead – except for two baby girls."

Jaden gasped and grabbed his arm. "William, what are you saying?"

"I can't tell you more while you are here in Alexandria, but I need to ask you a few questions."

"Of course."

"What do you know about where you came from?"

"Nothing really but what has come to me in dreams and intuitions or feelings." Jaden could barely keep one thought in her mind at a time. "My earliest memory is being sold by pirates to the king and queen of Yamis."

Arran looked at William and nodded.

"I believe I know the rest of your story. Unfortunately, I have sworn to King Alfred that I will not speak of The Third Daughter Prophecy in Alexandria."

William stood. Jaden, with tears welling up in her eyes, stood in front of him, looking straight into his hazel eyes. "You cannot tell me that you know everything I have suffered and fought for my whole life and then tell me you can't tell me!"

William did something that completely caught Jaden by surprise. He gently took both her hands in his and said, "I desired only to give you hope. I am sorry I caused you more pain."

Jaden pulled away. "Miss Betty!"

"She is my sister."

"What?!" Jaden was stunned silent.

"There is much that I must tell you, but now is not the time or place. Do not fear. I believe I know of a way to tell you everything soon, but you must pretend as if you know nothing for now. And please don't speak of the prophecy again."

Confused, angry, and sad, Jaden turned to Arran for comfort.

"Jaden, I couldn't tell you about William and only had hunches that your stories might connect. It was William, Miss Betty, their younger brother Roderick, and the remaining village elder from Rosehannah whom I met all those years ago when I buried the Silver Elf on the shores of the North Sea. But I fear I must also stop my story there."

Jaden glared out to sea wishing she could follow a silver light somewhere or flee anywhere, rather than stay here.

"I can't handle this, I really can't. I have come so far, sacrificed so much! You can't expect me to..." Jaden trembled and felt that if she didn't sit down she would faint.

William put his arm around her, but she shook it off.

"None of this is okay. I barely know you. I don't know right now if I even like you. All I want to know is who I am and where I am from. Arran, you have to tell me!"

"Jaden, please sit down. You look pale."

Jaden listened only because her legs buckled under her. William and Arran helped her land softly. She pulled her knees into her chest and rocked back and forth saying nothing for a long time. Neither of the men knew quite what to say or do, when all of a sudden, Jaden stopped rocking and said, "I know. I will continue asking about The Third Daughter and MaryAnne will send me to the Highlands. Isn't that what you said Arran?"

"You mustn't," William said quickly.

"No, Jaden, that isn't the best way. William has another plan, a better plan, but you must hold on until after the wedding."

"But, Arran, how can I possibly keep from talking about this. Danae will surely see through me!"

"Jaden," William was now on his knees in front of Jaden pleading with her. "No one must know any of this, Danae especially. I have kept this secret my whole life and sacrificed more than I can bear to relate in order to protect it. Arran begged me to share a piece of it with you so you would have hope and so that you wouldn't speak of it anymore.

"I wish I could help you understand, but you are simply going to have to trust me and Arran. Please be patient. I know I have been cold and distant since you have arrived, and I am sorry. I will be more of a comfort to you. It is just that I felt I knew you from the first moment we met, and in order to keep this secret,

I couldn't get close to you."

"Why can't Danae know?"

"No one can know. But Danae would be in special danger, for she will eventually return to Jeremiah and Xannellion. There are too many people between here and there who would kill her for this information or return to Alexandria and seek our destruction. And if Daman ever knew..." William touched the top of a scar near his collarbone.

Arran sighed. "William has risked everything since he was a child to protect The Third Daughter and the secret of your village. Even talking about this now could draw Daman to this land and put everything and everyone at risk. For the sake of all of Trivar, please heed our warning. If I had known what I know now, I would never have let you bring up this subject here in Alexandria. Too much is at stake. But trust us. We have a plan to get you to the Highlands and to share with you everything you need to know. It will finally answer all your questions, Jaden, I promise."

Jaden put her head in her arms and felt that her heart would burst. This was worse than knowing nothing. Now she was in the presence of men who knew everything, and she could still learn no more! And she had to pretend they knew nothing, as if everything were the same as it was before this meeting.

William sat down next to her again, put his arm gently around her shoulders, and sat there quietly waiting. When Jaden felt that she would no longer burst into tears, she lifted her head and looked at him.

"I have so many questions. I don't know how I will do what you ask of me, but if it is possible, I will. Of all the dangers I have faced, Xzavier's cruelty, my dragon sacrificing her life for me, black gryphons pursuing me as my son lay dying in my arms, watching Zachariah suffer near death, bulbanes, the desert, the flooding of the Zikong... Nothing, nothing compares to the anxiety and pain I feel being this close to the truth and freedom but being unable to obtain it. I feel as if my soul will twist inside out and burst, but I will bear it. Please promise me that you will tell me everything soon."

"I promise," William said solemnly. And Jaden believed him.

****

After they had climbed the boardwalk in the direction of the castle, Danae approached them. William politely excused himself. Jaden watched him go, feeling her face flush, to her frustration.

"Danae, are you feeling better?"

"Yes, I was so terribly tired this morning. It looks like you found some company after all?"

Jaden tried to laugh off the inquiry. "Not really, I spent most of my time alone, I only ran into these two on my way back..."

Arran could tell that Jaden was at the end of her bluffing and took up where she left off.

"I was actually looking for both of you. I came to tell you that we are leaving sooner than we had planned. Early tomorrow, in fact. And 7,000 of King Alfred's troops will head toward Jeremiah. They will be a great help to Gideon, which I told King Alfred. King Alfred replied that he 'stands on the shoulders of far greater men who were always prepared and taught him to do the same.'" Arran laughed.

"That sounds like him all right, 'standing on the shoulders of greater men.' I think I have personally heard him say that ten times since we came," Danae said. "I really like him and MaryAnne. Not to mention Lillian, Jordan, and Miss Betty. Alexandria has treated us well."

Jaden tried to act normal, but the reality that MaryAnne wanted her to be sent away made her heart sink. Danae didn't seem to notice.

"How can we ever thank you and your kinsmen for your kind and gentle care in our behalf?" Danae said. "Please be careful." Danae gave him a long hug.

"You are welcome," Arran said. "May the blessings of Gillantri shower down upon you for your goodness, Danae, and may you find the questions your heart is searching for, Jaden. We will meet you both again soon."

Arran gave Jaden a hug. To Danae he gave a tender kiss on the cheek. Then he returned quickly to the castle.

36

Light and Dark

Gideon's anger escalated. "Zachariah, what in Trivar are you doing here?"

"I have to be here, Gideon, you know I do. Besides, I obtained information that you need. Xzavier's troops are on their way, and I poisoned some of Xzavier's dragons."

The words spilled out of Zachariah's mouth. Gideon's exhaustion was tangible, and for a moment Zachariah felt bad, as his trusted mentor tried to gather his strength.

"Listen to me," Zachariah said. "I saw with my own eyes Xzavier's preparations. I know the number of his men and dragons. I even saw the tunnels under Xannellion."

Gideon stared at him, trying to put the pieces together.

"When did you get here? By how long did you beat us? We traveled as fast as possible with men on horses…You got the dragon? Zachariah, tell me you didn't."

"Yes, Justine is alive." Zachariah decided to leave out the part about Daman.

Gideon frowned as he walked toward the young man. "If you want to be a knight of Jeremiah you must be more than a good fighter. You must be honorable. You must keep your word. If I can't trust you to follow simple orders, how can I trust you will follow me when the danger is imminent?"

Zachariah felt desperate. "You know the only reason you didn't let me come back is because my mother feared sending me to battle. If she had supported it, would you have stopped me?"

"But she doesn't support it. You left her in turmoil, worried sick about her son who too recently almost died! Whether I want you here or not is not the point!"

"Yes, it is the point. I am supposed to be here. You and your men need me. You need the information I have. You need my dragon. You needed my help decreasing the number of Xzavier's dragon army. My mother knows I need to face Xzavier, and in the end she will support this. I know she will."

Gideon slouched, and he put his hand over his eyes. "I asked you to protect Danae and your mother."

Zachariah had no quick answer for that and felt a trace of remorse. He reached in his mind for sound justification but found none. Without a lot of heart behind his words, he finally said, "Arran and his brothers will provide more than adequate protection for them. You know they are in good hands."

"All right," Gideon sighed, accepting what he could not change. "I can't be anything but grateful that there will be fewer dragons to face. And seeing as I can't send you back to Alexandria, you have to stay, but you may not fight."

"What?" Zachariah was incredulous.

"What did you think I would do? Did you really think I would let you risk your life? I care for you and your mother. I watched you nearly die. I felt your mother's pain. I know that pain intimately, and she can't bear it again. You were foolish, very foolish. Promise me that you will never disobey my orders again."

"Never. But please reconsider. Let me fight!" Zachariah fairly begged.

"Let's get some food. I am tired and hungry. Richard, send word to our scouts that I need updated information about Xzavier's army. How fast they are traveling, when they will arrive and any other information they can gather. After we eat, Zachariah, we will discuss the intelligence you have gathered and what we are going to do with a dragon."

Gideon shook his head. Hope surged through Zachariah. "Thank you. I hope you can forgive me and maybe someday understand why I had to do this."

"I already understand. I just don't agree. Revenge isn't something men can control. It is far too powerful."

Richard and Franklin came forward and welcomed Zachariah back. Richard left to fulfill Gideon's order. Everyone except Richard returned to the house for dinner and spent the rest of the evening by candlelight listening to Zachariah share all the information he gathered from Xannellion, including what he discovered in the tunnels. The most shocking piece of intelligence came at the very end. Zachariah finished describing the underground lake. He slowed down and wrinkled up his face.

"I know this may sound strange, even false, but I swear to you it is true." He looked at the ceiling, shook his head, and stared straight into Gideon's eyes.

"The humanlike creature that kept burning the bulbanes turned his face so that the light of the crystals shined on him perfectly. I panicked when I saw him and had to take another good look to be sure, but..." Zachariah couldn't say it. He bowed his head and shook it again.

"Tell us," Gideon urged.

"It was Cannote."

"Cannote? But I thought he was dead? Has he just been hiding?"

Zachariah shook his head emphatically. "I watched him die, not two feet away from me. He was dead. And yes, it was him in the cave, but he was walking, holding a poker, and torturing the bulbanes. It was so sickening to me that I ran from the tunnel and the castle and never looked back."

"I can plainly see that you are not lying, but I don't have any explanation for this." He paused, then asked, "Franklin?"

Since Zachariah had begun his account of Cannote, Franklin had been thumbing through one of his large Histories of Trivar. Everyone in the room waited anxiously.

"Yes, here is our answer. The consequence for not following Gillantri... written by Alexander. There are only two paths in Trivar to follow, Gillantri or Daman. It has always been that simple, even in the Arwavian War before we came here."

Zachariah interrupted, "The war before Trivar?"

Gideon answered, "Yes. Before we came to Trivar there was a great war in Arway. Gillantri's children were presented with a simple way to return and live with him, but Daman didn't like his father's idea and wanted to force everyone to follow his own idea instead. A great war ensued."

Zachariah shook his head and Franklin went on. "If the children of Gillantri choose to follow Gillantri, they will live with him in Arway surrounded in beauty and peace and progression, but if the children of Gillantri reject his teachings and choose anything besides Gillantri, their default choice leads them to Daman."

Zachariah looked at Franklin. "I don't get it."

Gideon answered, "There are two ways. Gillantri or Daman. Cannote chose Daman and is now a slave to him forever."

Zachariah scowled. The undead slave Cannote that he saw in the cave disgusted him.

****

The next morning, Gideon, Zachariah, and Franklin met in front of the barn. "So we're all agreed, then?" Gideon asked.

When they emerged from the barn, Zachariah was on a horse, followed by Franklin on his horse. They set off quickly toward the east gate. Gideon mounted his horse and rode off toward the south encampments.

Franklin's assignment was to help Zachariah bring Justine to his cabin in the eastern forest behind Jeremiah. Gideon would begin training the men in regard to the underground threats of bulbanes and trolls.

The morning was cool with thick clouds marching steadily across a stormy sky. Zachariah and Franklin rode fast. The roads to the jungle behind Gideon's house weren't long, but Zachariah was worried about his dragon because he wasn't able to return the night prior to get her.

They turned north just before they arrived at the east gate and rode into the jungle behind Gideon's property. The cooler weather had subdued the jungle sounds of animals and bugs. As they approached the pool with the waterfall, Zachariah motioned for Franklin to stop.

"Let me go and find her. I'll bring her to you."

Franklin nodded and got comfortable in his saddle to wait.

Zachariah dismounted and faded into the flora. He called quietly, "Justine, Justine. Where are you, girl?"

"She isn't here," a voice said, sending prickles up Zachariah's spine.

"Daman."

"Yes, you know my voice," he said arrogantly. "Why did you leave her unattended? My spies located her flying around east of Jeremiah. You can't go off and leave a dragon like that if you expect to keep her out of Xzavier's hands. I expected better of you, Zachariah."

Zachariah worked to contain his anger. "Daman, where is she?"

"Safe. Cared for. I have her."

"She is my dragon. Give her to me."

"I rescued her and restored her to health."

"She was my mother's first."

"Oh, I think your knowledge is incomplete, my son. Do you know where dragons came from before your grandfather in Yamis found them?"

Zachariah hated being called "my son" but was more concerned that Franklin was behind him and might hear them. He also didn't want to give away Franklin's presence to Daman. He kept alert and deliberately fixed his eyes on the dark lord.

"I didn't really come for a history lesson..."

"They came from Kastinov. Have you heard of the place?"

"Kastinov is just a place mothers use to scare bad boys into obeying them."

"Oh, Kastinov exists, I assure you. I have spent thousands of years there."

"Thousands of years, huh?" Zachariah felt impatient. This man looked younger than Gideon, but Zachariah decided not to challenge everything Daman said. There was a fierce unpredictability about him that made Zachariah nervous.

"Yes. It is a dangerous place filled with dark, filthy creatures, but thanks to Gillantri, who, let's say, donated two of Arway's monarch eagles, I was able to create one of my many miracles. The miracle commenced on my first day in Kastinov when I saw what I call the drake. You see, one of the eagles that Gillantri donated was dying and making all sorts of racket, when, before long, the drake emerged from its cave to find out what type of meal was calling him.

"The drake looked very much like Justine but was bigger and flightless. He lit up the darkness with flames that came from glands near his mouth. He found his way to the eagle and disposed of it quicker than Justine disposed of the Twin Shaumas."

Zachariah's eyes opened wide in surprise.

"Yes, I was there the day you had your unfortunate accident. I know more of what goes on in Trivar than might be comfortable for you Trivarians to accept. Anyway, the drake ate the eagle. But I had a thought about the other eagle. What if I could breed the drake with the eagle? They were close in size and, well, there you go, one of my amazing dragons. They are quite fierce enough for this filthy world, don't you think? It took a lot of patience, which of course I have, and a lot of work, but it was worth it, wasn't it?

"Now, about whose dragon Justine really is. She came from my original dragons, my original creations. Justine is mine and has always been mine. I watched over her since your mother first set eyes on her, grateful that your mother took such good care of her and eventually shared her with you. But after your flight to Jeremiah, Justine nearly died and I saved her. Thus, she became mine again. I gave her to you to take care of and you lost her. Now she is mine yet again.

"Something else you should know. I never give my dragons away for free. I was pleased when Teeku found those first dragons and bred them. I needed Xzavier to find them and find Jaden. I hoped Jaden would have a son, to keep Xzavier in check, and, well, look how nicely things turned out."

Questions collided in Zachariah's reeling mind, and before he could clearly formulate one, he heard the light step of someone behind him. Franklin came out of the jungle with a staff in his hand. Daman shot Franklin a fierce look and hurled a bolt of black lightning directly at him. Franklin calmly blocked it with a white flash from his staff. Zachariah ran past Daman to find cover.

"Daman, so nice to see you again," Franklin said, smiling serenely.

Daman responded with a fury of black electric bolts, the last one sending Franklin flying backward. But Franklin maneuvered his staff behind him, expelling an energy wave below him that cushioned his landing and prevented him from crashing into a tree.

Daman sent out another surge of dark power. Franklin leaped into the air twenty feet to avoid the blows, and as he did, he blasted white hot lightning at Daman, slamming him to the ground. As Franklin landed, he released another shower of light which smashed Daman into a gigantic root tangled with vines.

Zachariah watched Franklin nimbly and fiercely fight Daman. Never would he have guessed Franklin could move with such agility and speed. His thickness only seemed an asset of strength. He was neither clumsy nor slow. Franklin nodded for Zachariah to make his escape.

Without questioning him, Zachariah ran deeper into the jungle to search for Justine. Zachariah peeked over his shoulder as he ran and saw black and white flashes and heard Daman yell. He nearly collided with Justine. He discovered her towering over the remains of a deer. She jumped forward to greet him.

"I am so glad you are here." He ran to her, hugged her, and got on her back. "Don't ever fly off like that again. I need you girl."

They flew above the trees, tracking the flashes of light and dark, and dove into the woods toward them. Justine swooped down, and Franklin hopped on her back. As they tore into the sky, Zachariah looked back to see Daman throwing his head back and laughing. Heavy rainclouds gathered and blocked out much of the daylight.

"When did you sell your soul?" Franklin asked.

"Justine has no strings attached and we need her," Zachariah said, but Daman's words haunted him, I never give my dragons away for free. Now he understood that Daman wanted Jaden and him to have Justine. It turned his stomach.

"Oh, there are always strings attached. Do not think you are more powerful than Daman or can manipulate him."

"I already have, though. Don't you see? We have Justine." His statement lacked the confidence he intended to display.

"But why?" Franklin asked.

"We need her to defeat Xzavier."

"Gideon was right when he said that revenge is a force better left to higher powers."

Zachariah felt foolish and angry. Nothing more was said as they flew south of the waterfall to Franklin's cottage.

37

Deeper into Alexandria

Seven days after the elves and Alfred's troops left, making it a fortnight after Jaden and Danae arrived in Alexandria, the weather turned from partly sunny to a constant drizzle with only random breaks throughout the day. And the days were rapidly growing shorter.

Jaden and Danae couldn't explore Alexandria or the beaches as much as they liked, though Jaden found a place she enjoyed almost as much. For the upcoming wedding, a golden gazebo was constructed in the back gardens of the castle that overlooked the ocean.

Many afternoons when the sun was low in the sky and painting the clouds in pinks and yellows, Jaden stood under the gazebo facing the wind, losing her soul to the skies and troubled seas while she thought about the Highlands and what they must be like and wondered how The Third Daughter Prophecy related to her.

She thought more and more of William and found comfort in knowing that he was likely a member of her childhood village. Her longing to have all of her answers wrenched her heart, and she became withdrawn, desiring more and more solitude. When the sun finally set, she often lingered under the gazebo until darkness drowned out every last glimmer of light. On clear nights the Aurora would take over where the sunset left off. Jaden slept little on these nights.

During the day, Danae and Jaden spent time with MaryAnne and Lillian preparing for the upcoming wedding. In some ways, it was a welcome diversion from her growing need to be alone. She found that the other three would keep the conversation going without much help from her, and the two young women's youth and enthusiasm for life was invigorating.

MaryAnne wasn't cold to Jaden, but a distance had grown between them that pained Jaden. Unfortunately, there was no way to fix it, so she suffered in silence. Her only solace was the hope that soon she would know all she had been searching to know.

The day before the wedding, MaryAnne, Danae, and Jaden sat folding little pieces of fabric while Lillian paced the room in a fury.

"Mother, there is no possible way that we will ever be able to complete everything for my wedding! Everyone will know. I am ruined."

Jaden laughed at young Lillian's feistiness. Lillian had been blessed with a protected upbringing abundant with everything good. Love and laughter were the hallmarks of their family and castle. Besides being spoiled, thanks to her father, and having a tendency to look on the negative side, thanks to her mother, Lillian was a delightful young lady with great abilities. Jaden's initial jealousy toward Lillian was fleeting. Once she got to know her, Jaden loved her.

MaryAnne said, "Lillian, everything is ready, but it will be a miserable occasion if the bride is so frazzled that the groom no longer wishes to marry her!"

Lillian's eyes flew at her mother. "This dress still needs its trimmings. The wedding's tomorrow. Why did you let me do this? Oh, I know it isn't your fault... I determined to make this silly dress! Thank goodness for Jordan. At least I know there is no fear of him backing out. If he didn't want me, he would've gotten out a lot sooner than this, like the day he proposed."

MaryAnne laughed. "Have you two heard this story?" she said to Danae and Jaden.

They shook their heads, no. "But we would love to," Danae said, turning to Lillian.

Lillian looked up toward the ceiling and rolled her eyes. "I was in such a foul mood that night, it is a wonder that we are even engaged," she smiled to herself. "He was so sweet, even after I berated him for being late, and then argued with him about what we were going to eat, and then complained about the difficulties of living in a castle.

"And just when I was about to start up again, he gently covered my mouth with his hand, pulled a bouquet of stunning lilies out of thin air, and with a look of amusement waited for my response. I gasped, felt instantly foolish, and gave him a big hug.

"Instead of hugging me, he jumped back. I pulled away and realized that there was something glittering on the stem of one of the lilies. It was a ring. Fortunately, the ring didn't fall off of the lily. Once he was satisfied that all was well, he got down on one knee and proposed gallantly.

"I know I didn't deserve it, that night of all nights, but I also knew that Jordan knew exactly what he was getting himself into and would love me unconditionally. No, mother, there are many things that I can worry about before this difficult event, but he won't be one of them. Jordan is totally committed. I just hope I don't look like a beggar-woman in this dress!"

"Dear, why don't we have my seamstress take a look at it? It is all right to admit when you have gotten yourself in over your head. You haven't sewn anything like this before. I still don't know why you had to start with your wedding dress..."

"Mother, please! I will make my own dress!" With that Lillian stopped pacing, picked up her dress, and started where she left off.

There was a knock on the door.

"Come in," MaryAnne said as she headed for the door.

Before she got there, it opened, and Jordan poked in his head. All the women in the room gasped and ran to stand in front of Lillian. There was quite a commotion as everyone shooed him out. Jaden looked at MaryAnne and then ran to Jordan.

"I'll distract him," Jaden whispered as she passed.

When Jaden got to the door, MaryAnne and Danae fell back in front of Lillian to block her dress from his view, and Jaden said, "You know you aren't supposed to peek in on your bride's preparations, especially the day before the wedding."

"I was just coming to offer you a tour of the ship yards, like you have been requesting. The rain let up and I need some fresh air. Would you like to join me?"

Jaden glanced back over her shoulder and both MaryAnne and Danae waved them on, pleased to have Jordan distracted.

"Yes, I would love to see the famed Alexandrian ship yards."

Jordan smiled and pretended to look past her toward Lillian, eliciting more protests from the women. Jaden quickly shut the door. He threw his head back and laughed in complete amusement.

"That worked out better than I had planned."

Jaden laughed, as well. She was getting used to his youthful sense of humor. But when Jaden turned around, William was standing there.

"Thank you, Jordan. I will take it from here."

"You are welcome. It was my pleasure," Jordan said with a wink.

Jordan bowed politely and left, leaving Jaden and William in the hallway. William shuffled awkwardly.

"I promised to show you the shipyards," he managed.

Jaden noticed a smile cross William's eyes as he put his hand on her lower back and led her through the castle.

"Thank you for remembering. My son would never forgive me if I didn't at least see your navy. He loves the sea like your people do and wants more than anything to have a strong navy in Xannellion when he is king."

"It would be a great blessing to Alexandria and the Highlands to have a sister navy to the south. We could rid our oceans of pirates and sail the seas in peace," William said sincerely.

They exited from the west side of the castle and walked to the shore of the great ocean. Even after a fortnight in Alexandria, it still took her breath away every time the ocean came into view.

"You know, ever since I was a boy I felt drawn to the ocean," William said. "Up north we live and die by the sea. Some of my earliest memories were at the docks watching the village elder preparing ships. He always wanted to be part of building them, even though the Steward of the Highlands was technically in charge. But shipbuilding was the village elder's passion. He is too old now."

"How old is he?"

"He will be ninety-seven years old this spring," William said. "My favorite times were testing out new ships. I would beg him for days to be allowed to come. When he'd finally agree, I could hardly sleep until the event."

"You sound like Zachariah. Even as a young boy, he only ever wanted to sail ships, even though his father had him training with chariots much of his waking hours. His father tried ruthlessly to convince him the sea wasn't worth his time and attention. It never changed the boy."

"I guess it is something you are born with."

Jaden looked a mile down the ship yard.

"Oh, William, your ships are exquisite." Hundreds of large and small ships rested at port or anchored in the harbor, some with their sails up and ready for great adventures, others with sails tied down, bobbing up and down waiting for their next turn at sea. "How many are you building?"

"Well, we have 140 ships ready. We usually have anywhere from five to ten of them on the dry docks being repaired. We replace one to three a year, unless we have a battle or bad storm and need to repair or build more." William smiled with pride.

"How long have you worked here in Alexandria with their navy?"

"Nearly twenty years."

Jaden stopped to watch workmen on a ship that was nearly finished. "Can we see what they are doing?"

"That is why we are here." William motioned for Jaden to go first up the gangplank. "They are carving some aesthetic details, which I will need to examine and pass off if I determine they are acceptable. Maybe you could help."

Jaden looked at him to see if he was taunting or mocking her, but William laughed good-naturedly. As they got to the top of the gangplank, Jaden let William go ahead of her so he could inspect the work. The sea breeze that tossed his hair and cooled her skin smelled sweet and salty, and she felt deeply contented.

He smiled at Jaden and nodded his head for her to come closer. There was something about seeing him among his men and his ships that gave new insight to Jaden. He worked naturally, effortlessly, moving from one spot to the next, laughing with the men and enjoying himself. With no stifled emotions or facades, he seemed so genuine.

Jaden loved the smell of the damp wood and wood shavings. And mixed with the smell of the salty air and the wind off the water, it felt like a cleansing tonic to her soul. William crossed to the cabin where a craftsman was carving a scene of Alexandrian ships sailing into a sunset. The details were exquisite.

"That is simply elegant," Jaden whispered.

"Do you think I should pass it off?" William said with a twinkle in his eye that reminded her of Franklin, who always wore that gleam in his countenance.

"I can't pretend to know the technicalities and principles of woodwork and art of this caliber, but that is some of the most brilliant work I have ever seen, and the emotions it evokes in me... It is splendid."

William passed off the carvings on the main mast and motioned for her to follow him. He went up the steps where the artisans had finished their work carving entwining ivy vines into the helm. He pointed to the mast behind the helm. Lilies set in threes were carved in swirls up the mast.

"That is breathtaking, really, William. It is."

"I agree. These ships are almost as intricately designed as ours. You know, Alexandria's ships were very plain before I came."

"What do you mean?"

"Well, twenty years ago when ships were built in Alexandria, they would get them sea worthy and call it good. After being here a year or so, I suggested to Alfred that we could add some beauty to them. He took a trip with me to the Highlands and toured our shipyards. Alfred fell in love with our ships. Jordan's grandfather agreed to send down fifty of his most skilled carvers. They trained the Alexandrian men and helped them complete the elaborate carvings on twenty-five of the Alexandrian ships before returning north. Over the next few years we finished all two hundred ships in the fleet."

William was animated. He obviously loved these ships. She loved being by the sea as he did and rejoiced with him in every detail.

His hazel eyes were more blue than green. He had suntanned skin, but it was lighter in color, more like Jaden's. He had freckles like Benjamin and medium brown hair that was receding around the hairline. William was strong, but not as large as Gideon. And he had softer features and a more gentle personality when he allowed himself to be less guarded.

He seemed more open and easier to read than Gideon had been. Maybe she was just better at reading men after Gideon, or maybe not, but it all felt more natural, as if she had known William for a very long time. Jaden found herself wanting to stay, even when it began to rain.

Twilight settled in by the time William finally finished the inspections. Everyone had gone home except the guards near the entrance to the shipyard by the castle. They would remain there all night.

After their visit to the shipyards, she felt an increasing fondness for this sphinx of a man. Who was he really? Why did he end up here in Alexandria? How could she ever get close to him, shrouded in all this mystery and these facades, as he was? As she was wondering about William, Jaden heard deep breathing directly behind her, right before she was hit hard on the back of the head.

She woke with a throbbing headache in a dark cave with glowing amber light. She was tied with rough rope back to back with someone who was leaning his or her head against her. She wiggled and said, "Is that you, William?"

"Yes, it is," an unfamiliar voice said, "but he may be out a little longer than you. The weaker of my men thumped you."

Jaden could barely focus her eyes. What she could see was blurry because of her mild concussion and headache. "Where am I? Who are you?"

"I am a friend," he said in a sugary voice. "I knew you in Arway before you came to Trivar. You don't remember, but you followed me, until Gillantri tricked you into turning away from all we could have been together."

"I don't believe you. I would never follow someone like you," she said, but she thought of Xzavier and felt some truth in his words.

"Don't you remember being in a cell, dark like this cave, when Gillantri came and manipulated you into following him?"

Jaden's dream of Gillantri unlocking her chains came to mind. "No one tricked or manipulated me into anything."

The voice laughed mockingly. "Whatever you say, Jade."

She fidgeted and squirmed again to get William to wake up.

"Retch, wake the man."

A dark, ugly bulbane walked over to William and kicked him, sending a wave of pain through Jaden, as well. William didn't stir. The monster kicked him harder and William moaned. Jaden could not stand it.

"Stop it. Don't hurt him." Another kick brought tears to Jaden's eyes. "No more! Stop!" William continued to moan.

"I was just trying to help you wake your friend. Isn't that what you wanted? I've always given you what you wanted, Jade. It was you who turned on me."

"Stop calling me Jade. I don't know what you are talking about. Who are you?"

A dark figure came close but didn't touch her. "You are still so beautiful," the voice said.

As he came nearer, Jaden trembled. William shifted and groaned.

"William, wake up, please, wake up," Jaden tried to say calmly, but her voice trembled.

William lifted his head and said, "Jaden, where are we?"

"You are here to finish your story," the voice said to William. "I love stories. I'm in the mood to hear the one you were telling Jade on the beach not too long ago. I want to hear the ending, William of Rosehannah, or should I say, Frederick of Rosehannah?"

"Who are you and what is it to you?" he said.

"That isn't important, really."

Frederick paused for a second and asked, "And if I don't tell you, what then?"

"Retch," the voice said less sweetly.

Something grabbed Jaden's leg and hammered it hard with its head. She felt it break near the shin. She yelled and began to pass out. Thrashing around, she managed to stop the hyperventilation and gain control of herself by trying to breathe deeply. Then nausea overwhelmed her. She tried to control it but failed and vomited to her right against the wall.

"No more!" Frederick ordered.

When Jaden got control of her breathing again, she said, "Don't tell him, William...or Frederick? Please."

Jaden's body shook as she worked to breathe deeply. She tried to stifle a groan in vain.

"Jade, I have waited for this moment for a long time." The voice was sweet again.

"You don't scare me, whoever you are," Jaden said. She was angry now. "Break all my bones."

"Don't touch her!" Frederick said. "Agree to let us go, and I will tell you what you want to know."

"You have already caused me too much trouble."

"I will tell you everything but you have to let us go." Frederick's authority resonated in the cold darkness.

Silence filled the cave: eerie, damp, dark silence. For a minute, Jaden didn't know where the voice went, or the Retch for that matter. Then the icy voice broke through the shadows. "All right, Frederick, tell us all you know."

"We are agreed then?" Frederick demanded.

"When you are done, I will let you go," the voice stated with an undertone of controlled rage.

William started with the prophecy and history of The Third Daughters. Jaden's leg hurt intensely, but she tried to distract herself by listening and trying to escape. She felt around on the ground below her hands, found a sharp stone and worked to cut the ropes from her wrists.

"Duchess Roslyn was born in Wallace to a warrior family, the McGregors. They were a good family but one that had to sacrifice everything to survive while protecting the northern borders of Alexandria. The land up north is unforgiving and wild. The heathens that live in the Highlands are as wild as the land they live in, not much different from the Vikings to the west.

"The only thing that kept the wild clans in the north from coming down and destroying Alexandria were a group of knights. They were a splinter of the Jeremian knights in the eighth century who fled from Xannellion's ruler King Basilius. Basilius, under Daman's cruel hand, decided to exterminate all knights in and around Xannellion."

Jaden's dream played over in her mind. She could picture the knights fleeing because her dream had been so vivid. And of course she easily visualized the green, deep lakes. She wondered how all this related to her. If she could only go into the Highlands!

"Yes, those were days filled with glory," the voice said, bringing Jaden back to her pain.

"Daman, is that you?" Jaden asked, suddenly remembering all Franklin had said about Daman's tunnels and treachery.

"Does it matter, my dear Jade? Frederick, keep talking."

Frederick took a shallow breath and finished telling the story. "The main group of knights fled in ships to the Highlands where Stephen McGregor, Roslyn's paternal grandfather many generations back, invited them to come and live. He offered refuge to the knights in return for protecting Alexandria from the wild people of the north. At the time, it was all Stephen McGregor could do to keep the Vikings out of his Highland cities, so having reinforcements provided him and his forces great relief.

"Knights from all over Trivar flocked to the McGregor banner, and to this day there is a strong group defending the Highlands, now led by Jordan's father, Steward of the Highlands. Only a handful of knights stayed in the jungle behind Jeremiah waiting for Basilius to die. And when Basilius did die, those knights in the jungle returned and rebuilt their beloved city. Duchess Roslyn was born into the pure ancestral line of knights. She escaped death in her early childhood and married Duke Roderick of Wallace."

"I am familiar with Roslyn and her childhood near-death experience. Two Highland babies escaped me that time. I am even familiar with her death, and I am familiar with Duke Roderick's death...and Frederick of Rosehannah...that would be you."

There was silence for some time. Jaden's leg hurt like it was on fire with shooting pains.

"Yes," Frederick said sadly.

"Frederick, you know what I need."

Daman's Retch came close to Jaden again.

"No, I will finish." Frederick sounded as if he would cry. "My brother, Roderick, and his wife, Roslyn, had two children who were mercilessly murdered by the dark lord of this land."

"I am also familiar with that failure of yours," Daman said impatiently. "Retch," he summoned.

"Stop! I mean it," Frederick cried. "Their third daughter was named Lillian of Wallace."

"Princess Lillian?" The voice was no longer sweet. "So that is where the cursed baby ended up. How clever. Right under my nose and I couldn't see it. Retch, let's go."

"Don't you want to hear the rest?"

"No. No more stories. Maybe we will meet again another time, and then you will tell me more."

"But you promised to let us go."

"I'm leaving you and not killing you, therefore, I let you go. Thank you, Frederick of Rosehannah. Until we meet again, fair Jade."

With a flourish, the dark voice was gone. Only the dull auburn light of the cave and the excruciating pain remained.

38

Stand With Us

By the time Franklin and Zachariah arrived at Franklin's cottage, the dark sky released its burden. The rain fell in sheets as Franklin and Zachariah dismounted Justine behind the cottage. They ran toward the cottage past dragon bones that Franklin had been drying and cataloging. Zachariah stopped to examine the large spine drenched by the deluge.

"I have it, let's get this on her and then get back to Gideon quickly." In Franklin's hands dangled a dragon harness connected to a large chain, probably found on one of the now-dead dragons. Zachariah put down the spine, took the harness, and ran over to Justine. Her mane, which was usually full-bodied, was dripping wet and straight. Her slippery, shiny body almost glowed in the gathering dark.

"Here, girl, I know this isn't your style, but we need to keep track of you. Come on. Bend down." Justine turned her head to see how serious he was, but Zachariah didn't give up until she bent her head down and he secured the harness. Justine raised her head and shook it, finding the restriction unfavorable.

Leash in hand, Zachariah led her to the edge of a meadow behind the cottage. She settled in to finally digest her deer while Zachariah chained her to a tree. With one last plaintiff whine of dissent, she laid her head down. Zachariah patted her head and left.

Back at Gideon's stables, Franklin and Zachariah found their frightened horses, which had returned home. The two men sloshed through the mud to put their horses safely in the stable. Next, they mounted fresh horses and rode to the south gate where they met up with Gideon.

Already the knights had constructed replicas of the bulbanes and trolls according to Zachariah's description and were using them to practice archery and fencing. With rain dripping off their faces, shooting was difficult, but these weren't ordinary soldiers. Zachariah was impressed with their accuracy and skill.

As Zachariah and Franklin approached, Gideon said to a young knight, "Keep the men working. I'll talk with these two and be right back."

The young knight nodded and turned back to the other men.

Gideon asked, "How did it go?"

"We need to talk to you," Franklin said without looking at Zachariah.

Gideon looked at Zachariah and then Franklin. "Did you get Justine?" he asked.

"Yes, but there was a slight complication," Zachariah offered.

"Well, let's move over here. The rain should muffle our sound." They followed Gideon to the east side of the field and found a spot beneath an enormous tree with roots that an entire garrison could hide behind. They stood in a small circle under the protection of the tree's large branches. "Tell me," Gideon said.

Franklin turned to Zachariah. "I think you ought to explain this."

Zachariah said, "I never told you exactly how I got Justine." Without waiting for a response, Zachariah plunged, "Daman followed us through the rainforest on our way to Alexandria. He often came to me trying to get me to take Justine. I told him to go away and didn't believe him at first, but he was persistent. Eventually, I realized how much of a help Justine would be to me, to us..."

At that moment, Gideon spotted Richard, thoroughly drenched and out of breath, running toward the tree. When he was near enough to be heard, he shouted, "Our scouts spotted dragons!"

Gideon bolted out of their hiding place first. The rain pelted them harshly. "What else?"

"It looks like Xzavier and his army is nearly to Jeremiah."

"They must have traveled through the night. Why have we only heard about this now?"

"Only two of our scouts made it back. Xzavier captured all ten of them and held them, killing eight and leaving two barely alive to return. We are tending to them now, but they are in bad shape."

Gideon said to Zachariah, "We'll talk about Justine later. Right now we need you. Stand with us."

Zachariah felt a surge of excitement and satisfaction.

Next, Gideon said to Franklin, "I need you to get the flying tigers ready. Use whatever means you have to aid the troops."

Franklin nodded, his eyes bright.

Gideon ran past Richard shouting commands to every garrison leader. "Get your archers ready. Send for ammunition. Mobilize the remaining knights out of Jeremiah..."

Zachariah said to Franklin, "I am going to get Justine."

"Be careful." Franklin looked deep into the young man's eyes. "Remember your mother loves you."

Zachariah felt a twinge of remorse for leaving her but pushed that away and ran to his horse. He rode as hard as he could through the blinding rain toward Franklin's cottage. Behind him he could hear the beat of the Jeremian drums organizing the troops. Adrenaline surged through his body as he rode. Finally, he arrived at the meadow where Justine was waiting.

****

By the time Zachariah and Justine arrived east of the battle field, having been careful to avoid being seen, the knights were fully engaged with Xzavier's foot soldiers on the ground and dragons overhead. The roar of battle was deafening. Zachariah couldn't see Gideon but knew he was near the south gate of Jeremiah overseeing the battle.

Earlier, the Mountain Elves were on the east side of the battlefield near the south gates of Jeremiah with Franklin, but Zachariah couldn't see them anywhere now. They were hidden well, and Zachariah guessed they were waiting for the right time to participate, as he was. The night that Gideon had returned to Jeremiah, Franklin explained to Zachariah that these were the elves who live quietly in the mountains behind Jeremiah. They were the ones who hid the Jeremian knights for a time before King Basilius died. Franklin spent a lot of time with them.

It took all of Zachariah's determination to stay out of sight. He knew that his restraint and obedience could mean the difference between success and failure, but it was so difficult to do nothing but watch the knights shoot arrows at Xzavier's dragons from below, while the flying tigers attacked them in the air. Justine could make a big dent in Xzavier's forces, but he needed to stay put until Gideon gave the signal.

The rain never let up, making the battlefield a virtual swamp. Soldiers and knights fought hand to hand in mud up to their shins. At one point in the late afternoon, Zachariah watched as two of Xzavier's biggest dragons took out several archers, opening a hole wide enough for three dragons to break the line. The three dragons dove directly into the ranks, flinging men and horses in every direction.

Jeremiah adjusted to this affront by sending in more flying tigers that weren't already engaged, but it wasn't enough. Archers shot at the dragons alternately from multiple directions, which eventually brought down two of the three dragons. Then Franklin appeared out of nowhere and shot arrows of light directly at the third dragon, sending it to the ground. This gave the knights the time they needed to fill the gap in the row of archers and secure their ranks again.

Franklin disappeared into the east jungle as soon as the dragon went down. As daylight faded, a guard from inside Jeremiah rode into camp and found Gideon, who sent word down the line from west to east: "Bulbanes are running through the streets of Jeremiah!"

Three hundred knights left the ranks from the back rows and entered Jeremiah. Shortly after the men left for the city, a scout from the southwest gate rode in.

"Black gryphons are coming!" As he said it, Gideon saw dark figures low on the horizon approaching fast.

Gideon didn't release the remaining flying tigers until the gryphons were right overhead. Zachariah couldn't stand it any longer. He climbed out of his perch, grabbed his sword, and left Justine tied to a tree.

"I'll be back girl," he said and ran toward Jeremiah. But as he got to the southeast gate, Franklin appeared from the shadows of the jungle.

"Where are you going, young man?"

"I can't stay in the woods. I am going to get some bulbanes!"

"What if Gideon needs you? What if Daman gets Justine again? I need you to think!"

"Why did you stop?" Zachariah deflected.

"It takes a lot of energy to use my magic."

"But the other day with Daman? You lasted longer than the elves did when we encountered bulbanes on the way to Ononzai."

"I have been around longer than most of those younger elves and have learned how to use my energy more efficiently. But I only have so much energy, and I am going to need that energy later when the troops run out of theirs. While they have strength to hold off Xzavier, I have to wait for my turn...just like you! Get back to your place!"

Zachariah knew he was right but didn't want to give in. "Just a few bulbanes. I'd feel so much better if I could have just a few. Watching is too hard."

Franklin stood his ground, and Zachariah turned back toward Justine.

Before long, it was dark, and Xzavier called back his dragons. Xzavier had lost three of his good dragons, but Zachariah could tell the losses were much higher in the Jeremian camp. He curled up next to Justine and settled in for the night.

39

She Didn't Flinch

Jaden worked at the rope, not too confident that it was doing any good. Her mind felt fuzzy and her head ached. The dull auburn light strained her eyes, adding to her pain. But all she could think about was getting free.

"What did he do to you, Jaden?"

"I think he broke my leg."

"We need to get out of this cave."

"I am trying to cut the rope with a sharp stone, but I don't know if it is making any difference."

"I'll try. Let me see if I can grab it." In the semi-darkness, Jaden tried to give Frederick the stone, but it fell between them. They both reached for it and after a moment's struggle, he grabbed it. "Got it. You rest."

"I feel dizzy."

"Lean against me." He tried to support her while continuing to work. Jaden talked to Frederick and tried to keep her mind off her injury.

"Lillian is not MaryAnne and Alfred's daughter?"

"No, my lady."

Jaden smiled weakly but insisted, "Is there more?"

"Roslyn, the mother of the second Third Daughter…"

"Roslyn was the first? Lillian is the second?" Jaden was shocked. She recalled the mother with blue eyes and blond hair from her dream.

"Yes, Roslyn was the first. When Daman found her, he killed my brother's first two children and did not spare Roslyn nor Roderick. This happened just after the birth of their third daughter, Lillian. He tried to kill Lillian, but I intervened. I was seriously wounded after our clash but was able to ride to Alexandria with Lillian. The King and Queen of Alexandria agreed to raise her as their own and protect our secret with their lives so that she would be safe.

"I chose them because I knew they could be trusted, and also because they were near to having their own child, and I hoped the two could be raised together. Sadly, their child was stillborn the very night I came with Lillian. By the grace of Gillantri, no one ever suspected, until now, that she was the child of prophecy. Alfred and MaryAnne raised Lillian as their own. No one knows her secret besides the King and Queen, my sister, and me."

"Doesn't Lillian know who she is?"

"Alfred thought it better not to tell her. He felt it was too much risk, but he trained her to be nearly as good a warrior as any soldier in Alexandria, as well as bringing her up with all the graces of a queen. But she isn't powerful enough to take on Daman. It was my job to protect her. I hope I have not failed her." Frederick worked more furiously as he spoke.

Jaden grew quiet. Her new knowledge and the cost by which she obtained it weighed on her.

"I don't know what to say, William." Jaden paused. "I mean, Frederick. I am so sorry. This is my fault."

"I didn't have to tell you. When you, Arran, and I were at the bottom of the boardwalk, I thought we were alone." Frederick's voice rose to an agitated pitch. "We need to get out of here. I have to protect Lillian!"

Just then, Frederick's rope gave way. Frederick worked furiously until his ankles were free. Carefully, he worked at Jaden's wrists, but when he got to her ankles she clenched her eyes shut and buried her chin in her chest. Every swipe at the rope sharpened the pain.

"Should I leave the ropes on your ankles?"

"No, being bound hurts more than cutting the rope does."

"I am trying to be careful."

"It is all right. Just get us out of here."

Frederick finished. He stood up and groaned.

"Are you all right?" Jaden asked.

"I am fine, just a few bruises."

"I felt every one of that bulbane's kicks," she said.

"Bruises heal." As he said this, he picked her up in his arms and walked in the direction opposite Daman's exit. She hoped they were heading toward the opening of the cave. Eventually, they found a large door cut out of the black, rough cave stone, which opened to the ocean.

When they emerged from the cave, it was night. Frederick looked toward the docks and the castle. All was quiet except the lapping of the waves on the shore. Jaden's leg was blood-stained and misshapen, probably a compound fracture.

"We need to get you help."

"After we tell Alfred," Jaden said and put her head on Frederick's shoulder. Frederick carried Jaden off the beach and up the docks to the castle. Jaden tentatively asked, "What are you going to tell Lillian?"

"I am not going to tell her anything that I don't have to until after the wedding. She has been looking forward to this day her whole life."

Frederick spoke paternally and more tenderly than she expected. She wondered about the heartache he must feel for having to keep all of these secrets for so many years.

"Was that really Daman?"

Frederick breathed heavily and answered quietly, "It was."

Jaden shuddered.

As soon as two guards near the castle saw them, they came running. "William, what is wrong? What happened?"

"We ran into some trouble. Can you take Jaden? I am injured," Frederick said and gently handed Jaden over to the larger guard. To the other he said, "I need you to run ahead and tell Alfred to put Alexandria on high alert from above and below. He will know what I mean. When I get there, I will explain the rest."

The second guard hastened to deliver the message. Jaden's pounding head made her heart feel heavier. The rain drizzled upon them in the darkness. By the time they reached the castle door, guards stood at every entrance and soldiers were running across the castle grounds to strengthen the perimeter.

When they reached the medical chamber, Jaden was struggling to stay conscious. The guard laid her down on a soft mattress. Frederick said, "Are you going to be all right, Jaden? You are pretty courageous, you know. I don't know if I would have argued with the fallen lord."

"I am so sorry that Alexandria is in danger, Frederick. I mean, William. Go to Lillian." Exhaustion was setting in. Jaden felt devastated that yet another Arwavian land was being attacked by darkness because of her. Frederick brushed her hair out of her eyes and left.

Early the next morning, Jaden sat on her mattress feeling almost comfortable when Frederick returned. His brow furrowed with concern.

"How are you?" he asked tenderly.

Jaden smiled. "Aren't you supposed to be at a wedding?"

"Well, let's say that it has been delayed for a day or so. We need to secure the kingdom first."

Jaden nodded. "It is good to see you. They worked on my leg last night. I won't be walking for some time. The pain is tolerable, but I feel responsible for this trouble. I have delayed a royal wedding, caused injury to you, and compromised the security of Alexandria."

Frederick put up his hand for Jaden to stop. "Enough. It is Daman who compromised the security of Alexandria, not you. You are a hero. You would have taken more punishment to protect Alexandria."

Jaden tried to smile, but she knew how MaryAnne must feel about this and wondered if she would be shipped off to the Highlands straightway. Frederick seemed to sense her thoughts and said quietly, "It is not your fault. It is mine."

Jaden's head dropped. She knew he was covering for her. Frederick sat next to Jaden and put his arm around her shoulders.

"You don't know me," she said. "You don't know anything about my life. You are too good."

Frederick held Jaden and said, "I don't know much about your life before you came to Jeremiah, but since you arrived here in Alexandria, I've seen a woman who risked her life for her son, traveled hundreds of miles under great peril to leave darkness behind her, turned her back on her former life and accepted Gillantri and his love, and faced Daman himself and didn't flinch! I know we all have weaknesses, but I hope that I can be as strong as that someday."

"Thank you for your kindness. I'll have to think on that."

"I am not being kind. I am speaking truth."

Jaden hugged him, grateful for his encouragement.

Frederick cleared his throat. His eyes were smiling. "Before I forget, Danae is going to be here in a few minutes. She is very worried about you. Last night she went to sleep assuming you would just be in late. When she woke this morning and everything was upside down, she panicked. Fortunately, Miss Betty got to her early."

"I am glad. She is very dear to me." Jaden decided to change the subject. "I am extremely curious about everything going on through the night. I heard all sorts of unusual sounds: men in armor marching, bomb blasts, warning horns. Can you explain any of these?"

Frederick smiled, "You don't miss anything do you? All of our armed men who aren't in Jeremiah, including many reserves, have been called up to secure

Alexandria. We have more than quadrupled the number stationed around and outside Alexandria.

"The bomb blasts... The cave and three other underground tunnels suspected of being used by Daman were destroyed. We have men searching every inch of Alexandria, including underground, to look for more passageways. Daman will not have easy access to Alexandria when we are done.

"The warning horns are being tested all over the city and throughout the countryside, all the way into the Highlands, to make sure we can warn our people and our allies to the north if Daman reappears. Our accidental find yesterday has proven to be a great blessing to Alexandria. We had no idea Daman was so entrenched here in the north. We owe many thanks to you for your bravery." Frederick took Jaden's hand and kissed it.

Frederick urged her to rest. He stood to leave, which caused Jaden to feel a bittersweet tugging sensation in her heart. Jaden sighed, wondering what in Trivar was happening between them.

****

The next day, all preparations for the safety of Alexandria were finished, and the wedding was under way. Soldiers lined the streets, and though the procession was shortened in order to adequately protect all involved, everything was elaborately decorated and well suited for a princess and her prince.

Jaden dressed in a lovely gown of midnight blue and gold. Instead of marching in the wedding procession, she reclined in a litter carried by four Alexandrian soldiers. She held a bouquet of lilies, as did the other bridesmaids. The day was clearer than it had been since winter had settled in. Wispy clouds paraded above in the pale blue sky.

Jaden thought of Gideon and hoped Gillantri watched over him and his troops. She wondered if Zachariah reached Gideon safely and if there would be a wedding in Jeremiah for her son and Danae when they returned.

She admired Danae, who radiated gentle beauty in an emerald green dress with gold accents. Yes, she wished for a woman like that for her son. But she wondered if he would come around, or even be alive? She shook off her recollections of his collision with the stadium wall. She noticed The Third Daughter statues as they passed and wondered if she would ever get to the Highlands.

So many questions hung in her mind about where she came from. Frederick was another question in her mind. And how would she keep all this from Danae? So many times she almost gave it away. It felt lonely knowing what she knew without being able to share it with anyone. Her admiration grew as she thought of Frederick here for twenty years with only Miss Betty to speak to about these things that were obviously so dear to his heart.

Jaden forced herself to remember more pleasant times, like this morning's activities. Danae had kept busy with Lillian. Lillian was vibrant as everyone fussed about her dress, jewelry, hair, and makeup. Jaden saw wistfulness in Danae's eyes and thought of Zachariah. Danae was radiant as she served her new friend.

Despite the threat to Alexandria, the whole kingdom came out for the ceremony and winter gala. White candles tied with deep green, midnight blue, or gold ribbons were placed everywhere throughout the city. Some candles were as tall as The Third Daughter statue. Others were small enough to be carried by children in the procession to the castle.

Many of the candles were ornate. They were created by professional candle makers who layered white, gold, green, and blue wax before carving them into elegant figures of lilies, swans, and ships. When they were lit, the splendid colored layers glowed. Trees were adorned with candles, ribbons, and white lilies made of glass. Garlands strung from street to street were wound with ribbons of emerald, gold, and midnight blue.

Jaden followed the wedding procession around the castle where large gold candelabras lined the way to the back gardens and the gazebo that Jaden loved so well. Evergreen garlands with streams of ribbon connected the candelabras in breathtaking beauty.

Jaden was carried to the front of the group and sat in a place of honor near Queen MaryAnne, who, with a slightly forced smile, nodded her greeting. Jaden nodded back. She glanced at the choppy, wintry sea that glittered periodically with gentle escaping sunlight.

After a simple marriage ceremony, Jordan kissed Lillian softly. Jaden breathed a sigh of relief, glad they were married without any interference from Daman. Lillian and Jordan crossed over to MaryAnne and Alfred and embraced them. Next, they embraced Jordan's father Samuel, who was Steward of the Highlands, and Loralee, his wife. Shortly after, Frederick hurried everyone to the Great Banquet Hall for a smaller, less formal celebration with family and close friends.

"Wasn't that lovely? I am so glad for them," Danae said.

"Then what are these?" Jaden asked, wiping tears from Danae's cheeks.

"I hope someday things will work out that well for me. Jordan is a good man."

"Things will, Danae, I am sure of it."

The procession of close friends and family followed Jordan and Lillian into the castle and through the halls, where smells of vanilla, cinnamon, and citrus wafted. They entered the great hall where musicians were playing a lively tune not common to Alexandria and unknown to Jaden, although it rekindled in Jaden that feeling of remembering, like when she saw the Aurora Borealis for the first time and first smelled the northern pine forest. The familiarity brought her emotions to the surface.

Danae noticed and offered, "The music was provided by Highlanders. Isn't it wonderful?"

"Though I've never heard it before, it seems so familiar. I am touched deeply by it. I don't want to cry at the wedding." All of the trauma of the past few days hit Jaden, and she worried she wouldn't be able to control her emotions. "I should go back to my room."

"Oh, no, please stay. We could just sit somewhere out of the way and enjoy ourselves."

Jaden agreed, realizing that she couldn't just disappear. The soldiers accompanying the two women set Jaden down at a table on the outer edge of the group and then retreated to the door to wait until they were needed again.

Once the room was filled, the doors were shut and guarded closely. King Alfred stood in the middle of the room and raised his hands. All noise ceased, and everyone gave him full attention.

"Welcome, Samuel and Loralee, friends and family! What a glorious occasion that brings us all together. Now the Highlands and Alexandria are once again united, never to part. During the past few days, Alexandria felt the fear of Daman, but we have received the peace of Gillantri in our time of distress.

"To prove our determination and courage, we carried on as if nothing happened! We stand on the shoulders of great ones who have shown us the easiest and simplest way to live. There are many roads to travel, many paths to choose, but thanks to the great ones who have gone before, we are blessed to observe how they lived their lives, worked out their struggles, and overcame with faith in Gillantri.

"Now a few words about my dear Lillian... From the time I first held you, I loved you. You are perfect, simply perfect, and you deserve all the goodness, courage, and purity that Jordan has to offer. You have been trained in all the affairs of the kingdom, yet you are still gentle, gracious, and kind. I consider it one of the greatest opportunities of my life to be able to help raise and love you as my daughter..."

A commotion broke out in the back of the room by the door. By the time Jaden swung her head around, two soldiers lay dead on the floor and Daman arrogantly swaggered in. Jordan stepped in front of Lillian, while Alfred stepped in front of MaryAnne.

Daman sauntered past Jaden and smiled.

"How nice," he said. "A family gathering. You really did a good job at distressing my tunneling project, but there are many ways for me to travel, and the tunnels can be rebuilt. I don't believe I was invited, but I have a toast for your new bride, as well. She will be mine." Daman laughed leisurely.

"Not if I have anything to say about it," Jordan said, drawing his sword.

"Nor I," said Samuel as he stood by his son.

"Nor I," said Alfred.

"Nor I," repeated Frederick, who stood in front of them all.

"Nor I, Nor I, Nor I," echoed through the hall as one person after the next added their support for Lillian's safety. Eventually all of the men and women chimed in. Daman looked shaken.

"Well, you have friends, Lillian, but unlike me, they don't know who you are – who you really are."

Momentary silence was followed by low murmuring from the crowd.

"I know who you are, Third Daughter! And now that I know – know this: I'm watching you. Don't delude yourself into thinking that you or your daughter will survive. I know you, and I know where to find you. Trivar will be mine!" With a blast of black lightning, he was gone, but his eerie laugh lingered and his voice was heard repeating, "I know where to find you."

Jaden couldn't stop trembling. "I think I'm going to be sick," she told Danae.

"Me, too. How awful."

Once the shock wore off, everyone in the room buzzed about the surprise and horror they felt. They especially questioned and discussed the new information about Lillian: "I never knew...I always wondered...I can't believe it..." Men and women gazed at Lillian in amazement and disbelief. So she is The Third Daughter, all their scrutinizing stares said.

"Danae, get me some help to get over to Lillian. I have to see her."

Danae found the two soldiers who had earlier accompanied them and returned. They carried Jaden to the front of the room with Danae by her side and set her down near Lillian. MaryAnne and Alfred were talking with the bewildered Lillian.

"Why didn't you tell me?" Lillian cried. She seemed deflated by the news.

Alfred took Lillian's hand. "My dear, it was my decision. We tried to protect your identity. I told Jordan so he would understand his role as your husband. It is an added responsibility for him to be the husband of the second Third Daughter and father of the future Third Daughter. Of course he accepts this fully."

Alfred searched Lillian's eyes to see how these new facts might impact her as they began to sink in. "And William...well...he is the captain of the guards and...well..." Alfred stumbled, trying to find the words to explain, when Frederick himself walked back into the room.

His presence hushed the group. He raised his hands to get everyone's attention, though it wasn't needed. "The kingdom of Alexandria is secure. We apologize for the disruption."

After his announcement, he walked straight over to Lillian and knelt in front of her. "Lillian, I am personally sorry that your wedding has been thus interrupted. I have done everything in my power to avoid this but have failed. Will you please forgive me?"

Lillian looked at him tenderly. "William, you have protected me since I can remember, and I will always be grateful. I love you. Daman surprised you, and if he surprised you, there isn't a man in Trivar who would have seen him coming!"

She threw her arms around him and gave him a hug. He hugged her back lovingly, and Jaden saw tears in his eyes. When they stopped, Alfred said quietly, "William, I was having a difficult time explaining about your role...and well..."

Frederick bowed his head, reached for Lillian's hands, and looked up into her eyes. "My dear, this isn't the place or time I wanted to share this with you, but I am your uncle. I knew your mother, and your father was my brother."

Lillian looked quickly at MaryAnne, who nodded in the affirmative with tears welling up in her eyes, then at the king, who smiled with a deep sigh.

"But I don't understand."

"It was our cover so that I could watch over you but keep the secret from those who wanted to thwart the prophecy."

"Who is my mother?" Lillian asked.

"Her name was Roslyn. Her hair was the color of summer wheat, like yours, and her crystal blue eyes were lively and compelling. Your father, Roderick of Wallace, and Roslyn met in the Highlands. You are a lot like her, feisty but quick to laugh. She embraced life fully. When they were married, she knew she was the first Third Daughter because of a blessing bestowed upon her by Franklin."

Jaden gasped, interrupting Frederick, who turned to her.

"Do you know Franklin?" he said. "Well, of course you do. He spends most of his time in Jeremiah. You would have met him."

"Yes. I know Franklin, but I didn't know he knew about the prophecy or had spent time in the Highlands," Jaden said. She felt bewildered. Her mind raced to put the pieces together. "I am sorry for interrupting. Please continue."

Frederick smiled kindly and went on. "Your parents knew that their life together would be different because of this. Your father was to be Duke of Wallace and had full access to the knights of the Highlands, all the protection they needed. But when it was known that Roslyn was pregnant with you, people began talking. I don't know who leaked information about the prophecy, but it became apparent that Daman meant to try to thwart fulfillment of the prophecy.

"Consequently, we took extra precautions. It was cramped in the little manor house with my brother, your mother, and their two young children. It wasn't Roslyn's style to stay around the house. Your mother was too free-spirited. Before her pregnancy, she spent her free days exploring the hills and valleys near our city. But no longer. There was too much danger.

"The night of your birth arrived, and we tried to keep it from everyone. I doubled the guard around the house, but bulbanes overran the home in the middle of the night soon after you were born. They killed many people, but somehow I was able to rescue you and flee to Alexandria. I knew that the Highlands were no longer safe for you." William appeared ashen, and Lillian openly wept.

"How did you endure it?" Lillian said.

Frederick seemed to be far away as he answered her. "My most important job was to protect you, and the only way to protect you was to hide you. The people of the Highlands were aware that an heir to the throne of Alexandria was about to be born. I came in hopes that MaryAnne and Alfred could pretend they had twins, but as Gillantri would have it, their precious baby had been born that same night and died before I arrived. No one knew that you weren't the heir."

People in the room quieted and Frederick looked around. "Let's talk about this more later. Would you like to send everyone away?"

Lillian grabbed his hands and looked at him carefully, her deep crystal-blue eyes narrowing into her most determined look. "Daman will not destroy my wedding celebration. I will mourn another night, but tonight I want to dance with my guardian uncle, my father, and my husband!"

Alfred smiled and motioned for the band to pick up again. Music filled the room, and Alfred nodded toward Frederick.

Frederick wiped the tears from Lillian's eyes and said, "May I have this dance?"

Lillian closed her eyes and inhaled deeply. She replied, "I would be honored."

They danced joyfully while everyone looked on. Some quietly voiced confusion as to why Frederick was the first to dance with Lillian. But then MaryAnne and Alfred began to dance, and then Samuel and Loralee, followed by others. After a time, Alfred cut in to dance with Lillian to a lovely ballad, and everyone watched.

At the end of the song, Alfred escorted Lillian to Jordan, who took her in his arms and danced the next slow song with her. The young couple whispered to one another happily, moving softly to the music. Jaden couldn't help wishing her leg was better. Danae, who had tears in her eyes, said, "I miss Zachariah." Jaden put her arm around Danae and turned her attention back to the dance floor.

40

Patience Is Not One of My Strengths

The next morning before light, the battlefield was quiet. Zachariah left his hiding place to get some breakfast, check on Gideon, and find out how things ended the night prior. The rain stopped sometime during the night, and in the early morning a few stars peeked out where the thick clouds were breaking up. He approached Gideon, Richard, Franklin, and some knights and elves, including Porter, who stood in a group at the south gate guard station making plans for the day. Porter greeted Zachariah.

"Hello, my friend."

"Porter, it is good to see you." Zachariah grabbed his forearm and gave him a hug. "I wish I had been able to use some of the skills you taught me yesterday."

Franklin turned around. "You did as you were told, and that is better." He winked and returned to his conversation with Gideon.

Zachariah shook his head, feeling irritated. But Porter said, "Yes, you need to avoid giving yourself away. You will play an important part in this war before it is over. Xzavier can't know you are here just yet."

"How did things go with the bulbanes?"

"We contained them, caved in their underground entrance points, and placed guards around the city to warn us if more show up. Using the bulbanes was a clever diversion, but the knights have a handle on them."

"Where are all the Mountain Elves? I didn't see any of them yesterday," Zachariah asked.

"Well, two are in front of you and the rest have a future role to play. We don't want to play all our cards at once."

"What were our casualties?"

"It is too early to guess, but there were many, unfortunately. The remainder of our men are strong and ready to go at first light. We are optimistic about today. How is Justine?"

"We are both chomping at the bit to get involved, but she is fine. I will get back to her. I just needed to know what was going on."

"You are doing well, Zachariah. Be patient. Gideon knows when you will be of greatest use to us. He is a cunning man. Don't underestimate him."

"Patience isn't one of my strengths..."

Gideon turned sharply, "But you have the help of Gillantri at your disposal, which is peacefulness and power that will fortify your patience, if you accept it. Is everything all right?"

"Yes."

"Good. You wait for my signal.

"Of course, but remember to give it, then."

Gideon laughed his deep laugh. "I'll remember."

Zachariah turned back toward Justine. He took notice of the men as he walked through the ranks. He saw a mixture of fear and determination in their eyes. They looked sharp with their chain mail and white Jeremian knight robes shining in the darkness. He was proud to be among them.

He heard Richard readying his troops. "You are the best of Jeremiah! You are the most seasoned and best trained soldiers in all of Trivar. For centuries you've defended the Arwavian way of life! Generations of your fathers and grandfathers have given their lives for the cause of freedom and protection of our people! It is no different today. You are ready. You know how to overcome these dark monsters! Show me what you have!"

The men roared mightily. The knights were arranged in seven companies of horsemen. Behind each company stood a row of archers in a semicircle. Each group was prepared to face a dragon. At the front of the knights were one third of the flying tigers.

Zachariah returned to his perch on the eastern side of the battlefield as daylight spread across the field. The winter sun wasn't strong, but after yesterday's miserable deluge, it felt good. Minutes after the morning light graced the field, black gryphons led seven dragons toward the battlefront. Xzavier's men followed on the ground. All of the knights on the field stood firm, anticipating the attack. The knights were patient and waited for their enemies to charge into their long spears before unsheathing their swords.

The flying tigers engaged the gryphons in the air. The flying tigers were larger than the gryphons by almost double and picked them off easily. But then the dragons came and tore into the flying tigers, so the flying tigers retreated behind the archers, who let the dragons and remaining gryphons feel the power of Jeremian arrows. Many gryphons crashed to the muddy field, and many a dragon roared in pain before the arrows stopped and the flying tigers returned.

Over and over the flying tigers dove at the gryphons and dragons and then retreated behind the archers, who fired as many arrows as they could in the time the flying tigers needed to briefly rest. Then the flying tigers would engage again while the archers reloaded.

The dragons sometimes grabbed the flying tigers, knights, and their horses like rag dolls and tossed them in whatever direction they chose. But the archers and flying tigers were eventually able to bring down two dragons, and the horsemen slew both by midday. When the second one finally succumbed, a roar went up from the knights.

In time, Zachariah's invention was wheeled out from behind the archers. It was a gigantic crossbow with three-blade broadhead tipped bolts. Ten draft horses pulled the beast of a machine into position. Zachariah could hardly wait as he watched six knights place a huge arrow, called a bolt, into the flight groove. The knights in charge of the horses directed them to cock the bow. Gideon ordered the launch. The bolt sailed straight and true and skewered the nearest dragon, which fell to the ground.

"Perfect!" Zachariah said to himself out loud. The knights cheered and worked to get another bolt in position as quickly as they could. The flying tigers were sent out in the interim to keep the dragons and gryphons at bay. The flying tigers did their job and retreated behind the archers, who let a shower of arrows fly, which distracted and disoriented the dragons until another enormous bolt was let loose. It flew straight, as well, but missed hitting any dragons and fell into the Xannellion army.

Again the flying tigers were released, followed by a barrage of arrows. But as the massive crossbow was being readied again, three twelve-foot cave trolls crashed through Jeremiah's city wall behind the knights, smashing everything in their path. Draft horses went flying. As knights scrambled to get the other horses unharnessed, the trolls crushed the crossbow.

While everyone's attention was at the back of the ranks, the remaining four dragons devastated the knights at the front of the battalion. It had taken too long for anyone to realize that the flying tigers were needed again because the archers were in disarray and unable to organize. Some of them shot at the trolls and others fought hand to hand with Xannellion troops.

Once the flying tigers were unleashed, no one called them back because of the ensuing chaos. Zachariah noticed the flying tigers beginning to tire, and some fell to the dragons, while it appeared that the trolls and dragons were in control at the back of the ranks. Xzavier's foot soldiers at the front became emboldened by the destruction of the crossbow and the knights' confusion.

Zachariah's face reddened. He looked toward Xzavier, who watched from a safe distance seated on his dragon, Danthor. Zachariah wanted to ride Justine and take out Xzavier right then, but he resisted the impulse.

"Promise me that you will never disobey my orders like that again," Gideon had asked when Zachariah returned to Jeremiah.

"Never," Zachariah had replied.

He lowered his head and submitted to his higher reasoning.

41

The Enchantment of the Highlands

Frederick allowed the dancing to go on until just before dark, when he called an end to it and sent people back to their homes. Jaden and Danae were personally escorted to their rooms and expressly told that no one was to be out until morning light. But just as Jaden was getting settled in her bed, there was an intense knock at the door, and the door opened slightly before she could move.

"Jaden, it's me, William. I mean, Frederick."

Jaden pulled the covers over her and said, "Come in. What is wrong?"

Frederick came in, shut the door behind him, and moved to the side of her bed.

"MaryAnne is determined to have you sent away from Alexandria. She believes all the activity with Daman is your fault. There are other concerns she has that I will have to relate to you in the Highlands, but King Alfred tried to talk sense into her without success. I tried to convince them that I was responsible for everything that happened, but they won't believe me. I offered a compromise. Instead of banishing you, I would take you to the Highlands... But we have to leave now. It was the best I could do."

Jaden found herself between despair and ecstatic joy.

"Oh, Frederick! But what about Danae? I can't leave her. And what will Lillian and Jordan think? Will they hate me? And how can I travel with this broken leg?"

Frederick looked kindly upon Jaden. "You have wanted to find out where you are from all your life. It isn't always the perfect path that gets you to your dreams, but when it opens for you, you really should take it."

"Okay, but please make sure they take good care of Danae and that she has everything she needs."

"Of course. And Lillian will explain to her that, because of security issues, the group from the Highlands needed to leave right away and you went with them because it is your only opportunity to get there, and you will likely be back in time to return to Jeremiah with her when Gideon has won the war. She will understand."

"I do hope they defeat Xzavier. Do you believe they will?"

"Jeremiah is a blessed city, and if anyone can win against these powers of darkness, Gideon will."

Jaden said a silent prayer for her son and Gideon and asked, "What do I need to do?"

"Miss Betty is coming to help you prepare your things, and when you are finished, we will begin our journey. We won't be traveling with Samuel and Loralee, since we need to remain as inconspicuous as possible. But we will be protected." He bent down and kissed her on the forehead before he left.

Flustered by his boldness and yet thrilled with the idea that she would be going to the Highlands at last, she could barely think what to do next. Fortunately, Miss Betty had her dressed and packed in short order.

"Thank you, Miss Betty. You have always been kind to me."

"We are from the same village, and that makes us family," she said. Tears formed in Miss Betty's eyes.

Frederick knocked and entered again, picked up Jaden in his arms, and nodded for Miss Betty to bring her baggage. There wasn't much. They walked through back-passageways that Jaden had not yet seen, which led to the northeast entrance of the castle below the gazebo.

A chestnut mare fitted with a shiny emerald green lazy-back buggy lined with plush pillows and heavy blankets and a cover in case of rain waited for them. Frederick set her down carefully and wrapped her in one of the thick blankets. Miss Betty fit the bags against the inside edge of the buggy and hugged Jaden before she returned to the castle. Frederick shook the reins and off they went into the night. Jaden fell into a deep sleep and didn't wake until the horse stopped the next morning.

"How did you sleep?" Frederick asked.

"Better than I expected to, thank you," Jaden said. "Do you need to rest?"

"No," he said, though Jaden thought he must surely be exhausted. "I don't want to give Daman any chance to catch up."

"Is he following us?" Jaden gasped.

"We are hoping that he won't have any idea where you are for a few days. But he will be aware that MaryAnne blamed you for his appearance. I only hope he doesn't guess the rest of the story."

"The rest of the story?"

"I will tell you when we get there."

They ate their food quickly and were on their way again. Frederick told Jaden that they wouldn't make it to the moors until late afternoon, but Jaden still kept watch for the land to change from woodlands and marshes to the expansive moorlands that had been described to her by Miss Betty shortly after her arrival in Alexandria.

Miss Betty said that all the land north of Alexandria was collectively called the Highlands because they were higher in elevation than Alexandria, which was at sea level. But within the Highlands, the moorlands were considered the lowlands. Pristine lakes and breathtaking mountain ranges comprised the true Highlands, where Jaden was born. She could hardly wait to see it. It was widely viewed as one of the most beautiful regions of Trivar.

It rained most the day, but Jaden remained dry and warm in her blankets under the buggy cover. Her leg began to throb the longer she sat, but she didn't complain, since she considered that Frederick was taking on the biggest burden by having to drive the buggy all night and day.

At midday they stopped again, though Jaden wasn't sure how Frederick knew it was midday, given the weather. He must have heard her growling stomach.

"Everything is so beautiful," Jaden said as she looked around her.

"It only gets more and more breathtaking as we get into the true Highlands. There is no place on Trivar as exquisite," Frederick said as they prepared to eat the lunch Miss Betty had provided them.

"Miss Betty told me there were lakes and mountains where we are from."

"Yes. The deepest lakes you have ever seen, some the color of emeralds, and others crystal clear to the bottom that reflect the blue summer sky." Frederick's thoughts were far away now. "Do you know that when the knights were being expelled from the lowlands of Trivar, many of them fled to the Highland lakes in their ships?"

Surprised, Jaden couldn't respond except to nod.

"They were able to sail their huge fleet of ships from the sea straight into the lakes where no one could find them."

"Then they are the ones I saw in my dream."

"We will be able to talk about everything soon. You have been patient, more than I probably know, but your waiting is nearly over, Jaden."

He said her name so lovingly that Jaden couldn't look at him for fear of giving away her growing feelings for him. Sensing her discomfort, he said, "Look toward the north as we travel. We are on the edge of the moorlands. Before the light is gone this night, you will get to see your moors."

Finishing the last bites of their midday meal, she said, "Frederick, you have done everything to protect me and help me find where I am from. I don't know how to thank you."

"You don't know how pleased I am that you have been found. I have spent my whole life knowing that a baby girl from our village was lost and needed to be found, for her roles were great in Trivar. Now you are here. It is I who am grateful."

Jaden colored but didn't look away. They held their gaze long enough to make it hard for her to breathe. She wanted to know what he meant by saying that her "roles were great in Trivar," but she contented herself to wait until they were in Rosehannah. There were so many things she hoped to learn while in Rosehannah, and now this, too. She was almost there.

Frederick had the reins again. On this leg of the journey, Jaden kept her eyes on the moorlands. Because of the rain, everything was green and glowing with patches of purple heather still blooming. The few deciduous trees that were scattered over the moors had almost all lost their leaves. The sky was a broiling mixture of light and dark grey. To Jaden's eyes, the gently rolling landscape covered by a blanket of clouds was a piece of Arway in Trivar that caused her heart to swell.

Off in the distance, large flying creatures circled above the moors. As they drew closer, Jaden wondered if the Highlands had their own flying tigers or were they gryphons? When they were close enough, she realized that they were golden gryphons, similar to the black gryphons but with lion bodies and eagle heads. Frederick pointed to them and she nodded. They were spectacular. She missed Old Trapton.

The sky darkened, which meant the sun was going down somewhere above the grey. By the time it was completely dark, Frederick stopped for their evening meal.

He asked, "Did you see those golden gryphons? It isn't often that I see them this far south."

"They are magnificent. Very grand, not creepy like those black gryphons."

Frederick chuckled. "They are prevalent north of Rosehannah where the Trivarian population is sparse. The village elder spent years living among them."

Once Frederick took care of the horse, he brought her a stick with a glowing ball at one end that emitted a pale blue light. It reminded her of the elvan light that led them out of Jeremiah.

"Did you get that light from the elves?"

"No, it belongs to the village elder. He gave it to me for times like these. We need to keep traveling after our meal until we get to Rosehannah. Didn't you notice the light last night?"

"I was exhausted last night. I didn't notice anything but the insides of my eyelids," Jaden said. Frederick laughed a genuine laugh that connected with Jaden's soul, lifting it. Jaden asked, "How are you doing without sleep for this long?"

"I have gifts that you will learn about shortly. I am doing well."

"When you say that the village elder gave you this light for 'times like these,' what do you mean?"

"You never miss a thing, do you? The light is a protection, as well as a way to see in the dark. It sends out a vibration that creates the illusion that all is still. If Daman's spies are about, they will only see an undisturbed moor. Only beings with strong senses can perceive our movements when this light is shining around us."

Jaden began to wonder what sort of a man this was. Could all his mystery be a magical vibration to cloak who or what he was? Could she be in danger? How did she let herself get cut off from known and trusted friends and allies out here alone on the moors? She had no way of fleeing, no way of calling for help, and now no one could even find her because of this light.

Frederick attached the stick to the top of the buggy cover so that the light shined around them for some distance. Without explaining himself, he pulled a hand shovel from the pouch on his horse's saddle, walked a few paces away, and began digging in the mossy brambles. He dug until he found a box of considerable size.

He removed the box from the ground with some effort. It seemed heavy. From the box he retrieved clothing, a staff, and various trinkets that sparkled in the light, but because of the surrounding darkness Jaden couldn't see clearly what they were. Little flashes of light, like fireflies, darted in and out and about all around him. Jaden was frightened, but with nowhere to go and no way to get there, all she could do was hold her breath and pray for protection.

Frederick emptied the box and reburied it, then walked toward Jaden with his arms wrapped around the contents of the box. Each step closer sent a chill down Jaden's spine.

"Stop," she said. He halted.

"I need more answers," she continued. "I can go no further with you until you tell me what is happening. Frederick, I am scared."

"I know I have asked a lot of you, but my purpose is not to frighten you. It is to protect you. I can only imagine what you must think of me. It upsets me more than you know. But for the first time in my life since our village was destroyed, I am going to be able to tell someone everything I know. You will get to know everything."

"All of a sudden I don't want to know everything."

Frederick laughed kindly. "I can understand your feelings, but I promise it will be all right. Let's just get to our village where we will be safe..."

Jaden let out a muffled scream, and Frederick looked around to see why. A prowling creature moved on the ground outside the edge of the light in the darkness. Frederick put down the contents of the box in the buggy and, without asking permission, picked up Jaden.

"Where are you taking me?" she whispered accusingly.

"Trust me."

"I am at the end of my trust, Frederick. I am scared."

"That is why they are here. Let me show you."

Inside the ring of light beside the buggy, he set her down on her good leg, while supporting her with one arm. Jaden bit her lip, trying to force herself to feel trust, but she had been pushed so far for so long, it took all her strength to resist yelling out for help. Then considering that there was no one to hear her, anyway, she calmed herself enough to remain still. Frederick reached out his hand to beckon the creature, which reticently stepped into the light. To Jaden's complete surprise, she recognized it.

"El-kirin," she whispered in delight.

"Yes, this is Malatore. He is the leader of el-kirin, their king. You must be a special woman, indeed, to draw the golden gryphons and, especially, Malatore near. And this far south!"

"I drew him?"

"Yes. I did not summon him." Frederick said this as if he were trying to tell Jaden something without saying the words, but she didn't understand his meaning.

Jaden turned her attention to Malatore, awed by this majestic creature. She remembered that Ozella had told her that some el-kirin still existed in the wild of the Highlands but never thought she would see one herself.

"He has offered to carry you to our village."

Jaden wondered how Frederick understood Malatore.

"I am honored," she said, though she worried her leg would not handle this form of travel. But Malatore had appeared for her, and she didn't feel she could turn down such a gracious offer. Malatore sat down on the ground while Frederick gently set Jaden on his back, and to Jaden's complete surprise she was comfortable. Malatore's back was so wide and long that she could stretch her leg out and still hold onto his cottony mane.

Frederick touched Jaden's broken leg and said something in a language that she didn't know. A silver light from within the el-kirin radiated through Jaden's leg and up into Frederick's hand. It warmed her leg, and within moments her pain was gone.

"What did you just do?"

"It was Malatore who suggested it. You are healed. Move your leg. It should be better than before it was injured."

Jaden moved her leg around and could hardly believe it. It was healed. "I don't know what to say. Please let Malatore know of my gratitude. I am overwhelmed."

"He will do anything for you."

Jaden wondered what other things he could do and how she could be remotely worthy of such treatment. But she knew questions would go unanswered until Rosehannah.

"We will arrive by nightfall tomorrow, now that Malatore is here. Allow his peace and magic to heal you." In response to her unasked question about how to do this, Frederick added, "Whatever emotional or physical pain is hurting you, instead of ignoring it, fighting it, or burying it, allow that pain to come to the forefront of your heart, mind, and body.

"This takes courage because it hurts. But if you truly desire to be free of your pain, it is worth it. You must be present with the depths of your pain. Feel all of it. It is only then that you can release it. Releasing pain is the hardest part because, for some crazy reason, we Trivarians hold onto our pain fiercely.

"I don't know how to teach you to release pain... It is more of a feeling than an action, but I know a symbolic image that might help. Holding onto pain would look like someone tightening all their muscles around the center of an injury. Once you are present with your pain and have allowed it to surface, releasing that pain would visually look like you were relaxing all your muscles around that pain.

"This relaxing allows the pain to simply dissipate. Once you have learned to release pain, it becomes easier the next time. To complete your healing, you then allow Malatore's peace, which is simply an uninhibited extension of Gillantri's peace, to wash away every last trace of that trauma and pain."

"I have been running from my pain for so long. It is hard to believe it is even possible."

"You watched him heal your broken bones in moments instead of a moon."

Jaden thought on that for a moment and realized that maybe it was possible.

"I have seen so many wonderful things on my journey, and I want to believe you."

"That is all it takes at first, the desire to believe. And great miracles can occur."

It was all too strange and foreign, but something about being here in the Highlands with Frederick and the el-kirin king felt good and familiar, and her fears were gone.

"I promise things will be more right than you can imagine," he said, "but I cannot promise there will be no change. Some of the wonders that you will see and learn about may challenge you, but do not give up now. You have faced all the darkness of Trivar. Now you get to learn of the light and goodness of Arway.

"Gillantri sent healing creatures like Malatore to Trivar to remind us of the beauty and peace we can have in Arway if we are faithful. It is time for you to learn to rejoice, for great things are coming!"

A thrill surged through her soul. What sort of a journey was she on where bones are mended, men are gentle, gifted animals and creatures appear when you need help or comfort, and where the answers to your deepest questions are found?

Suddenly she wanted to rush into Frederick's arms and dance like she had not been able to do at the wedding because of her broken leg. But instead, she asked, "Will you help me down? I want to see how this leg of mine is working."

Malatore must have understood her because he knelt down, and Frederick reached around her waist and helped her off, steadying her until she stood by herself comfortably.

"I have no pain in my leg at all."

Frederick chuckled in the darkness. "I am so pleased." As if reading her thoughts, he asked, "May I have this dance?"

Grateful for the cover of darkness to hide her pink face, Jaden gracefully curtsied. Frederick bowed gallantly and held out his arms for Jaden to fill. She needed no encouragement, and there in the middle of the Highland moors with only the el-kirin king to watch, they danced.

The little flying lights darted around them. They were much larger than she had been able to perceive from afar.

"Faeries, Frederick, they are faeries!"

Frederick laughed happily. "Yes, of course they are."

She could hardly dance for wanting to stare at the little creatures. They were all different colors with a variety of hair and clothing styles, each one gloriously unique.

"Tell me this is not a dream."

"Welcome to the Highlands. This is not a dream."

She stopped dancing and watched one little faerie twirl up into the night sky and disappear. Jaden smiled from the depths of her soul, breathed in the joy of it, and then realized that Frederick wasn't watching the faerie but was watching her. Her heart tripped over itself as she dropped her gaze to meet his. He took her face in his hands and gently kissed her lips. He lingered for just a moment, then pulled away.

"Yes, this is a dream," she said.

Frederick laughed and brushed her hair away from her face, kissed her again and said, "Dearest Jaden, you have no idea what is coming. If this feels like a dream...Well, I hate to interrupt it, but we have to keep moving."

"That is all right. I am content."

42

My Turn

By mid-afternoon on the third day, the knights were heavily engaged below the dragons, gryphons, and flying tigers. It was a horrible scene of death and dying when a path opened up in the middle of Xzavier's army. Zachariah squinted to see Yamis warriors running at full speed toward the knights.

Just then, Franklin and his Mountain Elves on horseback appeared from the jungle in the west. The Yamis warriors marched on without acknowledging the elves. They were bent on wiping out as many knights as they could before being stopped. Franklin and the elves focused their path toward the warriors, felling many enemy ground troops.

For a time after the fierce confrontation began, Zachariah hoped Franklin could check the frenzied warriors. But they were more like bloodthirsty piranhas than men. Zachariah watched one warrior get stabbed in the side by a spear and carry that spear with him as he wiped out two well-trained knights before being overcome.

The powerful swords of the elves only seemed to anger the warriors and spur them to greater fury. Zachariah watched with deepening respect as the elves dug in and held their ground. Their minds and muscles were as well trained as the warriors, but the elves were agile and graceful. Their speed and agility kept the Yamis warriors' frenzy in check for awhile. Unfortunately, there were twice as many warriors.

By evening, the Xannellion troops and warriors were gaining ground on the muddy battlefield. Exhausted elves began to fall more frequently, and dragons and gryphons were sweeping the field, picking off weaker groups of knights methodically.

As daylight brightened before it faded away, Zachariah noticed a wave of communication move through Franklin's ranks. Franklin sat tall in his saddle and shot his white light directly into the warriors' ranks, shocking the Xannellion troops along with the warriors, and they all fell back a step together. Immediately, the elves shot light at the warriors, Xannellion troops, and any flying demon that got too close.

Zachariah shouted into the din, hopeful again. He watched as Franklin and his elves spread into a shield formation, their white light repelling even the warriors. It was magnificent to behold. But just as the warriors began to thin out, Zachariah noticed Franklin leaning forward in his saddle. He was wondering if Franklin had been hit from behind, when, one by one, the elves began to weaken.

"Get out of there," Zachariah said to himself, wondering why they didn't retreat if they were growing weak. Then he remembered what the Ononzai elves had told him: The way for us to return to Arway when we are finished here is to be willing to give our lives for a greater cause.

Zachariah felt sick as he watched the main body of elves plunge themselves and their horses in one final thrust toward the Yamis warriors. Pain surfaced in Zachariah's chest, making it hard to breathe, as the elves gave their last bit of strength to shoot white light at the warriors. But the warriors knew death when they saw it and became wild beyond their previous show of force, falling recklessly upon the weakened elves.

Arrows fell like rain on the Xannellion forces in effort to allow Franklin to get back to the Jeremian side. Xannellion ground troops closed in on their exit route. The elves' well-trained horses attempted to crash their way through as they unleashed the last of their white light, but they had waited too long. Zachariah watched Franklin's power weaken as he almost made it to the Jeremian side. Painfully, he noticed Xzavier look toward the Scorpion.

"Justine, we could save them! Why won't Gideon send me in? I can't stay here...but I have to! I hate this!"

Zachariah stared in horror as the Scorpion flew into the rain of arrows and dove directly at Franklin from behind. Franklin was knocked from his horse by the dragon's head, and he fell into the first row of knights. The Scorpion and his dragon weren't able to pull out of their dive and flipped head over tail into the crowd of knights, clearing a path in the battlefield.

The elf escorts gave their last effort to protect Franklin's broken body, and one by one they fell. Knights rushed to carry Franklin off the field, while others made short order of slaying the Scorpion and his dragon. The Yamis warriors charged into the ranks of knights. Zachariah ached to fight. He let out a deep throaty yell of helplessness but stayed in his perch and watched as the warriors slashed viciously in every direction like crazed men.

The knights were exhausted by the sheer numbers of Xannellion's inexperienced soldiers, and after watching the elves all go down with Franklin, morale was low. The sun gave its last help of the day and disappeared beyond the western horizon.

Zachariah started to climb down out of the tree, when another one of Xzavier's dragons fell. The knights all cheered and rallied against the Xannellion's troops, but not before long, they were pushed back toward the gates of Jeremiah.

At this point, with the men of Jeremiah losing ground, Xzavier let his bulbanes loose again. Thousands of bulbanes poured into the battlefield. They ran in, killing everything in their path, even men from their own army. Terror swept through the ranks of the knights who didn't know from which direction the bulbanes were coming.

In a brilliant countermove by Gideon, the entire herd of flying tigers was unleashed on the bulbanes. Xzavier directed his remaining dragon to attack the flying tigers. More animals and people died faster in this exchange than they had during the whole conflict. Everything seemed out of control. Zachariah raged.

As twilight settled in, Zachariah locked his sights on Xzavier, hate burning inside of him. Xzavier sat on Danthor with a despicable smile on his face, and all Zachariah could think about was killing him. Zachariah jumped the rest of the way down out of his tree and ran toward Justine. Justine raised her head and stamped impatiently as Zachariah removed her chain. He climbed onto her back and looked one last time toward Gideon, hoping that he would give the signal.

A hundred flaming arrows soared, lighting up the darkening sky. Zachariah's face beamed.

"He remembered! Justine, fly toward Xzavier!"

They flew out of the cover of the jungle, adrenaline coursing through Zachariah's body. Justine flew hard. Xzavier didn't see them, but Danthor did and lunged toward Justine as they got close. Justine dodged him and took a bite at his hind quarters, startling Xzavier, who unsheathed his sword.

"Son, you are here. I wondered if I would see you."

"Don't call me son. You tried to kill me."

"It was an accident..."

"That was no accident."

Zachariah and Justine dove at Xzavier. Justine missed. She and Zachariah spun quicker than Xzavier judged they would and hit Danthor again in the side. Xzavier and Danthor regained balance as Zachariah instructed Justine, "Bring me up close to them." Justine nimbly flew astride Danthor, allowing Zachariah to cut his father's right arm, which sent Xzavier's sword flying. Danthor lunged with his talons and inflicted a deep cut in Zachariah's thigh. Justine and Zachariah retreated.

"A little scratch," Xzavier cackled.

Zachariah bowed his head and inhaled deep, calming breaths. He raised his eyes to glare at his father.

"I wanted to kill you for many years when you hurt my mother and me, but now that I see how pathetic you really are, I pity you, Xzavier. I pity you."

Zachariah wondered what he should do. For the first time in his life, he felt his need for revenge cool. He realized how complicated revenge really was. The emotion of pity surprised him, aggravated him. In that moment, he understood more fully what many had tried to explain to him, including his mother and Gideon.

He looked toward Gideon. The knights were in disarray and darkness was falling. If he let Xzavier go, it could mean more destruction for the knights. But if he killed him for revenge, he'd have his father's blood on his hands. Zachariah chuckled quietly to himself to think that he, of all people, would hesitate when he was so close to his goal. If he killed Xzavier he could save so much suffering. If the Xannellion troops lost their leader, Jeremiah would gain the advantage.

Darkness and cold gathered around him now that the sun was completely gone. Only the knights' white robes and chainmail glowed, telling him vaguely how things were going. He was leaning in to tell Justine to withdraw, when he heard Danthor give a cry.

Zachariah whipped around in time to see Danthor and Xzavier diving at full speed toward him. Zachariah and Justine jumped aside as Zachariah stuck his sword down Danthor's throat. Both Xzavier and Danthor spun out of control toward the battlefield, ejecting Xzavier, who landed in the middle of a group of Xannellion soldiers. Danthor fell in a heap on the ground.

Zachariah grabbed Justine's mane and followed them, landing nearby. Zachariah dismounted.

"Watch my back, girl," he said as he headed for his father, sword in hand. Justine screeched and started leveling soldiers who came too close to her. Zachariah slowed as he approached his father.

"You couldn't let me turn away. I would have let you live. But now the roles are reversed. You, all broken on the ground, and I am standing here with power over your life. I only have one question for you. You forsook your wife and your son. Why?"

"I never loved you or your filthy mother. She was good-looking and knew everything I needed to know about Yamis to overthrow it. That is all. You were a mistake, a big mistake." Xzavier coughed up blood, his body in a spasmodic combination of hateful laughter and pain.

Zachariah glowered darkly, "That makes my job a lot easier."

He pushed his sword through his father's chest.

"A quick death is more than you deserve," he said then hurried over and picked the crown up that had fallen from Xzavier's head. As he placed the crown on his own head, he noticed an amber stone glowing brightly from a bracelet on his father's wrist. Zachariah unclasped it and put it on. He ran toward Justine and didn't look back as they flew away to aid the Jeremian troops.

43

Prophecy

Frederick drove the horse and buggy behind Malatore and Jaden. It soothed Jaden to run her fingers through his soft mane. She felt giddy and free, like she had never felt in her life. It all felt too good to be true, but no matter how much she pinched herself, she didn't wake up. In fact, she hardly slept that night because her mind and heart would not let her.

Jaden thought about her conversation with Frederick the day before when he had spoken of their village, Rosehannah, and Wallace interchangeably. It confused her until he had explained that Rosehannah and Wallace were two distinct villages at the time of her birth, separated only by a hill.

Wallace had grown and spilled over the hill into Rosehannah until they became one and went by the name Wallace. It was where the knights of the Highlands resided and where Jordan's father, Samuel, ruled as Steward of the Highlands. Wallace was the center of life in the Highlands today, but it would always be Rosehannah to him.

When he had spoken about the village elder, he laughed lovingly and mentioned that the village elder insisted on living in his own cottage in Old Rosehannah. It had been there for hundreds of years before the bulbane attack when Jaden had to flee as a baby. Though it was mostly destroyed during the attack, the village elder had rebuilt it and wouldn't live anywhere else. Once she heard about this cottage, it became one of the places Jaden longed to see most.

As day dawned, they moved out of the moorlands and into the lake territory of the Highlands. The ground became grassier and mossier with fewer brambles and wild brush. Hills and valleys replaced the never-ending rolling of the moors. Even the trees changed. Though there were still deciduous trees sporadically dispersed throughout the land, the unusual evergreen trees from Jaden's dream appeared in patches all over.

Every once in awhile they passed a golden gryphon perched on one of the sturdy branches of a tree. Jaden felt a thrill every time she saw one of these creatures. A growing excitement kept Jaden from feeling the exhaustion she knew would hit eventually.

If she had thought the land was green before, she repented! The grass and moss fairly gleamed in the early morning sunlight, while little rivulets and streams sparkled down to the lake before them. Frederick said, "Welcome to the Highlands, Jaden. This is your homeland!"

Without knowing why, tears formed at the corners of her eyes and trickled down her cheeks. She didn't dare turn to answer Frederick for fear of exposing her emotions. She nodded, hoping he saw her acknowledgment.

But Malatore turned his head as if he knew her feelings. A warmth traveled from his mane up her left arm to her heart, and she was able to be present with all the sadness that she had carried her entire life, from the first time Talla told her to not think about where she was from, to being trapped in Xannellion, to facing the fury of Xzavier and Daman, even to being sent away from Alexandria. As she fully accepted her pain, she felt her whole soul release that horrible burden and embrace the joy of finally reuniting with the homeland of her birth.

By the end of the afternoon, they had traveled through the valley of the first lake and up the next hill before Frederick announced, "Rosehannah is the village at the far end of this lake, and Wallace extends over the ridge down to the next lake in the adjacent valley. Jaden, you are home."

Such a mixture of dark and light emotions flowed through her, but with the help of Malatore, she faced each dark emotion, accepted it, and released it, leaving her with a feeling unlike any she had experienced before. She felt truly alive. There was no fear in her, just peace. Every dark emotion had been confronted, and now she was free to rejoice. She never wanted Malatore to leave her. He shook his mane as if to say he would always be with her, and she believed him.

Jaden glanced back to see Frederick slouching in the saddle. She knew he hadn't slept for nearly three or four days and had to be completely spent, but in making eye contact with her, he straightened and waved. She waved back, feeling joyful and content. Every one of her senses was alert, and her soul reveled in the surrounding beauty and the feeling of remembering as she rode into the village of Rosehannah.

It was still a small fishing village on this side of the ridge and appeared to be sparsely populated. Three golden gryphons circled over the village. From what she had been told by Miss Betty, Wallace was nearly as large as Alexandria but more modern. Nearly forty years earlier, Wallace was a small fishing village like Rosehannah, but due to the bulbane attack and the loss of so many precious Highlanders, knights from all over the Highlands gathered to Wallace to protect the center of their culture and people until the two villages connected on the top of the rise between them.

There were still villages all over the Highlands with clan leaders who were determined to argue and fight against one another, but once Wallace became as large as it was now, most clans at least pretended to cooperate for fear that the knights of Wallace might come down to stop their argument for them.

Frederick told her she could visit Wallace once Samuel and Loralee returned, but they would be a few days behind them. Wallace sounded interesting, but truly her love was Rosehannah. Frederick was taking her by a back route so no one would see her coming because he wanted her to meet with the village elder before news spread that she was there. It sounded overprotective to Jaden, but Frederick knew things she didn't know and she was learning to trust him.

Being so close to her destination, she wanted to hasten their arrival. Feeling her urgency, Malatore began running. Jaden held on and smiled with her whole soul. They followed an el-kirin trail along the lake between ancient oak trees, mossy rocks, and over rivulets dancing to the lake. She could hear Frederick and the horse behind her but didn't dare look for fear she might fall off. The clean, cool, sweet air filled her lungs and invigorated her. Once they reached the end of the lake, Malatore slowed, rounded a bend, and entered a meadow.

In the darkening twilight, this meadow captured all the feelings of Jaden's longings for the Highlands of her birth and gave her a sense of closure. The meadow was surrounded by ancient oaks with one large oak tree standing by itself near a stream that spilled forty feet beyond the oak into the lake. A cottage situated at the base of the hill opened toward the meadow but rested on high ground far enough away from the stream that it would be protected from even the worst flooding. The cottage seemed to Jaden like a castle in its own enchanted world.

Frederick pulled up beside Malatore, who let out a gentle bellow. In a few moments, the door of the cottage opened. A tall and once-muscular man with white flowing hair who was dressed in a simple homespun robe shuffled slowly out into the meadow.

"Frederick. You have returned. Welcome."

"Siranta, it is good to see you." Frederick dismounted and greeted the old man with a gentle hug, then stood back while Siranta approached the el-kirin and Jaden.

"And Malatore, my friend, it is good to see you. You have a queen with you, but not just any queen. You have our queen for whom we have waited since she was removed from our company nearly forty years ago." Jaden's eyes widened.

He began to prophesy. "We lost you, and now you are found. You will be protected by Alexandria's banner and lead our people into a thousand years of peace. By your courage and wisdom, generations of our people will be blessed. Like the phoenix of old, all of Trivar will be made new through your influence and through your blood. Though you have tasted the darkness of Trivar, your light will forever shine. Your light will fill all those who will open their hearts, with the same light."

The old man trembled with power and Jaden felt the truth of his prophecy. Malatore sat down comfortably, and Jaden stepped onto the ground before Siranta. The old man looked straight into Jaden's green eyes and said, "RoseAura, you are the promised Third Daughter of The Third Daughter of The Third Daughter. I have been waiting for your return all these many long years. Welcome."

****

Trembling, Jaden bowed her head as tears trickled down her face. For the first time that she could remember, she didn't feel to argue, but even if she could have spoken, the emotions that swelled within her overcame her. Siranta embraced her as a grandfather would his grandchild. Frederick walked over by her side, put his arm around her, and walked with her into the cottage. He walked her to a chaise lounge. It was situated across the room from where the village elder sat in his own large, plush chair with his eyes closed.

It was growing dark outside, and Frederick lit two lamps. Jaden turned to Frederick.

"I admit I wondered if I was The Third Daughter from the time I learned about the prophecy because of my dreams, but when Lillian was named,

I doubted my feelings." Jaden asked, "When we arrived, Siranta called me RoseAura. Is that my given name?"

With his eyes still closed, Siranta answered for Frederick, "Yes, your mother named you after our village and your grandmother, Aurora." A little thrill ran through Jaden's heart.

Jaden turned back to Frederick. "When did you know that I was The Third Daughter?"

"I knew you would ask me that one day," Frederick chuckled. "I knew the first day you arrived at Alexandria. I had seen you before in a dream and knew you would show up there someday. I just didn't know when. Do you understand now why I was flustered that day and unable to answer your questions well?"

"I was so irritated with you. I had been traveling for days and had to put up with the drizzly rain and your terribly poor answers." The next question that came to her mind rocked her soul. "But if you knew then, why did you tell Daman that Lillian and Roslyn were The Third Daughters?"

It horrified her that he had allowed Roslyn to suffer and die and Lillian to be put in danger in order to protect Jaden. She recalled one of her dreams where a blue-eyed, blond woman was being beaten and was seething with hatred for Jaden. A sense of foreboding sent terror through her soul, for she had grown to love Lillian. She shook her head and dismissed the improbability.

"Why Daman was led to believe Lillian and Roslyn were The Third Daughters is one of the many questions that you have come here to have answered, and we can now answer them. But you will need to listen carefully and try to understand. Many of the answers may bring you more pain than relief, but you are in a position where you must know, and in time, grieving shall pass and the truth will make you free."

Frederick looked to Siranta for support. The village elder did not open his eyes but seemed to be aware of Frederick's need and nodded. "More pain, yes. Truth does not always bring immediate peace. The peace we receive is contingent upon us accepting the truth and being willing to realign ourselves with it. Often we have to change our way of thinking or living to right ourselves with truth as it comes to us. This process can cause deep pain, at least discomfort, until we reconcile ourselves with that truth. That is when the peace comes."

Jaden thought about the new truths she had already faced, accepted, and realigned herself with since she arrived in Jeremiah and remembered the pain that had caused her before the peace came. It frightened her to think what would now be required.

"Long ago, during Alexander's reign, Daman had shown himself in Alexandria and threatened to destroy Alexander's people and all of Trivar. Alexander's people were afraid and needed guidance, so he took a Nightflight, and when he returned, he brought with him the blackberry faerietale. Have you heard it?"

"Yes. Actually, I don't understand how it applies to me."

"In time you will." He opened his eyes, slowly stood, and hobbled to a large bookshelf. He picked up a thin book, hobbled over to Jaden, and handed it to her. "This is yours."

"You mean it is for me?"

"It is yours and it is for you."

"I don't understand."

"It is your faerietale and your book. Your mother saved it for you."

Jaden felt tears threaten again. "It is so unreal to be listening to you speak about my mother and grandmother. I have spent so many years wondering about these dear people, and here you are telling me about them from your own memories."

"Your mother was much like you. Her name was NightenGayle because her singing was so ethereal. She had black hair, but you inherited her green eyes and her spice for life."

"I don't know what to say. Please tell me more."

She lovingly picked up her book, almost unable to believe that her mother had touched it at one time. The cover was delicately painted with a picture of the little blackberry faerie looking into the water while the silvery fish jumped out of the water and ate the firefly. She tenderly leafed through the pages feeling enraptured by the paintings. She wondered what details the complete tale offered her. Maybe the message the story was trying to teach her would be clearer in this book.

The old man began again. "On the return from his Nightflight, Alexander also brought with him The Third Daughter Prophecy." Jaden held her breath as he spoke.

"This is the prophecy: 'As Daman swore he would destroy any who followed Gillantri, and eventually all of Trivar, so Gillantri promises that he will make all who will follow him truly free. Darkness will grow until it nearly destroys the land, but The Third Daughter of a Third Daughter of a Third Daughter will rise and sacrifice all so that light will overtake the darkness at the last hour before Arway consumes Trivar and restores those who will.'"

Siranta fell silent, as if he were asleep. Jaden tried to digest the prophecy.

Frederick leaned forward and said, "I can now share with you how I could let Roslyn and Lillian be decoys. This is one of the most painful secrets I have been required to carry, but it is also the most important secret for the eventual peace and freedom of Trivar.

"When I was five, as I told you, the bulbanes destroyed our village. My mother threw her body over Betty, Roderick, and me before our house collapsed. When Siranta found us, the three of us were unconscious but alive. No one else in our entire village survived besides you and Roslyn, but at that time we didn't know for certain if either of you were alive.

"Siranta hoped and even believed you survived. It was nearly a moon before Arran arrived with news that you were indeed alive but lost to pirates. It was a year before word came that Roslyn was being raised on one of the northernmost islands of the Highlands by the Silver Elves. Even though I was young, I was the oldest survivor besides Siranta and felt a personal need to protect my siblings, Roslyn, and you, RoseAura."

Hearing her given name again filled Jaden with a thrill that made it hard to concentrate on Frederick's words.

"Siranta wisely saw your being lost as a way for Gillantri to keep your true purpose hidden from Daman, and though Daman has obviously targeted you as one of Gillantri's most powerful children, he doesn't yet know your true purpose here. That is why we have done everything that we have done. Daman knows that his only chance at completely destroying Trivar is to destroy The Third Daughter.

"Many years before the bulbane attack, when Siranta was a young boy, Daman began to prowl around Rosehannah looking for The Third Daughters. It was then that your grandmother, Aurora, came up with the suggestion to establish a line of decoys. Roslyn and her mother came from a line of fierce knights who protected their women better than anyone else, and it was agreed upon by Siranta's father, who was the village elder before him, that Franklin would falsify a prophecy claiming this line of women to be The Third Daughters.

"Unfortunately, it worked too well. One of the more prideful knights, Roslyn's father, shared the prophecy with a friend and Daman caught wind of it. It is why we ended up losing all of Roslyn's family, except Lillian." Frederick stopped.

Siranta had wakened and picked up there. "And Frederick nearly lost his life saving her. Fortunately, he had spent his youth with me training in all the arts of wizardry and was able to fight Daman's dark light with pure light."

"A wizard?" Jaden's mind was spinning. "Why didn't you fight when we were in the cave with Daman?"

"He would expect me to fight for The Third Daughter but not give myself away for a common woman. To play out my bluff was my only defense for you." Frederick didn't move. Jaden felt so badly for him and all he had been through over his lifetime. She put her arm around him.

To her surprise, he leaned toward her taking comfort while the village elder spoke. "All village elders from Rosehannah are wizards and have been since the time of Alexander. Franklin's father is my father. Franklin is my younger brother." Again, Jaden wondered at the revelations pouring from Siranta and Frederick. "I took Frederick, Roderick, and Betty in and raised them. I secretly trained Frederick."

"Does Betty know all...this?" Jaden didn't know how to qualify what 'all this' was.

"Betty was sent to Alexandria as a young woman before Frederick was fully trained, but I believe she has some idea, though she won't speak of it, even to Frederick. She does know about The Third Daughter Prophecy and the decoys, though."

Frederick nodded in agreement.

"Why was Betty sent to Alexandria?"

"As another layer of protection for you. When Frederick had his dream that you would someday show up in Alexandria, we realized that we needed someone there to greet you. We didn't realize at the time that Frederick would end up in Alexandria, as well. But that, too, was a blessing for both Frederick and Betty to be reunited, especially after the trauma Frederick had been through in losing Roderick and Roslyn. Betty was able to be with him as he healed and heal with him. Eventually, he was able to take his place as Captain of the Guards in Alexandria. Frederick has made a huge impact on their navy, as well as their other defenses in the time he has been there."

By this point, Jaden was completely overwhelmed. She could feel the weight Frederick had carried his entire life and could not comprehend all he had sacrificed for her. "I am not worth all this bloodshed and pain."

"You do not fully see your purpose, RoseAura. When you do, you will realize that the blessing you will bring far exceeds even these terrible sacrifices." Siranta trembled as he stood, tottered over to Jaden, and painfully knelt in front of her. "I have one final protection to bestow on you. It is one that I saw in a vision the night you were taken by pirates and I found Frederick. I knew that Frederick must be trained as a wizard and become our future village elder for the purpose of protecting and marrying The Third Daughter. I now give you to him, and him to you."

Jaden removed her arm from around Frederick and pulled away, the thought of being his wife suddenly repulsing her. This wasn't how she wanted to fall in love – a prophecy that Frederick obviously knew about. He tricked her. All of this was now too fantastical.

"How could you do this? All these lies. All these secrets." Jaden got up and left the cottage. She was walking over to Malatore and feeling irritated with him, too, when a shadow caught her attention from the corner of her eye. Before she understood what was going on, Malatore let out a near-silent warning cry from his horn that the wizards somehow heard, for they rushed out of the cottage.

Siranta moved faster than Jaden expected. He didn't hobble at all while shooting three fierce arrows of light into the forest, killing the shadow instantly. Frederick leaped lightly onto Malatore, who ran full speed into the forest. More light flashed and more yells echoed around her from the dark bulbanes. Siranta rushed Jaden into the cottage and insisted that she hold his staff, instructing her to focus her energy at the tip of it if any darkness entered. He said light would flash and protect her. Without saying more, he left her alone and followed Malatore and Frederick into the forest.

In the dark of an unfamiliar cabin with both men gone, Jaden felt the full weight of fatigue and fear. Every noise, every creak, every breath of wind startled and unnerved her. How could this be her lot? A tiny cabin in the woods of a forsaken village with bulbanes sniffing around, an ancient village elder and his apprentice who had lied about everything from the moment she met him, and now, a second relationship of convenience to a stranger. She couldn't deny that if she had had enough time with Frederick and fully trusted him, she might have decided to love him on her own, but this? They must be crazy.

Fast-paced footsteps approached the cabin. Jaden wondered if the staff would work as Siranta instructed. Her palms were damp and she shook as she waited for the door to open, but it didn't. After what seemed a lifetime, Jaden had to look outside. Not knowing seemed far worse than finding out. Peeking out the front window revealed nothing because the light from the inside of the cottage reflected back onto her instead of shining outside, but she heard muffled voices that sounded like Frederick and Siranta. Gathering up her exhausted courage, she opened the front door.

What she saw made her nearly faint. Frederick was holding Siranta across his lap while trying to put pressure on his chest and shoot short bursts of light into his heart. Blood was draining uncontrollably from Siranta onto Frederick, who was crying. Malatore knelt by their side.

Siranta said, "It is finished. Frederick, let me go. I knew I wouldn't live long once I saw The Third Daughter. But you will see this through. A Nightflight will help you both. RoseAura will play her role. All will be…well." He gasped for air and shared one final thought: "Everything…I have taught you…follow. The Third Daughter will succeed."

And then he fell silent.

The old Jaden would have shut the door, leaving Frederick to his pain, but she had changed. Her heart filled with empathy. She had been through too much on her journey and learned too much about how Gillantri would have her respond. She felt the old struggle within her, compassion versus the justice she wished to dish out to this man who had lied to her and who put her in this vulnerable position.

But Jeremian charity overtook her childish desires, and she remembered that the same man who lied had also lost everything he ever loved to protect her. She brushed her fingers through Malatore's mane for strength as she walked past the serene el-kirin and put her arms around Frederick and simply let him cry.

It was as if Frederick's heart had broken with Siranta's. But Frederick had not only learned the lessons he taught Jaden – he lived them. As she held him, Jaden could almost feel him facing each overwhelming emotion in turn, being present with them, accepting the horrific pain, and releasing it. Jaden didn't let go until the moon was going down over the meadow and he lifted his head from her shoulder.

"I needed you. Thank you," was all he said.

Through the night, Frederick prepared the body for burial. Jaden helped where she could. By first light, they were both exhausted but finished and slept where they landed, Frederick in Siranta's chair, and Jaden on the small couch.

44

King

As Zachariah flew over the battle field, he saw that the Yamis warriors were still gaining ground. But from the west side of the field the Ononzai Ancients poured out of the jungle. The Yamis warriors were immediately drawn toward the elves. As they met, the elves battled gracefully and efficiently with their elegantly crafted swords. Some fell, but most held their ground.

Zachariah spotted the last surviving dragon that was wreaking havoc on the archers from behind. They were still in disarray because of the bulbanes. Zachariah forcefully collided with the dragon.

"It pays to have a female dragon," he said with a laugh. The male screeched and turned on Justine. They locked necks and spun around, nearly throwing off Zachariah. He held on until his footing slipped and the saddle came loose. He gripped the saddle and yelled, "Justine, disengage, disengage! Find a patch of ground to land!"

Justine headed toward the closest clearing in the eastern jungle and landed. Zachariah tumbled to the rooty ground, stood, and shook himself off, removed the remainder of the saddle, and got on Justine bareback.

"Let's get back up there!" They flew above the field. Noticing a group of knights giving way to bulbanes, he dove toward them and took out a patch of bulbanes. He wheeled Justine around for a quick look at the battlefield.

As he and Justine began climbing into the air, the injured male dragon hit them again, sending Zachariah flying around to the front of Justine, hanging from the reins. This sent Justine off balance, and Zachariah realized that if he didn't let go, she would crash to the ground.

"Lower me, girl."

Justine was falling anyway, but when he got close enough to the ground, he jumped. Justine corrected her flight and turned on the male dragon. Zachariah fell in the midst of the knights he had just saved from the bulbanes, and they hailed him, "King Zachariah of Xannellion!"

The cheer spread throughout the battlefield. Even some of the Xannellion troops were heard to cry with the knights. With no one in charge of Xannellion's troops, the field was more easily controlled by the knights. Gideon had flanked both sides of Xannellion's troops with men he had reserved for such a time. The elves were using their white light and almost had the Yamis warriors under control.

Justine rammed the male dragon in the side, and dodging the dragon's angry teeth, she followed his course to another large patch of bulbanes. Zachariah laughed as Justine picked them up and flung them toward the wall of Jeremiah. The dragon pursued, but Justine reared up just in time for the male dragon to miss her. He let out a frustrated scream.

The archers rallied to give Justine cover, reforming their lines and shooting at the male dragon. The dragon had narrowly flown out of range of the arrow fire, when Justine attacked him again. This time Justine buried her teeth into the male dragon's neck, and he let out a death scream. Justine flung him toward the remaining group of bulbanes. The dragon was dead. Zachariah helped the foot soldiers clean up the remaining isolated individual bulbanes. Then he and Justine soared over the field. Xannellion forces were diminishing. Zachariah and Justine flew from battle to battle, helping where they could.

Zachariah witnessed the last Ancient lie down on the battlefield. He saw in the dusk a tranquil expression in his countenance. There were no more Yamis warriors either. The Ancients had completed their mission, and they were on their way to Arway. Zachariah felt deep admiration.

Then he realized he hadn't seen Gideon for awhile. He felt panicked. He was looking back and forth across the bloody field as he flew Justine toward the walls of Jeremiah, when he finally spotted Gideon.

Gideon was organizing knights around him to finish off a few stray bulbanes and Xannellion foot soldiers. Zachariah and Justine slew a handful of bulbanes and circled the field. The twilight was almost gone as the last skirmishes quieted. Gideon began organizing the removal of prisoners from the field.

45

Arway

When they awoke around noon, Frederick said, "RoseAura, may I call you by your given name?"

"I was given both names, but RoseAura feels more natural here in Rosehannah."

"RoseAura, we will need to have a funeral for Siranta when Samuel and Loralee return in a few days. Rosehannah villagers will be there in Wallace for the service, and everyone who wishes to see the burial will walk over the ridge into Rosehannah. There at the cemetery where all our ancestors have been buried, Siranta will rest."

Frederick stalled for a moment and Jaden read his thoughts. "I am not allowed to be there," she said.

"I would have you come but after the bulbane attack last night, Daman must know something is going on. He might have just been following you to scare you or he suspects we know something else. We don't believe any bulbanes got away but we haven't seen that many around Rosehannah since you left all those years ago. But then, Daman may not know anything..." Frederick paused for a moment.

"It's likely he can feel the increase of power that resulted from bringing you, me, the village elder, and Malatore together," he explained. "Power always draws Daman. And – I want to apologize for all the secrecy and having to share so much with you all at once." Frederick stood and walked out into the meadow.

Jaden pulled the blankets around her and followed him. It was cool as the fog gave way to the weak winter sunlight, but the dew still lay heavily on the grass.

"This meadow is enchanting."

"It calls to me, especially when I have been in Alexandria for too long."

Jaden stepped in front of Frederick and faced him, "Frederick, I don't understand why my life is what it is, but it is not your fault. You have done everything in your power to protect who I didn't even know I was. You risked everything. Give me some time. I will come around."

Frederick smiled weakly. "I wish you had time. I have to return to Alexandria after the funeral, or Daman's suspicions will be confirmed that I have married and refuse to leave my bride." Pain etched itself across his face. "RoseAura, I wish Siranta were here to say what I now have to say because it sounds so self-serving, but it is the truth. Siranta referred to it as he lay dying. We need to take a Nightflight, probably tonight. More will be revealed..."

Jaden groaned. She turned toward the meadow and looked to the sky, wondering what kind of a joke Gillantri was playing on her.

"No, Frederick, I won't be forced into all this, and please call me Jaden. I cannot go on a Nightflight when I have so many doubts and feel so overwhelmed. Danae told me all about Nightflights and I know they aren't for me."

"But..."

"I am sorry for your loss, but the answer is no."

Frederick turned sorrowfully and went back into the house, shutting the door softly. Jaden whistled for Malatore, who appeared at the edge of the meadow and pranced up to Jaden. He bowed. Jaden climbed onto his back and galloped away. She fairly flew to the other side of the lake, the side where they first saw Rosehannah upon their arrival.

She felt tempted to keep riding all the way to the city of Jeremiah. Maybe Gideon would take her back. She could be content living with him in Jeremiah. Even if dragon attacks continued to plague Jeremiah, it seemed a simple, safe life compared to what she faced here!

She jumped off Malatore and sat by the edge of the lake. Like a faithful friend, Malatore sat down beside Jaden as she played over in her mind all she had learned. She was The Third Daughter. She needed to marry Frederick for her protection, but he would be in Alexandria? She would save the whole of Trivar somehow.

And she needed to take a Nightflight! A Nightflight! Of all the things she never wanted to do! And how did the faerietale fit in? She had to become a fae? Surely that was not literal, but figurative, and, yet, what did it mean? How was she supposed to transform? Every time she went over the facts, it became more confusing. Why hadn't she brought her faerietale book outside with her? She ran her fingers through Malatore's mane, trying to calm down.

Then before her, as if in a waking vision, she saw her dream of The Third Daughters again. They looked like Roslyn and Lillian and a baby who looked like Jordan and Lillian's baby might someday look.

Justine's image, her purple body and yellow horns, entered the vision and came clearly to her memory. She appeared frightened as she flew to protect Jaden and Zachariah just outside of Jeremiah. Next, she saw Benjamin's smile and then his cold, dead face. She recalled vividly her travels through the jungle with Gideon, Danae, her son, and the elves, and their arrival at the Zikong Valley. She recalled Etheltread, Meadthel, and Arran laughing together.

Then Danae appeared in the litter carried by four elves who sang as they ran toward Ononzai. Ozella's silver laugh echoed in the valley of the lake. Gideon stood apart from her, rejected but strong. Zachariah looked betrayed when she wouldn't support his choice to fight Xzavier. MaryAnne and Albert's faces expressed fear and pain because of her questions in their throne room.

She saw Frederick dancing with Lillian, who learned that he was her guardian and that she had a different mother and father. And then last night, after all Frederick had already sacrificed, he found himself holding the man who had been a father to him, as he died. It nearly broke Jaden's heart. All of this was to protect Jaden or what Jaden was supposed to become.

But marriage and solitude was a high price to pay, indebted though she was. Then again, what else would she do with her life? And who else would fulfill the prophecy? Who would do what she was sent to Trivar to do if she didn't? Would all of Trivar be lost to Daman if she ran away? Maybe Lillian's third daughter could fulfill the prophecy?

After searching all her life to discover who she was and where she was from, Jaden was positive this wasn't what she had hoped to find. The pressure of merely thinking about doing these fantastical things made it hard for Jaden to take in a full breath. How could she actually do it all?

Unable to carry the weight of her burdens any longer, Jaden laid her head on Malatore's back. Words flooded into her mind: "You can never do it all. Not by yourself. But no one ever asked you to do it alone. Gillantri keeps calling to you. He beckons you but will never force his help upon you. Accept his help. Take a Nightflight and let him teach you."

Jaden lifted her head and looked at Malatore, who seemed to stare into her soul. "You are worse than Trapton! He never asked me to go on a Nightflight. You are all conspiring against me!"

Then Jaden really listened to herself. Every one of the faces she had just seen in her wakeful vision flashed through her mind again. Not one of these dear souls was mistreating her, abusing her, or manipulating her. Each one showed her more respect, care, and kindness, even MaryAnne, who struggled with her the most, than was ever shown to her before she came to Jeremiah.

"I am afraid," Jaden finally admitted.

Malatore nudged her. "I only wanted to know where I was from and that I had a safe place to call my real home. I wanted family and loved ones around me who understood me and treated me the way I deserve to be treated. I wanted to be free of abuse and darkness. I wanted to love a man with all my heart. I wanted a good man, a kind and generous man."

Malatore nudged her again. "I know. I have all of that don't I? It all came so fast, though. It is overwhelming. If I had more time... But I don't have more time. It is all here, all before me. Malatore, you are right. I need to release my fears. Help me, your Highness."

Jaden got onto Malatore's back, he rose from the ground and slowly made his way back to the meadow, giving Jaden the time and space she needed to face and release her burdens. By the time she arrived back at the meadow, it was growing dark. Her heart raced when she realized how soon a Nightflight would be required.

She didn't know what to say to Frederick, so they prepared their evening meal in silence and then cleaned up in silence. Frederick left the cabin and Jaden followed. Frederick knelt in the middle of the meadow and said a truly heartfelt prayer, ushering in two monarch eagles.

They climbed onto the backs of the eagles and silently flew out of the meadow, up over the great oaks and into the northern night sky under the Aurora Borealis. Jaden felt warmer and safer than she expected at that altitude. It wasn't like flying a dragon, which was colder and more awkward. The monarch eagle flew effortlessly, soaring through the heavens.

After too short of a time, they arrived in Arway, landing on a patch of the most luxurious grass Jaden had ever seen. Had she not felt so frightened, she would have laughed remembering Danae's description of Arwavian Grass.

Four elves greeted them. Two took the eagles, a third guided Frederick off in one direction, and the other directed Jaden in the other. She would have asked

Frederick for help, but knew she had bitten the hand that fed her one too many times to expect him to want to help her now.

Jaden quietly followed her guide through a grassy glade of aspens basking in the Arwavian sun. A crystal green stream meandered around the glade and beckoned to Jaden. She knelt down and splashed her face. She took off her shoes and bathed her feet, legs, and arms before proceeding. They passed crystal statues that looked alive and went into the open field through which Danae must have passed. An angelic voice sang an inspiring melody, filling the valley with music that lifted her heart. Mount Arway glowed in the golden sunlight with gleaming waterfalls.

From the field, Jaden crossed over a stone bridge that spanned a sparkling rivulet fringed with white lilies. She saw the ornamental garden pavilion of which Danae had spoken, and her heart fluttered, for a man and a woman stood there together watching her approach.

The woman had raven black hair and was singing the purest melody. It made Jaden want to dance. The closer Jaden got, the more peaceful she felt. As she approached the final small hill that led to the pavilion, Jaden took in the two people who were waiting for her. The man was the blue-eyed man from her dream, Gillantri. But he felt so much more powerful in reality. His gaze penetrated her soul, making her feel like melting.

The woman's soothing music stopped, and the man with blue eyes spoke.

"Welcome, my daughter."

Jaden felt stronger now that he was speaking to her. His voice was deep and resonant. "You have had a few challenges since we last spoke."

Jaden didn't know what to say. So much had happened since she first arrived in Alexandria. "It is like you disappeared," was all she could think to say.

Gillantri gently chastened her with his paternal look. "I don't disappear. I am always here. But I gave you the space for which you asked."

"I wanted you near. I was just tired."

"I remember clearly."

Jaden knew this wasn't an argument she would win, and she knew deep down that he was right anyway, so she quieted.

Next the woman who had been singing spoke up. "I won't get to meet with you often on your Nightflights, but Gillantri gave me permission to see you and speak with you. The night the elf took you from me, my heart broke before any bulbane killed my body."

"Mother?" Jaden hadn't considered who she was. Upon realizing, she began to cry.

The woman with raven black hair descended the three stairs from the pavilion and embraced her daughter.

"Remember your mother loves you," she said.

"I love you, too," Jaden said through her tears. She didn't want to let go. All those miserable years with Talla, wanting a real mother – her real mother – and wanting so badly to feel loved.

At that moment, it was as if the hole in her heart was filling up and the pain was leaving her. She knew she was loved, and it changed something inside her soul. The gaping wound – the longing, the pain, the sorrow healed in one embrace.

"Only one of us could come, so your father allowed me the privilege, but he loves you, too."

"What is he like?"

"He is a man much like your Frederick, a good balance for us spirited women of the Highlands. He is strong and brave, but kind. Your hair is the same color as his." She laughed like Ozella, a silvery, bell-like laugh. "Don't turn away from Frederick too soon. There isn't a man in Trivar who more deserves you, and you him."

Jaden not only heard but felt what her mother was saying. She realized that she hadn't let go of her mother yet and slowly released her, but they continued to lightly hold each other's forearms.

NightenGayle chimed, "I am proud of you. You have come so far."

"I have missed you so much. I didn't think anything could make me feel better...all those years without you... But being here with you, I can hardly remember the pain."

Gillantri kindly nodded, "All will be made better in the end. RoseAura, you have made the hard choices every time. That is why you are here with your mother and me. If you continue to make those hard choices you can be with us forever with all those whom you love."

"But what if I make mistakes?"

"Do your best. Never give up. I will help you overcome."

Jaden thought about Zachariah and prayed that he was safe and making those hard choices wisely.

Perceiving her thoughts, NightenGayle said, "My grandson is struggling to make those choices. But he is succeeding now. Stay close to him. Help him to see the joy you have found. Trust him. Love him. Right now, Zachariah is finally being hailed the rightful king of Xannellion. Xzavier is dead and balance has been restored."

"How do you know this?"

"We observe everything that is happening in Trivar and are closer to you than you are aware." NightenGayle added, "Gideon is safe and Franklin will recover." She pulled Jaden close and sang her a simple lullaby, causing her to feel more loved, if it were possible.

She kissed Jaden on the side of her head and stared into her green eyes. She left a mother's blessing upon her daughter: "May the rivers lead you to safety, may the mountains protect you, may all good creatures help you on your way, and may Gillantri's watchful eye be ever kind to you. My dear daughter, farewell until we meet again."

NightenGayle walked backward with her arms stretched out to her daughter while humming her lullaby. At the end of the song, she turned and ascended the steps to the pavilion, glided across the platform and down the other side. And then she was gone. Jaden held her breath, and with glistening eyes looked toward Gillantri.

"Do you have any questions for me?" he asked.

Jaden's mind raced. Her thoughts were so overloaded that nothing surfaced. Her thoughts settled upon her mother's face and voice, which she knew, gratefully, would be forever imprinted in her mind and in her heart.

"You are The Third Daughter. You play a critical role in the final scenes of Trivar. You have made many correct choices and done much good, but more is required."

"Can you tell me what I must do to save Trivar?"

"That will be revealed in time as you are ready for it."

"Will you not tell me everything now?"

"If I do, you could not handle it all."

Jaden discerned that this was true but still wished for more.

Gillantri continued, "It is enough for now that you realize that I know you will faithfully accomplish all you came to Trivar to accomplish. I have confidence in you. Remember that always and do not give in to discouragement. Ponder the meaning of the faerietale, for it will unlock the power within you to be able to perform all you came to perform."

Jaden felt frantic to remember even one of the questions on her list while she had this opportunity, but her pursuit was useless. Gillantri seemed to understand.

"RoseAura, all your questions will be answered when you are ready. I will always be there for you. Take Nightflights often. They will rejuvenate you and give you clarity. You will be showered with everything you need as you fulfill your roles and missions and continue to progress toward Arway. Do not forsake Frederick. You will rely on each other more heavily than you now realize, and none of your goals are attainable without each other." Gillantri's eyes softened.

"RoseAura, I must go, but rest in Arway. Take your time. You do not have to return to Rosehannah right away. Allow the peace that surrounds you and the peace that emanates from within you to unite. That is true power."

Gillantri turned to go.

"Gillantri," she said.

He looked over his shoulder but stayed where he was. Jaden felt her stomach tighten. How could she ask, but how could she not? She again saw the look in his eyes that made her feel that he was disappointed. But her heart couldn't hold her pain any longer. "Why, in my dreams, are you always so disappointed in me?"

Gillantri grinned, upsetting Jaden further.

"Now you are enjoying my distress?" After every beautiful thing that happened here, Jaden could not believe he would end their conversation this way. The old Jaden returned, requiring all her courage to not flee to protect her wounded soul. To add to her embarrassment, she began to cry.

Gillantri faced Jaden and opened his arms to her as he often did in her dreams.

"I am afraid," Jaden spat out angrily through her tears.

Gillantri again turned to go, like in her dreams.

Jaden angrily shook her arms at her sides wanting to run to him and wanting to run away, and not being able to do either. When would she be here again? Would he ever appear to her again if she insisted on pushing him away?

"Please. Please, help me." She shook as great waves of grief engulfed her.

Needing nothing further, he came back to Jaden and tenderly embraced her, allowing her sorrow to flow through her soul and dissipate into the clear Arwavian air. Not until Jaden pulled away did he release her.

Wiping the tears from her eyes, he said, "I have never been disappointed in you. I am only disappointed when my children stop trying, when they give up and turn their lives over to Daman. I know what he will do with them. He will enslave and destroy them. He cannot give peace, healing, nor true happiness."

Jaden felt enlightenment begin filling her mind, and misunderstanding gave way to peace.

"What you thought you read in my countenance is not disappointment in you," he explained. "It is empathy that I feel for you as my heart was breaking with yours. I could feel the pain you held onto that sometimes kept you from allowing me to heal you and fill you with peace. But you persevered and finally asked for my help. Now I can heal you. You are truly a choice daughter."

Jaden didn't know how to respond. She began to feel free, light, and gratified.

"I see your relief and am pleased. This is my only desire for you. I release you to return to fulfill your purpose in Trivar. I will be with you as often as you need, as often as you allow me." Sensing that all was well, he left Jaden deeply contented in simple joy.

Jaden sat down in the grass and thought about what she had seen and heard and what she now knew, which had been a mystery to her all her life. She found herself crying at times and resigned at other moments. But her crying was refreshing and not stifling, a continuation of the release of pain, which she had felt in Gillantri's embrace. Peace and light filled her in greater measure after she cried, and understanding replaced the old hurt. It was so clear and simple in Arway.

But dread began to grow when she realized her time was nearly up and she would need to return to Trivar. At that moment, a warm breeze engulfed her until her dread disappeared, her inner peace uniting with the warm breeze. Joy again filled her soul.

She thought, All will be well, as Gillantri said. He knows I can do this. He is not disappointed in me. He promised to help me, therefore, I can. And what is more, I will.

Jaden stood and shook off the rich, green Arwavian grass, smiling at the thought of Danae's reverie about this grass being the most exquisite thing. Jaden couldn't argue with Danae. She loved Arwavian grass now, as well.

Her guide had been waiting for Jaden to motion to her and now rose, leading Jaden back to where the eagles and Frederick were waiting. Something about her newly gained experience, knowledge, and peace, and seeing Frederick standing there calm and assured, made everything feel solid and right.

She began to see Frederick with a deepening love and respect and as a dear friend and companion. Thoughts of NightenGayle's description of her father being like Frederick, "a good combination for spirited Highland women," and Gillantri's admonition to not forsake Frederick opened a part of her heart not previously open. She saw Gideon as a true friend who helped her get to this place. She felt gratitude for him.

She walked toward Frederick, and when she got close said, "I accept my role. Everything is going to be all right." She blushed without dropping her gaze. "Frederick, I am not an easy woman to be with, but you have my heart for now and forever."

Frederick lifted his head to the skies and breathed in deeply while wrapping his arms around Jaden and bringing her into his chest. From the depths of this good man's soul, he laughed as tears fell from his eyes. Jaden put her head against his chest, reveling in the warmth, safety, and joy she felt there, and happy tears filled her eyes. After a time of holding each other, she raised her head and wiped the tears from his eyes.

"You have endured so much. Thank you for being faithful. You can call me RoseAura."

She ran her hands through his hair and raised herself up on her toes to kiss him tenderly on the lips. He brushed her tears away. Holding her head in his hands, he kissed her passionately like a man who had waited patiently for years for the promise of his true love to appear, and she was finally in his arms loving him. So deep and intoxicating was their love that nothing else existed at this moment. Jaden knew that he was the only man she would ever truly love.

46

Danae Loves You

On the docks west of Xannellion, Zachariah walked from one ship to the next, passing off inspections and giving orders.

"We can't afford flaws or delays. Do it right the first time," he said. He turned to his top advisor. "Claudius, I wish I could just spend my days on these docks, but there is so much else that needs to be done. Give me the list again so I can get it in my head."

Claudius said, "Your Highness, you have only been here a fortnight, barely long enough to see the whole of Xannellion. Take one thing at a time until the whole mess is cleaned up."

"That's just it. My father left such a mess. In fact, he didn't even clean up after Cannote! I've got years of messes to clean up. We need to get started right away. So give me that list."

Claudius didn't argue any further. "Go to the ship yard and inspect navy progress. Check. Give pirates the choice to fight for Xannellion in their own ships or be put to death. Follow up with demolition team. Get report on the army. Have they been paid adequately for their service? Check on business in Xannellion's markets. Has reducing the tax burden caused citizens to return to the market..."

"Claudius, I just had a thought."

"Yes, Sire."

"I want everyone to report to me here. I simply can't be in every place to check progress. I'll make occasional runs through Xannellion, but my first priority right now is to oversee the building of our new navy. In fact, make it a high priority to build a palace for me here by the coast. Move everything of value from the old one to the new one. Use the old palace as a dragon's keep and a base for my underground mining operation. Until the new palace is built, I want to stay here. Find a way for it to be done."

Zachariah sensed someone approaching behind him and turned from Claudius to see Arran.

"Well, Arran, how are you?" Zachariah tried to be polite.

"I am well, Zachariah. How are you?" Arran bowed deeply.

"What do you need?"

Arran nodded. "Two things. First, I have been sent by Gideon to let you know that Danae arrived from Alexandria. She wants to see you at your earliest convenience."

Zachariah went dark. He pursed his lips, took a deep breath, and said, "Danae means nothing to me now."

Arran looked at him closely. "I will relate the message," he said. He paused, then walked away.

Zachariah lowered his head. He turned to Claudius, but remembering something, he turned back to Arran. "What about your second request?"

Arran stopped. "If you really mean what you say – that Danae means nothing to you – then the second request is of no importance."

Zachariah squinted and cocked his head. "Why?"

"It doesn't matter anymore."

"Stop playing with me, Arran, and tell me your request."

"Stop playing with me, Zachariah, and I will."

"Look," Zachariah said with impatience. "You have Danae's heart, so stop tormenting mine!"

"So you do love her?"

"Why do you say that?"

"I need to know."

"Out here on the docks? Yes, I love Danae, and you won. Now you know. I loved her the moment I awoke from my injuries and loved her more every minute I spent with her. She is not like anyone I have known, but she has you, and I will have to find someone else. May you be blessed!" Zachariah whirled around to speak with Claudius.

Arran moved quickly to Zachariah and said, "May I please speak with you alone, your Highness?"

"Haven't you humiliated me enough?"

"Please, Zachariah. I know you have never liked me, but trust me for one minute and I will never bother you again."

Zachariah's arms fell, his shoulders slumped, and he looked at Claudius's papers for a long time. Thoughts of Danae with Arran made him angrier by the second. He turned toward Arran and whispered sternly, "I will give you five minutes, but after that I never want to see you again." To Claudius he said, "I will be right back." He turned to Arran and said, "Let's walk."

They walked toward the open sea. The sun danced on the gentle waves that lapped the shoreline. Arran looked at Zachariah for some time before he said, "I love Danae..."

"All right," Zachariah interrupted. "I didn't give you this time to rub it in my face more. I left her for you. Isn't that enough?"

"Please hear me out," Arran said. "She is so pure, but has been through so much. Danae was raised by a good mother, protected by a faithful father, and spent a lot of time with the elves. Though she is strong in her own way, her nature is soft and easily hurt..."

"I know she is good and pure, and I would be bad for her. Get to the point."

"The past couple of moons have been a great burden on her..." Again Arran looked at Zachariah, who was burning now because he was certain he had been her greatest burden. "When I saw her in the forest, though she was careworn and fatigued, she was vibrant – more glowing than I have seen her since before her brother died. It surprised me."

Zachariah heard Arran's footsteps stop, but he refused to turn around. "Arran, I don't know what you are trying to say," he said to the sky.

"I have watched you with Danae. Something about you enlivens her. She relies on you, trusts you...needs you. I saw it plainly in the jungle when I arrived. The only reason I share this with you is that she needs you to be true to her. This is the last thing I will say to you about the matter because I must fade into the farthest reaches of her memory as only a good friend. And you must take care of her with more than just your strong body and quick wit. She needs your love."

Zachariah felt stunned. He walked back to face Arran. "I don't understand. You love her. You just said so. What are you saying?"

"I do love her, but I can never be with her. Elves are immortal. I will be here in Trivar when her great-grandchildren die. It was never meant for us to be together." Arran's eyes were filled with sorrow.

"Are you telling me that I could be with Danae and you wouldn't interfere?" Zachariah didn't trust Arran completely but felt something unwrap inside of him, a carefully protected desire.

"I am telling you that Danae needs you. She needs your love and protection. Since she was a child, I determined that when she found this kind of love, I would support her. But if you ever hurt her, I will hunt you down."

Zachariah turned away from Arran. The sun warmed the beach where the sea washed upon the shore. He finally said, "Elves are curious creatures. Too good for your own sakes." Zachariah breathed in the sea air. "I never suspected this. I will consider what you have told me. Thank you."

Arran put his hand on Zachariah's shoulder. "Please take good care of her."

Zachariah turned to face him. Arran bowed courteously and left.

****

A fine evening seven days later, Danae was sitting in the garden when Gideon called out to her from the side orchard.

"He's here."

Danae didn't move. Gideon came to her side while Zachariah peered around the corner of the old house.

"Come with me. What's wrong?" Gideon said.

"I am suddenly very scared," Danae confessed.

"What are you talking about? Arran told you what happened. Zachariah loves you. You are going to be a queen."

"That is just it. How can I be queen?"

Gideon reached for Danae's hand. "You traveled all the way to the Highlands and back. You endured bulbane raids, desert heat and exhaustion, and even Daman himself at the wedding, and now you are facing your own greatest desire – and you're afraid?"

"I know," Danae laughed. "What am I afraid of?"

Gideon laughed his deep laugh. Danae reached her arms around Gideon and gave him a hug. Then she saw Zachariah.

Embarrassed to be caught eavesdropping, Zachariah walked over and said, "Hello, Danae. I am sorry... How are you? How was your journey?"

"Long. I am grateful to be home."

"Gideon told me that Jaden found her home in the Highlands?"

"Yes, William, the Alexandrian Captain of the Guard, took her safely to the ancient city of Rosehannah. William sent word that Jaden wants you to visit when you have time. I'm sure she has so much to tell you. I miss her."

"She is not coming back?"

Gideon answered seriously, "Not all of us have the luxury of having a dragon to make traveling the length of Trivar an easier, faster journey."

Zachariah darkened. "I don't know when I will have time."

Danae took Zachariah's hands. Gideon excused himself.

"Being a king suits me," Zachariah said. Mild arrogance tainted his laugh.

"It certainly does suit you. I always knew you'd be king. "

Danae wore the green dress Ozella gave her and looked exquisite. Zachariah kept hold of one of her hands, and they walked deeper into the garden. Danae glanced at Zachariah, but neither of them said a word. They walked to where Zachariah shot the arrow. It seemed like so long ago.

Zachariah opened the back gate and walked with Danae through the forest to the waterfall and pool. They stood there for a time before Danae said, "It is good to be here with you. In Alexandria I thought of you often and couldn't wait to be back, but when I heard you were gone to Xannellion and became king, well, I didn't know if you wanted anything more to do with me."

Zachariah turned away from her with his head down. Danae reached up and put her petite hand on his shoulder. He reached back and placed his strong hand on hers, then slowly turned around. He looked so intense, almost fierce, that Danae dropped her hand.

"I feel afraid when you look at me that way."

"I am only upset that I could have made you feel that I never wanted to see you again."

He reached for her hands. "Danae, I don't ever want to be without you. I thought you were in love with Arran. I didn't know. My mother tried to tell me, but I thought it was just what she wanted to see." Zachariah paused. "When Arran came, I treated him poorly. If you see him again, would you apologize for me? He did more than I would have done for someone who had been as rude as I have been to him."

"He didn't do it for you. He did it for me," Danae said blushing. "Zachariah, I do love Arran…"

Zachariah let go of her hands. "I don't think I want to hear this."

"Listen to me, please." Danae grabbed his arm. "I love him but can never be with him. We have always known that. I never considered marrying him. It just isn't right. Before he left to see you, we agreed to never see each other again."

Zachariah looked at her skeptically, but she pressed on. "What's more, I promise my heart to you and only you, Zachariah, King of Xannellion."

Zachariah stepped closer and said, "I am sorry for being abrupt, but…" he trembled. He took her hands again, inhaled, and sighed. "Danae, I am doing everything in my power to transform Xannellion into a city dedicated to Gillantri. I am removing the images of my father and everything else I can find that is vile or offensive. I know that the only way for Xannellion to have peace is for us to unite behind Gillantri, but I need the help of your pure heart in order to succeed."

"But what can I do?" Danae asked sincerely.

Zachariah laughed uncomfortably. "Would you consider…"

Danae looked at him closer now. "Zachariah, are you okay? What is wrong?"

He leaned over and kissed her strongly, and then he pulled away. He looked into her eyes and said, "Danae, will you help me transform Xannellion as my Queen?"

Danae's eyes dropped. She smiled bashfully. "I don't know if I am cut out for that." She paused and looked up into his eyes. "But I want with all my heart to be by your side."

Zachariah smiled and touched her hair while looking into her dark brown eyes. "You will be protected and safe under my roof. I will build you a garden, larger than you can imagine, where you can spend time when I am gone. You will be happy."

Danae threw her arms around his neck and kissed his cheek.

"I am. I really am happy."

47

Rosehannah in the Summer

Zachariah and Justine landed in the meadow by Siranta's cottage where Jaden was waiting for him. He dismounted and Jaden ran to him. Her hair was long and pulled away from her face like Ozella had done it in Ononzai with little sprigs of baby's breath interspersed. She fiercely hugged her son.

"Oh, Zachariah, it has been too long."

Zachariah laughed. "Mother, it is good to see you, too." He hugged her and spun her around. Justine nuzzled them both, making them laugh.

Jaden turned her attention to her old friend.

"You are alive, Justine! I can hardly believe it. Zachariah, she means so much to me."

"She helped us defeat Xzavier and his army. But Gideon wants me to send her back to Yamis with the other dragons."

Jaden looked thoughtfully at her son. He seemed worn. "Come sit with me. This summer has been so pleasant. I spend much of my time here." Jaden led him to two chairs situated near the front door. "Tell me how things are going in Xannellion."

"I don't have much time. There is so much to do. I have blocked off most of Daman's tunnels. I am doing all I can, but I need the amber."

"The amber? You mean the amber that Xzavier used?" Jaden was displeased, and Zachariah could feel it.

"Yes, Gideon doesn't understand either, but with many of our dragons dead and our army at only half strength, pirates to deal with on our northern shores, and so many changes happening, we are vulnerable. But never mind all that."

"How is Danae?"

"She is happy, I think. We are building a palace by the sea."

"Of course you are." Jaden laughed and tried not to worry about her son.

"I have made her a garden three times the size of her old one in Jeremiah. But she still visits Gideon often. That is all right because I am so busy, and she needs to be near him." Zachariah grew fidgety. "I need to check on Lillian."

"Lillian?"

"Yes, did no one tell you? William agreed that I could be a shadow guardian of The Third Daughter."

Jaden visibly started.

"What is wrong mother? I thought you would be proud of me?"

"Of course, I just didn't realize. You are very honored, son. So many large responsibilities for a new king." Jaden regained control. "Of course you are protecting The Third Daughter. Since I began having my dreams, you have always felt drawn to protect her." She turned her gaze aside. "Son, I am sorry."

Zachariah was confused.

"I am sorry I didn't give you permission to fight Xzavier. I was so scared I would lose you. Our life was upside down. Everything changed so quickly. We lost everything, even our way of life. You were all I had."

He put his head down.

"I am sorry, Zachariah. Can you forgive me?"

"Of course, mother. What is there to forgive? I wasn't exactly the perfect son. All is well now. Xzavier is dead. I am king. You are safe here in the Highlands…"

"And Danae loves you."

Zachariah looked up into the sky and sighed. Jaden put her arm around her son and gave him a squeeze. He put his head on her shoulder. He hugged his mother. "I need to get back."

"Thank you for coming to see me. I wish I could have been at your wedding."

"It was an elaborate wedding. Better than Lillian and Jordan's, Danae said."

"I am sure it was. I dreamed about it." Jaden gazed beyond Zachariah, thinking of the loneliness she had faced during her first year in the Highlands and what she had given up to remain there. Shaking herself out of the thought, she pushed Zachariah to arm's length and said, "I always knew you would be king, the greatest Xannellion has ever known. I love you."

Zachariah's eyes softened. "I love you, too, mother." He kissed her cheek and said again, "I have to go."

"Visit me again soon. Since you have to be here for Lillian, take the time to visit your old mother, too."

Zachariah laughed, mounted the dragon, and flew away.

****

Moments after Zachariah left, Frederick emerged from the cottage dressed in his rustic, brown wizard attire. He carried with him a white dress that was draped over both of his outstretched arms.

"Oh, Frederick." Jaden couldn't believe the beauty of the dress. "Made by the elves?"

From behind the large oak tree came the sparkling laughter that could only belong to one person in Trivar. "Ozella?"

"Yes, it is Ozella, and, yes, she made the dress," Etheltread answered, and Meadthel laughed, both appearing from behind the tree.

"Careful, she isn't just a feisty Xannellion queen, she is a woman of prophecy now," Meadthel teased.

Jaden's sadness at Zachariah's short visit melted away into laughter. "You pesky elves, who invited you?"

Frederick coughed awkwardly in jest. "That would be me."

"You said this wedding would be secret. We have an audience."

"You made me wait until summer," he said joyfully. "I had time to invite some friends."

Jaden hugged each of her friends and returned to her dress. "Ozella. This is exquisite. I never would have..."

"I know you wouldn't have asked for it. That is why I took the liberty of making it for you. We come when you need us, not always when you want us." Her twinkling laughter filled the meadow.

"Oh, but I did want you to be here. More than anything. If Gideon, Franklin, Danae, and Zachariah couldn't be here, I did need you here."

"About that..."

"Hello, Jaden!" Franklin came out of the cabin behind Frederick and gave Jaden a warm hug.

"I thought you were severely wounded?"

"Malatore's son lives with the Mountain Elves and helped with that. I feel younger and healthier than ever."

"I wish Malatore could have healed Siranta," Jaden said sadly.

"His time was complete once he found you," Franklin said, resigned to his brother's passing.

Jaden walked over to Frederick. "I love it."

"I love you."

Jaden caught her breath. It still sounded sweet to her soul to hear those words. "I love you, too."

He handed her the dress. Quietly she asked, "Where is Miss Betty?"

"We both couldn't leave, or people would start asking questions. She sends her love." Jaden accepted his answer, pleased with all who could come, and carefully took the dress, saying in jest, "I assume there isn't anyone else hiding around here?"

"Only one," Franklin said with a twinkle in his eye.

Arran came out of hiding and kissed her on her cheek. "I wouldn't miss this for the world!"

Jaden felt tears at the corners of her eyes. "I am so glad you are all here," she said.

Evening began to fall. She came out from the cabin dressed in her white gown and found that elvan magic had been at work while she was getting ready. The meadow had been transformed into an enchanted wonderland.

Wood nymphs lit the meadow with their striking, varied colors. Three golden gryphons perched on three trees at the edge of the meadow like grand guardians. Faeries danced about the nymphs' heads adding sparkles of vibrant light everywhere. Tropical orchids, which were not common to the Highlands, hung from branches of old oak trees and were suddenly growing around the edges of the meadow.

High above, monarch eagles circled. Frederick's wizard outfit had been turned white and trimmed in the elvish fashion. The wedding guests were dressed in Jaden's favorite color, red. She didn't know for sure, but it sounded like her mother was singing from far away across the Highlands.

Frederick greeted her with a tender kiss. Looking truly regal, they walked hand in hand to the middle of the meadow where Franklin waited. Franklin extended his hand to Jaden.

"The Third Daughter and pure blood descendant of the king of the Highlands is among us."

Jaden's eyes widened, but before she could ask, Frederick interjected, "Remember when Betty told you that the son of the king of Alexandria, who carved the entrance door of the palace, was the king of the Highlands? She mentioned that his last remaining heir was killed by Daman not many years back. Well, that was your father, who gave his life defending your escape."

Franklin took up where Frederick left off. "Yes, that means you are the next queen of the Highlands. For now, we believe keeping this knowledge to ourselves will protect you. Are you okay with this?"

Jaden thought for a minute about Zachariah and worried about his thirst for power. "Yes, for now."

"You have proven yourself in every way, and we welcome you to the Highlands as our queen. You will be among friends for the remainder of your days. Together we will help you accomplish your weighty task. All of Arway is behind you. I crown you The Third Daughter of The Third Daughter of The Third Daughter and rightful queen of the Highlands."

At that moment, her mother's singing became voluminous, echoing through the trees and from the lake. Franklin placed a simple silver tiara with lily motifs on her head, and everyone silently bowed their heads. It took Jaden's breath away, but she stood there, gracious and true to the honor and responsibility that was bestowed. The peace she had accepted from deep inside of her connected fully with the powerful group of Arwavians in the meadow and in Arway. It felt as if all goodness was united and made them one.

"Now it is my heartfelt honor," Franklin said, "to wed these two glorious beings. Frederick, you got lucky, my friend!"

Etheltread and Meadthel snickered before Ozella could give them the motherly "behave yourself" look. Arran and others smiled or laughed softly, while maintaining the dignity of the occasion. Franklin enjoyed the response and left it alone for a moment before continuing.

"RoseAura, that is such a splendid name, my friend. It fits you perfectly. Now let me have your hands."

Franklin took one of each of their hands and said, "Together you will travel through the travail of Trivar, hand in hand. Much will be required of these hands, but as you fulfill all you came here to do, miracles, too, will come from them."

Franklin opened their hands and a white dove appeared, which morphed into a glowing faerie that rose into the night sky between the circling monarch eagles high above. Jaden watched it disappear and wondered at the beauty all around her.

"You are now united before all of Arway and Gillantri himself, for all time in Trivar and beyond Trivar in Arway, never to part."

Behind Ozella, Malatore came prancing into the meadow. He nuzzled Ozella and bit at Meadthel's trousers, causing more snickering. This time, Ozella had to cover her mouth. Jaden smiled, grateful to have such dear friends. Frederick kissed her once more and then lifted her onto Malatore's back and got on behind her.

Ozella, with tears in her eyes, said, "If you ever have a need, you know you have friends in Ononzai. May Arway smile kindly upon you both."

She blew a kiss to Jaden and Frederick. Arran and the others waved and bid the couple adieu. Frederick leaned in and kissed Jaden as they and Malatore disappeared from the wedding party into the moonlit forest accompanied by nymphs and faeries who flew above and before them to light their way.